Defense and Deals

Defense and Deals

Goshawks Hockey Romance #2

Dee Marie

Conceptual Images Publishing

Defense and Deals: Goshawks Hockey Romance #2

Published by Conceptual Images Publishing
PO Box 654
Clear Lake, South Dakota 57226

Cover Design and Interior Illustrations © 2026 D. M. Haskell
Paperback ISBN: 979 8 9909182 5 2
Epub ISBN: 979 8 9909182 6 9

Library of Congress Control Number:
Printed in the United States of America

Steve Haskell
my favorite hockey player
Elise Holt
for believing in me
Moritz Seider and Lucas Raymond
for breathing life into Axel and Etan

Portland Maine Goshawks Roster

FORWARDS

Etan Eklund #56 Right Wing: Age 20 – 5'11"/188lbs – Sweden
Trey Moss #80 Center: Age 20 – 5'10"/185lbs – Maine
Finn O'Connell #63 Left Wing: Age 32 – 6'4"/220lbs – Canadian

Steve Sturman #74 Right Wing: Age 27 – 6'/188lbs – Czech Republic
Eddie Bennett #18 Center: Age 27 – 5'10"/181lbs – Michigan
Daniel Murphy #11 Left Wing: Age 26 – 6'/203lbs – Canadian

Henry Kennedy #21 Left Wing: Age 33 – 6'3"/217lbs – Massachusetts
James Thompson #39 Center: Age 26 – 5'9"/178lbs – California
Vavrin Pavel #91 Right Wing: Age 24 – 6'/210lbs – Czech Republic

Aidan Casey #17 Left Wing: Age 34 – 6'/203lbs – Florida
John Cash #17 Center: Age 21 – 6'2"/209lbs – Canadian
Roger Meyer #52 Right Wing: Age 22 – 6'3"/198lbs – Texas

DEFENSE

Ryan Mitchell #73 Age 24 – 6'3"/200lbs – Canadian
Axel Berger #25 Age 20 – 6'3"/205lbs – German

Matthew Presto #62 Age 26 – 6'1"/209lbs – Michigan
Liam Armstrong #28 Age 30 – 6'3"/224lbs – Texas

Dylan Gallagher #27 Age 30 – 6'4"/224lbs – Canadian
Jake Carter #17 Age 25 – 6'1"/209lbs – New York

GOALIES

Hunter 'Ice Wall' Griffin #1 Age 23 – 6'2"/198lbs – Maine
Lane Wilson #34 Age 21 – 6'5"/218lbs – Canadian

Chapter 1
Against the Buzzer

Wednesday, October 4th
The cost of fame kills dreams.

The gate clanged shut, metal on metal, the sound ricocheting across the empty rink. Ryan Mitchell, the Goshawks' first-pair defenseman, pushed off the boards, steel ripping as they carved the first scars into fresh ice. Cold air stung his throat, sharp with the bite of shaved ice, the faint tang of gasoline still hanging from the Zamboni. The driver gave a quick wave as he disappeared through the tunnel, leaving a sheet that gleamed under the overhead lights.

Ryan's gaze flicked upward. Portland University banners hung from the rafters, their colors dull against the worn wood beams. Scuffed boards framed the ice, bleachers in place of padded seats. The place carried history in every scrape and dent, a far cry from the Goshawks' polished practice rink. For today, this sheet was theirs. Hunter Griffin's college coach kept the doors open for his former star goalie, making sure the crease stayed his whenever needed.

For the past month, this had been their ritual ... quiet mornings before the city stirred, when the rink felt like a cathedral and every sound carried. He studied Hunter crouched low in the crease, mask hiding his face, scowl etched in the lines that showed. Movements tight. Controlled. After five seasons as the goalie's D-man, Ryan recognized the storm brewing beneath the calm.

Pads thudded as Hunter dropped into a butterfly, tracking Ryan like prey. His voice cut sharp through the empty rink. "So, what's the plan today? More sympathy shots, or are you gonna test me this time?"

Ryan carved a slow arc around the net, snow curling up from his blades. "Plan's simple. Keep you sharp. Keep your head in the game. You know ... in case that chip on your shoulder slows your blocker side."

Hunter slammed his stick against the post. The clang cracked like a gunshot in the empty rink. "I don't need sharpening. I need a contract."

Ryan coasted to the faceoff dot, stick resting across his knees. "Yeah, well, until that happens, I'm your personal shooter and unofficial therapist."

A low growl rolled out of Hunter's mask. "You forgot punching bag."

Ryan's grin tugged sharp. "That too." He snapped a shot, the puck screaming for the crease. It hammered into Hunter's pads, the smack echoing as the puck died in the blue paint.

The return came violent as Hunter rifled the puck back, no warning. It hissed across the ice. A black blur aimed at Ryan's skates. No warmup clears. No friendly taps. Practice was turning into a brutal duel.

Teeth clenched, Ryan absorbed the hit, ripping it back low. Once more, Hunter's pads cracked on the ice. The puck ricocheted off his blocker, hammering the glass, echo rattling through the rafters.

Ryan looped wide. "Little slow there, eh?"

Hunter reset quick, crouched low, fury etched in his movements.

Stick rapping ice, Ryan barked, "Come on. You sulking, or you showing me something?"

Hunter answered with a cannon. The puck hit Ryan's blade with enough force to sting through the shaft, vibrating bone-deep.

They fell into a rhythm. Shot. Block. Reset. Over-and-over, the puck cracked off pads, rang off the glass, thudded against the boards. Every sound stacked, a drumline pounding through the rink. No matter how hard Ryan leaned into a shot, Hunter turned it aside. Nothing slipped past him.

Between exchanges, Ryan studied Hunter. Even though the goalie blocked every shot, he was a split-second slow on the reset. Shoulders wound too tight. A faint hitch before dropping into the butterfly. Every detail told the same story. This wasn't just about the contract. It was the silence from management, losing his longtime goalie coach, the isolation from his teammates, no crease of his own. The season loomed closer every day, and his best friend was stuck in limbo.

Hunter lifted his mask, breath breaking into sharp puffs that fogged in the cold. With a sudden shove, he knocked the net off its mooring, the scrape of steel pegs shrieked across the rink. "This is so wrong. You know it."

Ryan coasted in, chest heaving. Sweat cooled against his skin as he leaned on his stick. "Yeah, it sucks. But you can't let it mess with your head. You're better than that."

He skated in, grabbing the tilted post, bracing his shoulder as Hunter shoved the net back into place. The pegs locked in with a dull thud. Ryan gave it a testing shake, then tapped Hunter's pad. "Don't take your frustration out on your home."

Before Hunter could answer, the scrape of skates cut through the cold, sudden and sharp enough to make both men glance up. A dozen young players spilled onto the ice, helmets bobbing, sticks rattling, their chatter echoing off the boards.

Logan, the leader of the group, pointed his stick at the crease. "Careful, man, you're gonna hurt your only teammate out here." Laughter broke out behind him.

Hunter straightened, mask still high on his forehead. "Funny," he shot back, grin tugging at his lips, "but I don't see any teammates rushing to bail you out when I smother your shot."

"Hey, Griffin, you ready to show us how it's done?" one of the younger players called out, his voice caught between nerves and bravado.

"Tell you what. Twenty bucks to whoever puts one past me."

"Yeah, right," the player chirped. "What're you gonna do, get cash out of your blocker?"

Hunter's grin widened as he pulled his mask down. "Don't worry about my money, Camron. If you score first, I'll double it."

The kid flushed when his teammates howled, sticks rattling against the ice.

Ryan skated backwards to the boards, content to keep in the background. Better to let them work, see Hunter find his edge again. As always, he'd give the kids time to sweat. Sharp passes snapped across the ice. No half-hearted practice. They came to work. To learn. To prove they could hang with pros.

"Hey, old man, you just gonna stand there or you actually playing?" Logan called out, his grin as cocky as his tone.

Ryan skated into the group, stick low, angling pucks their way. He monitored Hunter. With every shot, the tension in his frame eased. Shoulders loosened, eyes lit sharper. Each save came with a barked order, each command dragging him deeper into the rhythm. The clatter of pucks off pipe, the scrape of steel carving hard turns, the ragged bursts of breath ... every sound stacked into something raw and real.

He had to keep reminding himself that these weren't college skaters. They couldn't be. NCAA rules barred any crossover with pros, no exceptions. By the end of summer, word of Hunter's situation spread to the local high school, and the players stepped up. Three mornings a week, they arrived early ... chasing every puck like it might change their future.

"Quicker!" Ryan barked, skating into a kid's lane, hip-checking him off the puck. "You think a defender's gonna wait for you to decide?"

Another forward deked as he snapped the puck. It thudded against Hunter's pads, dying in the crease.

Hunter scooped it up with his stick, flipping it back with a snap. "Not bad. Next time, aim high blocker." He rapped the pipe above his right shoulder, tugging up his mask long enough to splash water across his face. By the time it dripped from his chin, he was set again, crouched low, daring the next rush.

From the edge of the circle, Ryan let out a low laugh. That was the Hunter he knew. No sugarcoating. No slack. Just raw drive and demand. This wasn't his goalie's barn, but for now, he owned the crease.

After an hour, the players shuffled to the bench, skates scraping, gear clattering against their tired frames. Most looked wrecked, sweat dripping down their faces. Yet every one of them wore a grin.

Camron lagged, circling back to the crease. He gave Hunter a sheepish grin. "Guess it's a good thing you kept your money, huh?"

Tugging his mask up, Hunter leaned on his net. "You've got skill, Camron. Next time, you'll drain my bank account."

Camron's grin widened. He tapped Hunter's pads with his stick. "Gotta jet. First period starts in twenty. See you Friday?" He hesitated, then smirked. "Hope we didn't wear you out."

Hunter snorted. "That'll be the day. Bring your game next time. We'll see whose legs give out first."

With a sloppy mock salute, Camron pushed off to join his teammates, disappearing down the tunnel.

Hunter turned to Ryan, his smile wide and genuine this time. "Thanks for showing up," he said, voice rough but real.

"Always. We'll figure this out."

The stubborn set returned to Hunter's jaw, the familiar ice wall snapping back. "I just need to get back with the team. Back where I belong."

Ryan didn't answer. He didn't need to. The ice stretched empty before them, a cold sheet that gave nothing back. Hunter's fire burned hot, ready to consume anyone in his path. But fate played its own game. The call would come ... or it would bury him.

Chapter 2
Diamonds and Doubts

October 6, Friday

Ryan burst through the double doors of the Westin Portland Harborview ballroom like he was late to practice. His shoulder brushed a waiter balancing a tray of champagne flutes. The clink of glass trailed him as he threaded through sequined gowns and tuxedos, tugging at the knot of his bow tie. In his head, it was a game-winning breakaway ... only, the net was a table of teammates waiting at the front of the room.

Jessica, his long-distance summer romance, was already there, lips curved in a teasing smile as she tapped her fingers against the linen. Next to her, last year's star rookie forward Etan Eklund, chatted up Patty, voice low, eyes glinting with mischief. Patty laughed, swatting at him with the folded program. At the head of the table, Hunter waved him over.

Ryan slid into the last empty chair, catching his breath. "Tell me I didn't miss my name."

"They wouldn't dare start without you," Sage said.

Hunter's smile morphed into a smirk as he added, "Kind of out of shape for someone who's been training all summer."

Ryan shot the goalie a look that could kill, but Jessica cut in, brushing her hand down his sleeve as if smoothing him into place. "The only thing you missed, is me missing you," she said, sliding a glass filled with Macallan 18 on ice in his direction.

He leaned in for a quick kiss, savoring the faint sweetness of champagne on her lips. "You taste good."

Settling back, he froze at the sight of two empty chairs at the far end of the table ... one draped with Olaf's goaltender sweater, the other with the sweater of their longtime captain, Chase. The stitching on the C frayed. Against the glitter of crystal and chandeliers, the uniforms looked stark, defiant. His teammates' absence hit harder than he expected.

Jessica's champagne glass glinted in the light as she leaned an elbow on the table. "So, Hunter ... isn't there a rule about unsigned players not being allowed at team functions?"

Ryan groaned. *Typical Jessica ... always ready to jab where it hurt.*

Hunter's shoulders squared, his jaw flexing once, hard. Ryan recognized the look. It was the same one Hunter wore before a scrum in front of his crease. He braced, waiting to see if his friend would retaliate.

Instead, Sage's hand covered Hunter's. Ryan caught the quiet steadiness in the gesture. He wished she could be on the ice when Hunter needed grounding.

"I got this," she murmured, leaning forward. Her voice carried the weight of an old friendship. "Jessica, you know darn well this isn't just any Goshawks function. This is the Cup ring ceremony. Hunter dedicated his whole life to this moment. No one would dare keep him from attending."

This time it was Hunter who slid an arm around his fiancé's shoulder, his hand resting against the soft velvet of her gown. From Ryan's angle, he couldn't miss the way Sage's posture eased ever so slightly under his touch.

"It's okay," Hunter whispered.

Sage drained her glass of champagne before firing back. "No, it's not okay. The organization's been treating you like an outsider since last season ended." Her gaze cut to Ryan. "Tell me, would this team have won the Cup without him?"

The question struck hard. Ryan knew the truth, just like everyone at the table. Without Hunter standing on his head in the playoffs, none of them would be here tonight, waiting for the final reminder of what they'd earned.

Hunter kissed Sage's cheek, his words soft. "It's a team sport. Games are not won by one person."

Unless we lose, then everyone blames the goalie, Ryan wanted to say but kept the words to himself.

Patty cocked her head. "Sage, I know this is a silly question, but if Hunter's here ... why aren't Olaf and Chase?"

Ryan intercepted the question. "They're Nashville Reapers now. When you get traded, you're expected to assimilate into your new team. No time for looking back, especially when you're less than a week from opener." He motioned to a waiter, signaling another round before Jessica found a fresh target. The night was not going as planned. He'd just got here, and it was turning into a gongshow.

Then, he breathed in a familiar bite of perfume ... a blend of complex sophistication. Without looking, he knew its wearer; the Goshawks' no-nonsense media manager, Margret VanAlen. She stopped behind Hunter, her hands settling on his shoulders.

"And it just keeps getting better," Ryan grumbled, twirling the ice in his glass before taking a long swig.

"What was that, Mitchell?" Margret's head tilted.

"Nothing," Ryan said, feeling the heat rise to his neck.

"Good of you to join us," she said, her tone smooth as a rink freshly cleared by the Zamboni. "I thought I might have to mail you your ring."

"I wouldn't want the Goshawks' organization to dip into the salary cap budget for postage," Ryan answered, his voice edged with a dry bite.

Margret's hand lingered on Hunter's shoulder, her manicured nails catching the light as she leaned close. From where Ryan sat, he caught the faint creak of Hunter's chair under her touch.

"Good to have you back where you belong," she said.

Hunter's reply was quiet, almost lost under the clatter of dishes at a nearby table. "Wish I knew it was permanent."

The ice in Ryan's glass clinked as he pointed it at the next table. Luke, the son of billionaire quarter horse rancher Sterling Wheatfield, was in deep conversation with Goshawks' owner Justin Caldwell. "So, Margret, what's your South Dakota cowboy doing at this ceremony rubbing elbows with management?"

Margret's smile curved as she looked around their table. "The same thing your South Dakota cowgirls are doing ... enjoying the company of the Portland, Maine Goshawks."

Patty smiled, giving a quick finger wave, while Jessica lifted her glass in a sly salute. The conversation ceased when a flurry of waiters converged on their table. Plates lowered onto linen with practiced grace. Ryan's stomach rumbled at the scent of prime rib seared at the edges, scallops glistening under a drizzle of lemon cream, and twice-baked potatoes crowned with melted cheddar.

"Margret," Luke called, his Midwestern drawl cutting through the hum of conversation, "your dinner's getting cold."

Her hands slipped from Hunter's shoulders, smoothing the satin of her gown as though she hadn't just unsettled half their table. "Enjoy your meals," she said, her tone clipped but composed.

She then glided to the VIP table, sliding into the empty chair beside Justin Caldwell. Their group's conversation resumed without pause, as if the aura of her presence alone anchored her in management's orbit.

Ryan returned to his meal. He carved into his prime rib, the edge of his knife dragging through the crisp sear. Around him, silverware clinked in a scattered rhythm. For a moment, their table seemed to exhale, everyone caught up in their dinners rather than pointed barbs.

It was Etan who broke the quiet, a mouthful of potatoes muffling his words. "So ... who's wearing the C this year?" He wiped his lips with the back of his hand, earning a side-eye from Patty. "Chase is gone, and we can't skate without a captain."

Axel Berger, last year's breakout rookie D-man, leaned back, spearing a scallop, popping it whole. His shoulders lifted in a shrug, casual but carrying weight. "My money's on Ryan."

The words hit like a puck off the glass. Ryan swallowed a sip of scotch, playing it cool, though the idea stuck sharp in his chest. He reached for a dinner roll, buying a moment. "I'm not captain material," he said, the dismissal automatic. "Chase was special."

"That's why I'd place my bet on you," Axel countered. "The team needs someone who can keep us grounded. Who else is it gonna be? Etan?"

Etan snorted, nearly choking on his soda. "Yeah, right. No way I'd take the C even if they offered it to me. I'll have enough pressure trying to hit fifty goals this season."

"Good luck with that. Especially with the new hotshot forward they traded Olaf and Chase for," Axel said, catching a waitress's attention. She slid a chilled pitcher against the rim of his glass, ice rattling as water spilled fresh.

"I'm not concerned," Etan said. "You just keep feeding me the puck and watch me work my magic."

The tension eased as Axel reached around Patty's back for a high-five, but Ryan caught Hunter's quiet glance. The look said more than words. Hunter wasn't laughing. He knew this wasn't a throwaway topic.

The captain controversy was interrupted when Justin Caldwell rose from his chair, adjusting the front of his tuxedo as he stepped to the podium. The microphone gave a brief squeal before steadying. Ryan set down his fork, watching the Goshawks' elusive owner sweep his gaze across the ballroom.

"Good evening, ladies and gentlemen. On behalf of the Portland, Maine Goshawks, it's my honor to welcome you to this ... hopefully not a once-in-a-lifetime ... celebration."

Laughter rippled through the ballroom, soft and genuine, easing the edge of anticipation.

"Tonight, we're not just honoring a championship season. We're also breaking with tradition. It's customary for the Cup ring ceremony to be held behind closed doors ... players, staff, a handful of guests. But this victory was bigger than the locker room. It also belongs to our Portland fanbase."

Applause echoed ... louder from the back of the room.

Justin waited for the applause to quiet before leaning closer to the microphone. "You, our loyal fans, carried us when fatigue threatened to break us. You filled the arena with a roar that lifted us higher than we thought possible. Tonight, we share this moment with you ... not as spectators, but as family."

The applause surged again, louder this time, rolling like a wave across the room.

Once more, Justin waited for the sound to ebb before continuing. "I know we're also bucking tradition by holding the ceremony before regular season. I wasn't about to make these men wait one more day. They left it all on the ice, and they've earned this. We'll raise the banner on opening night. This evening ... my team, and the people who support them, get their rings."

Subtle pride curved his smile as the room thundered in response. He turned, gesturing at Margret. "And now, I'd like to introduce the woman who ensures our stories are told with vision and pride ... our media director, Margret VanAlen."

Margret walked to the podium. Her heels clicked against the polished floor, the satin of her gown catching the golden light. She accepted the microphone from Justin as he stepped back.

Ryan's gaze tracked her smile. As always, it was polished, rehearsed, with the smug tilt she wore like a badge. He leaned back in his chair, shaking his head.

"This championship is proof of what happens when a city and a team push forward together," Margret began. "Our players gave grit and resilience. You, our devoted fans, gave them your voices, your belief, and your loyalty. For that, we owe you not just thanks, but an experience worthy of your devotion."

Applause filled the air again, the kind that rose and fell without breaking the formality of the room. Ryan tapped a finger against his glass, letting the sound blur into the clatter of plates, and the muted shuffle of trays as busboys cleared courses around them.

"This season," Margret continued, "you'll see more than goals and saves. We'll be opening new doors ... sharing the stories behind the sweat, the rituals before the puck drops, the moments that make these extraordinary players human. Campaigns that don't just celebrate hockey but make the Goshawks a defining part of Portland's culture. I promise you ... this is only the beginning."

The room murmured its approval, a few toasts rising. Ryan caught Etan leaning to whisper something to Axel, both grinning as Patty hushed them.

Margret wrapped up. "On behalf of the organization, thank you. Thank you for standing with us, for celebrating with us, and for being part of this historic night."

As she stepped back, Justin returned to the microphone. He dabbed his forehead with a folded handkerchief, his hand trembling as he adjusted his grip on the podium. A flush crept high on his neck. Ryan frowned, an unease settling low in his gut.

"Does he look ... off to you?" Hunter muttered.

Ryan gave the barest shrug as he scrutinized Justin closer.

"And now," Justin said, his voice steadier than his hands, "the moment you've all been waiting for. Tonight, we honor not only our triumph, but the unity that carried us here. It is my privilege to present to you ... our Cup rings."

The rattle of carts drew everyone's attention to the stage, where the service staff rolled rows of black-velvet trays into place next to the podium. On the trays, dozens of small silver boxes shimmered. A Goshawks' assistant handed Justin the first box with a name tag inserted. Ryan's smile widened. The tagged box reminded him of the fortune cookie he had last night.

Justin cleared his throat as the ballroom fell into an eerie silence. "Axel Berger."

A round of applause and cheers from both his teammates and fans broke out as Axel shot up. His glass wobbled on the table, sending a thin ripple of water across the surface. If not for Patty's quick reflexes, their table would have been drenched.

Scattered laughter rippled through the room as Ryan shouted, "Way to go, Axel."

Etan muttered something under his breath to Axel, earning a wry grin from his linemate. With a jerky tug, the D-man adjusted his tie. Axel strode to the stage, the sound of his shoes thudded above the good-natured chirping from the crowd. He accepted the ring box with both hands, wide-eyed, clutching it like it might vanish into smoke as a round of applause rang out again. Ryan's palms burned from clapping as Axel returned to their table.

Justin raised his hand to silence the crowd as he called out the next name. "Etan Eklund."

Etan took his time, wearing his signature smirk as if he were skating a victory lap. The applause grew louder, peppered with hoots and whistles from the back tables.

A female voice cut through the din. "I. Love. You. Etan."

Ryan noted Etan received his box with the same reverence he had shown when lifting the Cup for the first time.

One by one, names were called. Each player rose, walked to the stage, received their box, and returned to their table. With every step, every handshake, the anticipation thickened, like air pressure building before a storm.

"Ryan Mitchell."

Ryan pushed to his feet, the weight of five seasons with the Goshawks flooding his memories with jagged flashes ... ice fogging under the lights in training camp, the sting of blocked shots, the roar of sudden-death victories. The suffocating silence that followed each loss ... an emptiness that clung to him long after leaving the arena. He climbed the short stage steps, noting Justin Caldwell's handshake ... icy, weak, clammy.

"Hell of a year, kid," Justin rasped, his voice rougher than usual.

"Thank you, sir." Ryan gave a sharp nod, taking the silver box, cool and heavy in his palm. His legs felt weak as he walked back to the table. Sinking into his chair, he set the box in front of him, unopened. None of them would dare lift the lid. Not yet.

A hush fell over the room as Justin glanced from the Goshawks' roster to their table. Ryan knew only one player's name remained to be called.

"Hunter Griffin."

The goalie rose with the same measured composure he carried in the crease.

The silence in the ballroom broke as the applause swelled, rolling louder than before, punctuated by sharp whistles. Then came the fans and teammates calling out, "Ice Wall! Ice Wall! Ice Wall!" The same chant that thundered through the arena last season. The sound vibrated through Ryan, sharp as the buzzer on their winning Cup goal.

Hunter accepted his box with a subtle nod, though Ryan noticed the pause. The extended handshake. The glaring eye contact between the two men before Hunter turned away. The contract fight. His boyhood goaltender coach Viktor's departure. The weight of an entire city's expectations pressing down on the guy who had stood like a fortress between the pipes.

Hunter returned to the table, placing the box beside Ryan's. "Feels heavier than I thought it would."

"Maybe it's all the diamonds," Axel blurted, rubbing his hands together.

Hunter didn't smile. "Or all the expectations."

Ryan was about to console him when another name cut through the room.

"Margret VanAlen."

She stepped forward in an evening gown of deep Goshawks blue. At five foot eleven, and wearing three-inch heels, she stood eye-to-eye with Justin. She accepted her box with poise, her expression unreadable, her gaze skimming above the crowd without landing. She returned to her seat, spine straight as steel.

More names followed ... coaches, trainers, key staff ... until one box remained. Ryan watched as Justin picked it up, placing it on the podium. He then returned to the microphone, the Goshawks' owner's voice steadier now, though a sheen of sweat still glistened on his forehead.

"You've all worked hard to earn this. Now ... I think it's time to see your reward."

A current rippled through the room, anticipation snapping tight like static before a storm.

Justin picked up his box, followed by dozens of silver hinges creaking as lids snapped open in the hushed ballroom. A collective gasp followed, whispers ricocheting like pucks clanging off the boards in a game warmup.

Ryan's heart raced as he removed the ring from its velvet bed. Forged from white gold, the Portland Goshawks' championship ring was a monument to the battle fought and won. At its center, a goshawk soared, wings spread in eternal hunt, sapphire eyes flashing beneath the light. Around it, arcs of dark and pale blue stones glimmered, framed in a blaze of diamonds.

On one side, the Cup and the year. On the other, his name and number etched deep. Inside the band, against the skin, the words that bound them ... Brothers on Ice. Along the outside band, bold and unmissable, the mantra that had carried them through every war on the ice ... Strike First. Rule the Ice.

Ryan turned the ring in his hand, cool and solid against his palm. In it he felt every sacrifice, every bruise, every drop of blood and sweat left behind in pursuit of this moment. He slid it onto his finger. The metal first chilled his skin, then grew warm, settling as though it had always belonged there.

This wasn't just a ring. To him, it was the Cup, pressed into metal. It was their legacy.

The microphone shrieked. Everyone's attention snapped to the stage. Justin stood frozen, lips parted, expression blank, as though his next words were caught in his throat. The ballroom stilled, heavier than the diamond rings weighing down their hands. He cleared his throat; the sound rolling raw and jagged in the hush.

"Tonight is a night of celebration, but it's also a night of change." Justin's words carried to every corner of the ballroom. "As we look ahead, there are important developments I need to share."

Ryan and Hunter's gazes locked. The tension from earlier no longer simmered beneath the surface. It sparked, sharp and dangerous.

Justin leaned forward, hands gripping the podium. His voice boomed with authority. "This offseason, the team has undergone significant changes." He paused, letting the murmurs ripple and fade. "These decisions weren't made in haste, but with long, hard, thoughtful consideration. They were made to keep the Goshawks at the top where they belong."

Ryan's fingers tightened on the empty ring box. Something in Justin's tone pricked the back of his neck, a warning he couldn't quite name.

Justin's lips curved in a knowing smile. "And with that, I'd like to announce that Sterling Wheatfield, a man of great vision and resources, is now the co-owner of the Goshawks organization."

The reaction hit like a puck ricocheting off the pipes. Voices rose in disbelief, chairs shifted, heads craned. Justin raised a hand in a request for calm. When the noise refused to settle, he cut through it with a firm edge. "Sterling couldn't be here this evening, but he's entrusted his son, Luke Wheatfield, to speak on his behalf."

Everyone in the room shot glances at Margret's table. Luke took a beat before rising. Adjusting the lapel of his tux, he squared his shoulders and walked to the stage.

"Thank you, Justin." His voice was steady, though his knuckles whitened around the microphone. "My father sends his regrets that he couldn't be here, but he's honored to join this organization. He believes in what the Goshawks have built. More importantly, he's committed to ensuring this team continues to soar to new heights."

Luke's gaze swept the crowd, landing for a moment on Hunter, then Ryan. "I know I'm not a hockey expert," he said, ignoring the ripple of laughter from their table. "But I've grown to admire the dedication and passion the Goshawks bring to the ice. On behalf of my father, thank you for allowing us to be part of your journey."

"Well, that explains a lot," Ryan grumbled as he watched the South Dakota cowboy take his place next to Margret.

"Thank you, Luke," Justin said, wearing a forced smile as he reclaimed the microphone. "We're excited to welcome you and your father into the Goshawks family. Now, let's raise our glasses to the future of this team."

Crystal chimed as glasses lifted. Justin lowered his mic to join the toast. His face drained of color. His hand twitched as he reached for his glass, then froze midair.

A sharp inhale tore from him, followed by a strangled gasp. His features twisted in agony. The microphone slipped from his hand, hitting the stage with a crack that echoed through the ballroom.

"Justin!" Margret cried out.

Justin staggered, clawing at the podium. He grabbed his chest as he crumpled to the floor.

For a beat, silence gripped the room. Then chaos ensued as chairs scraped, shouts overlapped, screams echoed.

"Ryan!" Jessica's voice cut through the panic. "You're a doctor. Go help him."

Ryan shot to his feet, Hunter on his heels.

Sage clutched Jessica's arm. "He's not that kind of doctor."

Ryan didn't slow. Instinct took over as he vaulted onto the stage. Justin lay on his back, chest rising in shallow, erratic jerks.

Hunter dropped beside him. "You know CPR?"

"Yeah," Ryan said, already starting compressions, his palms pressing hard against Justin's sternum.

The team's medical staff, championship rings flashing under the lights, surged forward. One knelt beside Ryan, gripping his shoulder. "We've got him. Step back."

Ryan obeyed, his chest heaving as he and Hunter crouched nearby, helpless spectators to the desperate rhythm of compressions and shouted commands.

The ballroom's air grew thick, choked with fear and perfume, and the metallic tang of adrenaline sharp on Ryan's tongue. Voices tangled in panic. Beyond the room, sirens wailed.

Ryan's pulse hammered in his ears. His new ring, meant to symbolize victory, pressed heavy against his finger. Whatever future Justin had envisioned for the Goshawks hung by the thinnest thread, trembling on the edge of uncertainty.

Chapter 3
Legacies and Deceptions

Monday, October 9th

Margret VanAlen sat in the leather chair like stone set in velvet, her fingers locked tight on her lap, the room's chill mirroring the grief of the day. She hadn't changed after the early-morning funeral. Her black suit still carried the faint scent of roses from the church, the fabric heavy on her shoulders, reminding her with every breath that this day was far from over.

The law firm's executive office was as imposing as it was sleek. Rich mahogany paneling lined the walls. On one side of the room, floor-to-ceiling windows framed Portland's skyline, the harbor glinting beyond. The late-morning light streamed in, a beam catching the fabric of her sleeve. Margret imagined it was Justin reaching down, reminding her she wasn't alone.

Her gaze drifted to the oak desk in front of her. It seemed too large, too heavy, echoing her sorrow. Behind it sat Anderson Griffin, Hunter's father and the Goshawks' new legal counsel. Not a strand of silver hair out of place, the sharp angles of his tailored suit cut a commanding figure. His stare pinned her, a quiet force impossible to ignore. The folder before him lay untouched; an anchor for the questions churning in her mind. She shifted in her chair, the squeak loud in the silence, her focus drifting to the others in the room, a fragile attempt to escape his hold.

Luke Wheatfield sat at her side. At the funeral, she had leaned on him, grateful for his support. But on the drive to the lawyer's office, when he reached for her hand, she kept hers folded in her lap. The space between them felt deliberate.

Next to his son, Sterling Wheatfield sat somber, one leg crossed over the other in a pose too casual for the tension in the room. His composure was ironclad. His presence filled the space without a word. Justin had trusted this man enough to sell him half the Goshawks, but that truth only deepened the knot in Margret's stomach. With Justin gone, would Sterling claim the rest? The thought made her shift in her chair, as if the leather itself had turned unforgiving beneath her.

On her left sat the Goshawks' General Manager, George Stonebridge. Next to him, Head Coach Stan Harrison. Their presence didn't surprise her. Justin had respected both. They had been key to the Goshawks' rise, shaping the team from an idea into a legacy etched in ice. What bothered her most ... beyond the brief greeting when she arrived, neither man had spoken to her ... or anyone. She'd shared five seasons with them, and their silence didn't fit the men she thought she knew.

The quiet became unbearable. Her words slipped out hushed, softer than she intended. "Mr. Griffin, I ... I don't understand why I'm here. What does this have to do with me?"

Anderson leaned forward, his attention fixed on her, steady and unblinking. "Margret, all will be revealed in due time," he said, his voice smooth, betraying none of the tension that thickened the air. "I assure you, your presence here is important."

Her stomach twisted. The three days since Justin's death had worn her down, each one chipping at her resolve. And now this ... summoned to a will reading she hadn't known she was part of. It was too much.

Margret tried to calm her breathing, but the ache in her chest refused to ease. Justin had been more than her boss. He believed in her, mentored her, shaped her into the strong, confident woman she was. He had felt like a father in every way that mattered ... and now he was gone. Sitting in this office, waiting to hear his last words, made the loss unbearable.

The faint scent of coffee lingered, rich and familiar. Usually, she would never refuse a cup. Today, she did. Instead, she rubbed her hands on the armrest, cool skin brushing against the warmth of the leather beneath her palms.

Anderson cleared his throat before speaking. "In normal circumstances, a will is not read this soon after a death. I think we can all agree these are not normal circumstances." His fingers tapped the folder. "Furthermore, the league requires every owner to file a succession plan. Mr. Caldwell's last revision, made after the Cup victory, provided that plan. Ownership may pass to immediate family without commissioner approval, yet the transfer must be finalized before the season begins. The first regular season game is three days away. That is the matter before us now."

The clasp of the folder clicked open, the sound echoed through the room. When Anderson flipped to the first page, Margret felt the air constrict, as if the walls themselves leaned closer. She braced for the secrets Justin's will would reveal.

"I, Justin Caldwell, being of sound mind and body, do hereby declare this to be my last will and testament," Anderson began, his voice measured, even.

"To my good friend George Stonebridge," Anderson continued, glancing at the GM, "I leave my collection of vintage hockey memorabilia. A reminder of the passion we shared for the sport that brought us together."

Margret looked at George for his reaction. He gave a small nod, his expression stoic, yet beneath it she caught a flicker of gratitude mixed with grief.

"To Stan Harrison, I leave my binder of notes and strategies from the Goshawks' inaugural season, along with the winning puck from the night we secured the Cup. These belong with you, Stan, a testament to the foundation we laid and the victory we claimed together."

Margret's focus shifted to the head coach. Stan sat taller, shoulders squared as though he could take the words like a blow and keep standing. For a breath he managed it, jaw locked, face unbroken. Then grief slipped past the armor. His hand rose, rough fingers dragging once across the corner of his eye, as if he could erase the evidence before anyone noticed.

The sight pierced her. In five seasons, she had seen him rage behind the bench, reprimand players, even laugh so hard his face turned red. She had never seen him cry. Her chest pulled tight at the quiet truth of it. *If a man like Stan could be undone, then none of them were as strong as they pretended to be.*

"I need to stress again that Justin's will was revised after the Goshawks secured the Cup. That was before certain transactions were completed." Anderson paused, giving the silence a chance to thicken before pressing on.

"To my childhood friend, Sterling Wheatfield," Anderson read, "I bequeath my Cup ring. Sterling, your friendship has meant the world to me. This ring is a token of our shared love for the game that shaped our lives."

Margret's fingers curled against the armrest. *Childhood friend?* Her pulse quickened. She had known Sterling only as Luke's father, a rancher with horses and money, a man whose world seemed far removed from rinks and hockey players. Yet here was Justin, binding their lives together with words she'd never expected to hear. The image unsettled her, puzzle pieces shifting into patterns she hadn't realized were missing.

Sterling leaned back in his chair, his posture too composed, too deliberate. It wasn't grief she saw or even pride. Just control. Too much control. To Margret, it didn't look like respect for Justin's memory, but a man claiming what he already believed was his.

When Anderson turned to her, a chill crept up her spine. His voice shifted; his expression softened. She both yearned for and dreaded what he was about to say.

"I leave the remainder of my estate, including my home, all personal belongings, and my ownership of the Portland, Maine Goshawks, to my biological daughter, Margret VanAlen."

Biological daughter? The air thinned. Faces blurred at the edges of her vision. The floor felt unsteady, as if it had shifted, leaving her untethered.

Luke eased an arm along the back of her chair, his palm settling on her shoulder. Margret went rigid beneath the touch. She did not want his comfort. What she needed was answers. Her fingernails pressed crescents into the leather armrest.

"Margret," Anderson said, removing his reading glasses, "Justin did not know of your existence until you became part of the Goshawks organization. Your mother, Mary Dubois, was a close friend of Sterling's late wife, June. Before Justin's pro hockey career began, the four of them spent a summer together. You were conceived during that time." He paused, his focus unflinching as he added, "Mary kept the truth from him."

Her breath came uneven. She had known so little about her birth mother. A name, a handful of facts, a gap she had taught herself not to chase. To learn the secret had been kept this long rattled her confidence. She leaned forward, glaring at Sterling. *Did he know? Was he part of this conspiracy?*

Sterling sat rigid, his hands clasped, knuckles white. His focus fixed on the paper in Anderson's hands.

A sound caught in Margret's throat, sharp as splintered glass. This was proving to be the worst day of her life. The ache in her head matched the ache in her chest.

Anderson leaned back, fingers steepled as he addressed the room. "The Goshawks meant everything to Justin. So did Margret. He wanted her future secure, as much as the team's."

Margret's pulse hammered. The implications of Anderson's words were staggering. She was now in a position of immense power. She had never asked for it. Yet, there it sat in front of her, twisted in the fine print of an incomplete transaction. *Would Sterling contest the will? What would this mean for the future of the team, the career she had built over the past five seasons?*

"I understand this is a lot to take in, and I'm sure you all have questions. But it's important to emphasize that Justin's will was drafted and revised before Mr. Wheatfield's acquisition of half the Goshawks organization. Given that, the matter of ownership will require legal review to determine how Justin's bequest will affect the existing sale."

Margret swallowed, her throat parched. "What ... what happens now?"

Anderson laid his glasses on the folder, pressing fingers to the bridge of his nose. "Rest assured, Margret, I will guide you through the process."

She nodded, though her thoughts churned without settling. The future of the Goshawks, once bright, now loomed uncertain, jumbled in law and shadowed by grief. Luke's hand slid over her hand. This time she didn't pull away.

Sterling turned to Margret. "Justin was a trusted friend. I'll honor his wishes. That being said, this is still a legal matter. The ownership must be clarified. The future of the Goshawks is something we all care about. I believe we can reach an agreement that benefits everyone involved."

The words sounded diplomatic, but Margret caught the steel beneath them. He wasn't offering a compromise. He was laying his claim.

Anderson replaced his glasses. "Indeed. There will be time to address these matters in detail. For now, it is important that Justin's wishes be honored."

Margret waited for Anderson to close the folder, instead, he reached for one last document.

Anderson scanned the paper. Looking up, he said, "Two months ago, Justin added one last codicil to his will, addressing a matter he considered vital to the future of the Goshawks." His tone shifted into something precise, as though each word he was about to read were carved into the page. "It is my express wish that, should the contract negotiations with Hunter Griffin remain unresolved at the time of my passing, this matter be given priority by the succeeding ownership. It is my intent that the Portland Goshawks secure his future with the organization, as I consider him one of its most valuable players."

He paused, resting the paper on the desk before going on. "While this codicil is legally binding within the scope of Justin's authority, it does not override existing contract negotiations."

Margret's pulse quickened. She felt the shift ripple through the room as everyone processed his words. *A will was one thing, but for Justin to commit this to writing ... it wasn't a request. It was a directive.*

"Dad," Luke whispered, leaning to Sterling, "isn't Hunter's contract a conflict of interest?"

"Not now," Sterling muttered.

Margret noted the slight tightening of Sterling's jaw, the throbbing of his temples. The calculation in his stare as he looked at her left no doubt ... *Hunter's future would be tangled in the larger fight for control.*

Anderson closed the folder with a snap. He glanced from Margret to Sterling. "See my secretary to set an appointment to discuss the next steps. For now, I suggest we all take time to reflect on what was revealed today."

A rustle of movement followed as chairs pushed back. Margret felt Luke's hand press against her waist, guiding her to the door, but her mind was trapped elsewhere.

The Goshawks, Justin's legacy, now rested in her hands. Could she carry it? Navigate the legal battles, the fractured loyalties, the uncertainty looming ahead? And what about Hunter? What would become of him if she failed to negotiate his contract?

The questions swarmed, unanswered and relentless. *The future of the Goshawks was hers now ... but it was a future balanced on the edge of a blade.*

Chapter 4
Fractured Ice

Tuesday, October 10th

Margret sat behind Justin's desk, her fingers drumming an uneven rhythm against the wood. The chair, the desk, the entire office didn't feel like hers. She belonged in the media wing, where her world revolved around press releases and marketing strategies, not ownership battles. Yet here she sat, twenty-four years old, thrust into power she hadn't asked for ... sharing it with a South Dakota cowboy two years her junior. Her fingers stilled as she looked across at Luke, irritation simmering hotter than grief.

"So, this is it," Luke said, breaking the silence. "We're in charge of a pro hockey team, and neither of us knows what we're doing."

Margret leaned back, her palms pressing into the armrests, her stare locked on him. "Remind me again, why you're here instead of your father? We've established Sterling and Justin were childhood friends, that your father followed Justin's high school and college games. But why in the world would he leave you in charge? You don't even like hockey."

Luke tilted his head, the faintest shrug loosening his shoulders. "Maybe not. But I know business. My father trusts me to run his quarter horse operation ... owning and running a hockey team isn't that far of a leap."

"Co-owner," Margret snapped, her voice clipped. "And running a professional sports franchise is nothing like managing livestock."

Luke stretched his legs, arms folding across his chest. His tone carried a cool edge. "I get it, Margret. I'm not here to pretend I'm some hockey expert. But I'm not clueless either. My job is to make sure this team is financially stable. We can't afford decisions based on sentiment."

Margret let out a dry laugh. "That's rich coming from you. You base everything on sentiment. We both know the real reason you want Hunter gone."

Luke's jaw tightened. "What are you talking about?"

Margret's stare didn't waver. "Oh, please. You've never liked Hunter. Because he's engaged to Sage. The girl you could never have."

Luke's response lost his easy Midwestern drawl. "This isn't about Sage. It's about making smart business decisions. Hunter's contract is a massive financial commitment. He's asking for more money than he's worth. Plus, he wants a long-term deal. Ask yourself, can the Goshawks afford to take that risk?"

Margret fought to keep composure. "Hunter Griffin is the best goalie in the league. Without him, there'd be no Cup. He sells tickets. He keeps fans in their seats. He's the backbone of this team. Securing him is a smart business move." She snapped a copy of Hunter's contract at him.

Luke leaned forward, the crease between his brows cutting deep. "I'm not saying let him go. We just can't bleed the budget dry just because Hunter's a fan favorite. Popular doesn't always equal profit."

Margret's voice dropped, her stare unflinching. "I don't know, Luke. This feels more like a personal grudge than a business decision. From where I'm sitting, it sounds like you're the one letting emotions cloud your judgment."

Luke straightened, his jaw set hard. "How many ways can I say this? My feelings about keeping or dumping your star goalie are not personal. It's about what's best for the team."

She didn't flinch. "Is it? Because if you want this team to succeed, you'd better start thinking about the long-term impact of losing a player like Hunter. We've already lost Olaf and Chase. Strip Hunter too, and you strip the soul from this team." Her voice softened as she added, "and Justin's last wishes."

The tension pressed in, suffocating. Neither would yield. Luke dropped his gaze to the papers. "Fine. We'll figure it out. The last thing this team needs is more chaos."

She hated to admit it, but he was right. "Agreed. But we're co-owners. I won't let your grudges or inexperience sink the Goshawks."

Luke gave a stiff nod, mouth drawn hard, eyes gone slate. His gesture gave the appearance of surrender. Yet, Margret knew him well enough to know better. This wasn't a resolution. It was the end of the first period, and neither of them had any intention of skating off the ice first.

The Goshawks' players, coaches, and staff packed into the team's training room. Last season this was where they broke down plays, dissected footage, and braced for battle. Today, the room buzzed with unease. The usual light banter was gone, replaced by mutters too low to catch, chairs scraping as players shifted in restless anticipation.

Margret stood at the podium, trying to project the authority she wasn't sure she felt. For five seasons she'd worked alongside these men, fought for them in her own way. Now every player was fixed on her, measuring her before she'd even spoken. Beside her, Luke crossed his arms, looking more like a man guarding a secret than sharing leadership.

She forced a smile. After straightening her suit jacket, she began in a calm, rehearsed voice. "Good morning, team. I'm sure you've heard the rumors. I've called you here today to set the record straight. There's been a major shift in the Goshawks' ownership. After Justin Caldwell's passing, his will appointed me co-owner of the team."

The squeak of sneakers against tile cut through the silence as bodies shifted. She felt like a rookie goalie, doing her best to prevent the puck from slipping into her net.

Finn O'Connell, the seasoned forward, kicked the empty chair in front of him, the crack of metal on tile reverberating like a check against the boards. His voice came out raw, gritty. "What the hell, Margret? You write press releases, plan events. That's not running a hockey team. And now you expect us to believe you're calling the shots? This has to be a joke."

Luke started forward, shoulders tensing as if to step between them. Margret's arm cut across his chest, firm and final. She glared at Finn, her tone sharpened. "You think I wanted this? That I asked to be standing here? Justin's will put me in this position. The same as Justin put you on the ice. You don't have to like it, Finn. Get used to it, because you're stuck with me."

Last season's alternate captain, forward Daniel Murphy, rose from his chair. He planted his feet wide, shoulders squared, pointing to his teammates. "Yeah? So, what's all this mean for us? What changes are you planning to throw at our team?"

The room stilled. Players grumbled. Their attention locked on the exchange.

Margret didn't flinch. She lifted her chin. "It means I'll be taking an active role in the day-to-day operations. Coach Harrison continues to command the ice. My responsibility is to make sure you have everything necessary to succeed, without distraction, without excuse."

Daniel's mouth tightened. He gave a short huff, dropped back into his chair, arms crossing, leaving his defiance hanging in the air.

Defenseman Liam Armstrong, leaned hard on the back of the chair in front of him. His chin jerked at Luke. A fleck of spittle caught the light as he spoke. "What about the frickin' cowboy? What's his role in all this?"

Margret's gaze locked on Armstrong. "Luke is representing his father, Sterling Wheatfield." She pointed a manicured finger at the D-man. "You. Know. The man who owns the other half of this franchise. Don't mistake Luke for a rich Midwestern boy coasting on a family name. His business degree, along with his experience running a billion-dollar enterprise, makes him qualified to handle the financial side of this team. My role is to run the rest. Together, we'll keep the Goshawks where they belong ... at the top."

"Bunch of kids," Finn muttered.

Margret leaned into the podium, eyes narrowing. "What's that, O'Connell?"

Finn shifted forward, elbows braced on his knees. "I said you're a bunch of wet-behind-the-ears kids." He swept a hand between her and Luke. "The two of you are playing grown-up with our futures and the future of this team."

"Geez, Finn, give her a break. She hasn't had time to screw anything up yet." Axel grinned. He turned to Margret, a wink flashing like an ally's shield.

Etan nudged Axel, letting out a loud snort. "Don't worry, Finn. Axel's just buttering her up so he doesn't get traded to the Florida Barracudas."

Axel snapped his head at Etan, eyes wide in mock horror. "The Barracudas? That's low, even for you."

"What? I hear they've got great beaches." Etan grinned, leaning back in his chair.

"Yeah, and zero chance of winning a Cup. I'd rather hang up my skates for good than play with Chucky," Axel shot back.

"Careful, man, say his name three times out loud and he'll pop out of the penalty box like a horror movie villain."

It was all Margret could do to suppress a smile as laughter skated around the room. The players' grim expressions softened. She felt it was the perfect opportunity for another puck drop faceoff. "There's one more change you need to be aware of," she said. "Sage Larson will step into the role of marketing manager and Nikki's backup photographer."

The announcement stirred a ripple of reactions. Daniel let out a low, skeptical laugh. "Hey, we all love Sage ... but how do you expect a small-town photographer from South Dakota to fill your high heels? Really? I just don't get where you're coming from."

Margret's scowl cut sharp. "Sage may not come from a media background, but don't mistake that for incompetence. She's a hard worker and a quick learner. She proved herself on every project I handed her last season. She's earned this. I trust her to deliver. Most important, she knows hockey. She knows the Goshawks."

Liam shifted in his seat, hands clasped, his voice rough. "And what happens if Hunter's contract doesn't get resolved? Where does that leave her ... and us?"

Margret drew in a slow breath, her words measured, carrying more steel than calm. "Sage was brought on for her skill, not her relationship with Hunter."

"Just like your cowboy," the shout came from the back, sharp as a split stick.

Margret did her best to ignore the heckler. "Hunter's contract is being handled. I'm confident it will be resolved in a way that benefits both him and the Goshawks."

Etan leaned forward, his tone darker than his usual good-natured banter. "Yeah, the GM said the same thing about the Snowman and the captain's contracts too."

Et tu, Brute? Margret thought, his words grating on her last nerve, bordering on betrayal.

A low rumble moved through the room, players shifting and murmuring in agreement. Once more the mood turned heavy, taut as a pulled skate lace.

Margret let her gaze sweep across the players. She knew trust had to be earned, especially with this group. Still, she wasn't here to be liked. She was here to lead them to another Cup. She squared her shoulders before delivering the final piece of news. "There's one more thing we need to discuss."

"The hits just keep coming," Liam muttered.

Heat prickled at Margret's cheeks as she pressed on. "As you all know, Chase Rutherford's departure left us without a captain. After conversations with the coaching staff, I'm pleased to announce Ryan Mitchell will wear the C this season."

Approval swept through the room, swelling into sneakers pounding the tile, hoots and howls echoing off the walls. A few players leaned over to slap Ryan on the back, shoving him to his feet.

Axel jabbed an elbow into Etan's side, his grin smug. "I won that bet."

Etan groaned, but his expression was impish. "Big surprise. No one in their right mind bets against the best defenseman in the league."

Margret nodded in agreement, watching her two favorite players slap a high-five.

Ryan turned to face his teammates, sporting a grin. He lifted his hand for quiet. The noise settled, though the energy still thrummed beneath the surface. "I didn't see this coming. Wearing the C isn't something I expected. But standing here now, with this group, it feels right."

He paused. "Chase set a high bar for what it means to be a team captain. He led with strength, with heart, and with class. I can't replace him ... but I can do my best to honor the standards he set."

Ryan's body relaxed, his tone firming. "I want you all to know, this isn't about me wearing a letter. It's about all of us pulling in the same direction. That's how we win. That's how we stay the Goshawks."

The room erupted again; their approval shook the walls. Margret felt her chest tighten, pride swelling as she watched Ryan's teammates surge around him, voices carrying praise. This was the Goshawks she knew and loved. For the first time today, she felt their pulse beating as one.

She waited a beat before announcing, "Daniel Murphy will continue as our alternate captain."

Another wave of approval. Daniel, other than his first outbursts, had spent most of the time perched forward like a spring wound too tight, now eased back in his seat, a faint smile tugging at his lips.

"What about the second A?" Axel called out, scanning the room.

"That goes to Finn O'Connell," Coach Harrison cut in from the sidelines.

Margret nodded to the head coach, waiting for the congratulations to die down before adding, "I know this past week has been filled with change, more than in seasons past. I believe in the Goshawks. I may not skate with you, but I've stood with this organization from the first day any of you put skates to our ice."

She paused, letting her gaze sweep across the players. "Every season you've shown grit, heart, and resilience. I expect nothing less now. Our first regulation game's tomorrow. When we face the Chicago Tempest, I want them to see the fire that defines this team." She stepped back, her words hanging in the air like the crack of a goalie's stick against the pipes.

D-man Dylan Gallagher, who'd been quiet until now, shifted in his seat. He turned to Finn, his words slicing through the rumble. "We'll need more than grit if we don't have a strong starting goalie."

Coach Harrison stepped forward, his voice cracking across the room. "You've all been practicing and playing with Lane Wilson during the preseason games. Until we have ink on paper with Griffin, we're covered. Wilson's been the Eyas' starting goalie for three seasons. If needed, we'll bring up another tendy from the farm team."

"Lane's no Hunter," Ryan called out, turning to the young netminder seated behind him. "No offense, kid."

Lane, gave a curt nod. "None taken."

Margret caught the stiff line of Lane's jaw. The bead of sweat slipping down his temple. The young goalie had been brilliant in preseason, winning every start ... stopping nearly ninety-five percent of the shots that came his way. Yet she sensed the tension beneath his calm reply. Preseason was practice. The real season began tomorrow. If Hunter's contract remained in limbo, the rookie's numbers would be tested against the league's best.

Coach Harrison clapped his hands, sharp and purposeful. "We've got a strong team. We focus on what we can control. Train hard, stick to the game plan, and show up ready."

Margret nodded, her smile just a shade too sharp, her voice lifting brighter than she felt. "We're all in this together. Let's make this season one to remember. For all the right reasons." She added, "Before we close, I'd like to welcome our new players. Along with Lane, two Eyas forwards, John Cache and Roger Meyer, have been promoted to the Goshawks."

"What about the hotshot you traded Chase for?" Finn's voice cut from the front row.

Margret sighed. "Due to last-minute contract negotiations, Trey Moss will join us later today."

Ryan pushed back his chair and rose to his feet. "Enough grumbling," he called out, his voice carrying over the rolling noise. "We're a family. Let's show it." He thrust a fist in the air. "Go Goshawks!"

The team roared back, voices uniting as chairs rattled, fists pounded the walls, shoulders slapped in celebration. The sound thundered through the training room, echoing in Margret's ears. Still, the morning's revelations hung like fog. Beneath it all, she felt a shift. It was thin, but real. Ryan's promotion, Harrison's strength, the spark of unity pulsing in the air ... the Goshawks were anchored once more.

Margret remained at the podium beside Luke and Harrison as the last of the players filed out. There was hard work ahead. Yet, for the first time since Justin's funeral, she let herself believe.

Maybe, just maybe, she could pull this off.

Chapter 5
Games Within Games

Wednesday, Oct 11th
Home Game: Goshawks vs Chicago Tempest

The roar inside the Portland, Maine Goshawks' arena pulsed like a living thing, shaking through concrete and steel. The Jumbotron swept across the crowd, catching faces painted Goshawks blue, jerseys stamped with favorite players' names and numbers, and signs waving tribute to last season's Cup win. Heat rose from the packed stands, thick with the smell of popcorn, hotdogs, and beer. A chant surged up, growing louder until it rattled the rafters. "Ice Wall! Ice Wall! Ice Wall!"

"I'm Tom Hughes, with John 'The Gatekeeper' Hamilton. Welcome to the season opener between the Portland, Maine Goshawks and the Chicago Tempest."

He adjusted his headset; his words drowning in the rising swell of the arena. "There's a lot to unpack before puck drop. The sudden loss of Goshawks' founder, Justin Caldwell, still looms large over this team. Now ownership is split between media powerhouse Margret VanAlen and billionaire cowboy Sterling Wheatfield, a man no one saw coming."

John gave a short laugh, disbelief threaded in his tone. "That announcement sent shockwaves through the league. Two weeks ago, no one in Portland, Maine knew Sterling Wheatfield's name. Now he owns half the franchise. Looks like tonight's game isn't the only thing this team is up against."

"And speaking of headlines," Tom glanced at the notes on his desk. "Let's talk about today's bombshell. Hunter Griffin signed an eight-year deal worth sixty-six million dollars. That's a cap hit of 8.25 per season. The news dropped just hours before morning skate."

"Footage was already circulating before practice wrapped," John added. "Griffin was in his crease at the Goshawks' practice facility, taking heat from the hashmarks, flashing the glove, tracking pucks like it was the playoffs. There was no doubt he was locked in."

"Even so, there's been no confirmation from Coach Harrison on whether Griffin starts tonight," Tom said, tapping his notes on the desk.

"You don't pay a man that much to sit him on opening night. But we'll know soon enough."

Tom gave a quick nod. "Of course, this season isn't just about Griffin. The Goshawks reshaped their roster in a single summer. They moved two fan favorites ... Olaf Svensson, the league's second-best goalie, and Chase Rutherford, their captain and leading scorer. Those weren't random deals. That was a calculated reset."

John leaned back. "They cleared cap space for a reason. You don't let go of veterans like that unless you're building around a cornerstone."

"Two words for you ... Trey Moss. The Goshawks' management did everything they could to lock down the twenty-year-old phenom."

"Can't disagree with you, Tom. The kid's got lightning reflexes and a high hockey IQ. I've studied his plays. The puck follows him around the ice." John let out a hearty laugh. "Plus, three seasons on a losing team left him starving for wins. That kind of hunger makes him a valuable asset."

John looked into the camera lens and shrugged. "He only joined the team last night. Even so, he turned heads during practice. Tonight's the first real chance to see if he lives up to the hype, maybe even become Portland's next favorite player."

"I'm not so sure," John countered. "Don't count Griffin out. The Goshawks' crowd loves their goalie. Plus, unlike Moss, Griffin's always been a team player. Add the Cup ring to his resume, and you've got a leader with pedigree. The challenge now, is he a strong enough to carry the expectations of an entire franchise?"

"Fans seem to be torn between the excitement of having Moss on the team and Griffin back between the pipes." John motioned toward the arena. "It's a different kind of pressure for both players when there's a multi-million-dollar sign next to their names."

Tom shuffled the notes on his desk. "And let's not forget the last piece of the puzzle, backup goalie, Lane Wilson. Fresh off a winning streak in the Goshawks' preseason. Some circles are calling him the next Hunter Griffin. That's a heavy label for any rookie to shoulder, the kind that can make every shot feel like sudden death overtime."

John leaned forward, scrutinizing the ice. "We'll find out soon enough. If Griffin isn't between the pipes tonight, the Goshawks are sending mixed messages about who really owns the crease."

Pregame Warmup

The arena lights dimmed, dropping the crowd into a tense, waiting silence. Everyone fixed on the tunnel, waiting for their first look at the revamped Goshawks' team to take the ice for pregame warmup.

In the darkness, Ryan shuffled his skates, chest tight with the same nerves he'd fought since his first season opener. Beside Hunter, twenty-one-year-old Lane Wilson hovered at the gate, mask tipped high, frozen in place.

Ryan smirked, snatching the mask off Lane's head, pushing him toward the opening. "No Bucket!"

"No Bucket! No Bucket!" The chant rattled down the tunnel, Axel and Etan's voices booming loudest. Veteran players stomped their skates in rhythm.

Lane looked like a deer caught in a truck's headlights. He glanced from Ryan to the bench as he tucked his catcher glove under one arm, running nervous fingers through his unruly long hair.

Coach Harrison stood with arms locked across his chest, head tilted back, eyes closed, jaw working overtime chomping his gum. He let out a low grunt followed by a slow shake of his head.

"Get out there, show 'em what you got," Ryan barked, giving the goalie a shove onto the ice.

The spotlight caught Lane as he pushed off. Raven hair streamed behind him as he cut long arcs across the fresh sheet, the roar of the crowd swelling with every stride. By the time he raised his stick in a wave, the fans were on their feet.

Hunter leaned close to Ryan, voice low, edged with dark amusement. "You know Margret's losing her mind right now."

Ryan lifted his glove to the owner's box, blowing a kiss. "Good. She always says, give the fans what they want."

Up in the booth, John shook his head. "And there he is, Lane Wilson. First pro-moment and already breaking the rules."

Tom jabbed at his tablet, scrolling fast. "Here it is. League rules say players entering 2019–2020 or later must wear helmets during warmups and rookie laps."

"It's a mask, not a helmet," John said, voice smug.

"Once a goalie, always a goalie." Tom snorted. "Either way, the Goshawks' new owners are paying for that moment. Big fine coming."

John gestured at the sea of Goshawks' towels whipping through the stands. "Worth every penny of that fine. You can't buy that kind of fan love. Kid hasn't faced a single shot tonight, and he's already got the barn on its feet."

Tom's brows knitted, his attention never left the rink. "Question is, does this lap mean Wilson's starting ... or is Griffin leading them tonight?"

"I don't know about you, Tom, but the suspense is killing me."

Ryan met Lane at the boards, tossing the mask back. The rookie jammed it on his head, a flush still burning under his cage as he hustled to the Goshawks' net.

Hunter followed the young goalie, mask tilted high, a grin cutting across his face. He stepped onto the ice with slow, deliberate strides. The arena thundered in response, the roar carrying the weight of loyalty. This wasn't curiosity like Lane had stirred up. This was worship of their goalie deity. "Ice Wall! Ice Wall!" boomed, reverent, weighted with memory. It pounded through the rafters, the chant rolling over the glass, rattling the boards. Hunter lifted his stick in a salute to his fans before skating to a corner. He tugged his mask down. His pads scraped the ice with a sharp rasp as he dropped into his stretching routine, every motion crisp and exact.

With a sweep of his arm, Ryan cleared the railing of pucks, the hollow clatter bouncing off the boards. He lunged after the scatter when a blur ripped past, close enough to rattle his balance. *Trey.* Heat prickled up the back of Ryan's neck as his pulse spiked. Narrow-eyed, he watched the new kid tear around the rink, tapping his stick along the glass where a knot of college girls pressed close, jerseys tight with his number stamped bold on their sleeves and backs. Their squeals cut high and piercing, rattling the glass like they rattled Ryan's nerves.

A smile replaced his sneer at the shout of, "Go, Captain!" He recognized Jessica's voice without looking into the stands. She'd stayed for his first game wearing the C. It struck deeper than he expected. He scooped a puck on his stick, flicking it over the glass in her direction. For a heartbeat, the sight of her softened him. His jaw locked, teeth grinding as he shook it off. No place for weakness. He cut hard to the crease, ripping a shot. The puck screamed past Lane, slamming into the net.

"And there's Trey Moss. First game in a Goshawks sweater and he's already playing to the crowd," John said, his tone edged with amusement.

Tom countered, his words laced with exasperation. "Pushed past the captain to do it. I'd pay good money to hear what's said in their locker room after practice." His glance met John's, a knowing look flickered between them.

On the ice, Axel skated alongside Trey, bumping into his shoulder. The big D-man leaned close, voice low and primal. "Don't ever disrespect our captain again." He let out a low growl, then peeled away.

In the booth, John whistled. "Did you catch that?"

The crease between Tom's eyebrows deepened. "Oh, yeah, I saw it. Whatever Berger said, those weren't words of encouragement."

"You can bet they weren't," John added. "Last year's top defenseman never wears a scowl unless he's looking for a drop-the-gloves showdown."

Tom straightened his tie. His voice slipped back into broadcast polish. "Judging by that exchange, folks, there could be more going on in the locker room than in the game tonight. We'll take a quick break before the puck drops. You can count on us to keep you updated on all the action ... on and off the ice."

Introduction

The house lights dropped, plunging the arena into semi-darkness as a low rumble rolled through the crowd. Strobes flared above the tunnel entrance. The bass of *The Phoenix* by Fall Out Boy rattled the rafters, vibrating through Ryan's chest.

A single spotlight slashed across the tunnel as the arena announcer's voice boomed deep and commanding. "And now ... *YOUR* starting lineup for the Portland. Maine. Goshawks! Starting in goal ... number 1 ... Hunter 'Ice Wall' Griffin!"

The roar in the arena hit ear-splitting levels as Hunter skated onto the ice, lifting his stick to the rafters. At the crease, he set his mask on the crossbar, then pushed out between the end zone circles. Under the sweep of lights, his frame cut sharp and unyielding, every movement carrying the weight of a man claiming his ground.

"On defense ... number 25 ... last season's breakout rookie ... Axel Berger. And number 23 ... wearing the C for the first time ... your new captain, Ryan Mitchell."

The crowd erupted again, the noise ricocheting through Ryan's chest. He cut across the ice, blades biting into the surface, taking his place on the blue line. A quick nod to the stands, jaw tightening as adrenaline burned hot under his skin. Every nerve hummed, sharp with the heft of the letter stitched on his sweater.

"At center ... number 80 ... making his Goshawks debut ... Trey Moss. On left wing ... number 63 ... Finn O'Connell. And on right wing ... number 56 ... Etan Eklund."

Trey skated out with the swagger of someone who expected the spotlight, his grin cocky enough to draw cheers that rolled through the stands. Female fans screamed his name, swept up as much by his star power as his skill. Ryan's gut clenched. Swagger was easy. What mattered was whether Trey could bury his ego long enough to play Goshawks hockey.

On the blue line, Axel glared at Trey, then leaned his shoulder into his captain. Ryan pressed back, the weight solid between them. The season might start with the puck drop, but for him, it always began with the heartbeat of the team.

First Period

"You can feel the rumble in the building," Tom's voice cut in as the anthem faded. Chants, cheers, jeers, and raw anticipation surged through the barn, nearly drowning the commentary. Cameras swept the arena, catching a sea of Goshawks and Tempest fans on their feet as the players skated to their faceoff positions.

Laughter filled the booth as John paused, letting the roar fade into tense silence. "New captain. New ownership. A rising star at center. Hunter Griffin back in net. Folks, if you're not staying for the game tonight, you'll be missing the start of what promises to be an epic Goshawks season."

At the first puck drop, Finn O'Connell fought the Tempest captain at the dot and won, snapping the puck to Ryan. He surged forward, carving across the neutral zone. He passed the puck to Trey before leveling a Chicago forward who strayed into Goshawks ice. A quick glance left, caught Trey slicing through the Tempest's defense with raw speed, the puck glued to his tape.

Damn, the kid had wheels. Ryan angled back, ready to cover if the rush collapsed. No need. Trey cut through the zone like it were his alone, blowing past sticks and bodies as if they were practice cones. One last stride, a snap of the wrists, and the puck tore past the Tempest's goalie, hitting the back of the net. Red light glowing.

Goal! Goshawks–Moss

"What a move by Moss!" John shouted. "I'm betting management's breathing easier after dropping big money to land him."

Tom cut in without missing a beat. "No doubt he can score. But the real test is whether he fits in with this team."

The barn exploded as *Chelsea Dagger* blasted from the speakers. Fans stomped their feet, belting out the opening refrain. The sound rolling through the rafters like thunder. Trey looped around the net, arms spread wide, soaking in the frenzy.

Standing next to Hunter, Ryan leaned on his stick watching Trey. The kid coasted by the bench, tapping gloves, but never once looked at his teammates. His gaze stayed fixed on the upper rows, basking in the chants of "Moss! Moss! Moss!

"He's got an attitude," Ryan muttered, tapping Hunter's pads.

"Yeah," Hunter tipped back his bottle, water streaking down his face. "But you can't deny it ... that was a sweet goal."

Ryan pushed off, scowling at Trey. *The kid had skill, no question. But the showboating, the crowd-first routine ... that could rot a locker room fast. If this kept up, the season was going to be a grind.*

The period pushed on with both teams throwing weight and speed into every shift. The Tempest pressed hard for the equalizer. Hunter held fast, turning aside shot-after-shot with quick pads and sharper hands. Some pucks he smothered, others he batted out, each stop clean and final. Every save was met with an eruption that shook the barn to its bones.

The clock counted down, the final seconds dragging. At the horn, Ryan shot a glance at the Jumbotron. 1–0, Goshawks. The burn in his muscles fed him as much as the scoreboard, proof he'd shown up, proof he still had fight in him. Standing near the gate, he tugged his jersey up to wipe the sweat from his face, only to feel Trey brush past.

"What a hoser," Ryan muttered, trailing his teammates down the tunnel.

"Smile, Cap, it's a solid start," Etan said, giving him a slap between the shoulders.

Ryan side-eyed Etan. "Not good enough. The Tempest are fast. Seasoned. Dangerous. You know they'll come out harder next period."

The tunnel swallowed them in a haze of sweat, damp gear, and the dull shuffle of skates on rubber matting. The adrenaline of the ice drained into the pause of intermission, heavy and unrelenting.

Third Period

"Folks, we're heading into the final period, with the Goshawks clinging to a slim lead," John said, his voice carrying over the restless crowd. "The Tempest threw everything they had at Hunter and his defensemen in the second, yet the score held at 1-0. It's been old-time hockey ... heavy hits, no room to breathe from the first puck drop.

Tom watched the players line up for the faceoff. "You're right, the Tempest are down, but not out. Thirty shots on goal. Everyone chipping away at Griffin's wall. The third will be the true test of his endurance."

The puck dropped. The Tempest surged, swarming through the neutral zone in waves. Ryan powered forward, tracking the puck's every move. "Stay Sharp! Stay Tight," he barked, cutting across the lane to seal the gap.

A Tempest forward barreled at him, the collision slamming through his ribs. He braced for the hit, dug in, and shoved back. His stick hacked low, jarring the puck loose, sending it ricocheting up the boards.

Just as Ryan cleared the puck, Axel tangled with a Tempest forward in the corner, his stick riding high across the Tempest's back. The whistle shrilled. Axel threw his arms wide in protest as he was ushered to the box for cross-checking.

"Check your eye prescription!" a fan bellowed, the jeers swelling from the stands, crashing down on the referee.

"That's a tough penalty to take this late in the game," Tom said. "The Goshawks were already under pressure, and now they're down a man."

John came in without missing a beat. "Berger's been solid all night, but he's got to be smarter. Discipline is everything in a one-goal game."

The Goshawks braced for the penalty kill. Thirty seconds in, Daniel Murphy reached to clear the puck, his stick hooking a Tempest forward's skates. The whistle shrilled. Daniel erupted, barking at the call. His spit flying as the linesman muscled him to the box. The Tempest's bench pounded their sticks, feeding off the chaos.

Ryan cut across the ice, sliding tight beside Daniel as the ref stepped between them. "Get your guy under control, Mitchell, or I tack on a ten-minute misconduct."

"One more word and you screw us all. Sit." Ryan crowded into Murphy's space, forcing the fellow Canadian back.

Murphy stormed into the box, yanking the door so hard the glass rattled. Axel glanced at the clock, shaking his head.

"Murphy's off for tripping! The Goshawks are in a real bind now. Five-on-three for the next ninety seconds." Tom groaned. "This could be the turning point."

Ryan's pulse hammered as the Tempest once more lined up. He planted himself at the top of the crease, body squared, stick low, ready to eat whatever came through. Protect the net. Protect his goalie. They were going to need every ounce of grit to survive the kill.

The Tempest snapped passes tape-to-tape, the puck zipping around the zone with impressive speed, forcing the defense to chase.

"Left Side! Stay On Your Man!" Ryan's voice sliced through the chaos.

Hunter dialed in, tracking the puck as it snapped from stick-to-stick. Shots came fast, pounding his pads, smacking off his blocker, stinging into his glove. Each save bought the Goshawks a breath, the crowd's voices rising louder with every stop.

The Tempest's captain broke free, cutting hard to the net with Trey riding him tight. Both barreled into the crease. Hunter caught the first shove, body jolting off balance. The puck kicked loose, glancing off Trey's stick sliding across the line.

Goal! Tempest–Dolence

"What a critical mistake from Moss," John's voice was a mix of disappointment and surprise. "That's got to put a pin in the kid's ego. Talk about knocking yourself off your pedestal."

Tom's voice followed, tinged with frustration. "By the way Griffin is striking his stick on the pipes, you know he's frustrated."

"Plus, his first shutout of the season gone." Tom let out a low laugh. "That's not the first time tonight Moss has gotten under his teammates' skin."

The Goshawks' fans fell quiet as the Tempest celebrated their tying goal.

Ryan skated to Hunter, rapping his pad with the blade of his stick. "We'll get it back. Stay locked."

Hunter nodded, tension tight across his frame.

With the score even, both sides dug in, every shift heavier than the last. Ryan felt the weight pressing hard as the clock counted down. The Goshawks needed a break, and soon.

With the final seconds slipping away, Ryan fed the puck to Etan, who streaked down the right side. His skates carved deep lines into the ice. Axel mirrored him on the left, ready for the pass. Etan faked the feed, then snapped a shot, the puck clanging off the post with a sickening ring.

"Eklund with the shot. Off the post!" Tom's voice rose then dropped. "That was inches away from a Goshawks win."

Ryan gritted his teeth as the buzzer sounded, signaling the end of regulation. The score remained tied one to one. They were headed to overtime. Now it was anyone's game.

Shootout

The horn blared, ending overtime. The scoreboard still 1–1. The players on both benches sagged with fatigue, yet every player braced for the ultimate test. The shootout loomed, best of three, the kind of finish where skill and nerve carried more weight than sixty minutes of grind. The crowd's buzz rose and fell, a mixture of excitement and dread, the whole barn knowing the game was about to tilt on a blade's edge.

In the booth, Tom and John adjusted their headsets.

"Well, John, as a Hall of Fame goalie, what's your perspective on Griffin's mindset right now?"

John arched a brow. "There's no way around it. The pressure on Griffin is intense. Especially with the new contract. Add to that he's only had one practice with the Goshawks this season ... I wouldn't want to be in his skates."

This time Tom's grin crept through, sly and sure. "I don't agree with you, John. With Griffin knowing his future's secure, his focus can be on the game. Right now, that's exactly what the Goshawks need."

John shrugged. "Contracts take a backseat to what he's about to face. Griffin's staring down the ultimate pressure in this shootout."

The camera locked on Hunter in the crease, tapping each pipe in steady rhythm, his body in constant motion.

Tom's voice carried through the booth. "The Goshawks are ready. They've chosen to shoot first, putting the pressure on the Tempest. This is going to be a nail-biter, folks."

John jumped in. "Etan Eklund steps up for Portland. Last season we saw flashes of his speed and skill. Let's see if he can deliver when it counts."

At center ice, Etan closed his eyes for a beat, chest rising with measured breaths. Silence gripped the arena as he launched forward. A quick burst left, then right, his stick snapped, sending a wrist shot screaming over the goalie's blocker and under the bar.

Goshawks–1 Tempest–0

"Eklund makes it look easy. What a way to start!" Tom shouted.

On the bench, Ryan's fists clenched tight, pride surging through him for his young forward. "That's how you do it."

The Tempest's first shooter glided to center ice. His eyes locked on Hunter. The tension thickened, the fans holding their breath. He snapped a shot low and

quick, but Hunter was quicker, glove flashing out, sealing shut like a steel trap.
Goshawks–1 Tempest–0

"Great save by Griffin!" John shouted. "He's totally focused tonight."

Next up for the Goshawks, Trey Moss. The young forward skated to center ice with his trademark confidence, shoulders squared, every movement calculated. He gathered speed, bearing down on the net, but a caught edge jolted him off balance. He snapped the shot, the puck ringing off the post before ricocheting wide.

Goshawks–1/0 Tempest–0

"Moss clangs it off iron!" Tom's call cut through the crowd's collective gasp. "Another big disappointment for the Goshawks and their fans."

Dolence came next. His stride sharp ... hungry, driving straight for the crease. The Tempest captain went for the quick drag move, but Hunter tracked him, shutting it down with a pad save.

Goshawks–1/0 Tempest–0/0

"Griffin, with another stop!" John barked. "He's absolutely in the zone."

"Finn O'Connell, the veteran, steps up for the Goshawks," Tom announced. "This is where experience shines."

Finn's approach was smooth, every stride measured. He sold the fake, snapping his shoulders as if ready to fire ... to draw the goalie out. But the Tempest's netminder didn't bite. He dropped low stuffing the shot wide with his pad.

Goshawks–1/0/0 Tempest–0/0

"Unbelievable, O'Connell comes up empty!" Tom shouted. "That keeps the Tempest alive."

The game rested on Hunter. The final Tempest shooter glided to center ice, stick tapping as he readied for the deciding shot. Hunter sank low in the crease, every line of his frame coiled tight, waiting.

The forward's stick snapped, sending the puck rocketing high. Hunter exploded across his crease, blocker stretched. The impact pushed him into the net as the puck bounced off his glove, coming to die at his skates.

Goshawks–1/0/0 Tempest–0/0/0

"Griffin stops it! The Goshawks win!" Tom hit the table with a fist. "What a game! What a finish! Hunter 'Ice Wall' Griffin is back!"

The arena shook as the Goshawks jumped the bench, flooding their goalie in celebration. Ryan skated to his netminder, taking his place near the end of the goalie appreciation line. They'd done it. The first game of the season was theirs. With Hunter's new contract in place, what could go wrong?

Chapter 6
Brewing Storms

Wednesday, Oct. 11th

The sidewalk glistened beneath the streetlamps, rain-slicked and alive with the leftover buzz of the Goshawks' first regulation win. Rounding the corner, Ryan caught sight of the Frosty Nest's glowing sign. The silhouette of a goshawk perched in a nest of hockey sticks blazing like a beacon above the crowded entrance. It tugged at something deep in his chest. Pride, maybe. Exhaustion ... without doubt.

A cluster of college girls in Goshawks jerseys lingered by the door, phones in hand, cheeks flushed pink, shrill voices calling their names. Ryan hurried to the entrance. *Some things never change.*

"Déjà vu all over again." Rapture, the Frosty Nest's bouncer, swung the door wide. His smile carried easy warmth, but his Grizzly bear's bulk filled the doorway. "You boys still know how to draw a crowd."

Ryan noticed Lane lingering at the edge, shuffling from side-to-side like he was guarding his crease. The rookie's hands stayed buried in his suit pockets, a mirror of Hunter in his first season with the Goshawks.

"What's with the kid?" Hunter shot Ryan a look heavy with questions.

"I don't think he's ever stepped foot in a bar." Ryan shrugged.

"Come on, you expect me to believe that? He's a college all-star goalie. You're telling me the Goshawks never celebrated any of his wins during preseason?"

"He just turned twenty-one last weekend."

Hunter huffed. "That never stopped Etan or Axel from celebrating at the Nest. Why didn't anyone tell me?" His last words dropped to a whisper.

"Hey, no one expects you to be up to speed on the team's dynamic. With everything that's gone down since we got our rings, we've all been slacking on the new guys."

"That ends tonight." Hunter snapped his fingers at Lane. "Hurry up, Wilson. Tradition says the captain buys my backup the first round after an opener win."

"Good thing we won then," Lane shot back, hustling to catch up.

"Wait, Lane!" A fan rushed forward. She shoved a Sharpie at him. When he took the bait, she spun around, tugging her hair aside to bare the back of her jersey. His name stretched across it in bold silver letters. "Sign right here? Oh my gosh, I loved your rookie lap."

Lane sucked in his bottom lip, glaring at Ryan, as if waiting for his D-man to step in ... but the captain stood firm near the open door. With a shaky hand, the young goalie dragged the Sharpie across the silver letters on the girl's jersey. The marker's squeak on fabric, matched her squeal that cut through the hum of the crowd. Her friend nuzzled next to Lane, capturing the moment on her cell.

Ryan leaned into Hunter. "Should we help him out?"

"Nah, I think he has it under control. The girls are harmless, plus he's young and single." He nudged Ryan's shoulder, letting out a low laugh.

"Alright, that's enough. Let the boys in." Rapture's voice cut through, his scowl talking louder than words. He tapped the mic clipped to his collar as he motioned the three Goshawks players forward.

The girls backed off, still giggling over the fresh ink, as Ron, the head of security, appeared. Dressed in black with wire-rim glasses, he always gave Ryan the chills ... as if he were Steve Jobs reincarnated.

"What a game, Hunter," Ron said, shaking his hand. "Great way to start the season," he continued as he escorted them to the VIP area.

Inside, the shift was instant. The Frosty Nest wrapped around them with its signature scent: spilled beer, hot wings crackling in the fryer, the sweet spice of cedar rising from paneled walls. Soft light pooled across the bar, glinting off glassware. Their team's jerseys hung from the rafters like battle flags. The Goshawks logo blinked from the beer taps. Tonight's game replayed on flatscreens angled from every corner, each one catching a fresh burst of cheers.

A waitress brushed past, tray high above her head, ponytail bouncing with each step. Her jersey carried WILSON #34 across the back.

Ryan elbowed Lane. "Look at that. Didn't take long to get your first fan club."

Lane flushed. His eyes locked on the jersey like it might lunge at him. "Is that normal?"

"The waitresses get to wear their favorite player's name and number," Ryan said, flashing a crooked grin.

Hunter laughed, clapping Lane on the back hard enough to jolt him forward. "Welcome to the show, kid."

Ryan let Hunter and Lane drift ahead, rolling the tightness from his shoulders. His thoughts kept circling. Hunter back in net. Lane, a solid backup. The Goshawks battling like they meant to take a second Cup. But beneath the pride, something colder stirred. He could still see Margret in the owner's box, arms folded, glare locked on him when he blew that kiss. That moment scraped down his spine. She looked like she owned more than the team. Ryan had a sinking feeling that she wasn't done with him yet.

He scrubbed a hand down his face as if he could wipe Margret's glare from his memories. Celebration awaited, Ron held the velvet rope aside. The hum of voices and clink of glasses rolled over him as he stepped into the VIP lounge, reserved for the Goshawks and their guests after home games. Axel and Etan jumped to their feet, waving him over to their usual table.

"Sit down, you ninnies," Jessica said, tugging on Etan's suit jacket while Patty wrangled Axel back onto his barstool.

"What?" Axel blinked at her, then at Patty. "We just wanted to make sure he knew where we were."

"This is the same place you guys sit every time you come to the Frosty Nest," Patty scolded, holding up the reserved sign for proof.

"Yes, but this is the first time we've been here this season." Etan leaned forward, directing his words past Patty and Axel to the far end of the table. "In the world of hockey, nothing stays the same."

"I saved you a place," Jessica cooed, nudging the empty barstool out with the toe of her cowboy boot.

"Thanks," Ryan went in for a kiss, when his gaze snagged on the far end of the table. Margret sat, champagne flute in hand, poised as if holding court. Beside her perched Luke, loyal as a lapdog. *Of all people, why was she planted front and center at their table, like she belonged? Like she'd earned the right to celebrate with them.* Ryan forced himself to press a kiss on Jessica's cheek. She smelled of vanilla and a faint trace of hops. He was halfway to claiming the seat when...

"Ryan." Margret's voice cut through the music like skate blades over ice. Sharp. Clean. Impossible to ignore.

He stared her down, one brow raised.

"I'm sure you know there's a fine for rookie laps without a helmet." She gave a sideways glance to Lane before lifting her flute of champagne in a mock toast. "So, Ryan, are you volunteering to cover it out of your salary?"

Ryan met her stare with a slow, sly smile. "No, that doesn't interest me."

A beat of silence lingered before the table broke into scattered laughter. Everyone except Luke, his features locked into a cold, hostile stare. Margret sipped her champagne as if she hadn't just taken a shot at the Goshawks' captain in front of his teammates.

Ryan leaned back, taking in the mess of half-empty glasses. The Frosty Nest was jammed shoulder-to-shoulder, like it always was on an opener. No waitress in sight. From experience, Ryan knew they'd be dry for another twenty minutes if someone didn't move.

His attention shifted down the length of the table. Between Margret and Luke, sat an ice bucket, a bottle of Dom Perignon propped inside like a trophy.

"I'm making a bar run. What's it gonna be, cowboy? Beer, or that sissy stuff?" Ryan prodded.

Luke opened his mouth, ready to fire back, but Margret's fingers closed on his arm before the words escaped.

"Sage, give me a hand," Ryan said.

Jessica's barstool scraped back. "I'll help."

Ryan flashed a quick smile. "That's okay, Jess. We've got it covered."

Jessica's boot heel tapped a sharp rhythm against the floor. "Sure. Take Sage." Her voice was syrup sweet, but the glare she leveled at Ryan carried the sting of a high stick.

Sage, caught mid-sip, set her glass down with a frown, confusion flickering in her eyes as she stood to follow Ryan into the crowd.

The noise swelled as they left the VIP section. Fans shifted aside, parting just enough to let the Goshawks' captain through. The Nest's air hung heavy with seafood poutine and the sweet tang of blueberry BBQ wings. Ryan reached back, catching Sage's hand in his. Her fingers curled into his palm, a quiet anchor as he led her between a pair of fans snapping photos on their phones.

With a wave of his free hand, Ryan flagged Joe behind the bar. Only then did he release Sage, settling his elbow against the counter.

The bartender hustled to him, a towel slung over one shoulder. "What can I get you, Mitchell?"

"Four IPAs, two colas, and two single malts neat." Ryan's tone was low, steady.

"Coming up." Joe disappeared toward the taps.

Sage tilted her head, arms folded. "You really needed me to help carry drinks?"

Ryan turned to her. "Nope. You're here because it's time you started earning that Media Manager salary."

Her brows furrowed. "What's that supposed to mean?"

"Lane," Ryan said. "He turned twenty-one last weekend. Nobody celebrated; nobody even mentioned it. Rookies don't get hung out to dry on my watch."

"You're kidding. No one did anything?"

Ryan gave a single shake of his head. "Not a thing. So tonight, we fix it."

"Okay ... so what exactly do you expect me to do?"

"Cake," Ryan said. "Twenty-one candles. Singing waitresses. The whole deal."

"You're out of your mind. How am I supposed to pull that off at this hour?"

Ryan nodded at the swinging kitchen doors where servers hustled through with trays. "We're in a bar that serves food, aren't we? Cake, pie, it doesn't matter. The manager knows us. You can make it happen."

She frowned, lips pressed tight. "Ryan..."

Joe returned with the order, setting the tray on the bar. "Anything else?"

Ryan shook his head. "That'll do." He dropped a couple of big bills on the counter. "Keep the change." Without a backward glance at Sage, he lifted the tray high and pushed back to the table.

"We have waitresses for that," Ron's voice carried exasperation as he unclipped the velvet rope.

"No problem," Ryan shot back, balancing the tray through the VIP section. The moment he set it down, Etan and Axel lunged for the IPAs.

Patty swatted their hands. "Not on my watch."

"Ow!" Etan rubbed his knuckles. "Just a sip."

"Please. I've seen you take harder hits without flinching. Besides, I'm looking out for you. I don't want to sit here alone because you two got yourselves banned." She shoved a cola toward each of them.

Ryan passed Hunter a scotch, then slid an IPA to Luke. He placed another one in front of Jessica. She accepted the ale without looking at him, jaw tight, fingers picking at the bottle's label.

Hunter raised his drink, then paused, scanning the table. "Where's Sage?"

Ryan took a sip of his scotch, setting it down with a quiet thud. He shrugged. "Ladies' room?"

As if on cue, Sage scooted beside Hunter, a satisfied smile tugging at her lips. She lifted her beer, eyes meeting Ryan's across the table. The faintest nod passed between them. Ryan tipped his glass, then turned back to the chatter around him.

Moments later, the lights flickered and dimmed, shadows sweeping across the Nest. The music cut off mid-beat, replaced by a ripple of hushed voices. Heads turned to the glow moving out of the kitchen.

The waitress with the bouncing ponytail, Lane's number on her jersey, carried a cheesecake blazing with twenty-one candles. Her voice rang out as she launched into *Happy Birthday.*

The table erupted. Etan and Axel pounded the wood in rhythm, players crowding around Lane as if he'd just made a game-saving stop ... taps on the head, slaps on the back. Fans throughout the bar picked up the song, rough voices rising off-key.

Lane froze, eyes wide at the blaze of candles. By the final chorus, his eyes misted before he blinked hard. He leaned forward and blew, snuffing all twenty-one flames in a single breath. Smoke curled upward, sweet with melted wax and sugar.

When the cheering eased, Lane cleared his throat, his voice rough around the edges. "Thanks, guys. Seriously ... this is amazing."

The waitress leaned close, planting a quick kiss on his cheek. "Happy birthday, rookie," she whispered before darting back into the crowd as the bar roared its approval.

Ryan tipped back his glass, biding his time, letting the laughter die down. His smile tight as he shouted across the table. "No disrespect intended, Margret..." He leaned in, elbows braced on the wood, a predator about to pounce. "...but why are you at our table?"

Luke straightened, his barstool scraping against the floor as he glared at Ryan.

Margret stilled the cowboy with a flick of her fingers. "Because I'm the owner," she said, calm and unbothered, the stem of her champagne flute steady in her hand. "Which means I can sit anywhere I please." She took a slow sip. "If you don't enjoy my company, you're welcome to move."

Ryan's gaze swept the room. The Frosty Nest was packed ... no open tables, not even a spare barstool.

Everyone at the table held their breath for a beat, tension coiled tight until Etan cut in. "Yo, Hunter. Tough break. Trey, blowing your shutout."

Axel jumped in. "That dink's too into himself. Unless he plays like part of the team, I'm not passing him the puck."

"Best trade this team's made," Luke chimed, lifting his beer.

Ryan snorted. "You don't know a damn thing about hockey. Let alone trades. Stick to horses, Luke. That's all you'll ever manage."

Luke's knuckles whitened on his bottle, his face turning scarlet. Margret's flute hit the table, bubbles splashing over her hand. Everyone stilled, the air tight as taunt wire.

After giving Ryan her fiercest *enough already* look, Sage turned to Etan. "Why didn't Trey come with you? Isn't he your roommate?"

"He doesn't like hanging out with us," Axel muttered.

Etan nodded. "All he talks about is Trey. Trey's goals. Trey's fans. Trey's abs." He dragged out a fake yawn. "Can't wait 'till he moves out. Place is too small for him and his ego."

Ryan caught Luke flick a glance at Margret. She answered with the faintest shake of her head.

Before the air could snap, their waitress arrived with a tray of shots and two virgin Goshawks' signature cocktails. She set them down, her smile aimed at Ryan. "Sorry about earlier. I'll keep your table top priority." She placed the blue drinks in front of Axel and Etan. "I remember you troublemakers from last season. I'll be watching you two." With a quick smile at Margret, she hustled back to the bar.

Jessica slid closer, her lips brushing Ryan's ear. "You hungry?"

"Starving."

"I'll grab you some lobster sliders and pretzel bites."

Patty pushed back her barstool, nodding to Sage. "We'll help."

Axel hopped up beside them.

Etan elbowed Lane with a grin. "Let's track down that cute waitress. Maybe she'll stick around for cake?"

The group peeled off to the buffet, leaving behind a tighter, heavier silence.

Margret lifted her champagne flute, watching the bubbles climb. "So, Hunter," her voice velvet-smooth, "how did it feel being back between the pipes tonight? First game since signing that monster contract."

Hunter took a sip of scotch. "It felt right. Good to be home." He smiled at her. "Thanks, by the way. I know you had a hand in making it happen."

"Don't thank her." Ryan drained his scotch in one pull, welcoming the burn. "Could've saved us a lot of drama if she'd done it sooner."

Margret arched a brow, but Luke jumped in. "That wasn't on her. She didn't even touch Hunter's deal until yesterday. You know that."

"Still," Ryan shot back, his tone all bite. "It's obvious she had influence over Justin. He wouldn't have left the team to her otherwise. Even a cowboy doesn't need skates to understand timing."

Margret leaned in, her elbow resting on the weathered wood. Her smile curled, sharp and deliberate. "What do you think of Trey, Ryan?"

Ryan met her gaze. "You sure you want to open that door?"

"No." She sipped her champagne, unbothered. "Not really."

"Then why ask?"

She didn't answer him directly. "Just hoping the team's giving him a fair shot. Next to Hunter, he's the team's biggest investment. It's not easy breaking into a core group that's been together five seasons."

Luke nudged her. "When are you going to tell him?"

Ryan's eyes narrowed. "Tell me what?"

Margret sighed, as if Luke had spoiled the punchline. "Trey's contract has a clause. He doesn't share apartments. He needs his own space."

Hunter frowned. "Isn't team housing full?"

Luke's smirk spread as he turned to Ryan. "You living with anyone?"

Ryan blinked, a cold weight settling in his gut. "No. Just me."

"Well," Margret said, her voice honey-sweet, "Trey will be moving into your place."

For a beat, Ryan didn't move. Then he eased back, a finger tracing the rim of his empty glass, shoulders tight. "You're not pawning that prima donna off on me."

"You're right," Margret replied, her voice smooth. "We're not. He's taking over your apartment. Temporary, of course. Just until we find him a place offsite."

Ryan slid his empty glass across the table, the sound swallowed by a burst of laughter from a nearby booth. Music thumped low from the speakers, the bass rattling in his chest. His head throbbed, the room blurring red at the edges. He stayed silent, his thumb worrying over the edge of his Cup ring beneath the table, shoulders sinking as if he carried the weight of a big game loss.

"Come on, Ryan," Margret said, calm, cool, collected. "You, of all people, should understand the pressure. He's young. He needs breathing room."

Ryan got to his feet, every line of him rigid with restraint. A low buzz rippled through the bar as the others returned from the buffet.

Margret lifted her glass in a mock toast, her smirk just shy of smug. Ryan met her eyes, unflinching, though his gut twisted as Jessica appeared with a plate stacked with sliders.

"Hope these are enough," she said, setting it in front of him. Her hand brushed his shoulder.

He shrugged it off. "Lost my appetite."

"Ryan..."

"I'm good." Still standing, he snatched a full shot glass from the try, tossing it back in one gulp. The liquor scorched his throat. "I need some fresh air."

Jessica leaned in, voice low. "I'll come with you."

"Don't." Feeling a tinge of guilt, he brushed a stray hair from her cheek. "Stay. Enjoy the night." He didn't wait for a reply. Just turned and walked off.

Hunter jumped up, trailing him past the VIP rope. Music swelled behind them, classic arena rock pounding as the warmth of the Nest gave way to the cooler air near the front. Ryan already had an Uber pulled up on his phone, the screen glowing in his hand.

"Crash at my place tonight." Hunter pressed his house key into Ryan's palm. He held it there for a beat longer. "What she did ... that was a low blow. Just remember, we've got you."

Ryan dipped his head, swallowing hard before he found his voice. "Thanks, bud." He pulled Hunter into a quick hockey hug, the same as after any game, win or lose.

Outside, the sidewalk buzzed with energy. The night air carried damp pavement and the faint tang of the harbor. A few fans spotted him near the curb, waving and calling his name. He didn't slow. Just ducked into the waiting car and slammed the door.

He leaned his cheek against the cool glass as the Frosty Nest slid past, neon blurring. The pride and heat of the win drained away, leaving only the dull ache of being displaced.

Ryan slouched against Hunter's apartment door, eyes closed, wishing he hadn't slammed that last shot.

"Don't bother. He's not home." Hunter's neighbor, Jill, stood a few feet away, all smart smiles in yoga pants and a hoodie, a gym bag slung over her shoulder.

"Really?" Ryan countered. She was too easy a target not to jab at.

"Yeah, really." Her mouth curved in that sharp little smirk that always grated on his nerves.

He wanted to ask how she knew about Hunter's comings and goings. Instead, he shot back, "Kind of late for a workout."

"I like having the gym to myself." She tilted her head, studying him. "Why are you here without Hunter?"

Ryan dangled Hunter's keys between them, the metal clinking.

Her brows rose. "Great. Now I'm stuck with you too." In a huff, she jabbed the elevator button three times. The door slid open. Then she was gone, leaving behind the faint mix of citrus and vape.

Ryan exhaled, leaning harder against the door. He hated the way his chest pulled after her, how he'd noticed the sway of her walk, the glint in her lavender eyes ... even when they were daring him to back off.

He didn't know what unnerved him the most ... Margret blindsiding him ... or the girl next door slipping under his skin.

Chapter 7
Fault Lines

Thursday, October 12th

Sunlight slashed across the countertops, bright and merciless, as if the house wanted to remind her it wasn't truly hers. Justin's kitchen. Her kitchen now. Margret cinched her silk robe tighter, slippers on cool marble, one finger tapping a jagged rhythm against the espresso machine.

"Stupid, arrogant..." she muttered. Coffee grounds smeared the white counter, a dark crescent marring perfection. Instead of wiping it away, she stared it down, imagining Luke's smug grin in the mess. Steam hissed. Her hand froze on the mug. She sensed him before she saw him. The faint shift of air. The slap of bare feet. *Luke.*

She turned at the sound of him, and there he was ... bare-chested, hair a tangled mess. Faded jeans rode low on his hips, worn soft at the seams. His abs tightened as he reached above her for a mug. Her hands flew up, flat against his chest. Heat surged beneath her cool fingers. She pushed. More protest than force.

"Clothes, Luke," she snapped, her gaze snagging on the stubble roughening his infuriatingly kissable jaw. "Try dressing like a grown-up before you enter my kitchen."

His grin curved into a half-smile, as if daring her to react. Ignoring the shove, he leaned past her and poured himself a coffee. He settled onto a barstool at the island with a sigh that filled the silence. "You're still mad."

Margret folded her arms. "You think?"

"Last night wasn't a team summit."

She scoffed, stalking to the opposite side of the kitchen island, the hem of her robe fluttering. "You humiliated me. In front of my team."

He sipped, the rim of the mug hiding a grin. "Our team. Last I checked, Sterling still owns half."

"You own nothing. Sterling left you in charge," she hissed. "A man who thinks a horse trailer qualifies as office space."

Luke glared at her. "We both know Ryan's a major jerk, but he's the Goshawks' captain. He deserved respect."

Margret's palms tightened around her mug. The heat bit into her skin. "You undermined me," she said, softer now. "In public."

"I only said what you wouldn't." His voice stayed calm. "Your golden boy needed to know you were about to kick him out of his apartment."

"I didn't kick anyone out. I was obligated to secure Trey a single apartment. It's in his contract. Goshawks housing is a short-term transition. Rookies, new signings. Not for a captain who should've settled in his own place years ago."

Luke shifted in his seat. "Didn't mean to make you look bad. But you can't run this team alone. You've got to share control. That's something that's difficult for both of us."

Margret turned, fury simmering under her skin like a too-hot espresso. She left her coffee on the counter, untouched. "If you're coming to New York, be ready in an hour." Without waiting for his answer, she stomped down the hallway, slippers striking sharp against the marble.

The Goshawks' jet sliced through a sky so smooth it felt indifferent. Not a cloud in sight. Not a bump in the ride. Just quiet pressure, the kind that built behind the eyes and never let go.

Margret sat in the front section, her tablet idle on her lap, its screen gone black. She'd claimed the aisle seat, a deliberate barrier to keep anyone from sitting beside her. The hum of the engines paired with the soft clinking of glassware.

One row up a flight attendant refilled Coach Harrison's ginger ale. Across from him, Luke and Sage sat shoulder to shoulder, heads bent over a glowing tablet. Promotional shots. Marketing slides. Sage's fingers skimmed the screen, pointing out edits, her blonde hair spilling forward. Luke leaned in, laughing at a detail Margret couldn't catch.

She wanted to hurl her coffee. Instead, she handed the cup to the flight attendant, unclipped her seatbelt, smoothed her skirt, and stood. Down the narrow aisle, the atmosphere shifted. She didn't announce herself. She never had to.

The team's section buzzed with a different energy ... voices louder, laughter unrestrained. A poker game rattled at the back. The scent of peppered jerky and popcorn hung in the air.

Margret spotted Ryan by the window, head tipped against the glass, eyes shut as if he were meditating. Or maybe just trying to block out Trey Moss. The young superstar sat beside him, rattling on about power-play formations, shot-attempt differential, ticking off shots on goal, misses, and blocks.

"I told Coach if we cycle behind the net more, the slot opens up for back-door..."

"Trey." Margret's tone was flat, unmistakable.

He froze mid-sentence.

"Etan and Axel are reviewing film two rows back. They might benefit from your insights."

Trey blinked. "Oh, yeah?"

She gave a practiced smile. "Plus, there's snacks. I think I saw wings."

That did it. Trey stood, smoothing his hoodie. "Cool. Catch you later, Cap." He clapped Ryan on the shoulder and headed to the back.

Margret slid into the seat beside Ryan before he could protest.

He didn't look at her. "Trouble in paradise?" His chin flicked forward.

Her gaze followed. Luke and Sage still leaned in close, their heads nearly touching. Her stomach tightened.

"Nothing I can't handle," she muttered, crossing one leg over the other until the sharp toe of her stiletto brushed against Ryan's shin.

He glanced at her shoe, then back up at Margret. "Why are you in my row?"

She huffed. "To apologize."

Ryan arched an eyebrow. "You?"

"Yes," she said, folding her hands in her lap. "I overstepped at the Frosty Nest. I should've handled it differently."

He studied her for a beat longer than necessary. "You think?"

Her tone sharpened. "I said I should've handled it differently. Not that I was wrong."

"Ah," Ryan said, twisting the cap on a mini water bottle. "The fine art of the half-apology."

She let the jab land but didn't bite. Instead, she plucked at a piece of lint on her sleeve. "I'm serious, Ryan. We both want what's best for this team. Nothing good is going to happen if we continue to butt heads."

"You gave away my apartment." Ryan snapped his fingers once. "Just like that."

“You disrespected me.” She uncrossed her legs, stilettos scraping against the floor.

He turned back to the window, a muscle ticking at his temple. “We’re not going to win a Cup by coddling egos.”

“I agree,” she said, her voice cool. “We’ll win it by pulling in the same direction. Are you capable of that?”

He let the question hang before answering. Then, with a nod to the front, he said, “Depends. Who’s really running the Goshawks’ organization?”

Before she could reply, a voice crackled over the intercom.

“Listen up Goshawks, this is your captain speaking. We’ll be touching down into Buffalo in approximately fifteen minutes. Please, fasten your seatbelts.”

Margret stood, smoothing her blazer. “Thanks for the chat, Captain.” She walked up the aisle like she owned it, reclaiming her seat as if she hadn’t served two minutes in the penalty box for sparring with her captain.

Luke looked back. A moment later he rose. When she slid to the window seat, he eased down beside her, brushing a kiss against her temple.

Margret sat statue still, her lips barely moving as she said, “I forgive you.”

Back in the players’ section, Hunter dropped into the vacated seat, handing Ryan a protein bar. “What was that about?” he asked.

Ryan tore back the wrapper, his expression unreadable. “No idea,” he said around the first bite.

The plane jolted as the wheels kissed the tarmac, a soft shudder running through the cabin.

Chapter 8
Breaking Point.

Friday, October 13th
Away Game: Goshawks vs Buffalo Rapids

Hovering above general seating, the Harbor Club Box was more vantage than luxury. Sage led the way to the small table pressed against the glass railing. The rink spread wide beneath them, an arena set for combat.

Margret slid into the seat near the glass; the chill from the ice curled up to greet her. A chair scraped as Sage settled across from her. Beyond the boards, the Zamboni moved in slow arcs, its wide blade shaving the surface. The scene below marked the hour clearer than the time clock. Pregame warmup ... over. She looked at Sage with an approving smile. "Thanks for the seating suggestion. Justin always opted for a suite for away games."

"I thought you might enjoy being closer to the action, feel the energy of the crowds ... but still have a fair share of privacy."

Luke appeared at the table, sudden as a shadow, balancing two pints of ale foaming at the rims in one hand and a single glass of sunlit wine in the other. He set them down with the easy steadiness of a man who'd once worked behind a country bar.

Margret lifted the glass, the color promising what she expected. One sip proved otherwise. Her mouth tightened, lips drawing in as though she'd bitten into something unripe. She lowered the flute with deliberate grace, eyes narrowing on Luke.

"You do remember I drink Chablis, don't you? This..." she tapped the base of the glass against the table, the pale liquid trembling inside, "...is not Chablis."

Luke dropped into the chair at the end of the table, adjusting the brim of his cowboy hat before letting it tip back. A faint smile flickered at the corners of his mouth. "I've got a great memory when it comes to pleasing you, Margret. But the bar only pours local stock." He leaned back slightly, shoulders loose. "Only white they had was Chardonnay."

A retort hovered on Margret's tongue, something sharp enough to sting. Then he flashed that unshakable smile, the one that belonged more in a boardroom deal ... or under a wide prairie sky ... than in an arena box. Her words dulled before they left her mouth. Instead, she tapped the glass once more, the liquid quivered.

"That figures," she said at last, her tone clipped but quiet. She hoped this wasn't a sign of what was to come. She needed a strong win. Nothing else would do.

Sage leaned forward, eyes bright as the house lights dimmed. "Hey, that's Kacey Rhodes," she said, nodding to the spotlighted singer at center ice. "I love her."

Margret rose with the others. She reached over to touch Luke's arm as he removed the cowboy hat, holding it over his heart. Across from her, Sage sang along, her voice sweeter, more genuine, than the country star's words echoing through the arena.

When they sat again, Margret lifted her wine. The first sip hit her tongue heavy and warm, the flavor clinging instead of cleansing. She swallowed, fighting the urge to grimace.

First Period

The announcer's voice boomed through the arena: "Tonight, for the Portland, Maine Goshawks, in goal, number 34, Lane Wilson."

Margret coughed, the wine catching in her throat as Luke reached over to pat her back.

Across the table, Sage blinked, confusion clouding her face. "I thought Hunter was starting."

"Looks like Coach Harrison listened to me after all," Luke said, leaning back, a slow grin spreading across his face.

Margret's gaze snapped to the bench where Hunter sat. No mask, just a Goshawks cap pulled low over his hazel eyes. Elbows on knees, jaw locked, staring straight ahead as if none of it touched him. Something twisted hard in Margret's chest. She turned on Luke. "The idea that you, of all people, could persuade Coach Harrison to do anything is absurd."

Sage leaned in, her brows drawn tight. "What are you talking about, Luke?" Her voice rose an octave. "Why would you want Lane in the net instead of Hunter?"

The grin slipped from Luke's face. "It's a strategic move. Puts the Rapids off their game. Lane proved himself with our Eyas farm team. Plus, he only let in a half dozen goals all preseason." He downed his ale in one long drag.

Margret inhaled. Four steady breaths, in and out, before her words came sharp. "Just stop trying to be something you're not. Stop meddling in a business you know nothing about." For a moment, she waited for his verbal retaliating strike.

Instead, Luke rose, his boots scuffing the floor. He tilted his head at Sage. "Want a refill?"

She glanced at Margret, hesitation flickering across her face, then gave a small nod. "Yes, please."

Luke headed to the bar without a backward glance at Margret.

She could feel the heat rise from her chest to her neck. Her voice chased after him, thin and cutting. "I'm fine, but thanks for asking?" The sarcasm dripped like poison into crystal perfectly poured.

"Shoot. The. Puck," The chant rolled through the arena, pulling Margret's attention back to the ice just as Lane made his first save ... a sharp blocker deflection that sent the puck skidding up the boards.

Then came the hit. The glass beneath them shuddered as a Rapids defenseman leveled Etan with a shoulder that rode far too high. The refs swallowed their whistles. *Of course they did. Home ice advantage was always more than the logo at center ice.*

Margret didn't flinch. She lifted her glass, chugging the too-warm Chardonnay like it was water.

"They're targeting the wings," Sage murmured, swallowing the last swig of her beer, as another crunch sent Finn sprawling after a quick dish to Etan. "That was interference."

Margret's eyes never left the play. "The refs need to pay attention to you, but we both know they won't."

The game turned gritty. Elbows high, sticks slashing, every shift a scrum waiting to erupt. Then the whistle split the noise. The ref glided to center ice, tapping his mic. "Tripping. Buffalo. Number 56."

Margret's fist snapped into the air. "Finally."

Another rush. Another whistle.

"High sticking. Buffalo. Number 22."

The Rapids' forward slammed his stick against the boards as he dropped into the penalty box, curses spilling loud enough to turn heads in the lower bowl.

Luke slid a pint glass across the table to Sage. He then sank into his chair, raised his ale, and took a long swallow. "What'd I miss?"

Sage accepted the glass, taking a sip, her head tilting at the ice. "Commercial break. Two Rapids in the box, five on three."

Around them, the arena noise swelled with chants, boos, and the restless shuffle of fans on their feet. Scattered in the sea of Rapids' blue and gold, a few brave Goshawks supporters in powder blue and silver jerseys lifted their voices for the away team.

Luke sat back, arms folded, his tone easy. "They need to run the umbrella from the top of the slot."

"Please stop pretending you know what that means," Margret growled.

"No, really. I'll show you." He tugged the napkin from under his glass. Looking at Sage, he snapped his fingers.

With the kind of shorthand only longtime friends shared, she dug a pen from her suit pocket, sliding it across the table.

Luke sketched fast, blocking out the end zone ... net, faceoff circles, the blue line. In the middle of the line, he wrote Axel. On the right circle, Ryan. On the left, Finn. Then, Trey and Etan planted in front of either side of the crease. He slid the napkin forward, grinning like a schoolboy. "I've been watching tape with the guys."

Sage gave a short gigglesnort as she plucked up the napkin. "Good for you, Luke." She crumpled the paper, lobbing it back at him.

Margret smirked, then lifted her empty wine glass to Sage in a silent toast. By the time her focus returned to the rink, the puck was in play.

A Rapids defenseman caught it clean on his tape before rifling the puck deep into the Goshawks' zone. Axel cut behind Lane's net to retrieve it, but two Rapids forwards pressed hard from either side of the trapezoid. No time. No space. Margret held her breath as Axel planted his skates. Putting his weight into his shot, he backhanded the puck. Her moan escaped when the hurried clearance caught too much edge, sailing into the stands instead of banking off the boards.

"Oh, for the love of..." She sat back, crossing her legs, shaking her stiletto. "Delay of game."

"Bad break for Axel." Sage sighed as the defenseman skated to the penalty box.

"I liked the five on three advantage a lot better too." Luke added.

As the puck dropped, Margret fixated on her goalie. The rookie dropped low, reading the plays as if every second was survival. The Rapids circled like sharks. Three quick passes cut the zone. A crack rippled through the arena as the puck

snapped past Lane .... top shelf, glove side. A shorty for the Rapids' captain.
Goal! Buffalo—Jackson

Margret's eyes darted to the Goshawks' bench. Hunter pushed to his feet, then sank back, coiled tight, waiting for his chance.

The buzzer sounded, closing the first period.

Margret slumped in her chair. Her fingers tightened around the stem of her empty glass before setting it down with care, as if the sound of glass on wood might betray her. She sat motionless, lips pressed thin, her silence carrying more weight than words. Friday the thirteenth had never been her favorite day for an away game.

Second Period

Buffalo won the draw to open the second, their forwards cutting through the neutral zone in smooth strides. A quick dump chased down hard, sticks banging against the boards pinned the Goshawks deep. The Rapids worked the puck high to low, cycling the zone with relentless pressure.

At six-foot-five, Lane filled the net when he settled into his butterfly. His pads flared wide to seal the ice as the Rapids peppered pucks into his crease. A wrist shot kicked off his blocker, ricocheting into the corner. Another came through a screen; pad save to the left. The next blast ripped from the point, tipped mid-air. Lane snapped his glove in a wide arc, snaring it clean.

Sage shot to her feet. "Let's go, Hunt..." The cheer broke in her throat. Her hands froze mid-clap. "Oh..."

Margret arched a brow. "Easy mistake," she murmured. "They have a similar style." She glanced at her empty glass, then reached for Luke's pint without meeting his eyes. The first swallow dragged a cough. She loathed the taste of beer, but right now she needed something. "Same gear. Same reach. Same focus." She exhaled slowly. "His size is the biggest difference. Lane takes up the whole net."

Sage dropped back into her seat. "For a rookie, he's just so ... calm."

"He's hungry for a win," Margret said. Her voice stayed smooth, though her gaze never left the crease.

Luke pushed back from the table. "What can I get you, Margret?"

"Ice water would be nice," she said. "Anything to wash down the memory of that Chardonnay."

The Rapids pressed again, a shot clanging off the post. Lane kicked out the rebound, then pushed across the crease to seal the far side just in time. Sage pressed her fingers between her lips, letting out a shrill whistle.

Luke returned, setting a crystal goblet of ice water in front of Margret. He stood behind her chair, clapping slow and deliberate. "Lane's putting on a show."

Margret's hands pressed against the glass railing as Finn intercepted a loose puck at the Rapids' blue line. He cut hard left, deked a defenseman so badly the Buffalo's player spun out. He skated to the Rapids' net, where he made a quick pass to Trey, who snapped the puck clean and fast through the goalie's five hole.

Goal! Goshawks—Moss

Three shifts later, Trey struck again. The faceoff win dropped to Etan, who slid it forward with a slick no-look pass. Trey, already in motion, caught it on his backhand, flipped it to his forehand, snapping it low between the goalie's skate and the post.

Goal! Goshawks—Moss

Margret rose, clapping twice. She glanced at Sage. "Back-to-back goals. Trey's on fire. That'll play well on socials."

On the ice, Trey glided past the bench, tapping gloves. He glanced at their section, giving Margret a quick salute.

Margret's smile tilted. "Gotta love that kid. Just enough cockiness to sell a highlight reel."

Sage bounced in her seat. "The fans are going to eat this up."

"They should." Margret's gaze swept the ice, her mind already pulling captions and clips together as if she was still the media manager instead of the co-owner. She turned to Sage. "Find Nikki. You two get down to the locker room. I want Trey mic'd-up and his footage online before intermission ends."

Third Period

Moments into the third, the second line struck. Alternate captain, Daniel Murphy, blasted from the point. The Rapids goalie sprawled, kicking the puck out with his pad. Lian Armstrong pounced on the rebound, burying it glove-side.

Goal! Goshawks—Armstrong

Margret's table erupted in cheers, drawing sharp looks from the Rapids' fans nearby. On the bench below, the Goshawks were on their feet, sticks hammering the boards.

Sage beamed. "Now that's how you start a period."

"Let's hope they remember how to finish." Margret's tone was cool, her expression unshaken, as she watched with the poise of an empress at court.

Thirty seconds into the next line change, a Rapids power forward barreled into Ryan at the blue line. The collision rattled the glass, the vibration shivering to the Harbor Club seats. Margret covered her ears, doing her best to blunt the roar of Buffalo's crowd.

The Rapids kept coming, charging into the Goshawks while the refs turned blind eyes to slashes and trips. Through it all, Lane held firm. Shot-after-shot, he tracked the puck. Pads sealed. Glove high. Blocker set. A wild scramble in front forced him into a full split, robbing a Rapids' sniper with a toe save that drew jeers from the Buffalo crowd.

Margret's nails pressed into her palms as she followed Lane's every twitch, every adjustment. Her expression, a mask of control, slipped. Eyes narrowed. Lips parted. Her breath caught as the rookie read a two-on-one like a seasoned vet.

The clock ticked down. With two minutes left, Buffalo pulled their goalie.

Six attackers swarmed. Lane faced a flurry of shots. One rang off the post. Another was redirected by Ryan's skate. Just before the end of the period, the horn blasted as Lane smothered a point-blank blast against his chest, making the final score Goshawks 3, Rapids 1.

The bench emptied as the Goshawks skated to Lane. Helmets bumped against his mask, gloves thumped his shoulders. Lane stood tall in the net, blinking like he couldn't believe it was over.

Hunter skated to the end of the goalie appreciation line, his stride measured. When he reached the rookie, it was only the two of them. He hauled Lane into a bear hug, the force lifting the younger goalie off his skates.

Margret's gaze never touched the scoreboard, the cameras, or even the cheers from the smattering of Goshawks fans. She kept her focus on Hunter, on the way he embraced Lane. She drew a slow breath, the knot in her chest easing at last. Hunter's net had been taken from him at the last moment. A decision that could have left him seething. Instead, he rose above it, celebrating the rookie who carried the night. Moments like this reminded her of why she loved hockey so much.

Chapter 9
Home Again

Saturday, October 14th

Ryan sighed. *Coming home should have felt better than this.* The lobby was quiet, echoing with the soft roll of his suitcase wheels over polished tile. Midnight air clung to their suits, stale from the jet, wrinkled with hours of wear. Ryan tugged at his loosened tie while Hunter shifted his garment bag higher, the hanger jutting against his shoulder.

Hunter muttered under his breath something about missing sleep. Ryan didn't catch it all, but he didn't need to. Hunter's scowl did the talking, quiet fury simmering under a creased forehead.

"Oh geez, eh?" Ryan said, pressing the elevator button with a knuckle. "It's only our second game. You almost got a shutout on the opener. Shake it off, bud, you'll be in the net next time."

"Can you guarantee that?" Hunter snorted, low and sharp. "After signing the contract, I didn't expect to be riding the pine this soon."

"Yeah, well, none of us did." Ryan rolled his shoulder.

"Hold the door!"

Ryan's hand shot out, bracing the steel edge just as Jill breezed in. Her black bob swung with each step, oversized coat cinched at the waist, pleated skirt whispering against her knees. Citrus and a trace of vanilla from her vape pen drifted in with her, a sharper counterpoint to the sterile lobby air.

"You boys are getting in late." Her eyes lingered on Hunter.

"Long night ... Buffalo," Hunter said, voice dry.

She hugged him, quick and familiar, her hand resting a second too long on his sleeve. Ryan jabbed the elevator button to their floor like it had wronged him.

"You just getting back from a date?" Ryan asked.

Jill smiled, slow, confident. "Something like that." She adjusted her purse.

As the doors slid shut, Ryan's gaze tracked down her outfit. From her coat to her skirt, stopping at her shoes. Penny loafers. He squinted. "Are those silver pennies in your shoes?"

"Steel, not silver," Jill corrected, lifting one foot, wiggling her toe. "They're a matched pair of 1943 Steel Lincolns."

Ryan crouched, lifting the toe of her loafer onto his knee for a closer look. "Are they real?"

Jill wobbled, catching herself on the wall. "Mint condition. My granddaddy was a collector. Uncirculated. I never wear them if it's going to rain or snow. Don't want them to rust."

"Made during the war when copper was scarce," Hunter added, like he was reading from a Wiki page.

Ryan frowned at him as he straightened, brushing his trouser leg.

Hunter shrugged. "Hey now. I know things other than hockey."

The elevator chimed, doors parting onto their floor. Jill stepped out first, turning back with a mischievous glint.

"Been meaning to ask, Hunter. Over the years, I've been stuck in this elevator with you plenty of times. You always smell nice after games ... never rank. Does the team have a laundry lady?"

Hunter barked a laugh.

Ryan bit the inside of his mouth, suppressing amusement. "We've got equipment managers for that. Not laundry ladies."

"They wash all your sweaty clothes?" Jill pressed.

"What do you mean by all?" The crease between Ryan's brows grew deeper.

"You know..." Jill's lips twitched. "Your outer and under things. Like the garments that protect your ... bits and pieces."

Another round of laughter rolled out of Hunter, deep and unrestrained.

"Jocks," Ryan said flat, no nonsense. "And yes. Those are included in the ... all." He waited for her cheeks to pink and was unsettled when she didn't blush.

Instead, she nodded as if cataloging the fact. "Well, now I know. Send my regards to your people for keeping the Goshawks' athletic supporters in good shape."

She hugged Hunter again, quick and easy, then flicked a finger wave at Ryan. With that, she strolled down the hall to her apartment, each step punctuating her exit.

Ryan stared after her, rubbing the back of his neck, rolling the stiffness out like he could shake her memory. When he caught himself half-smiling at the ridiculous *laundry lady* question, he scowled, jerking his suitcase forward, shaking his head, as if doing so would remove Jill from his thoughts.

The hallway stretched quiet except for the low rumble of his bag wheels. They stopped at the apartment door, Ryan's pulse still tight with leftover annoyance.

Hunter pushed inside first. His bag hit the wall with a dull thud, a sound too heavy for the hour. He kicked off his shoes without looking back, same as always. Ryan toed his off, leaving them where they landed. One of Hunter's rules. No shoes past the entry. He shut the door with his heel. The quiet click closed them in for the night.

The overheads softened under Hunter's touch, sinking the room into amber half-light. The liquor cabinet caught the glow, bottles lined up like players waiting for the national anthem. He went straight for the Macallan, pulled the cork with a soft pop, pouring two heavy measures. A rich wave of dried fruit, warm spice, and toasted oak drifted into the room.

Ryan dropped onto the couch with a grunt. The leather gave under his weight, sighing like it had been waiting all night. He stretched his legs, stocking feet claiming the coffee table without apology. His spine cracked when he leaned back. Hunter handed him a glass, warm and solid, the scotch glowing like fire caught in crystal. He took a sip. Heat uncoiled down his throat, leaving a lingering taste of ginger, toffee, and dark chocolate.

Hunter lowered himself onto the couch beside Ryan. He set the bottle of scotch on the solid wood table, its glass catching the faint shimmer from the skyline beyond the picture windows. "Food?" His voice came out low, almost an afterthought. "TV?"

Ryan gave a small shake of his head. He lifted the Glencairn crystal, twirling the amber inside. "Just this."

For a while, they let the silence breathe. The hum of the fridge carried from the kitchen, steady as background noise, while the city murmured faintly below.

"I don't get that girl."

Hunter's head angled, brows pulling together.

"Jill," Ryan muttered, scratching at his jaw through his short beard. "The smug, finger-waving menace."

"She likes getting under your skin." Hunter's mouth twitched though he kept his eyes on his glass.

Ryan harrumphed. "She's an expert at it. Too polished. Too ... perfect." The words came out rougher than he intended, half swallowed by the scotch.

This time Hunter looked straight at him, expression equal parts surprise and amusement. "Jill's our neighbor. You could at least try to get along."

"She's your neighbor," Ryan added quickly, like he needed the words out before Hunter could read too much into them. "Not mine. I'm only here temporarily."

Hunter leaned back, head sinking into the cushion, glass balanced on his stomach. His eyes tracked the ceiling as if it might offer a clean answer. The quiet stretched thin.

"Second game," Ryan said, tossing the words out like bait.

Hunter pushed forward, elbows braced on his knees. "Playing tandem with the Snowman felt right. Sharing my net this soon in the season with Lane..." He lifted the glass to his lips, then stalled. "I don't know how to put it."

"I get it. Lane's no Olaf." Ryan raised his drink in a half-toast. "It'll work out. It always does."

"Tell that to our new goalie coach," Hunter muttered. "Or should I say Lane's college and farm team goaltending coach? Guy's been treating me like a backup since the first practice."

Ryan shifted on the couch, one shoulder rolling to ease the ache. "That's brutal. But you gotta admit, the kid's solid."

"I never said he wasn't." Hunter continued, cutting the words short. "He's got instincts. Size. Calm."

Ryan tilted his glass. "But?"

Hunter rubbed a thumb over the Glencairn's rim, gaze locked on the amber liquid. "But ... he's played preseason and one regular game. That's it. This is my sixth season in this league. I've given my life to the Goshawks. Now I'm reduced to being the guy cheering for the rookie."

"He's only two years younger than you."

"Experience isn't measured in birthdays," Hunter snapped. "You know that."

Ryan didn't argue. He drained the last of his scotch, the warmth crawling down his chest. Hunter had a point, one that didn't need defending. Ryan let out a low groan, settling deeper into the couch. His glass dangled loose against his thigh, empty.

"I miss Viktor." Hunter's voice came after a long beat, quieter now. "That man knew how to push me without breaking me. This new guy ... I don't trust him. He's not building me. He's replacing me."

Ryan scoffed. "Are you serious? You just signed a solid, one-way, no trade, multi-year, multi-million dollar contract. We both know you're not replaceable.

Not to management. Not to the guys. Not to your captain." He gave Hunter the kind of look that left no room for argument.

Hunter's mouth curved into a tired half-smile, faint and fleeting. "Hope you're right."

Silence settled again, heavy but comfortable. The kind only brothers-on-ice could manage. A siren wailed somewhere in the city below, fading as quickly as it came, leaving the room in a pause of its own.

Ryan reached for the bottle, topping off both glasses. The Macallan slid warm down his throat, a slow burn that softened joints and loosened thoughts. It gave him courage to broach the next subject. "So ... where's Sage been hanging out lately?" His voice stayed low, casual, like he was testing the air.

Hunter didn't answer right away. His eyes locked on the black flatscreen, thumb running along the rim of the crystal. "Busy. Media crap. Promos. Meetings." He exhaled hard. "Now that she's around Margret and Luke all the time..."

Luke's name landed heavy. Hunter hadn't spat it, hadn't raised his voice, but Ryan heard the grind in his molars. He saw the way his friend's fingers flexed against the glass.

"Man..." Ryan gave his head a slow shake. "You know Sage is yours, right? Loyal to the core. That girl looks at you like you're constantly lifting the Cup."

Hunter's grip eased, the tension in his shoulders relaxed.

Feeling the need to change the subject, Ryan leaned back. "I hope that me crashing here isn't cutting into your Sage time. I appreciate you taking me in."

Hunter let out a quick snort. "It's been nice having someone around who gets me." He drained the rest of his drink, setting the glass down with a dull clink. "Jill said the place next to hers is opening up."

Ryan let out a throaty laugh. "She trying to collect the entire team on her floor?"

"Her friend's moving to London for a year." Hunter shrugged. "Figured you might want to check it out."

Before Ryan could respond, Hunter's phone buzzed. The sound cracked through the quiet like a puck off the post. He thumbed the screen. His expression changed in an instant ... brows easing, mouth tilting into a crooked, private smile.

"You gonna share with the rest of the bench, or just sit there looking like you blocked every shot on goal without help from your favorite D-man?"

Hunter tapped out a quick reply, then set the phone face down on the table. "Just Sage."

Ryan grinned, sprawling deeper into the couch. "Text that good?"

"She's got timing," Hunter said. He pushed to his feet, joints popping as he straightened. "We better get some rest."

"That's what I plan to do for the next two days. I'm sleeping until noon. Maybe longer." Ryan yawned, closing his eyes. "That's my plan."

"Nope," Hunter said, smug enough to raise a flag.

Ryan cracked one eye open. "Nope, what?"

"Car's coming at seven."

"Seven in the morning?" Ryan's eyes snapped open. "Have you lost your mind? You may have been sitting out the game, but I was busting my butt. I'm beat, I'm bruised, and now I'm boozed."

Hunter leaned against the hallway wall. "Sage convinced Margret to give us a long weekend. Luke's dad is flying us to South Dakota. Sterling's jet. Wheels up at sunrise."

Ryan jerked upright, his glass nearly slipping from his hand. "Wait. What? South Dakota? You serious?"

Hunter nodded. "Quick visit. Margret leaned on Coach Harrison, got us a pass. Time to reset before the next game."

Ryan blinked, then broke into a grin. "Well, dang ... I'm not mad about that."

"Thought you might balk at losing your beauty sleep." Hunter smirked. "You could use it."

"I was planning to complain," Ryan admitted, setting the Glencairn on the table. "Until you said South Dakota. That means time with Jessica."

Hunter gave a short laugh. "Figured that might sweeten it."

"Oh yeah. Haven't heard from her in almost a week. Neither of us likes to text. I could use some open sky ... maybe a night under the stars." Ryan shifted on the couch.

Hunter pushed off the wall, walking to his bedroom. "Look at you, going soft."

Ryan let out a sharp breath, half laugh, half scoff. "Says the guy who sleeps with his girlfriend's sweatshirt as a pillowcase."

"Don't knock it." Hunter's voice floated back as he disappeared into his room. "She smells like home."

Ryan stretched his arms wide, leather creaking beneath him. A smirk tugged at his lips. "Yeah, well, I'm not asking Jessica for a t-shirt. I've got an image to protect."

"Seven. Sharp." The words echoed from the hall, firm enough to erase any thought of arguing.

Ryan lingered a minute longer. He finished the last warm drops of his drink. Leaning back, the leather cool against his neck, his eyes closing as the thought pressed in. Something was shifting in the air tonight. He just wasn't sure what.

The guest room waited, travel bag abandoned by the door. Ryan went straight to the picture window. Portland stretched below, the skyline pulsing with energy, headlights threading through fog, neon signs cutting color over dark streets. He stood for a moment, trying to let the view anchor him. Wide sky. Quiet air. None of it helped.

He yanked the blackout curtains shut. Darkness folded over the room. Stripped down, Ryan slid beneath the cool sheets with a long exhale, head sinking into the pillow.

And just like that ... she was there. That daring smirk. Jill slipped into his thoughts like she owned the key. The lift of her brow. The lazy curl of her lip. Her voice in his memory, soft, sweet, yet grating on his nerves.

Ryan groaned, scrubbing both hands over his face. "What the..." he whispered, rolling on his side. Silence. Darkness. Nothing but the faint tick of the wall clock and his breathing. But Jill didn't leave. She lingered. That look she'd given him outside her apartment ... half challenge, half promise.

Fatigue pulled him down, reluctant but steady into restless sleep. Jill stayed ... stubborn in his thoughts. It didn't feel like she'd be leaving anytime soon.

Chapter 10
Roots and Cowgirls

Saturday, Oct. 14, midday

The dry South Dakota sun hit harder than Ryan remembered. His boots thudded on the cracked tarmac at Brookings Airport, heat waves rising in lazy shimmers. The scent of prairie dust clung to the air. It was high noon, with no city skyline in sight, only the wide stretch of cloudless blue.

He adjusted his ball cap, working out the crick in his neck from the long private flight. Ahead of him, Hunter yawned like a bear crawling out of hibernation. Sage was already halfway down the stairs, sprinting to the parking lot.

"Daddy!"

Jim Larson waited beside Sage's SUV, one boot propped against the bumper, arms crossed, a grin spread wide beneath his salt-and-pepper mustache. Dressed as always in faded jeans, flannel shirt, scuffed cowboy boots. Ryan grinned as Sage barreled into her father's chest. Jim caught her like it was second nature, lifting her off her feet.

Hunter hurried after her, stepping forward, posture relaxed, hand out. "Good to see you, Jim."

Jim took his hand in a firm, no-nonsense shake. "You too, son. Saw you stopping pucks again instead of sitting home watching the game from your comfy chair." A faint smirk tugged under his mustache. "About time."

Hunter huffed a quiet laugh. "I couldn't agree with you more."

"Where's your Stetson?" Sage teased, tugging the brim of her father's worn Goshawks cap.

Jim brushed her fingers away. "Figured I ought to wear the colors. Gotta support the family team now."

At the word family, Ryan's chest gave a quick thump. *Family.* Jim said it like it included all of them.

"Ryan!" Jim called, pulling him in for a firm handshake and a half-hug that smelled of hay, horses, and hard work.

"Good to see you again, sir," Ryan said.

They turned at the commotion behind them. Etan and Axel were clowning with the luggage, last year's rookies elbowing each other, laughing like they were at summer camp. On the flight over, they had claimed the back rows, headphones on, trading snacks while snapping selfies. Ryan hadn't known they were coming, but seeing them here, out of uniform, off the ice, they looked less like pro-hockey players and more like kids.

"Margret said we needed a break, and who's gonna argue with the boss lady?" Etan called, reaching out to shake Jim's hand.

"We're excited to spend it on the farm, Jim," Axel added with a grin.

"Nice ride." Etan let out a low whistle as a limo rolled up beside the SUV. Black. Sleek. Out of place in the rural setting.

Margret approached. On the plane, she'd traded her usual boardroom polish for skinny jeans tucked into riding boots that matched her silk blouse ... both were the warm color of good bourbon. Her brunette hair pulled into a messy ponytail.

Ryan squinted, studying her. She looked different. Like she belonged. He shut his eyes, convinced it was his imagination. When he opened them, the vision remained.

Luke trailed a few steps behind, a black carry-on in one hand, a large purple suitcase dragging in the other.

Margret offered Jim a polite nod, her fingers brushing his outstretched hand. She turned to Ryan. "Be here at five sharp Monday morning. I promised Coach Harrison you'd all be on the ice for afternoon practice."

She walked to the limo, then paused. Ryan caught the flicker in her gaze as it drifted over the group by the SUV. There was something in her eyes ... a sadness, maybe even longing, as she lingered on Jim's easy laugh, Etan's teasing, and Sage leaning into Hunter's side. When her attention shifted back to him, he gave a small nod, lifting his hand slightly.

She answered with a soft smile before slipping into the limo, swallowed by leather seats and tinted glass.

Ryan watched the car ease away, shrugging as he slung his duffel into the back of the SUV.

"Let me drive, Daddy. It's been months since I've been behind a wheel."

"It's all yours, baby girl." Jim winked, tossing her the key fob.

Etan and Axel folded themselves into the third row, knees jammed against the back of the bucket seats in front of them, where Hunter and Ryan settled. The engine rumbled to life, country music spilling from the speakers. Something twangy, raw, and gritty. Before they reached the main road, Etan and Axel were singing along.

Ryan leaned his head against the leather headrest, rolling down the window a crack. The warm breeze carried the faint lowing of cattle and the scent of sunbaked tilled fields. It was a stark contrast to Portland's salty air and crying gulls. Not like his hometown in Canada, but close enough.

The SUV's tires crunched down the gravel drive, dust billowing in the rearview. Ryan shifted in his seat; one hand hooked over the back of Hunter's headrest. A smile tugged at him as the red barn rose ahead like a sentinel at the edge of the fields. Beyond it, the big white farmhouse stood tall against the open sky, its wraparound porch dappled in sun and shadow as if it had been waiting for them. He hadn't realized how much he'd missed the place until now.

On the porch, Lilly waved a dish towel, snapping it like a victory flag. Patty stood beside her, rocking on her heels. Jessica perched on the railing, arms crossed, a wide smile eager for his arrival.

Sheriff Thor lounged in one of the porch chairs, legs kicked out like he owned the horizon, a glass of lemonade in hand. His Malinois, Hammer, tussled with a golden blur in the yard.

Crease.

The big Yellow Lab locked onto Hunter the instant he stepped from the SUV. Then, like a flipped switch, he exploded forward, ears flapping, paws tearing up dirt.

"Watch out, Hunter!" Sage cried.

"Hey, buddy." With the instinctive ease of a goalie, Hunter dropped to one knee just in time. Crease body-slammed into him, A wet tongue swiped across his face, tail thumping. Hunter let out a raw, unfiltered laugh, deep and real, the kind Ryan hadn't heard since July. It was the laugh of someone who wasn't just back on the farm, but back where he belonged.

Ryan stepped out, barely shutting the door before Crease lunged again, launching at him like a golden torpedo.

"You're huge." Ryan grunted as the Lab reared up, paws thudding against his chest. Slobber smeared his cheek before he could shove the dog off. "Alright, alright. Down, ya moose."

Crease wagged like an idiot, tongue lolling, until he froze at the sound of a familiar voice.

"Back off, mutt. This one's mine."

Jessica.

Before Ryan could blink, her arms were around his neck, legs wrapped tight at his waist like last summer. Like it hadn't been only a week since he'd seen her. Her scent hit him first. She smelled of horses, sun-warmed cotton, and that faint trace of strawberry shampoo that always lingered. Her barrel-racer strength held him firm.

"Missed you," she whispered, pressing her forehead to his.

He looked at her, voice dropping low. "You're the only reason I got on the plane."

Her arms tightened. Then she kissed him, quick, firm, full of promise.

Sheriff Thor rose with a grunt, setting down his lemonade. "Gotta get back to the grind. Just came by to say hello." He tipped his hat to Lilly, gave Sage a quick hug, shook hands with the boys, then headed for his patrol car, Hammer trotting at his side.

Lilly clapped her hands. "Dinner's on the table. Don't let it get cold."

Jessica caught Ryan's hand in a grip that didn't ask ... it claimed. "Come on. You're not getting through this meal without telling me every details about your week."

The screen door creaked as the group filed inside, boots thudding against worn floorboards, laughter chasing them into the farmhouse. In the dining room, the long wooden table sagged under the weight of the feast. Not a catered spread. Not a team cafeteria buffet. This was food that stuck to your ribs, the kind that made you want to unbutton your jeans halfway through.

Roast chicken with crackling skin. Biscuits the size of hockey pucks. Corn on the cob dripping butter. Potato salad with just the right bite of dill. Pumpkin pie already sliced, daring someone to jump early.

Ryan claimed his usual seat. He was about to reach for the potato salad bowl when Jim cleared his throat, stretching a hand to Hunter. The table quieted. Ryan took Sage's hand on his left and Jessica's on his right, bowing his head as Jim began the blessing.

At "Amen," bowls passed as plates piled high.

The conversation drifted between farm chores and hockey plays. Ryan plowed through a second helping like he had something to prove. He washed it down with a long pull of Jim's homebrewed porter. Malty. Dark. A little sharp at the finish. Perfect.

Beside him, Jessica nudged his thigh with her knee, melting into his arm as if she could erase the space between them.

"You planning on eating that or should I put it out of its misery?" Ryan muttered, eyeing the untouched food on her plate.

She sighed, threading her fingers into the crook of his elbow, resting her head against his shoulder. He kept chewing as his free hand found hers.

At the head of the table, Jim leaned in, fork stabbing the air at Etan and Axel. "So what do you boys make of that new kid, Trey Moses? Real deal, or just a pretty boy with fast hands?"

"*Moss,* Daddy," Sage cut in, giving him a look. "His name's Moss, not Moses."

Jim waved her off with a grin. "Close enough."

"Unfortunately, he's both pretty, and good," Etan said through a mouthful of corn. "Worst part is, he knows it."

"Faster than Chase," Axel added, reaching for the bottle of Draugr's Demise hot sauce.

Ryan frowned as he watched his D-man twist off the cap, drowning his potato salad in the thick red liquid. "Careful," he warned.

Too late. Axel shoveled in a bite, froze, then went wide-eyed as his face flushed crimson from the neck up. He coughed, sputtered. "Scheibe!" he choked out, grabbing for a glass of water.

"You shouldn't swear at the table," Etan said, nearly toppling out of his chair with laughter. Patty snorted into her beer. Even Hunter cracked a smile.

"Jim!" Lilly shot up, patting Axel on the back. "I told you not to put the heat on the table." She whisked Axel's plate away, vanishing into the kitchen. A moment later she reappeared with a clean dish and a pitcher of milk, sliding them in front of him before leveling her husband with a look sharp enough to cut.

Jim leaned back in his chair, unbothered, tearing a biscuit in half. He took his time buttering it before glancing at Axel, his tone flat. "Serves you right. Never trust a label with an undead creature on it."

Ignoring her husband, Lilly plopped a second helping of potato salad onto Hunter's plate. "You're too skinny," she scolded, before settling back into her chair at the far end of the table.

"Mom! He just signed a sixty-six million dollar contract, and you're worried he's wasting away?"

"You can't earn a paycheck if you're too weak to defend your net," she shot back. "Hunter. Eat."

Jim dabbed his lips with a napkin, setting it back on his lap. "Speaking of which, how's it feel, son? New contract. New goalie coach. No more Olaf backing you up."

Ryan noticed the way Hunter stiffened, shoulders tightening before he dropped his gaze to his plate.

Etan jumped in fast. "Hunter's carrying the whole team now. No pressure, right?"

Axel, still red-faced, swiped his eyes. "Ten-year winning streak coming up."

Hunter grunted, head down, forking into his food.

Sage reached around him, giving her dad a playful slap on the arm. "Can you please leave him alone and let him eat?"

"Alright, alright." Jim threw his hands up. "Can I at least ask if you've set a date?"

Hunter choked mid-sip, spraying beer into his napkin.

"Dad!"

Patty clapped her hands, bouncing in her chair. "I'm so excited. Have you figured out your wedding party yet?"

Sage twisted the diamond ring on her finger, eyes darting around the table. "I've been thinking about asking Margret to be my maid of honor." When the table went still, she added quickly, "Maybe."

Forks hovered mid-air. Even Crease perked his ears.

"Margret! Are you kidding me?" Jessica grabbed her fork, stabbing a piece of chicken twice before stuffing it into her mouth.

"Nothing's set in stone. Just thinking," Sage shot back.

"We'll look at colors and flowers this weekend," Lilly said, stepping behind her daughter to wrap her in a hug. "I bought a stack of bridal magazines for inspiration. You've got time, sweetie." She moved to Hunter next, squeezing his shoulders until his tension eased.

Ryan sat back, finishing the last of his Porter. He took in the table, each moment pulling at him in a different way. Etan and Axel bickered over the final biscuit while Patty refereed. Lilly's steady hand kept Sage calm. Hunter eased into a sports conversation with Jim. Jessica clung to him, her touch more possessive than comforting.

They made him miss his own family more than he cared to admit.

On the porch, the boards creaked under Ryan's boots as he dropped into one of the Adirondack chairs. South Dakota sunsets never disappointed. Tonight, the sky burned with streaks of red and violet, the kind of colors Portland never gave him. Gold lingered at the edges, spilling over the fields like a last embrace. The air carried that sweet post-harvest chill, dry corn stalks brittle in the fields, mixed with the fermented sweetness of silage drifting from a nearby silo. A breeze stirred the prairie grass, whispering secrets no city could hold.

He jumped at the slam of the screen door. Jessica crossed the porch, closing the distance until she slid onto his lap, all legs, heat, and strawberry shampoo. She settled against him like she belonged, denim pressed to denim as she nuzzled her nose beneath his jaw.

He tipped his beer bottle "Wanna sip?"

"Not tonight." She wrinkled her nose, shaking her head.

Ryan cocked an eyebrow. "Since when have you ever said no to a homebrew?"

She shifted, fingers playing with the strings of his hoodie. "Got a barrel race tomorrow. I have to leave tonight."

Ryan froze, his beer halfway to his mouth. "You're leaving?" His voice came out flat, hard. "How long?"

Jessica sat up straight, winding a lock of his hair around her finger as if she could soften the blow. "The weekend. Big event out west. Qualifier."

He set the bottle down harder than he meant to. The thunk against the small metal table cut through the night air. Pulling her closer, he brushed his lips against her neck, his voice low. "Don't go."

She stiffened in his arms, then eased back, sliding off his lap. "Ryan, if I'd known you were coming ahead of time, I wouldn't have entered."

He rose, the warmth of her body leaving a ghost on his thighs. With both hands braced on the porch railing, he stared out over the fence lines. "How could I have told you? I didn't know myself. Margret dropped the weekend on us last minute."

"Well, right back at you," she said. "I signed up months ago. Sterling's footing the bill. I'm riding one of his horses. He expects me to compete."

Ryan felt his pulse quicken. "I flew halfway across the country to be with you."

She folded her arms across her chest, chin lifting. "I'm glad you did." Her voice was tight. "But I can't just blow off my season because you showed up."

"It's just one race." His hands curled against the railing.

"Would you skip a game if I turned up in Portland the day before an away match?"

His jaw clenched. "That's different."

"Why?" She stepped closer, boots striking hard against the porch boards. "Because hockey is your life?"

"Yes."

Her reply cracked like a taut rein. "Right. And barrel racing is mine."

The words split the space between them, sharp and final. In the distance, a horse neighed, cattle mooed. From inside, the screen door squeaked then slapped open with a wooden clap.

Wide-eyed, Patty whispered, "Hey, you guys ... you're gettin' kind of loud." She stood in the doorway, Jessica's worn leather jacket dangling from one hand.

Jessica planted her feet, shoulders squared. "I need to go."

Patty hesitated, glancing between them. Taking a small step forward, she held out the jacket.

Jessica snatched it without looking. Her voice came low, bitter. "You don't get it, Ryan. You never will."

Ryan reached for her. Not thinking. Just needing to stop her somehow. But Jessica was already beyond his grasp, long strides carrying her off the porch. Her boots clacked down the steps like gunfire. She hit the gravel, yanked open her truck door, slamming it shut.

The engine roared to life. Tires spit a gritty spray of dust and sharp rock. Ryan stood frozen, the cloud hanging in the air like a spray of ice after a hard stop. His stomach twisted into knots.

Patty lingered at the edge of the porch. With a nervous glance at him, she slipped back inside, easing the door behind her just as Crease nosed through the gap.

The Labrador bounded forward, nails scrabbling on the floorboards; a slow "woo, woo" emerged low in his throat. He shoved his head under Ryan's hand, nudging his knees until Ryan gave way and dropped into the Adirondack chair. Crease sprawled half across him, chest heaving, tail thumping once before stilling. His head rested heavy on Ryan's chest, golden eyes searching his face for answers Ryan didn't have. His pulse slowed as fingers slid into the dog's fur, scratching behind his ears.

The porch creaked as Jim stepped beside him, a beer cap snapping open. He held it out without a word.

Ryan took it, the glass cooling his palm. Jim's hand settled on his shoulder, a brief squeeze carrying all the comfort Sage's father chose to give. Crease lifted his head, watching as Jim lowered into the next chair. The steady quiet between them was enough to say it all.

Chapter 11
Bourbon and Bombshells

Saturday, Oct 14th

The South Dakota sun dipped low, throwing amber light across the sweep of Sterling Wheatfield's quarter horse estate. Leather, hay, and the musk of hard-ridden horses lingered in the air. Margret rode her mare along the pasture's edge, stirrups polished, heals down, posture straight. She moved in rhythm alongside Luke, a quiet duet on horseback.

The hush of evening shattered when tires spat gravel across the drive. A black truck tore past, dust curling in its wake. Margret's mare jerked sideways, ears flattening, hooves scattering dirt. She tightened her thighs, adjusting her grip on the reins. Her voice calm but stern, authority born from a childhood astride temperamental thoroughbreds. The horse steadied beneath her.

Luke cursed under his breath, swinging off his gelding in one smooth motion, boots crunching against dirt. His fists tightened as he studied the retreating truck.

"Who drives like that with horses around?" Margret asked, smoothing a hand over her mare's neck.

Luke's expression darkened. "Jessica."

Margret raised a brow. "Your Jessica?"

"She's not mine. Never was."

"Oh." Margret frowned. "She should know better."

"She does." His grip tightened on the reins. "Jessica's ego's gotten too big since Dad's sponsorship. I'll have him talk to her."

They led the horses into the barn, the scent of straw and oiled leather wrapping around Margret like an old memory. Every halter hung in its place. Each stall raked to a crisp line. She passed her reins to a teenage stable hand, who took both horses with a polite, "Ma'am. Sir." followed by a nod.

She brushed the dust from her jeans, then tucked a loose strand of hair behind her ear. Another clung to her cheek. She caught Luke watching. "What?" she asked.

He brushed the strand away, fingers lingering for a breath. "Nothing. You just … fit in here."

Was he right? She had grown used to her city life in Portland, yet the scent of horse, hay, and leather made her question her choices.

"Come on." Luke reached for her hand.

She laced her fingers through his, giving a small squeeze. Her pulse quickened as they followed the flagstone path to the main house. This was all too new. During her six years with the Goshawks, she kept to one-night stands, never risking commitment. Yet here she was, edging too close to a South Dakota cowboy.

Margret had been to Sterling's mansion before, but never to this more intimate part of the house. The bar looked carved out of an equestrian dream. British racing green walls framed shelves of cut-crystal decanters and top-shelf liquor. Amber sconces cast a low light across marble tile and a cowhide rug.

Luke slipped behind the bar. With a sly grin, he set a tulip-shaped Riedel glass before her, gold trim catching the light. He opened the wine fridge, the soft click breaking the quiet, then turned the bottle so she could see the label.

Margret leaned forward, breath hitching. "Domaine Gérard Duplessis Montée de Tonnerre."

Luke cocked his head, pride flickering in his grin. "I hope this is to your liking," he said, slipping into a thick French accent as he draped a towel over his arm in mock ceremony.

Her laugh came easy, light and genuine.

He poured the pale gold wine in a slow spiral. The stem of the glass cooled her fingers as she lifted it. She inhaled, eyes closing. "Lemon oil and orange blossom … with a hint of hay and sea spray. Like Brookings and Portland in a bottle."

Luke leaned on the bar, his gaze steady. "It's fate. Even the wine thinks our lives are meant to intermingle."

After the first sip, her lips parted in a sigh she hadn't meant to release.

Luke's laugh rumbled low. "Makes me wish I could be reincarnated as that Chablis."

She arched a brow, but the corner of her mouth softened. "That so?"

"From where I'm standing, your first taste looked like a spiritual awakening."

Her thumb traced the stem of her glass, slow and absent. For once, she let the silence linger. "How'd you find this in South Dakota?" she asked at last.

Luke picked at the label on his beer bottle. "I wish I could take credit. It was all Sterling. When he heard you were co-owner of the Goshawks, he ordered a few bottles in case you visited."

Margret blinked. "I didn't think he remembered what I drink, let alone that he'd stock it. I'm impressed."

"Don't be. Dad's a businessman. You're his new partner." Luke gave a half-shrug. "That wine fridge is full of bribes."

She nodded. "Will Sterling be joining us for dinner?"

Boots rang against polished marble, slow and deliberate. "Where is everyone?" Sterling's voice boomed from the main hall.

"Guess that answers your question." Luke cracked the top of another IPA. "In here, Dad!"

Margret swiveled on the barstool as Sterling stepped through the archway, all six feet of tailored confidence in a navy suit. His white shirt crisp, the tie a subtle paisley knot. Italian leather cowboy boots, oxblood rich yet dusted with trail grit. He looked like a man who had conquered two empires before breakfast. She didn't doubt he had.

"Margret." His smile was tight. "Welcome back."

"Sterling." She extended her hand. His grip warm and firm. Cedar clung to him, softened by leather and cologne she was certain cost more than her first car.

His gaze dropped to her boots, then lifted in a measured appraisal. Calculated, not leering.

Margret glanced at her dusty designer jeans and boots. "Should I change?"

Sterling's mouth quirked. "You're perfect as you are."

It was a line, but the steadiness of his gaze made it feel more a decree than flattery.

Luke handed his father a glass of deep mahogany bourbon. "I figured you'd want to ease into the night."

Sterling nodded, lifting the glass slightly in Margret's direction before sipping. His sigh after the first taste was near reverent. "Now that," he said, "is how you start a conversation."

Margret studied them in profile. Father and son, same eyes, high cheekbones, squared jawline, same air of command. Dangerous in different ways.

"Let's retire to the library." Sterling's words carried more command than invitation.

The air shifted as both men turned their attention to her. Whether it was the wine coursing through her or the weight of their gaze, her gut told her the evening was about to take a dangerous turn.

Margret's breath hitched as she crossed the hall into the library. Oak smoke curled from the hearth, rich and sharp. Dark wooden panels rose from floor to ceiling, lined with shelves of books stamped in gold leaf. Gilded frames held paintings of horses frozen mid-stride, their eyes seeming to follow her as she moved deeper into the room. Overhead, a chandelier glimmered, its light catching on crystal and brass as the fire snapped in the grate.

Margret trailed her fingers along the edge of a green marble end table before settling into a floral-patterned wingback chair. Luke took the seat opposite, a bottle of craft beer sweating in his grip. Sterling moved to the wet bar, refilled Margret's glass, then poured himself two fingers of bourbon with deliberate ease.

The wine had already softened her thoughts, its warmth wrapping her in a loose sort of confidence. The fire's heat seeped into her bones. For the first time since Sterling's arrival she felt at ease.

Sterling dropped into the chair across from her, his movements unhurried. He sipped his bourbon. "So," he said, "you two survived your ride?"

Luke snorted. "Barely. Jessica damn near ran us off the trail."

Margret cut him a side glance. "It wasn't that dramatic."

Luke leaned forward. "She came tearing up the drive like she was running from the law. Your mare almost unseated you."

Margret raised a brow, silence answering for her. *Her mare had flinched, yes, but nothing as dramatic as Luke made it out to be.*

Sterling swirled his glass. "I'll speak to her when she gets back."

Luke huffed. "She's getting out of control."

Sterling's expression cooled. "And how would you know what she's doing when you're in Portland?"

Luke sat back, caught off guard. "I know."

"You want me to fire her?"

"No." Luke's gaze dropped. "Just talk to her. She listens to you."

Sterling took a long, thoughtful sip. The fireplace crackled as silence spread again.

Margret stared into her wine; the golden liquid catching the firelight. Her voice emerged quiet, but firm. "So, you knew my birth mother?"

Sterling set his glass on the table, the crystal clinking against wood. His features, bold a moment before, softened into something distant. When he looked at her, the faint lines around his eyes deepened. "I did," he said at last, his voice lower than before.

Margret leaned back, slowly twirling the stem of her glass between her fingers. The Chablis offered no comfort against the truth she'd just invited into the room.

Sterling exhaled. Not a sigh. A reckoning. His voice, when it came, was stripped of the easy swagger it always carried. "Justin and I grew up in Upstate New York. A little town near Saratoga, you'd miss if you blinked at the signpost." He sipped his bourbon, turning the glass once, then set it down. "My family raised thoroughbreds, bloodstock for the racetrack. Old money, tight reins. Justin's dad worked for mine as a stable manager. His mom taught grade school."

He paused. "None of that mattered to us. We were inseparable. He dragged me to his first pee wee hockey game. I made him stay up with me all night when my mare foaled. Neither of us belonged in the other's world, but we carved out space for each other." He shifted in his chair.

"In college we stuck together. My parents wanted me at an Ivy, but I insisted on following Justin. He landed a spot at a D1 university in a nearby town. One of the rare few with a full hockey scholarship. I wasn't about to let distance break what we had. While there, we double dated. Rebecca, Luke's mom, was mine. Justin was with your mother, Mary. The four of us laughed, made plans, thought we could take on the world." He paused, taking another sip of his drink.

"Mary and Rebecca were roommates. Like us, they were inseparable. Then, one afternoon, Rebecca handed Justin an envelope. Inside was a note from Mary. *It's too complicated. I need to go home.* That was all she wrote. No call. No goodbye. She packed her things and left for Tennessee. Justin was wrecked. He never understood why. Thought he'd driven her off." Sterling' gaze lifted. "She never told him about the pregnancy."

Margret stared into the fire, the heat pressed against her skin, though she felt nothing but cold inside.

"Life moved on. I married Rebecca. My parents passed. I inherited the estate and turned it into something different. Sold the thoroughbreds, built the quarter horse operation. Rebecca..." His voice quivered. "She died giving birth to Luke."

Margret glanced at his son, searching for a reaction. Luke turned his beer bottle in his hands. When he finally looked up, he gave her a sad smile before Sterling continued.

"Justin turned pro. Played for several teams before he retired. During that time, calls became texts. Then nothing."

Sterling swirled the bourbon in his glass, the firelight glinting in the amber. "The truth of your birth began to unravel last spring, when Luke brought you here for the first time. That was when I learned you worked for the Goshawks ... that Justin owned the team."

He shifted in his chair. "When you came here after visiting the Larsons, it was like a memory I couldn't place. The way you moved, your laughter, even the turn of your head ... it all felt familiar, as if I'd known you in another life. It wasn't until after you left that I realized why. You were Mary's mirror image at that age."

The fire snapped, sparks scattering up the chimney. Sterling's gaze held her so sharp it sent a shiver through her body she couldn't mask.

"When did Justin know?" Margret forced the words past lips gone dry.

"A couple months after the Goshawks won the Cup, I flew to Portland to congratulate Justin on the win. That was when he told me about you." Sterling tipped the bourbon in his glass, watching the fire catch on its surface.

"He said he'd first suspected the truth during your internship interview. Seeing you was like being transported back in time. He almost called you Mary. When he read the background check, his suspicions deepened."

Sterling took a long swig of his drink. "Your birth date fell nine months after Mary left for Tennessee. The report listed a contact number. When he called, Mary's sister answered. After some coaxing, she confessed the truth ... that you were his daughter."

Margret's voice cracked into a whine. "He knew all those years and didn't tell me?" She stood, pacing in front of the fireplace, then sank back into her chair as if the weight of Sterling's words shoved her down.

"I asked him the same question. He said when he took you on as an intern, he didn't know how to tell you. When he hired you full time, he was afraid you'd quit. He couldn't bear the thought of you leaving." Sterling's lips curved into something that wasn't quite a smile. "I told him I'd keep his confidence ... if he sold me half the Goshawks franchise. The team had become a sound investment under his leadership. All it took was a handshake between old friends."

Luke shot to his feet, the bottle slipping from his hand, crashing onto the imported Oriental rug. He gave no regard to the beer bleeding dark into its intricate weave. "You blackmailed him!"

Sterling glanced at the stain spreading across the rug. His lips thinned, nostrils flaring like a bull about to charge. In an instant he was on his feet too, fast and hard, closing the distance. Nose to nose, boots braced against his son's, he squared himself to Luke. "I saw a business opportunity and took it. Nothing more."

Margret rose, her legs betraying her with a faint wobble. The last thing she wanted was to stand between two angry cowboys. Her voice cut through the tension, low but sharp. "Enough. Both of you."

She rested a hand on the back of her chair before sinking into the cushions. Tears welled, though she refused to let them fall. "Justin was a grown man. He knew what he was agreeing to. It's done." She turned to Luke, more plea than command, she said, "Please, pour me a double bourbon. I need something stronger than wine."

Sterling brushed past Luke, moving to the wet bar. He poured a generous measure, placing the heavy tumbler in Margret's hand. No garnish. No ice. Just unfiltered truth, distilled.

"You deserved to know," he said, voice low, calm. "He wanted to tell you himself. He just ... ran out of time."

Margret stared into her glass. Firelight bent, fractured in the amber. A hundred thoughts battered against her mind, none of them whole, all of them aching.

Chapter 12
Luck and Loss

Sunday, October 15th

Ryan stood in the Larson's front room, brushing aside the curtain as rain tapped against the glass, a rhythm that settled into his bones. A sip of Jim's craft beer only deepened the weight. The maples out back, bright with orange and red, pulled him home to Calgary, to autumns that always promised hockey and fresh starts. He cocked his head, listening to the chatter floating from the kitchen.

"Patty, I swear, if you eat another cookie, there won't be enough to share." The clatter of a tray punctuated Sage's warning.

"I'm helping with quality control!" Patty shot back.

"Interference." Etan crossed both arms in front of his chest, fists closed. "Denying sweet treats to the rest of the team is a five-minute major."

Axel reached over, stealing a cookie from Patty. "You'll be out on a game misconduct if I don't get my share."

Lilly stepped into the front room without warning, one hand on her hip, the other wagging a finger at her husband. "Are you going to sit around all day watching TV, or are you going to engage in some family time fun?"

Jim popped his recliner upright. "All right, all right. How about we play some poker? Rain like this calls for cards."

Hunter reached for the remote, but Jim growled, "Leave it on. I want to keep track of the score."

"Okay." Hunter set the remote down like it burned his fingers.

Jim squinted at the enclosed back porch. "Lilly, how are we supposed to play poker with all those magazines and doodads piled on the card table?"

"I'm not moving anything," Lilly shouted back.

"How about the dining room table?" Ryan suggested as he walked to the kitchen.

Jim grunted, already crossing to a cabinet for a deck of cards and the poker chips.

Etan and Axel step in without being asked, clearing the dining room table, wiping it down with the urgency of a line change.

In the kitchen, Lilly and the girls laid out wooden platters stacked with cheeses, crackers, veggies, cold cuts and olives. The sharp bite of mustard mingled with something smoky and sweet, maybe candied bacon, drifted through the room.

"Your house always smells so good." Ryan leaned on the island counter inhaling deeply.

"Everything Mom cooks is made with love." Sage untied her mom's apron as she gave her a tight hug.

"Stop dilly-dallying and let's get this game started." Jim took his seat at the head of the table, cracking open a new deck of cards stamped with the Goshawks logo.

"I see Sage's been sharing team merch with you." Ryan dropped into the chair at Jim's right, a place reserved for Hunter. Taking it tonight meant he'd be dealt last, a slight advantage he wasn't about to surrender. Hunter took the seat on Jim's left, giving Ryan a brief nod, followed by a knowing smile.

Jim gave the deck a hard shuffle. Ryan caught the subtle side-eye Jim slid his way before the cards snapped back into place.

Chairs scraped against the wooden floor as Axel slid in beside Hunter. Etan claimed the seat next to Ryan. Followed by a shuffle of small plates, snacks and drinks being set down within easy reach. Lemonade landed in front of Etan and Axel ... beer for everyone else.

"How come you get to sit by Patty?" Axel's brows furrowed.

"Haven't you heard? She likes me the best."

"Enough," Jim grumbled, giving the table a slow scan. "Do you boys remember how to play Five-Card Draw?"

Etan leaned forward with a smirk. "I just remember Axel taking all your money last summer, Jim."

Ryan felt Axel's foot slide past his leg as the defenseman kicked Etan under the table.

Etan's chair screeched on the wooden floor as it jolted back. "What was that for?" He winced, rubbing his shin.

"Never poke the bear, especially after you win," Axel said with a heavy German accent. "You're no longer a rookie. Time you stopped making rookie mistakes."

Laughter broke loose. Axel and Etan slapped a high-five that sent a stack of poker chips skittering across the table. Crease pounced on one that fell on the floor.

"Hey!" Axel shoved his chair, chasing the Lab as he trotted off, tail wagging like he'd just won the pot.

Lilly rubbed Patty's shoulders as she sat next to her at the far end of the table. "You want to trade seats?"

"What? And not be in the middle of chaos?" She winked across the table at Sage.

Jim gave a long-suffering grunt, dealing out the first hand. "And I thought raising one child was a chore."

Ryan leaned back, fingers brushing the edge of his cards. He almost asked Jim if the old deck was still around. This one was too slick, too clean, carrying the wrong kind of luck.

As the day wore on, his shoulders relaxed. The game opened steady enough, chips stacked, cards snapping against wood, a couple of decent hands. The hum of conversation, the rain, the faint clink of glasses ... all of it grounded him. For a while, there was no pressure, no press, no questions about leadership, or team politics ... no Jessica drama. Just family. Just cards. He glanced at Hunter, who raised his beer in a silent toast. Ryan returned the gesture.

Before long, the table drifted into two teams. At the far end, it was all sunshine and cake dreams ... Lilly, Sage, Patty, Axel, and Etan in full-on wedding chatter. On Ryan's end, it was down and dirty poker, with Jim treating the game like a playoff final.

"Are we playing cards or planning a wedding?" Jim barked.

Sage laughed. "Multitasking, Daddy. It's a skill."

"I'm not convinced any of you even looked at your cards." Jim tossed two down like they'd betrayed him, waiting as Hunter slid replacements across the table.

Sage's laughter pulled Ryan from his cards. She glowed as she giggled about centerpieces and lace versus satin. Axel tossed out a wild idea about camo tuxedos, earning a smack on the arm from Sage. Etan countered with matching cowboy boots for everyone in the wedding party.

Crease sprawled under the table, his head resting on Ryan's boots. The Lab's tail thumped once, then again when Ryan slipped him a baby carrot.

Jim sighed like the outcome of the game was riding on his shoulders. "At this rate, I'll be drawing social security before we finish a hand."

Etan lifted his cards with a grin. "You're already the oldest person at the table, Jim. How much slower can you go?"

"Fold!" Jim slapped his cards down.

Ryan laughed. Winning or losing didn't matter today. Some games were less about the cards and more about keeping the people you loved close ... even if the talk was fondant frosting and twinkle lights instead of flops and full houses.

From the front room, the murmur of the golf tournament drifted. Shouts of "get in the hole," hushed commentary, the crack of a driver meeting a ball, floated over the half-hearted poker plays like white noise.

Jim took a long swig of his beer, then shuffled the cards for a new round. "You boys ever golf?"

Hunter smirked, shoulders rising in a lazy shrug. "Few times," he said. "Turns out I'm better at stopping pucks than sinking putts."

"He's being modest. First time out, he birdied a par four with rental clubs. No clue what he was doing." Ryan laid down three cards, sliding the replacements Jim dealt across the table.

Hunter shook his head. "That was luck."

"No," Ryan countered, studying his new hand while taking a sip of beer. "That was dumb rookie magic. You've got some kind of weird body awareness. It's annoying."

Jim and Hunter checked.

"I've seen it," Axel said, eyes glinting as he doubled his bet instead of drawing. "Guy's annoyingly good at everything."

Sage, Lilly, and Patty were too busy chit chatting to play.

Etan tossed chips into the pot, grinning at Ryan. "You can carry my bag anytime, Cap. I'll even tip."

"I'm more caddy than golfer. Hockey's my first and only love." Ryan pushed chips into the pot.

Hunter gave a small nod, sliding his cards away too. "I never had time for anything else," he said, quieter now. "Since I was five, it's just been hockey. Training. Tournaments. Travel. Rinse, repeat."

"Yeah, no, for sure." Ryan's voice dropped low, his beer bottle clinking against Hunter's. Two teammates in sync, no explanation needed for the weight they both carried.

"You've got to be kidding me." Jim groaned as Axel fanned out his hand. A royal flush.

Etan shook his head, grinning. "Unreal. You've got the kind of luck guys spend their careers chasing ... and the skill to back it up."

Jim pushed up from his chair with a hand on his lower back. "I need a break. Going to the basement and grab the good stuff." He didn't need to explain. Everyone knew what *the good stuff* meant ... his guarded stash of home-brewed ale and experimental lagers, he swore were better than anything bottled commercially.

"Bring me one!" Axel called, raising his empty lemonade glass in mock hope.

"Me too!" Etan chimed in.

"In your dreams!" Jim hollered over his shoulder as he disappeared down the creaky steps.

Lilly stood. "Axel, Etan, since you're so full of energy, clear the table, then come help me in the kitchen with dessert."

Axel groaned in mock protest. "This feels suspiciously like punishment."

"Think of it as cross-training," Lilly called over her shoulder, already halfway to the kitchen.

Etan followed, nudging Ryan's arm as he passed. "You want anything?"

"Yeah," Ryan said, arching a brow. "A winning hand."

"Good luck with that," Hunter muttered, shuffling the deck.

"Hey!" Ryan called to the kitchen. "Remember, sweets slow you down. Watch your sugar intake."

"Or our trainer will kill us," the boys sang out in unison.

"Everyone needs a sweet treat once in a while, Cap," Axel mumbled through a mouthful of cookie crumbs.

"You've had enough sweet treats since we got here to fill your quota for a year." Ryan shook his head, a grin tugging at his lips despite himself.

Sage leaned into Hunter, her gaze finding Ryan. "You okay?"

He picked up a poker chip, twirling it on the table. "Haven't heard anything from Jessica since she left last night."

Patty nudged him. "Jesica didn't mean what she said. She gets intense before big events. Always has."

Ryan glared at Patty, then turned away. "Nerves?" He let out a snort, fingers closing tight around the chip. "You think that's an excuse for not getting back to me?"

His phone vibrated. Just once. Just enough to snap him back. Out of habit, he pulled it from his back pocket.

Jim stepped to the room, a six-pack in each hand. He stopped mid-stride, eyes narrowing. “You know the rules.” Putting the beer down with a soft clunk, he added, “No phones at the table. Take it outside.”

Ryan nodded, already rising. Crease trotted after him as he pushed through the screen door onto the porch. The hinges creaked louder in the sudden quiet. Rain hissed against the eaves, the air thick with damp soil and wet leaves.

The boards groaned under his boots as he paced. Phone in hand, thumbs moving fast ... swiping, typing, deleting, trying again. His fingers froze when a message blinked at him. Just two words. His breath hitched. Shoulders sagged.

Crease pressed against his leg, eyes lifting with quiet concern. Ryan gave the Lab a soft pat before slipping the phone into his pocket. The door creaked again as they stepped inside.

Hunter looked up. “Everything good?”

Ryan pulled out his phone, turned the screen toward his best friend.

JESSICA: We’re done!!!

“She blocked me.”

Chapter 13
Split Roads

Sunday Night October 15

"Remind me again why we're not using the dishwasher. More importantly, how'd we get stuck on kitchen duty?" Water swooshed in the sink as Ryan handed Hunter a soapy dish to rinse and dry.

"Better question, how did Etan and Axel score TV privileges with Jim?" Hunter scrubbed a plate until it squeaked, the sound sharp against the cheers drifting from the front room.

"Didn't know you followed football. If you want to watch the Vikings game, I can finish up here."

"Nah." Hunter rinsed the plate in a stream of steaming water. "Not that into football. Just wondering how the young bucks weaseled their way out of dishes, and why Sage is serving them carrot cake like they've just scored winning goals."

"Where's Lilly?" Ryan let the water drain as he wiped his hands on the back of his jeans.

"She's tucked in her rocking chair in the reading corner, earplugs in, engrossed in a mystery novel," Sage said, stepping into the kitchen. "Looks like you're all done here. Why don't you grab some cake? I'll get the coffee."

Ryan didn't wait to be asked twice. He cut three slices, handing a plate to Hunter. They were halfway to the dining room when Margret and Luke stepped in from the mudroom.

She was pulled together as always, cashmere sweater, riding boots traded for stilettos. Luke looked like he'd wandered straight out of a *Cowboy Lifestyle Magazine* shoot as he draped his Stetson on a peg.

"Great timing," Sage said, hurrying back into the kitchen for two more slices of cake. "Glad you guys could make it." She placed a piece in front of Margret, then one beside Luke.

Ryan caught the flicker of tension on Hunter's face the moment Luke sat down. First Jessica. Now Luke. So much for a drama free evening.

Crease trotted under the table, sniffing for crumbs like a Roomba. Ryan reached down, gave the Lab a quick scratch behind the ears, then slipped him a fingertip of cream cheese frosting.

Sage cleared her throat as she set a cup of coffee in front of Margret. "So ... the reason I asked you to come over tonight ... I need to bring my SUV back to Portland."

Ryan heard Hunter sigh. Across the table, Margret set her fork down with care. Luke leaned back in his chair; arms folded like he already knew where this was headed.

Sage continued, her tone light. "I need a car for work. I'm tired of bumming rides. Besides, Crease misses me, and I miss him."

Hunter scoffed, wiping his lips with a napkin. "You're not driving across the country alone."

"Excuse me?" Sage blinked, her fork paused halfway to her mouth.

"You heard me." Hunter's eyes narrowed, the crease between his brows deepening. "Twenty-six hours on the road by yourself? Not happening."

"I'm not a child, Hunter."

"You're not a long-haul trucker either."

Margret glared at Sage. "Look, I agreed you need a vehicle in Portland. That's not in question. I just didn't realize you meant your SUV ... now."

"When would be more convenient?" Sage asked, her tone sharp.

Luke lifted his fork, voice easy, like he was talking about a weather delay. "I'll go with her. It's not a big deal."

Ryan took a slow bite of cake, letting the cinnamon heat linger on his tongue as he side-eyed his best friend. *Here we go.*

Hunter shot up as if he'd taken a puck to the ribs. "Over my dead body."

"Whoa," Ryan said, reaching for Hunter's sleeve. "Sit down, Bro."

"She needs someone with her," Luke started.

"She doesn't need you." Hunter dropped back into his chair, tossing his napkin on the table like he was challenging Luke to a duel.

Sage pushed her plate away, voice rising. "You, Hunter, do not get to control what I do because you're ... because you're ... you!"

Margret groaned, pinching the bridge of her nose. "Can we all agree that Sage shouldn't drive alone? Also, Hunter shouldn't be the one choosing who does, or doesn't drive with her."

"Thank you." Sage scoffed.

Silence settled, heavy as a locker room after a hard loss.

Ryan leaned forward, rolling his coffee mug between his palms. "Okay. Look. I've got an idea. You three drive together."

Margret frowned. "What?"

"Hear me out," he said. "Margret, Luke, Sage. Three drivers. You can tag-team the whole way. No one's alone. You'll get there faster. If you leave tomorrow morning, you'll make it to Portland in plenty of time before the puck drops Wednesday night."

From the living room, shouts of discontent rolled in as Jim and the boys protested a call against the Vikings. The noise rose, then faded, leaving a hollow quiet in its wake.

Margret straightened, folding her napkin with careful precision, as if order could hold back the chaos around her. "I'm needed in Portland tomorrow. There's media. Sponsors..."

Ryan cut her off, calm but firm. "It's a home game. Late one. If you leave tomorrow morning and share the driving, you'll be golden. What's so urgent for any of you to be in Portland Monday morning, that the whole team falls apart without you?"

A whistle blew from the TV, sharp as the silence that followed his words.

Margret opened her mouth, then closed it again. Luke's eye ticked, fingers drumming once against his plate before going still.

"This could work." Sage clapped her hands, the sound too bright for the tension in the room.

Hunter growled. "I still don't like it."

"Tough," Ryan muttered, wrapping both hands around his mug, the coffee now lukewarm.

Margret nodded once. "Fine. But I'm not stopping at every roadside antique shop you pass."

"Deal," Sage said before Hunter could object again.

Ryan leaned back. The football game's noise dulled to a low rumble. The air around the table felt heavy, charged, like the last seconds before a storm breaks. He didn't care. He'd take the win.

The early morning sky looked like it hadn't slept. Low gray clouds pressed against the South Dakota horizon, smearing the light into a dull wash. The air tasted of turned soil and leftover rain, the kind of morning that clung to your skin, making everything feel heavier than it should.

Ryan toed at the gravel, hands shoved deep in the pockets of his hoodie watching Sage load the back of her SUV. Crease bounded into the back seat like he was heading to training camp.

Margret and Luke pulled in right on time ... because of course they were. Sterling's limo made the whole thing feel more formal than it needed to be; the engine a low purr, paint gleaming despite the clouds. The driver stepped out to pop the trunk. Luke grabbed their bags, tossing them in the SUV beside Sage's. The thud fell flat in the still air.

Hunter stood stiff near Sage, his Goshawks hoodie wrinkled like he hadn't changed since the night before. His jaw worked side-to-side, chewing on words. Ryan knew that look. Something was about to snap.

"Don't make a scene," Ryan warned as he passed, voice low.

Hunter ignored him, eyes fixed on Sage. "You really think this is smart?"

Sage leaned in, refusing to back down. "We've already had this conversation."

"No," Hunter said, stepping back. "We yelled at each other. That's not a conversation."

Her fingers tightened on the strings of his hoodie, pulling him closer. "It's a done deal, Hunter. I'm driving my car. You're flying to Portland this morning."

Hunter's laugh came hollow. "Right. So that's it?"

Ryan watched Margret slide into the SUV's passenger seat without a word, sunglasses slipping into place like armor. Luke lingered near the back door, letting the moment play out.

Sage's voice dropped. "What do you want from me, Hunter?"

"Not to watch you drive away while everything still feels broken."

Ryan shifted, a lump in his throat. This wasn't the place. Not with goodbyes hanging in the air like smoke. "Hunter," he said, his voice low, "you want Lane starting next Wednesday because your head's not in the game?"

Hunter's lips pressed thin. For a second, the anger in his eyes faltered.

Ryan stepped closer. "You know the fans. You get one bad start, and they'll come for blood. Don't give them a reason."

Hunter nodded once, sharp and bitter.

Lilly walked to the group. She hugged Axel, Etan, and Ryan like it might be the last time. When she reached Hunter, she held him a little tighter, a little longer. "We'll be rooting for you boys on Wednesday."

Ryan paused at the limo door as Lilly turned to Sage, wrapping her arms around her daughter with trembling hands. Jim had left for work an hour earlier. Ryan suspected he wanted to avoid the goodbyes.

Crease gave Lilly a sloppy kiss. Dabbing her eyes with a hankie, she said, "Take good care of our girl."

Ryan slid into the limo next to Hunter, across from Etan and Axel. The vehicles rolled away from the house, moving in opposite directions.

Through the tinted glass, he watched the SUV heading east, taillights glowing faint in the misty morning. In the rear seat, he caught one last glimpse of Crease's yellow head bobbing beside Luke.

Ryan leaned back, closing his eyes. A clean split. Different roads. No guarantees they'd ever merge again.

Chapter 14
Down the Rabbit Hole

Tuesday, October 16th

The dashboard light blinked like a smug little beacon, warning her the road to control always ended in fumes. Margret tightened her grip on the steering wheel, glaring first at the glowing gas pump icon, then at the gauge needle wobbling on the big green E.

Sage reached back from the passenger seat to comfort Crease. "I know, baby. Just hang on a bit longer, okay?"

He whimpered, front paws prancing, tail thumping against the seat in a restless rhythm ... the canine version of a potty dance.

"We just passed Erie," Luke said from the back seat, cracking sunflower seeds between his teeth, looking far too calm for someone minutes away from being stranded. "There was a sign a few miles back." He leaned through the gap between the front seats. "Gas down this road."

"Yes, because nothing says dependable fuel supply like a hand-painted sign on the side of a highway," Margret grumbled.

"There's the turn." Sage pointed ahead.

The SUV rolled through the curve, gravel pinging the undercarriage as trees closed in above them, knitting a tunnel of shadow and damp leaves. The air smelled of wet bark and old pine, heavy with the scent of rain-soaked earth. Somewhere nearby, a crow called out, its cry echoing through the woods.

The gas station appeared at the bend, or what remained of it. Faded lettering clung to a sagging sign. Windows cracked, clouded with grime. Plywood sheets covered the pumps like a child's makeshift fort.

"Oh, fabulous," Margret muttered.

"Should we turn back or keep going?" Luke asked, popping another sunflower seed into his mouth.

Margret twisted around and glared. "Back to the interstate. Obviously."

"We could keep going," Sage said, her voice calm in that irritating way that always sounded sensible. "I bet it's only a few miles to the next town."

"Or a few more miles to a backwoods documentary," Margret shot back. "Do you want to be found by a hiker next spring?"

Luke shrugged. "I vote we keep going. Turning back wastes gas."

"Sorry, Margret, you're out voted. Let me drive." Sage scrambled to the driver's side.

Margret stomped to the passenger door. Once inside, her eyes narrowed at the road ahead. It was a single lane of patchy gravel, bordered by thick woods and the occasional leaning mailbox. "If this road turns to dirt, I swear..."

Sage drove a short distance before easing the SUV onto a small gravel pull-off beside a cluster of trees. "We have to stop. Crease is about to implode."

Margret frowned. "Why didn't you let him out when we stopped at that ghost station?"

Sage tightened her grip on the wheel. "I didn't want him getting into anything. You saw that place. He'd have found trouble in under a minute."

When the engine shut off, Margret glanced at her pristine white wool slacks and buttercream cashmere sweater, then out the window at the muddy forest floor. "I am not stepping foot in whatever fungus-friendly bog this is."

When Luke opened the back door Crease shot out of the SUV, chasing a rabbit like it was a playoff puck.

"Luke!" Sage shouted, lunging from her seat. "I told you to buckle his harness!"

"I forgot!" Luke yelled back, already sprinting after the Lab.

The woods erupted with snapping branches, startled birds, and Sage's voice cutting through the chaos as she disappeared into the trees.

Margret closed her eyes, inhaling deeply. The air smelled of wet moss and the tail end of a bad idea. She stayed seated, fingers tightening around her phone. She would not chase a dog. Not in designer flats. Not in Prada. Not in Pennsylvania. She tapped her screen to check for a signal. One bar. Maybe.

Somewhere in the distance, Luke shouted Sage's name. Crease barked like a maniac. A squirrel shrieked ... hopefully in protest, not pain.

Margret sank deeper into the seat. "Just a few more hours until we're back in Portland," she muttered, "assuming the wilderness doesn't finish us off first."

She jerked awake to a *low battery* warning from her cell that felt more like mockery than help. Blinking at the screen, she frowned. *Had it been an hour?*

With deliberate care, she climbed out of the SUV, hoping for a better signal. The woods had gone still, damp and green in that heavy late-afternoon way. No shouting. No frantic bark-chasing. Only a hush laced with the slow drip of water from the branches, as if even the forest had lost interest.

She tiptoed to a dry rocky mound a few feet from the SUV and adjusted her stance, peering down the path where Sage and Luke had vanished. Nothing. No Sage. No Luke. No Crease. No resolution. With a sigh, she unlocked her phone and began to type.

Margret: Luke. Where are you? Please don't be lost.

She was mid-message when something yellow and brown burst through the brush. "Crease?"

She blinked twice. "CREASE!"

He bounded at her like a joyful missile, ears flapping, tongue out, tail beating the air like a riot baton. His entire underside was streaked with mud, clumps of wet leaves plastered to his chest like swamp armor.

Margret stared in horror, then made a beeline for the SUV. Over her shoulder she shouted, "No. No. No. Stay there! Stay. STAY!"

Crease did not stay.

Margret slid behind the partially opened passenger door as Crease jumped against it from the other side. Wedged in place, she gripped the door like a shield, the reluctant commander in a one-woman standoff. Lifting her phone, she tapped out two frantic texts:

Margret: Luke, Crease is back

Margret: Sage. Your dog is here

Both replies arrived at once.

LUKE: Secure him before he bolts

SAGE: Tie him up. Don't let him run off

She doubted the big goober would wander off again, but the lost time gnawed at her. Deciding to take one for the team, she pushed the door with all her strength, expecting Crease to step back and settle.

Instead, eighty pounds of Labrador joy launched straight at her. His paws hit square on her chest, his tongue slapping her chin as he shoved her away from the door's meager protection.

"OFF! OFF! YOU GIANT SWAMP RAT!"

She stumbled, one cream-colored shoe twisting off in the mud, arms flailing for balance. Her shoulder struck the door. It slammed shut with a hollow thud. She hit the ground. Cold, sticky muck seeped up her back. Her cashmere sweater gave a sound that could only be described as a soggy betrayal. Her other designer flat sailed through the air like a fleeing dove.

Crease, thrilled by this new game, scooped the shoe into his mouth, shaking it like a chew toy.

"Drop it!" she shrieked. "That cost more than your neutering surgery!"

He shook his head harder.

Mud crept into the waistband of her white slacks. Her sweater clung to her ribs like damp tissue. The elegant fabric sagged, stained beyond salvation. She sat in stunned silence, staring up at the pale sky, chest heaving, face speckled with bits of something she prayed wasn't a worm.

Crease padded over, dropped the mud-caked shoe in her lap, then stuck his tongue up her nose. She didn't flinch. "This day just keeps raising the bar," she muttered.

Branches cracked in the distance like popping corn. Voices followed, faint at first, then louder.

"Did she catch him?" Sage called, breathing heavy.

"Hope he didn't get away," Luke added as the two stepped into the clearing.

Margret didn't move. She couldn't. Not with mud seeping through the seat of her designer slacks, one bare foot coated in grime, the other jammed inside the shoe Crease so generously returned.

Luke froze mid-step. Sage clapped a hand over her mouth. Both went statue still, the kind of stillness reserved for people trying not to laugh in church.

Margret's glare could have melted steel.

Luke cleared his throat and stepped forward, hand extended. "Let me help you up?"

She swatted at him with a mud-smeared palm. "Touch me and you'll lose that hand."

Sage turned her attention back to Crease. "Okay, bud, time to settle down." She grabbed his collar. "Let's get you in the..."

She yanked the handle. Nothing. She blinked and tried again. Still locked. Color drained from her face, a shade at a time. Her hands moved from her pockets to her waistband, searching. Her breathing quickened, eyes darting in confusion.

"Sage..." Margret growled. "What's wrong now?"

Sage's voice rose. "The doors have an auto-lock. When everyone's out of the vehicle and the fob's not inside, it locks."

"So, unlock it," Margret snapped, swiping at the mud on her cheek with her sleeve, only smearing it more.

Sage didn't move.

"Sage."

"I … I can't."

Margret froze mid-swipe. "Why not?"

"The key fob's missing." Sage whined.

Luke blinked. "What do you mean it's missing?"

"I must've dropped it when I pulled out my phone to answer Margret's text."

Margret's mouth opened, closed, then opened again. This time she screamed, "Go. Find. It."

Sage bolted into the woods.

Luke turned to follow, already moving when Margret shouted, "Where are you going?"

He stopped. "To help her."

She pointed at Crease, who was busy rolling in the mud he hadn't already smeared across her. "Secure the mutt first!"

Luke glanced at the SUV. "His leash is in the car."

They stared at each other, then at the dog, then at the locked vehicle.

"Think, Luke!" Margret barked.

He tore off his flannel shirt. threading one sleeve through Crease's collar, securing the other sleeve to the SUV's hitch. It was messy, but it would hold.

Margret's scowl deepened as Luke studied her mud-caked sweater, tangled hair, streaked makeup. He stepped closer, pressing a kiss to her muddy cheek.

"You're beautiful," he whispered, then sprinted after Sage.

Stunned, Margret watched him vanish into the grove of trees. Tears pooled as she looked down. A maple leaf clung to her chest like a wet slap from Mother Nature. Crease settled beside the bumper, tail thumping, wearing a big grin. She looked skyward, arms wrapped around her knees. "I swear, if I ever get back to Portland, I'm driving the Zamboni over all three of them."

Margret slumped against the SUV as her world collapsed. Mud dried in streaks along her sweater and slacks, stiff patches clinging in all the wrong places. Her neat bun, once the perfect twist of professionalism, now sagged to one side, flecked with bits of leaves and indignity. The toes exposed on her barefoot looked like they'd been painted by a toddler using river silt.

She wiped at the sludge on her phone with the cuff of her sweater. No signal. Dead battery. The surrounding silence pressed in ... mossy, sticky, judgy. A crow called again, its cackle mocking her from an unseen tree branch.

Her head thumped against the SUV with a dull thud. Tears burned but didn't fall. There was no crying in hockey. She'd never stepped onto the ice, yet she had always been part of the team. Five seasons beside Justin. Five seasons of fights, strategy, pride. Now she sat here, stranded, soaked, smudged, and benched.

Her gaze shifted to Crease, who lounged nearby with her other designer flat clamped in his jaws, tail thumping, flinging bits of dirt her way.

"Thief."

He wagged harder.

She closed her eyes. Maybe the universe was finished with her. Maybe she'd stay here and become a forest spirit, the patron saint of Mud and Misplaced Dreams.

The slow crunch of gravel broke the silence. Tires rolled to a stop. Her eyes snapped open. "What now?"

Crease perked up, tail drumming against the bumper. A pair of polished boots appeared beside him. Their owner crouched to scratch behind the Lab's ears.

"Well now," the words came out, deep and masculine. "What are you doing out here, boy?"

"He's pleading the Fifth," Margret called.

The man straightened, tall and broad in a khaki uniform, a silver badge catching the light across his chest. Sheriff. Of course ... because humiliation, like comedy, thrived on escalation.

He had just rounded the SUV when Sage and Luke burst from the woods. Luke shirtless. Sage's blouse untucked. Her long blond hair tangled with twigs.

"Stop!" The sheriff's hand snapped to his sidearm.

Luke froze mid-stride. Sage stumbled into him, clutching his waist.

The sheriff's gaze swept from Luke's bare chest to Sage's wild hair, then to Margret, still dripping mud.

"Can someone tell me what is going on here?"

They all started talking at once.

The sheriff lifted a hand. "One at a time." He looked at Margret. "Ma'am, are you all right?"

Margret blinked up at him. "Do I look alright?"

Sage stepped forward. "We're about out of gas. My dog had to go. He saw a rabbit and bolted. I chased him, dropped my key fob, had to find it." Lifting the offending item, she clicked the locks open, her smile triumphant.

The sheriff grunted, shifting his attention to Luke. "Son, where's your shirt?"

Luke pointed at Crease. "The leash is locked in the SUV."

The sheriff scratched his chin as if debating whether this circus warranted a written report.

Luke reached his hand to Margret. She flinched, swatting it away once more.

Sage plucked a bug from her hair. "Is there a hotel nearby? Something not ... forest-adjacent?"

The sheriff gave a slow nod. "My aunt runs a place down the road." He removed his hat, raked a hand through his hair, then settled it back in place. "There's a youth hockey tournament this week. Families started arriving this morning. It might be booked."

"Could you please call her?" Margret asked, a rough laugh catching in her throat. Hockey, as always, determined her destiny.

The sheriff glanced at Crease. His lips twitched. "Not sure she takes dogs."

Luke pulled a hundred-dollar bill from his wallet. "I'll make it worth her while."

The sheriff squinted. "Put that away, son, and get your shirt on."

Luke untied one end of his flannel from the hitch, securing Crease in the backseat of the SUV. He shut the door before slipping on his damp shirt, brushing away clumps of mud.

The sheriff's fingers moved across his phone. A grin tugged at his mouth. "Looks like you're in luck," he said. "She's got one room left. Two queens. She'll take the dog for a sizable, non-refundable deposit."

"Thanks, Sheriff. That's great news." Sage checked the time on her phone. "We can get cleaned up, grab some food, gas up, and be back on the road tonight."

The sheriff shifted his stance. "About that ... there's a bait shop next door to the motel that sells gas. He opens at nine sharp."

Margret moaned. "Nine? In the morning? With minimum stops, it'll take us at least eleven hours to get back to Portland. If we can't leave until after nine, we'll miss the first period."

Luke pulled out his wallet again, fanning a handful of bills. "Could you call the owner? Offer something extra to open early?"

The sheriff folded his arms. "Son, I don't know how many ways to tell you to put your money away. Owner's out of town. He won't be back 'till morning."

Margret didn't think she could sink any lower in the mud, but somehow she did.

"Follow me," the sheriff said, motioning to his cruiser. "Stay close. It's not far, but since you're running on fumes, I don't want to waste more of my time calling a tow truck."

Sage tossed the fob to Luke. "You drive. I'll buckle Crease in."

Margret stood, legs unsteady. "Luke, can you get my clean clothes?"

A light sprinkle of rain tapped the leaves overhead. Ahead of them, the sheriff's taillights blinked as thunderclouds rolled in.

"Get in, Margret," Sage called. "You can clean up when we get to the motel."

She hesitated, then climbed in. "Why not ruin the seats too."

"Good thing they're leather," Luke said, lowering his voice he added, "I'll clean them once we get you inside."

Margret stared at the sheriff's taillights, lips pressed thin, broken nails digging into the dash.

Luke started the SUV. The fuel light blinked. The engine wheezed. They rolled forward, chasing the red glow on fumes and what was left of her patience.

Chapter 15
The Cost of Loyalty

Wednesday, Oct 18th
Home Game: Goshawks vs Nashville Shredders

The house lights dropped in perfect unison with the rumble of the Goshawks' entrance. Blue and silver lasers rippled across the glass, chasing through the sold-out crowd. The sound hit next, a rolling surge that rose, collided with itself, then crashed down in waves. Ice fog drifted through the lower bowl. Skates bit the surface, cutting clean white arcs as the team poured from the tunnel for pregame warmups.

High above the ice, the camera light blinked. Tom Hughes adjusted his mic, voice carrying a polished calm only years in the booth could give. "The Goshawks hope to continue their winning streak with this second home game. You can feel the crowd's energy all the way up here. Welcome back, folks. The defending conference champs are on home ice once more. Tonight, they'll be facing a pair of familiar faces."

"Too familiar, Tom," said John, his voice lower, gravelly. "The Nashville Shredders got stronger this offseason ... a lot stronger. Chase Rutherford and Olaf Svensson, both fan favorites here in Portland, now wear Nashville black and red. You think that's awkward for the Goshawks? Try looking your old captain in the eye across the faceoff dot."

"Don't forget the other side of the equation." Tom nodded to the Goshawks new addition. "I don't see any love going to Trey Moss from his former teammates."

"I saw a few Shredders glare at Moss when he skated onto the ice." John tilted his head and shrugged.

Ryan pushed off from the boards, looping past the blue line. He glanced at Hunter stretching near his net, loose and quiet behind his mask. Across the sheet, Olaf skated with that same deliberate calm Ryan remembered from practice drills. Hunter drifted out of his crease, gliding to the red line. No theatrics, no hesitation. Olaf spotted him. The two goalies met, sticks tapping before pulling each other into a heavy, thumping embrace that drew a pulse of reaction from the arena.

"And there it is," Tom said as the camera zoomed in. "Olaf Svensson, and Hunter Griffin. The former tandem goalies sharing a moment at center ice."

"Yeah," John added, "but we'll see how friendly they stay once the puck drops."

Ryan coasted nearby, resting on his stick, letting the moment sink in. He remembered those long nights when Olaf's calm steadied every storm. Hunter's balance came from that. But tonight, Hunter stood alone.

A flash of motion drew Ryan's attention. Chase Rutherford broke from his stretch routine, gliding toward him. They slowed near the neutral zone, skates scraping a fine mist between them. Chase gave a quick tap to the front of Ryan's sweater where the stitched C caught the light.

"Congrats, kid," Chase said, his grin quick but genuine. "You earned it."

"You set the bar."

Chase's laugh was brief, easy. "Then keep it high." He turned, coasting back to his side of the ice.

Ryan felt the weight of that moment linger ... respect without rivalry, history without words. He shrugged it off, skating in front of the net. He glanced at Hunter. "You know she'll be here."

Hunter raised his mask, taking a slow drink from his water bottle. "Yeah? Then why hasn't she called?"

Ryan straightened, meeting his gaze. "No cell service?"

Hunter's laugh was tight. "Sure. That's always an excuse. Before it all goes sideways." He set the bottle down hard, water squirting over his glove. The mask came down, sealing him off.

Ryan tapped Hunter's pads. "Keep your head in the game."

Trey coasted by, his stick flicking a puck through a slick spin pass near the blue line. The puck slid wide of his reach, tapping the boards before settling flat. Etan's slow clap echoed across the ice, his grin wide enough to catch the light. Axel skated up, giving Trey a light shoulder check, the kind of bump that spoke more attitude than muscle.

Up in the booth, Tom's voice carried over the broadcast. "Boys are already getting chippy. That's the second time Axel's nudged Trey during warmups. Look at Coach Harrison's face. He's not loving this."

The camera panned to the bench. Harrison's jaw tight, his posture rigid, his focus locked on the ice.

"In-house tension brewing," John added. "Not the tone you want before puck drop. Forced chemistry always looks this way. You trade away your captain and your backup netminder for a player whose talent matches his attitude; you better hope the gamble pays off."

Ryan skated to center, blades cutting thin grooves into the ice. The echo of pucks striking the boards faded into background noise. He adjusted his chin strap, spat once near the blue line, jaw tight enough to throb. All that mattered now was the puck drop and guarding his goalie.

First Period

Tom adjusted his headset, eyes on the crowd as the last of the lights settled into place. "Welcome back, folks. Warmups are in the books here in Portland. You can already feel the charge in the air. The crowd's ready for this one to start."

John tugged at his mic, his tone measured. "Yeah, this one's got the weight of history on it. Let's see how both sides handle that emotion once the puck drops."

Tom nodded, his voice carrying the handoff. "Let's go rink side for the starters."

The arena speakers boomed with the Shredders' starting lineup announcement. "Starting in goal, Number 30 ... Olaaaf Svenssoooon."

The crowd rose to their feet. The standing ovation hit like a blast of wind, echoing through every tier of the arena. Even from the tunnel, Ryan felt the vibration in his skates.

When they announced, "Number 88 ... Chaaaase Ruuuutherford," the noise swelled again, louder, sharper. Fans stomped their feet. Whistles cut through the roar. A cluster of homemade signs waved near the lower bowl, their glittered letters catching the lights. *Once a Goshawks. Always a Goshawks.*

Ryan expected it but hearing that kind of love for his former teammates, now wearing Nashville colors, burned deep. He moved side-to-side listening to the rest of the Shredders' starting lineup names called.

There was a slight pause before the announcer's voice cracked over the roar. "And now... your Portland GOSHAAAWKS!"

Blue lights swept across the ice. Pyro hissed from the tunnel, filling the air with smoke and the faint scent of sulfur. Hunter skated out first, leading the charge as the crowd thundered.

The volume climbed again when the announcer called out Ryan's name. He pushed off, shoulders squared, stick gripped tight like an extension of his arm. The stands rattled under the weight of thousands stomping their approval.

Across the rink, Chase and Olaf waited at the far blue line, the neon red of their sweaters catching the arena lights. For a brief second, the noise blurred. The years they had shared, the flights, the locker rooms, the victories, all flickered through Ryan's mind before vanishing in the glare of now.

This was no reunion. It was a revolution, where former brothers on ice now battled against each other. *Hockey can mess with your mind.*

The first shift fell apart in seconds. Winger Finn O'Connell misread the breakout, dumping the puck deep with no one chasing. Nashville swarmed. Their forecheck pressed high, cutting off passing lanes, slicing through Portland's zone exits like a practiced ambush.

Ryan barked at Etan to swing wide. His voice lost in the noise. The puck hit the boards kicking out clean onto Chase's tape.

Edges bit deep as Ryan pivoted to recover.

Chase faked the shot ... sliding it to his trailing D-man. One touch. Bar down.

Goal! Shredders—Patterson

The red light flashed behind Hunter, casting quick bursts of color across the glass. The sound hit a heartbeat later, a full-throated roar from the visiting bench. Ryan coasted to the crease, where Hunter stood frozen, glove half-raised, eyes vacant.

Two line changes later, Ryan dropped into the lane, guarding the crease. A ninety-mile-an-hour slap shot ripped from the point, cutting through traffic. He dropped to a knee, the puck hammering his shin guard with a crack. It ricocheted wide, spinning out of the zone. Pain throbbed deep in his leg, bright and searing. He pushed to his feet, skating hard to the bench, each stride a pulse of heat.

From the booth, Tom's voice carried over the broadcast. "Mitchell blocks a rocket from the point. That's a captain putting his body on the line to assist his goalie."

John leaned in, his tone rough with approval. "That's a defenseman willing to wear one to protect his net. You can't coach that kind of loyalty."

On the bench, Ryan breathed hard, sweat cooling against his neck as he watched the action at the far end of the rink. Olaf kicked away a backhander from Axel with his right pad, popped up quick, then sprawled sideways to rob Trey on the rebound. His glove flashed like a cobra strike.

A single gasp swept through the crowd, followed by a groan that rolled across the arena.

Ryan stood in the bench, breath still heavy as Trey skated past. Grabbing a fistful of jersey, he said, voice low, teeth clenched, "Start playing Goshawks hockey. Ignore the team that let you go."

Trey's jaw tightened. He gave a quick nod, then pushed off down the ice. Ryan watched him go, unsure if the warning landed.

Next shift, Nashville came again. Harder. More Precise. Playing like a well-oiled machine.

Chase cut across the high slot. Ryan shadowed him, stick angled wide to close the lane. The puck never came. Instead, it went low, a sharp-angle shot from a winger hugging the boards. It slipped past Hunter's glove, catching the corner clean.

Goal! Shredders—Atwater

The sound in the stands shifted from anxious to uneasy, then broke into scattered boos.

Hunter slammed his stick against the post. Once. Twice. Three times. The cracks echoed through the rink. He turned to Ryan, breath fogging in the cold air, shoulders heaving like a bull ready to charge.

Ryan skated to him, tapped a glove against the top of Hunter's mask. "Stop thinking about Sage. Start thinking about keeping your home safe."

Hunter jerked back like he'd been struck. "How about you guys get the puck in Olaf's net?"

His tone cut deeper than the words. Ryan glared at him, then turned away before he said something he'd regret.

By the time the buzzer sounded, the Goshawks headed to the tunnel trailing by two. The scoreboard didn't show how badly they'd been dominated. Nashville was faster. Tighter. Grittier.

Ryan skated to the gate as he unclipped his helmet. He stayed silent, eyes fixed on the ice, shoulders rising and falling. His breath fogged in front of him, fading like the hope they'd carried into the period.

"End of the first here in Portland. The Shredders came ready, taking advantage of every Goshawks' mistake." Tom shook his head.

John followed, his tone lower, measured. "You can see the frustration building down there, especially in the crease. Griffin's fighting the puck. When a goalie starts overthinking, it spreads fast. Portland needs a reset in that locker room."

Second Period

"Welcome back folks." Tom turned to John. "The Goshawks trail two to nothing."

"They need someone to set the tone early," John countered. "This team runs on emotion. They get on the boards, they'll get the building back. But first, they got to clean up the turnovers and, more important ... they need to calm Griffin down in net."

The puck dropped. Ryan's legs felt heavy, his shoulders tighter than they should've been. That sick churn in his gut, the one that usually faded during the first period, stayed with him.

Four minutes in, the Shredders took a holding penalty. *A gift.*

Ryan readied for the puck as Goshawks' second-line center Eddie Bennett won the draw clean, feeding back to Murphy, who slid it to Ryan, who caught it on his tape.

One stride. Two. Ryan didn't think. He just ripped it. The puck screamed off his stick, low and clean, as Axel blocked Olaf's sightline. The puck slammed into the back of the net the same instant the crowd rose to its feet.

Goal! Goshawks—Mitchell

The horn blasted. Lights pulsed. Fans cheered. Goshawks towels waved.

In the booth, Tom's excitement bled through his mic. "Captain Ryan Mitchell breaks through with a laser from the point. That's how you answer."

John's laugh came rough but approving. "That's how you lead. You don't talk your team back into the game. You show them how it's done."

After being jumped by Etan, Ryan gave a quick glove bump on the bench. No big celly. This was business. A one-goal disadvantage left no room for comfort.

Two line changes later, a high sticking call on the Shredders. *Another lucky break*, Ryan thought.

But Nashville caught them mid-cycle, lazy and wide. Trey wobbled a pass high in the zone. A Shredder pounced, taking off with four strides on second-line winger Steve Sturman. Trey chased but couldn't close the gap.

Ryan rushed to stop the shorthanded breakaway but came up short.

Hunter stayed set, knees squared, waiting too long. The puck beat him ... five-hole clean. Like he forgot to close the front door.

Goal! Shredders—Atwater

The arena went quiet, the silence louder than any cheer.

"A brutal shorty. That one hurts. The Goshawks had a chance to tie it, but one mistake turns into another two-goal hole." Tom leaned back in his chair.

John leaned forward. "You can't leave your goalie naked like that. Griffin's fighting it, but that's not all on him. That's on his teammates."

"Griffin. You. Suck." Reverberated from the seats behind the net. Fans pounded the glass.

Hunter sprayed his face with water, repositioning for the next onslaught.

The coach didn't pull Hunter. That made it worse.

The Shredders smelled blood. They came harder, hammering the corners, grinding down the clock. Ryan blocked two shots with his body in one shift, the second ringing off his ribs hard enough to rattle his breath.

Near the end of the period, Axel boarded a Nashville winger at the end of a shift ... too high, too late. The player spun, arms flailing, selling the hit. The whistle shrieked. Axel barked at the ref, jaw tight, eyes wide.

Ryan skated over, shoving him into the box. "Shut up. Sit down."

Axel glared but didn't argue.

Power play, Nashville. They didn't waste it.

Goal! Shredders—Rutherford

The arena deflated like someone put a needle in a balloon.

Tom cleared his throat. "Chase Rutherford's always been the king of power-plays. You knew he'd find the net. That makes it four to one, Nashville."

John sighed. "You never want to see your former captain score on your home ice. That one's got to sting for the Goshawks."

Three minutes later, off a scramble in front of the net, Ryan's stick got tied up as he lost sight of the puck in the traffic. Black jerseys crashed the crease, sticks stabbing, skates chopping the ice. Hunter crouched low, fighting through the mess. A Nashville player, jabbed once, twice, then pushed it past the blue crease.

Goal! Shredders—Johanson

Sweat stung Ryan's eyes as he stared at the scoreboard. This wasn't a loss. It was a massacre.

He skated back to the bench as the horn blared the end of the second period. The crowd barely moved. Those who stayed sat in silence, heads shaking. Others drifted to the concourse, their hope of victory left on the ice.

Tom's voice carried the weight of it. "That's five for Nashville. Portland looks out of rhythm, out of sync, out of answers."

"I've seen games get away before, but this is different. You can feel the confidence bleeding out of that bench. The Goshawks need more than adjustments right now," John said. "They need a miracle."

Tom shook his head. "This period exposed every crack in Portland's game. If they can't regroup, the third turns into damage control."

Second Intermission

Ryan entered the locker room, chest heaving, eyes on his skates. His shoulder pads shifted with each breath, heavy as armor that no longer fit. Inside, silence waited. Players adjusted gear. Steam hung low. No one spoke. There was nothing left to say.

The door burst open, the slam echoing like a slapshot. Coach Harrison's voice hit before he crossed the threshold. "Eklund! Berger! What the hell was that out there?"

Etan's head snapped up, lips parting to answer.

"Don't even," Harrison barked, clipboard swinging at his side. "Over-skate the puck one more time, you'll be buried so deep in the roster you'll need a rope to climb out."

Etan's jaw flexed. "Coach, Trey..."

"I'm not finished!" The clipboard cracked against a locker. "Berger, you forget how to play the body? You let a rookie winger skate through you like it's a men's-league scrimmage."

Axel lowered his head.

Harrison's glare shifted. "Mitchell."

Ryan straightened, the word freezing him in place.

"You're the captain now. Act like it. I saw you floating out there. The puck's in your zone and you're coasting like it's a charity game."

Ryan started to lift his sweater. "I can show you the bruises that prove that's not true."

"Oh, you were giving a hundred percent?" Harrison's laugh came out cracked and bitter. "Then that's worse."

The room went dead. Only the slow drip of a leaky water bottle broke the silence.

"And. You." Harrison turned to the far corner.

Hunter sat still, head leaning back on his stall, eyes closed.

"I fought for you in that office. Told the board I'd walk if they let you go. What did I get for my efforts? A goalie who couldn't stop a beach ball."

Ryan's voice cut in, low. "Coach..."

"No!" Harrison roared, stepping forward, the veins in his neck drawn tight. "He needs to hear this."

Hunter looked up, eyes empty.

"You're not worth the ink on your contract. And you, Moss ... don't think I didn't notice you gifting your old teammates goals."

Trey froze, one skate half-laced.

"You want to be a superstar?" Harrison snapped. "Start by finishing a pass."

Trey's temper broke. "Maybe if I had linemates who could keep up."

Etan shot to his feet, pointing. "Maybe if you passed once instead of trying to make every play a highlight reel."

Axel joined in, voice rising, "You cost us that shorty. You froze at the blue line."

Trey spun toward him. "Maybe stop playing like you're scared of the puck."

"Enough!" Ryan's voice thundered through the room. "All of you."

Silence snapped tight.

Harrison stepped closer, nose to nose with his captain. "You think protecting them makes you a leader?"

Ryan didn't blink. "Someone has to do something. You're tearing everyone apart."

"Because someone needs to. You want to keep that C? Earn it." His finger jabbed Ryan's chest, hard. "Right now you're just a sweater wearing a letter."

Ryan's fists curled at his sides.

Harrison's voice dropped, quiet but cutting. "This isn't a slump. This is collapse. Keep it up, I'll mail your Cup rings to the Shredders."

He turned. "Griffin, you're done." He pointed at the rookie beside him. "Wilson, third's yours."

Lane nodded once, calm amidst the storm.

"Git it together." Harrison shouted to his players before slamming the door, rattling the metal hooks along the stalls.

Ryan's breath came quick, sweat cooling against his skin. Hunter rose, silent, pulled on his ball cap, gathered his mask and gloves. He walked to the exit.

Ryan caught his sleeve. "Don't let him get into your head."

"He already did." Hunter pulled free, disappearing down the tunnel.

Ryan stood in the doorway, the air thick with defeat, the sound of wrapping tape marking every second until the next period.

Third Period

Tom's voice carried over the hum of the crowd. "We're underway for the final period. The Goshawks made a change in net. Lane Wilson takes over for Hunter Griffin."

John's tone softened, the edge of an experienced goalie in his voice. "Tough spot for a rookie, coming in cold, down four. But this is how you earn your place on the roster."

Ryan noted how Lane stood tall between the pipes, unblinking behind the cage of his mask as the third period clock ticked down like a slow drip. The young goalie tracked every puck, cut angles with precision, slid post-to-post like he was born there.

The Shredders didn't score again. Didn't get close. It didn't matter. The Goshawks couldn't buy a goal.

Finn missed high. Trey hit the post. Etan got robbed on a wrister that should've buried itself top shelf. Every Goshawks stick seemed cursed. Every rebound bounced the wrong way. Every cycle collapsed under its own weight.

Throughout the period, Ryan kept yelling. Kept clapping. Kept trying to keep the fire alive. His words fell flat, but he kept up the banter, because silence would hurt worse.

By the final five minutes, the fan exodus began. Slow. Silent. Like a funeral procession. When the buzzer sounded, it felt like mercy.

From the booth, Tom closed the evening with weary professionalism. "Tough night for Portland. The Shredders take it five to one. A lesson in composure, discipline, and execution."

John's tone dropped lower, reflective. "You don't win every game, but some losses cut deeper. The Goshawks have to regroup after this one."

Ryan didn't look at the opposing bench. No acknowledgement of his old teammates. That would come later, maybe at the Frosty Nest. For now, he skated off the ice, nodding once to Lane, who tapped a glove to his shoulder as they passed. No celebration. Just acknowledgment.

In the tunnel, the air cooled. Quiet. One light flickered overhead. A bitter voice rose from above. "Eight million a year for that?"

Another followed, rougher. "Should've sent Griffin to the farm team."

Then a kid's voice, small but sharp. "I want my jersey money back."

Something hit the floor near Ryan's skates. A Goshawks jersey, with Hunter's name and number stitched on the back. Crumpled, tossed like garbage ... the price tag still dangling.

He bent, picked it up. Mid-stride he saw her.

Margret stood in the middle of the tunnel, arms crossed, back rigid, her presence radiating fury without a sound. Her face flushed, lips drawn tight, eyes locked on his. Behind her stood Luke, stone-faced. Sage lingered a few steps back, arms wrapped around herself. Her gaze restless.

Ryan met Margret's glare. Neither blinked. The air shifted between them, charged and silent, like lightning before the crack of thunder.

Chapter 16
Boxed In

Thursday, Oct 19th

Ryan woke to darkness. For a split second, he thought it was still night, until his eyes adjusted, catching the faint glow leaking around the edges of the blackout curtains. Hunter's guest room felt weightless, like time hadn't moved since the night before.

Rolling over, he flipped on the nightlight, instantly wishing he hadn't. Cardboard boxes lined the far wall, stacked in uneven towers. Some taped shut, others slouched open with clothes spilling out. The air smelled of dust and hockey tape. Over five years of his life, folded away, waiting for a decision he still hadn't made.

He swung his legs over the side of the bed, fingers raking through his beard. The itch to wash off last night still clung to his skin. The urge wasn't just physical ... it gnawed deeper. Disappointment did that. It always happened after a loss in their barn.

Crossing to the bathroom, his bare feet slapped the cold tile. Steam filled the air a minute later, the shower hissing to life. Hot water hit him like a dare. He braced both hands on the wall; the spray cascading down his back, eyes closed as flashes from the game replayed ... missed coverages, wild passes, Hunter being pulled. That final buzzer still vibrated in his bones.

When he stepped out, he wiped a streak across the fogged mirror. Bruises mapped his ribs in deep violet and fading shades of yellows. Another branded his shin, angry and raw where the puck had struck. He flexed the leg, wincing at the pull. The mirror gave him back a stranger's face with shadowed eyes.

Dressed in sweats, Ryan padded into the kitchen. The scent of coffee lingered thick in the air, laced with chocolate and a trace of cinnamon.

Hunter sat at the island, elbows on the counter, shoulders slumped as if bracing for impact.

Ryan poured himself a cup without speaking and took the seat across from him. The first sip scorched his tongue. He welcomed the sting. "Hey. Don't let last night eat at you," he said. "It's only one game."

Hunter didn't look up. His gaze stayed locked on the mug in front of him, spoon tracing slow circles in the dark liquid. "You've got to be kidding me," he muttered. "I was a sieve out there." He set the spoon down, metal clinking against marble. "I let five goals in at home. Crowd turning. Coach ready to ship me to the farm team." The words came low, half to himself.

Hunter grabbed his phone off the counter, thumb flicking across the screen before he shoved it at Ryan. "Did you see what the fans are saying?"

Ryan pushed it back without a glance. "You know better than to check those sites after a loss."

"They're not wrong." Hunter's voice thinned at the edges. "Sign a big contract. Suddenly, I forget how to play net."

Ryan took another sip, holding off a response. Last evening, they rehashed this conversation during the drive back from the rink. Margret's shouting still echoed. So did Coach Harrison's threats.

He would have loved a day off to ease his sore muscles. Instead, Harrison had made it crystal clear ... practice at two o'clock sharp, no excuses. Ryan's body ached in places that weren't even bruised. Across the counter, Hunter looked like he'd aged ten years overnight. Thirty-plus saves, yet he'd skated off the ice like the villain.

"You regroup today," Ryan said. "Next time you're between the pipes, you shut the door."

Hunter stood, drained his cup. He leaned against the counter, gaze drifting to the ceiling as if searching for a reset button that didn't exist. "I feel like I've been constantly waiting for a next time. Feels like Gray and Harrison are ready to hand the net to Lane full-time. I'm not blind. Wilson and Gray finish each other's sentences."

Ryan folded his arms. "I get it. Lane and Cal have history."

Hunter eased back onto his barstool. "Kind of like Viktor and me."

Ryan hesitated, eyes narrowing. "So, what did Sage say? Did she explain the late arrival?"

Hunter stared into his empty mug. "We didn't talk," his words emerging cold and flat. "I shut off my phone."

Ryan's cup hit the counter with a sharp clink. "No, way."

Hunter didn't look up. "I knew she'd call or text. I didn't want to hear her excuses. If she wanted to support me, she'd have been there before warmups. Instead, she spent three days cooped up with that South Dakota cowboy."

Ryan bit his lower lip. He could've said Sage wasn't alone, that Luke hadn't been her only passenger. None of it would land right this morning. "Yeah, no, for sure," he said instead. "It's why I've stuck to casual dating once I went pro. The game's gotta come first."

Hunter nodded, looking out the window. Beyond the glass, the Portland skyline shimmered pale under the early light.

Ryan smirked. "Still, there's something about those South Dakota girls ... hard to resist."

Hunter's lip twitched. "No kidding."

"Look at Jessica," Ryan went on. "She weaseled into my life. Thought she was just a summer distraction, someone to hang with while the rest of you were golfing. Then she tried to worm her way into my heart, only to stomp all over it."

Hunter let out a breath that might've been a laugh, or maybe just disbelief.

"Thing is, you and Sage are different. She gets the game. She gets you. She respects your space. Jess got hockey, but she never got me. Not really. We never had what you and Sage have."

Hunter stayed quiet, staring out the window.

The sound of a key turned in the lock. "Are you decent?" Sage called from the front door, her tone light, almost teasing. She didn't wait for an answer, stepping inside to toe off her sneakers at the mat.

A leash stretched from her hand to a squirming yellow blur beside her. Crease lunged forward the instant he spotted movement, his body wagging with excitement. Once unclipped, he barreled straight for Hunter, every muscle quivering with joy.

Hunter didn't move. Didn't glance down.

Crease froze, ears dropped, confusion flickering across his face. After a beat, he spun to Ryan, bounding across the kitchen, paws thudding with renewed joy.

"Hey, buddy," Ryan murmured, fingers sinking into soft fur.

"Hey, Ryan." Sage finger waved.

He looked up. She was all sunshine and good intentions, walking like the air wasn't thick with tension. Ryan gave her a polite smile. The energy hit him sideways. She was too bright, too calm. Trying too hard to pretend.

Sage circled behind Hunter, draping her arms around his neck. Her lips lowered close to his ear. "I don't care how bad the game was," she said, tone sweet ...

until it wasn't. "Never block me again." She bit his earlobe, sharp, then turned away without waiting for a reaction. In the kitchen, she poured a mug of coffee, every move deliberate. Like she hadn't just pulled a grenade pin and walked away.

Silence stretched until he couldn't take it anymore. Ryan stood, rolling his shoulders to shake off the weight of the room. "Looks like you two could use some alone time." Crease's ears perked, tail thumping against his bruised shin. "Not now, boy. I'll take you for a run later."

Ryan stepped barefoot into the hallway. His hand hovered over the doorknob before his brain caught up. Two quick knocks on Jill's door.

"Come on in. It's open," she called, her voice slicing through the hum of printers.

He pushed the door open and stepped into her lair ... because that's exactly what it was. Similar layout as Hunter's place, only it looked like a mad scientist shacked up with a hacker, neither willing to give an inch. The room temperature was so cold his toes curled.

In the front room, three giant monitors flickered along a long desk. LED lights glowed like runway beacons. Piles of paper blanketed the floor like scattered snowdrifts. Post-it notes clung to the walls. The air smelled of lemon and ozone, the kind of charge that builds before a storm.

"Why is your floor covered in paper?" Ryan asked, stepping carefully, like one wrong move might trigger an IED.

Fingers hovered over the keyboard. Jill twisted in her chair, adjusted her oversized glasses as she tugged on the sweater slipping off one shoulder. "Oh. It's you. I thought it was Hunter," she said, then turned back to the screen, typing again in rapid bursts. "What can I do you for, Ryan? Need to borrow a cup of sugar?"

He shifted his weight, suddenly self-conscious. Jill always had that effect, like he'd walked into a test he hadn't studied for. "I came to see if your friend's apartment is still available."

Her fingers froze mid-stroke. "How did you hear about that?" she asked without turning. "And why do you care?"

"Hunter," he said. "I need a place."

This time, she spun her chair fully. Narrowed eyes scanned him like he was a barcode. Without a word, she yanked open a drawer, rummaged through it, and came up with a ring of keys, lobbing it at his chest.

It hit with a dull thud as he fumbled to catch it.

"Geez. For a hockey player, your reflexes suck."

He arched a brow, recovering fast. "You throw like a girl."

She smirked. "Thank you for the compliment."

He stood, keys dangling. Jill, of course, filled the silence.

"My friend moved last weekend. A few people were interested, but I didn't want them as neighbors." Her lips quirked into a slow smile, followed by a wink. "Want to see the place?"

"Sure," he said, a little too casual.

She rose with a long stretch, hips swaying as she crossed the room. For half a beat, Ryan forgot how to walk. She plucked the keys from his hand, rifling through them with flair. "Ah-ha. Here it is ... I think."

Across the hall, she turned the lock, pushing the door open with a theatrical flourish.

The interior was a blend of high-end art gallery and Scandinavian furniture showroom. White walls. White furniture. White appliances. A massive shag rug covered the front room floor. Splashes of color from oversized abstract paintings broke the sterile calm.

"Oh geez, eh? Who lived here?"

"Sandra," Jill said. "She still technically does ... subletting it for a year. Artist. Those are hers."

Ryan tilted his head at the canvas. "Is this one upside down?"

"Maybe. It stays that way regardless. So does everything else. It's in the contract."

He stepped deeper inside, the rug swallowing his bare feet. "I suppose that includes this polar bear underfoot?"

"Yep, faux fur tundra included." Jill's loafers squeaked down the hallway. "Come on. I'll show you the rest."

The bedroom was just as blinding ... white bedspread, white accent chair, white silk roses in a too-perfect milk glass vase. The only color came from more bold artwork.

Ryan scratched the back of his neck. "Not sure I see myself living here. I'm a hockey player, not a tennis pro."

Jill gave him a slow up-down look. "How could I forget? Also ... why are you barefoot?"

Ryan wiggled his toes. "Hunter had a bad game. Gave him and Sage some space to work things out."

Jill shrugged.

"All that's missing is a scalpel and a pair of scrubs," Ryan said, eager to steer the focus away from his feet.

Jill motioned to the bathroom like a tour guide. "This way, Dr. Mitchell."

Back in the kitchen, it mirrored the rest of the apartment ... immaculate, restrained, every detail controlled. It reminded him of the woman holding the keyring in front of him. Ryan leaned against the marble countertop. "How much?"

"Three grand." Jill said, pulling out her phone, thumbs tapping across the screen.

He didn't flinch. "I'll take it."

A satisfied hum escaped her as she detached a key from the ring, setting it on the counter.

"You can Venmo first and last. Sandra's a Goshawks fan. I just texted her. She said If you want it, she'll waive the deposit."

Ryan arched a brow. "Hard to picture you being friends with someone who's a hockey fan."

She reached to take the key back. Their fingers brushed. A sharp crack of static jumped between them.

Ryan flinched. "That rug's a menace."

Jill rubbed her palm, staring into his eyes. "You think that was the rug?"

He held her gaze. "What else would it be?"

She stepped back, smoothing her sweater. "So ... when do you want to move in?"

He opened his mouth, then forgot why. Lavender eyes. Lashes too long, too dark. His focus slipped for half a breath before he yanked it back, giving a quick shake of his head, pulling himself to center. "Today," he said, regrouping. "I'm off until two, then we head to the west coast on Saturday. My boxes are at Hunter's."

Jill drifted to the doorway, shoulder in the frame, posture pure noir. The ring of keys dangled from her finger, swinging once. "I've got a spare. Just in case you lock yourself out."

He stepped close, voice dropping low. "Do I look like a man who locks himself out?"

Her perfume met him halfway; citrus laced with steel, bright over something darker. It pulled a sharp breath from his chest.

She said nothing.

He pocketed his key, lips curving into a smirk, walking away barefoot, confident, leaving behind nothing but charged air.

Chapter 17
Wild, Wild, West

Saturday, Oct 20th
Away Game: Goshawks vs San Jose Shockwaves

An usher guided Margret, Luke, and Sage into one of the smaller luxury boxes overlooking the rink. San Jose marked the first stop on the Goshawks' west-coast run, less than twenty-four hours after a late-night flight. The three-hour time change clung to Margret like a weighted blanket.

She breathed in the air, a mixture of the musky scent of leather with a faint whiff of gourmet meats and cheeses from the catered charcuterie spread. Soft lighting cast a warm glow across walls accented in the Shockwaves' team colors of teal and burnt orange. Pregame commentary murmured from hidden speakers above. Plush carpeting muted every step as they moved to the front row of seats close to the glass.

Below, the Shockwaves' logo blazed across center ice. The crowd's restless hum rolled upward, softened by the insulated pane. The contrast of the rink's cold air meeting the dry warmth of the suite made the space feel too still, too large ... a hollow stage built for twenty now holding only three. Margret sank into a front row leather seat; her gaze fixed on the expanse of ice below.

"Remind me again why we're not sitting glass side like Sage wanted?" Luke looked around the empty suite. "How much is this costing us, Margret?"

"Since when did you worry about the cost of anything?" She patted the empty chair to her right, hoping he'd settle.

"That's why I'm here, to control spending." Luke dropped into the seat, stretching his legs. "Besides, this is a lot of room for only three people."

"It's a matter of safety. You've never experienced what it's like for the visiting team in the Shockwaves' barn."

"How bad can it get?"

"Trust me, you don't want to find out," Margret said. Years of sitting with Justin at West Coast games taught her how ruthless San Jose fans could be to visiting teams. She'd chosen safety over proximity.

Sage slipped into the seat on her left. "Have you heard if Hunter's starting?"

Margret shook her head, arms folded, gaze fixed on the ice. "Lane's in net tonight."

Moments later the Goshawks flooded out of the tunnel, pucks flying, blades cutting clean arcs over the blue line. Lane skated out last, his mask askew as if jammed on in a rush. Something in the way he moved set off Margret's internal alarms.

Players snapped pucks into the net. Others stretched along the boards. Lane lingered in the crease, using his stick more for balance than defense.

Margret retrieved mini binoculars from the pocket of her suit jacket. She zoomed in on Lane as he raised his mask to drown water on his pale face. She passed the glasses to Sage, nodding at the net. "What do you think?"

"Not good," Sage murmured, handing them back.

"What are you two talking about?" Luke reached across Marget to pluck the binoculars from Sage. He let out a low whistle. "Why is he starting?"

"That's what I'd like to know." Margret retrieved the binoculars from Luke. She tracked Lane as he skated back, forward, stumbled, then caught himself. His glove hand drooped. On unsteady legs, he pushed to the bench, tore off his helmet mid-stride, then doubled over. A heartbeat later, a splash of bile hit the ice a foot from the Goshawks bench.

Margret groaned. She prayed the cameras had missed it. Experience told her they hadn't. Seconds later, the Jumbotron confirmed her fears, looping the replay. The crowd erupted in laughter, cruel and thunderous. San Jose fans hooted, clapped, stomped their feet, feeding on the spectacle.

Margret shot up. Luke rose too but sat when she snapped, "Stay."

She bolted from the suite, racing down the stairs, weaving through the lower concourse. Within seconds she reached the corridor near the team entrance, flashing her Goshawks lanyard at a security guard who stepped aside as she stormed past. No time for questions. She wanted answers.

The team poured in from warmups, sticks clacking against the floor. Margret followed them into the locker room. Lane sat hunched in his stall, half dressed, mask beside him, head bowed. A trainer wiped his mouth with a damp cloth. Another draped a cold towel across his neck. Lane's chest rose in quick, shallow bursts, a trash can between his knees. The team doctor hovered, checking Lane's pulse, before unwrapping an electrolyte packet, shaking it into a water bottle.

"What's wrong with him?" Margret's voice cut through the clatter of sticks and gear.

Coach Gray looked up from his tablet, eyes narrowed, brow furrowed. "Why are you here?"

"Let's get one thing straight, Cal." Margret's gaze locked on him, her tone low and sharp. "I own the Goshawks. That means I own the players. That means I. Own. You. I go where I want. Get it?"

"Got. It." His nostrils flared. His jaw set hard.

"Good."

Their standoff broke when a muffled exchange rose from the corner between the head referee and Coach Harrison. Margret angled closer, catching only fragments of their words.

"That's a lot of nerves spattered on my ice." The referee glared at Lane with an expression caught between skepticism and indifference. Then he shrugged, slipping a folded note into his pocket, muttering, "I'll let the booth know."

Margret waited until the door closed. Harrison's scowl deepened as she stepped forward, hands on hips. "Nerves? That's rich."

Coach Cal Gray closed his tablet, cleared his throat, stepping into her path. "Routine with young goalies," he said, his tone flat but practiced. "I've been a goaltending coach since before you could walk. Sometimes the pressure hits hard. He'll push through it."

"He puked on the ice, Cal." In three-inch heels, she faced him eye-to-eye. "In front of a sold-out arena ... under national broadcast cameras. That's not something you fix with a pep talk and mouthwash."

Her glare didn't waver. Cal shifted his weight, shoe-checking. She recognized the telltale twitch of a man who knew more than he'd admit.

"That's why we're starting Griffin," Coach Harrison said. "It's covered. Lane will stay on the bench, hydrate, and back up if needed. No more discussion. You saw me send the change upstairs."

Margret met his stare for another beat, then shook her head. "I don't care if we pull the Zamboni driver to sit on our bench. That kid's not collapsing in my crease."

Harrison gave a quick nod. Gray let out a snort, turning back to his tablet.

Margret let out a deep sigh. "Men," she muttered, scanning from the coaches to Hunter. He sat in his stall, taping the blade of his stick, mask lifted. His shoulders stayed rigid, every movement deliberate. He never looked up. *Of course he knew, even before Lane folded on the ice. They all had. They'd risked the kid, risked the game, to avoid putting Hunter between the pipes after their last loss.*

Coach Harrison turned to Lane. "You okay to play backup?"

Lane groaned from his cubicle, lifting his head just enough to meet the coach's eyes. "I'll be fine, Coach." A faint grin tugged at his lips. "Must've been the sushi I ordered from room service late last night."

"You can use Trey's bucket if you get another urge to toss your cookies," Etan said.

"Thanks, buddy. I'll remember that next time you expect a pass." Trey adjusted the laces on his skates, head down, tone dry.

"Since when do you pass a puck?" Axel muttered.

"Knock it off," Murphy snapped, tossing an empty roll of clear at Axel. "Save it for the ice."

Margret kept her focus on Hunter. Their eyes met across the room. He gave a slow nod. She answered with a quiet shake of her head.

Ryan rested a hand on Hunter's shoulder. "Go time."

Back in the suite, Margret dropped into her seat. "Lane's out. They've got him sipping electrolytes." The lights dimmed as the pregame fanfare swelled. Lasers cut through the air, flashing across the ice while a mash of guitar riffs and bass drops rolled through the arena. The Shockwaves' intro hit with pure spectacle and bravado.

Luke whistled under his breath, looking at the tunnel where the Goshawks waited. "Talk about high-stakes pressure on Hunter."

Margret nodded. "He's got the weight of that contract on his shoulders."

The crowd roared as the announcer introduced the Shockwaves' starting lineup. The bass from the speakers vibrated through the floor of their suite.

Luke shifted in his chair. "If Hunter wins tonight, the media spins it as a redemption arc. If his ice wall cracks..." He turned to Sage. "It'll be a media nightmare for you."

Margret raised the binoculars, scanning the Goshawks' tunnel. "She knows," her voice tight. "So does Hunter."

When the Goshawks took the ice, the boos swallowed their introduction. Margret spotted Assistant Coach Scott Smith pacing the bench. The backup goalie chair remained empty. No Lane.

First Period

"What's with the fans' aggression toward us at away games?" Luke scanned the arena.

"You'll get used to it." Margret lied. Her hands folded tight against her lap.

Lane entered the bench late, slumping into the goalie chair. Margret studied him through the binoculars. Concern swept over her as she gazed at his ashen complexion, and the tremor in his hand as he gripped the water bottle. Slouched over, his six-foot-five frame seemed to shrink into itself, a giant reduced to fragility.

Her focus shifted to Hunter. He stood at the lip of the crease, pads squared, shoulders set. He bounced once on his skates, then sank into his stance, tapping his posts with the blade of his stick ... left, right, left again. The ritual pure muscle memory from years of repetition, honed to calm his mind.

The puck dropped with the Shockwaves winning the first faceoff. The Goshawks winning the next. Within seconds of the third-line change, Trey burst onto the ice. A quick backhand toe-drag around a defenseman, then a roof shot glove side that snapped the Shockwaves goalie's water bottle off its perch. The arena groaned. Margret's lips curled in satisfaction.

GOAL! Goshawks—Moss

Trey dropped to one knee, stick lifted in a salute to their box before skating to the bench, chin high, tapping gloves in stride.

Minutes later, Trey struck again. A steal at center ice, a feed from Axel, a sharp wrister past San Jose's sprawling goalie. Two goals, five minutes in.

GOAL! Goshawks—Moss

Throughout the first period, the Goshawks remained focused. The puck moved tape-to-tape with precision. Etan found his lane at the top of the slot, ripping a shot blocker side, burying it in the Shockwaves' net.

GOAL! Goshawks—Eklund

The home crowd turned venomous. Boos swelled, thick and raw. A drink hit their suite, yellow foam streaking the glass. Margret turned to Sage, then to Luke. "That's precisely why we're not sitting unprotected in the lower bowl."

For the remainder of the period, Hunter held firm. Shot after shot, he tracked the puck like it owed him money, dropping into a butterfly, snapping up rebounds, redirecting traffic in front with crisp glove signals. Nothing got through. Every save stopped with purpose.

Ryan took a hit along the boards but bounced up fast, shoving a Shockwaves forward out of the crease. Margret's pulse raced watching the play. She glanced at Sage, who sat rigid, eyes wide. "Ryan's in full alpha mode."

"Thank goodness he's protecting his goalie." Sage added in a whisper, "Everyone's waiting for Hunter to fail."

"He won't." Margret eased back into her seat exhibiting more confidence than she felt.

Second Period

At the first puck drop, San Jose came out fighting ... sticks slashing, bodies slamming, cheap shots flying in Trey's direction. The refs' whistles stayed quiet. When Ryan flattened their left winger behind the Goshawks' net, Margret sat straight-backed, regal, her focus locked on both creases while the chaos raged between.

Hunter continued to own his net as if it were sacred ground. The shots came in hot, but he stopped them all. Every rebound denied. Stance solid. Glove hand quick. His movements fluid, controlled. Margret knew he was hungry for a win.

The Shockwaves remained relentless as they mounted a three-on-one rush. Ryan dropped back, forcing the shooter wide. Hunter stayed low, baited the wrister, then snapped it from the air like it belonged to him.

Margret gave Lane a passing glance. He shifted in his gear, restless. The ball cap sat low, hiding his face. Her focus returned to the crease. After watching Hunter for five seasons, she knew her goalie well. This was the Hunter who wanted to win, who wanted redemption. The goalie destined to lift the Cup again.

The horn sounded to end the second period. The score held at three to zero.

As Hunter skated off, helmet up, Sage leaned toward Margret. "He's locked in."

"About time." Margret smiled.

Third Period

On the opening play of the third, Armstrong flipped the puck over the glass, earning a two-minute delay of game. Across the ice, Murphy tossed his gloves, grabbing the San Jose captain's sweater in retaliation for an uncalled slash to his ankle.

Margret groaned as the Shockwaves' captain turtled while Murphy kept throwing punches. She didn't like it but expected five minutes for fighting, plus a two-minute instigator for Murphy. Her voice rose in protest when the San Jose captain stayed in the game.

"Wait," Luke said, "why isn't San Jose getting a penalty? He slashed Murphy first. The coach should call for a review."

"Doesn't work like that, cowboy," Sage replied, leaning around Margret. "It's an on-ice judgment call. The ref didn't see the slash, and coaches can't challenge a penalty."

"Hockey is full of stupid rules," Luke muttered, slouching in his seat, stuffing a handful of spiced nuts in his mouth.

"Five-on-three power play. Not good." Margret chewed at a manicured nail.

The Shockwaves' crowd erupted, stomping, howling, clapping like it was a playoff game.

"I can't watch this. I'm hitting the ladies' room." Sage pushed up from her seat.

"Coward," Luke called after her.

Margret kept her eyes on the ice. "She'll be back, wishing she'd stayed when we score a shorty."

Luke's grin crept in. "That confident?"

"I know what this team's capable of under pressure when they're in the zone."

The siege on Hunter came hard, quick, unrelenting. Full-on assault. Blasts from the point, deflections from the slot, traffic everywhere. Three shots fired in rapid succession. Hunter blocked high, dropped to his knees, flared out his pads for a save that drew a gasp then moans from the crowd.

Two minutes into the power kill, Trey snagged a rebound off a weak shot, tearing up the ice like a missile. Etan chased close behind, picking up speed. The Shockwaves' defense scrambled.

Margret rose, pressing her palms to the glass.

Trey blew past the last man, open lane ahead. It was his shot to take. Margret waited for the hat trick celebration from the small pocket of Goshawks fans. Instead, without a glance, Trey slid the puck behind him. Etan collected it clean, roofing it into the Shockwaves' net.

GOAL! Goshawks—Eklund

"What a shorty." Luke fist pumped the air as he jumped up, twirling Margret off her feet.

The Goshawks' bench erupted. The Jumbotron caught it in slow motion. Etan grinning as Trey hugged his fellow forward.

Sage returned, eyes wide. "What just happened?"

Margret smiled. "Looks like our little egomaniac's becoming a team player."

"You must be so proud," Luke said, setting her to her feet, placing a kiss on her cheek.

"You bet I am. All the way to the bank."

Margret watched Trey now on the bench. He sat breathing hard, as if giving up a hat trick for a teammate was nothing out of the ordinary. She leaned to Luke. "You can tell your father ... Trey's worth every million we paid for him."

The clock ticked down to the final minute. The score held at four to zero.

The Shockwaves stopped playing for goals. Now they played for payback. The game turned ugly fast.

An uncalled cross-check sent Goshawks third-line forward Dylan Gallagher spinning. The crowd roared its approval. Then came the hit from Axel, a full-body collision with San Jose's biggest bruiser. No hesitation. The Goshawks' D-man lost his helmet, curls flying as fists flew.

Margret cheered from her seat as Axel landed two clean shots to the Shockwaves' jaw before taking one to the ribs. The refs swarmed, whistles shrieking. The punches kept flying until the linesmen forced them apart.

"Yesssssssssss!" Margret shouted. "That's how you answer."

The referee's voice boomed over the chaos while both players were escorted off the ice.

Four-on-four. No uneven power play. No empty net. Just space and spite.

Hunter stayed locked in, tracking every play. Margret could feel it from her seat high above the ice. He wasn't just defending the net ... he was guarding his redemption.

The final horn blared. No last-second goal. No desperation plays. The Goshawks' bench erupted. Players vaulted over the boards to mob their goalie.

Etan and Axel reached him first. Then Trey ... Lane came last, bumping helmets with Hunter in a quiet show of respect. Hunter let it happen. No raised arms. No theatrics. Just the steady weight of acknowledgment from his teammates for his shutout.

Margret watched from her perch. She knew this was more than a win. It was a reckoning.

Chapter 18
Sleepless In Portland

Thursday, Oct 25th

The engines of the Goshawks jet thrummed beneath Ryan's feet, a low vibration that settled deep in his bones. He slouched lower, staring through the oval window at a thin smear on the glass, only black sky beyond. His body ached like he'd been run over by a Zamboni. Three time zones. Four games. No rest. He pressed his head against the glass, chasing stillness that refused to come. Every sound ... the shuffle of cards, the rise of voices ... clawed against his skull. *Next trip, bring noise-canceling headphones.*

A few rows back, chaos reigned around the mid-plane table. The younger players' voices tangled in a mess of laughter, shouts, and the slap of cards. From the sound of it, Etan, Axel, Lane, and Trey had invented a new game ... half Go Fish, half Slapjack, all noise.

"Bender, you can't slap the Queen of Spades," Axel barked, a card snapping across the table.

"Says who?" Lane shot back, laughing.

"Says logic, Lane," Etan replied. "It's not even your turn."

"Sucks to suck," Trey added, followed by the slap of a card, then the clatter of chips raked across the table.

"You're cheating," Axel grumbled.

"You're just jealous because, once again, I'm the GOAT." Trey snorted, his laughter rising over the shuffle of cards.

Ryan stood, leaning over the back of his seat. "Shut it. All of you. It's three in the morning. You guys are getting on my last nerve."

Silence dropped like a curtain. Cards stilled. Trey raised both hands in mock surrender. "My bad, Cap."

Etan mumbled, "Forlat."

Lane grimaced and shrugged.

Axel ignored Ryan, glaring at his hand before slapping a card onto a new pile, the motion hard and deliberate.

Ryan sank back into his seat, shoulders tight, jaw clenched. He closed his eyes ... exhaustion cutting too deep for sleep. Giving up, he glanced across the aisle. Hunter sat with Sage curled against his side, her head resting on his shoulder, fingers threaded through his. Her breathing slow and even. Hunter's gaze locked in a blank stare. Ryan knew the look ... his best friend was lost in a faraway place where goalies replay every save and every miss.

An hour later, the cabin lights flared bright as the seatbelt sign chimed. Around him came the click of trays locking. Seat buckles snapping shut, followed by the heavy thud of wheels meeting tarmac. The plane hit once, bounced, then screeched down the runway.

The second the door opened, he jumped to his feet, grabbing his duffle and suit bag, moving down the aisle without a word. The airstairs delivered him into Portland's twilight. The frigid temperature bit his skin. The salt air stung his face, clinging to the back of his throat sharp, after hours of recycled air.

He crossed to his Tahoe, jabbing the key fob. Taillights blinked, trunk popped. He leaned against the SUV, arms folded, breath curling in the cold as he waited for Hunter to deplane. Four wins. A black eye. Bruised ribs. Mentally exhausted. *Who created this schedule?*

They trudged out of the apartment building's elevator. Hunter's shoulders sagged. Ryan gave him a once-over. *He's running on fumes. We all are. Another game tomorrow. At this rate, we'll be playing on pure adrenaline and muscle memory.*

A hallway light flickered overhead, coupled with the dull thud of their footsteps, feeding Ryan's unease. At Hunter's door, they paused.

"Later." Ryan waited until Hunter disappeared inside the apartment before he ventured down the hall. He hitched the duffle higher on his shoulder. His garment bag trailed behind him. This place didn't feel like home. How could it? He'd left on their road trip the same night he'd moved in.

When he reached his door, he dropped his bags, rolling a shoulder to ease the weight. He pulled out his car fob. The apartment key wasn't attached. His hand went to one pants pocket, then the other, then his suit jacket. Panic edged in as he unzipped the duffle, digging through it like a hungry dog searching for a buried bone.

Nothing.

He stuffed everything back into the duffle, then sank to the floor. Hands on his head, he muttered the mantra his mother drilled into him ... "If Ryan can't find it, Jesus can."

Then it hit him ... the kitchen counter. He'd left the key there during the move in, meaning to loop it through his fob's chain. *Brilliant.*

He let his head thump against the door, squeezing his eyes tight. *Jill's going to love this.* For a half-second, he considered curling up on the hallway carpet, using the duffle as a pillow. Instead, he pushed off the wall, trudged back to Hunter's door, knocked. Waited. Nothing. Knocked harder ... no answer. Of late, his life was feeling like a series of nothings.

Of course, Hunter's dead to the world. Ryan exhaled a long breath.

He pulled out his phone. 5:03 a.m. Too early to call maintenance. Too late to pretend this wasn't happening. His gaze drifted down the hall to Jill's apartment. He rubbed the back of his neck, pride heavy as lead.

A second after his first knock, the door opened.

Jill stood framed in the soft hallway light, dressed like she was going on a brunch date with a senator. Slim-fit khakis, a pale sweater over a collared shirt, boat shoes looking too clean to have ever touched a dock. Owl glasses perched on top of her head like a crown. Makeup perfect. Not a hair out of place.

She blinked once. "Geez, you look awful. All-night celebration?"

Ryan squinted, voice flat. "Plane just got in. Late game."

"Ah." Her gaze swept over him with cool, academic curiosity. "That explains the 'I've-seen-better-days' couture." Her eyes shifted from his rumpled suit to the bags slumped across the hall. The corners of her mouth lifted. "Don't tell me..." Her tone brightened with cruel delight. "You're locked out?"

His jaw flexed. "Not in the mood, Jill. Just let me in."

She crossed her arms. "Magic word?"

He stared, dead-eyed.

She tilted her head, mock serious. "Please?"

"Please." The word came through clenched teeth.

Jill walked back into her apartment, unhurried, as if she had all day. After far too long, she reappeared along with a cluster of keys, which she held high, her lips twitching into a smirk.

She crossed the hallway, stepping over his bags like she was dodging sidewalk gum. The keyring jingled as she sorted through the mass of keys. On the third try, the lock gave a relenting click. "Ta-da," she said as the door swung open.

Inside, a white shag throw rug leaned in a corner, half-rolled as if caught mid-eviction. Two walls were lined with mismatched moving boxes, still taped shut. Hockey sticks jutted from opposite corners like they'd grown out of the drywall.

"Nice." Jill's gaze swept the space. "Very Hockey-Boy Chic."

"Sorry for the mess. I didn't have time to unpack before leaving." Ryan grunted as he dragged his bags past her.

"Need help?"

"Got it." The bags thudded to the floor. He stayed hunched for a beat.

Jill lingered in the doorway; one hand braced on the frame. "Don't I get a thank you?"

Ryan turned to her. "Yeah. Sorry. Thank you. I mean it."

She squinted, studying him closer. "What happened to your face?"

He sighed, lifting the hem of his dress shirt. His abs tensed, a sprawl of bruises blooming across his ribs ... purple, yellow, and dull green, leftovers from checks, slashes, maybe a fist or two. He wasn't sure why he needed to show her more, only that he did.

Jill stepped closer. Her fingers traced the edge of one bruise, brushing the skin. "That has to hurt."

Her cool touch sent a shiver through him. He caught her hand, his thumb brushing her knuckles before letting go. "It's part of the game," he said, voice low. "You don't want to see the rest of me."

She froze, lips parted in a half smile, gaze flickering over his body. Whatever witty reply had been on deck vanished.

"Thanks again, Jill. Right now ... I need to pass out. I owe you big time."

"I'll hold you to that." Jill stepped back, the moment folding in on itself.

She turned and walked away, stride easy, though he caught the subtle sway. The faint scent of her lingered, a trace of citrus and coffee drifting in her wake. He watched the door close, the quiet pressing in. Sleep pulling at him almost as much as Jill did.

Chapter 19
Mascot Mayhem

Sunday, October 29th

Margret tapped her stylus against the edge of her tablet, eyes flicking down the checklist for tomorrow's game. Parking logistics, media access, pregame warmup schedule ... every box ticked. As co-owner, she had staff to handle these details, but old habits died hard.

Across the kitchen island, Luke sat sideways on a barstool, one leg stretched long, the other bouncing slow in time with his scrolling thumb. The faint buzz of his phone cut through the quiet, a lazy rhythm matching his mood. He looked like a man on vacation, not someone whose father recently acquired half a professional hockey team.

Then came the sharp clatter of nails on marble.

Crease stormed into the kitchen, oversized paws sliding on the polished floor. Sage followed, breathless in pursuit. The large ball of fur skidded to a halt, a blue-and-silver t-shirt clinging tight to his frame, the Goshawks logo stitched haphazardly on the back.

"He should be our mascot," Sage said, pointing to Crease as he spun in gleeful circles. "I'm serious."

Margret blinked. "Good grief, Sage. Where did you get his outfit?"

"It's one of my old t-shirts. I found a patch in the dresser, stitched it myself." Sage wiggled her fingers like a magician revealing a trick.

Luke angled his phone's camera at Crease. "You gotta admit, it's a solid concept."

Crease sat, butt wiggling, tail thumping the cabinet like a bass drum. His gaze locked on Margret, pure adoration shining back at her. She had to admit, it felt good. She leaned forward, fingers drumming on the countertop. "I don't know, Sage. Remember when he peed at Petco?"

"That was over a week ago." Sage patted Crease's head. "He felt bad and promised never to do it again."

"I know he won't. He's banned from the store." Margret turned her attention back to the iPad.

Luke slid his phone across the counter. "Check this out, Margret. A college team in Minnesota has a bulldog dropping the puck before home games. Over a million hits."

Margret squinted at the screen. A stocky dog in team colors trotted onto the ice, puck in his mouth. The crowd roared when he dropped it on cue.

"Think of last year's Goshawks' charity calendar featuring Portland's animal shelter," Sage said. "It sold out before printing. The players had too much fun at the shoot. I had to pry Hunter away from the puppies."

Margret's breath caught. The memory came back sharp and vivid, Olaf kneeling on the shelter lawn with an old Husky mix wrapped in his arms. The way the goalie's eyes misted still tugged on her emotions.

"Don't forget," Sage said, "last year you told Hunter if he won The Cup, you'd let Crease be the mascot."

Margret lifted her coffee, hiding a smile behind the rim. "That doesn't sound like something I'd agree to."

Sage's tone softened. "I know it's silly. But being reigning champions has everyone wound tight. They need something light, something that reminds them why they love the game."

"I'm well aware of the pressure the team's been under."

"Hunter hasn't been sleeping," Sage added.

"That makes no sense." Luke set his phone down, brow furrowing. "He's been on a winning streak since San Jose. He had another shutout last night against Detroit."

"That's exactly why he's losing sleep. He's afraid of breaking the streak."

Luke exhaled, lips pressed thin. "I don't think I'll ever understand goalie logic." His gaze drifted to the ceiling before picking up his phone, settling back on the screen.

"I think it would help their morale," Sage said. "Especially since they'll be playing Florida tomorrow. A dose of Crease might just be the trick." She slid onto the stool beside Luke.

Margret glanced at the Lab, belly-up on the tile, tail sweeping like a broom, paws twitching in expectation. "Fine," she said. "But he stays off the ice."

"Deal!" Sage gave Luke's arm a playful punch.

Luke raised his coffee mug in salute. "Next to Murphy, he'll be the hairiest Goshawk on the roster."

The crack of pucks against pads echoed through the Goshawks' practice rink. Margret stepped from the tunnel first, cold air biting her cheeks. This time slot was always reserved for goalie drills. Luke and Sage followed close behind, Crease trotting between them.

They stopped at the player's gate. On the ice, Hunter crouched low in the crease, head twitching with each shot, every movement tight and precise. Lane hovered to the side, stick ready, eyes tracking every rep. Coach Gray stood at the blue line, stick in hand, pucks lined across the ice like ammunition.

"Square up, Griffin. You're dropping your glove again," the goaltending coach shouted.

Margret leaned against the dasher, tracking Hunter's form. His stance stayed tight, coiled, every movement sharp. He looked like a goalie trying to impress, not one playing on instinct.

Cal wound up and fired. The puck slipped past Hunter's blocker, clanged off the inside post, rifling into the net.

"Out," Cal snapped.

Hunter skated to the corner, trading places with Lane.

Cal wasted no time as he shot three quick releases. Lane responded to three clean stops. One stick save. One glove. One chest smother.

"That's how it's supposed to look," Cal said, turning to Hunter. "You want to be the Goshawks' starter? Stop playing like you're Swiss cheese."

Margret's stomach turned. Hunter gave nothing away, though she caught the tells. The blade's quick pivot. His stick tapping sharp twice against the ice.

Luke leaned closer, voice low. "That's not good. Even I can see Cal's favoring his protégé."

"Lane's not the problem." Margret's reply came hushed but firm.

Crease lifted his paws onto the gate; eyes locked on Hunter. A low whine slipped out, ears high, body tight.

Sage pulled on the leash. "Don't even think about it."

Crease quivered, tail twitching in short bursts. When Hunter dropped to one knee and lifted his mask, the leash slipped from Sage's grip as if her hand were slick with grease.

Margret shouted, "No dogs on the..."

"Crease!" Sage lunged a heartbeat too late.

The yellow blur shot across the ice, paws sliding over the surface. Cal yelled, his words lost beneath the thud of fur hitting pads. Hunter toppled backwards, laughter echoing through the near-empty rink while Crease covered his face in sloppy kisses.

Luke watched with a smirk. "Well," he muttered, "looks like your mascot made a grand entrance."

"Sorry! Sorry! Sorry!" Sage called, leaning over the gate.

Hunter lay flat on his back, pads spread like broken wings, Crease sprawled across his chest. The dog's tail beat the ice, tongue sweeping across Hunter's face.

Margret's hand covered her mouth, doing her best to suppress a laugh.

Cal skated over, stopping fast, snowing the boards. His face burned red. "Are you trying to undermine our practice?" he barked. "What the hell is that dog doing on the ice?"

Margret straightened, one hand firm on the rail. Before she could speak, Luke stepped between them.

He met Cal's glare with a slow grin. "Tension breaker," he said.

Margret caught Luke's sleeve, before a wave of players spilled onto the ice.

Pucks clattered from a bucket, sticks snapped onto tape checks, blades cut hard lines across the surface. Their pace slowed when they spotted their goalie covered in a blanket of yellow fur.

Ryan glided over. "Need a hand up?"

"Nah, I'm fine where I'm at."

"Hey, look who's here," Murphy shouted. "Nice sweater."

"Crease," Etan called, gliding in close. "You're covering our goalie better than Axel."

Players circled Hunter, gently tapping sticks against Crease like he'd won a shootout. Axel slid a puck across the surface. Crease sprang after it, nails digging into the ice, body slipping and sliding. Another puck followed. Then another.

"Careful." Ryan laughed. "We'll have to sign him to a two-way deal."

"Watch out, Ice Wall," Axel called. "Crease is gunning for your job."

Hunter stood, adjusting his mask. The smile faded. "Someone's already gunning for it." He skated back to the net while Lane drifted to the bench.

The chaos found a rhythm. Pucks slid across the ice, players laughing as Crease darted through them like a puck-chasing pinball.

Margret ignored Cal, rested her elbows on the rail, her smile vanishing when she heard footsteps on the bench. Coach Stan Harrison appeared with Assistant Coach Scott Smith close behind.

Stan's brow lifted at the scene, the corners of his mouth tightening as if he were fighting a grin. "What's going on, Margret?"

Luke nodded at the ice. "We've recruited a new player."

Scott grinned. "Don't tell Ryan. He's just getting used to wearing the C."

"I figured the team needed a release valve," Margret said. "This is it." Her eyes narrowed, ready for pushback.

She was surprised when none came, instead Stan studied his players. Some passed pucks to Crease, other tapped sticks as the Lab chased and slid. Organized chaos rolled through the rink. Even Trey, always stone-faced during drills, was laughing.

"They were heads down in the locker room a few minutes ago," Stan said, murmuring to himself. "All grit. No joy. Look at 'em now."

A low growl cut through the air as Cal skated back to the bench, scowl carved deep. "If we're going to beat Florida tomorrow, they need focus, not fun," he grumbled. "This isn't beer-league practice."

Stan's jaw tightened. "Take the goalies to the far end. My boys are going to enjoy a few more minutes of laughter."

Cal's glare swept from Stan to Margret, then locked on Hunter passing a puck to his dog. "Griffin. Mask down. Break's over."

Hunter adjusted his gear without a word, eyes shifting not to Cal or the far end net, but to the yellow fur next to his crease.

Margret caught it, the flicker of defiance in Hunter's gaze. "Sage, get our mascot off the ice ... NOW!"

"Crease," Sage called, stepping with care onto the rink. "Let's go, buddy."

The Labrador darted left, then right, tongue flapping, tail in constant motion. It took Sage three near-falls, two failed sweeps with the leash, and one glove bribe before she could clip the leash onto Crease's collar.

Hunter crouched as Sage made a final pass, tilting his mask high enough for a quick kiss, smile crooked, eyes soft.

Hoots and chirps erupted.

"Get a room!"

"That's goalie interference!"

Crease answered with a sharp bark, chest puffed in triumph.

Margret shook her head, mumbling, "What have I agreed to?"

The last of the chaos faded. Players drifted into lines, breath clouding in the cold air. Crease trotted beside Sage, head high, tail up, leash drawn tight like he was taking a celly lap.

"Bye, buddy," Etan called. "See you soon."

Trey lifted a glove. "You're faster than half our forwards."

Axel leaned on his stick, grinning. "Bring him back tomorrow. I've got a few D-zone drills he can help with."

Margret's lips curved. She turned to Stan. "Sage's training him to drop the ceremonial puck during home games."

Stan tilted his head. "You're sure he won't eat it?"

"Won't make promises we can't keep." Luke nudged Margret.

"Alright, Margret. But if this blows up, it's on you and your cowboy, not me," Stan said, running a hand over his bald head.

Margret watched Crease trot down the tunnel, leash slack now, big yellow butt swaying. "What could possibly go wrong?"

Chapter 20
The Drop

Monday, October 30th
Home Game: Goshawks vs Florida Barracudas

The packed Goshawks arena throbbed with energy, the crowd on their feet, faces flushed with anticipation. Blue spotlights swept the rafters, spinning in rhythm with the bass-heavy intro that shook the boards. The air smelled of ice and popcorn ... sharp and sweet.

Ryan rolled his shoulders once, then again, attempting to grind out the knots. His skates whispered across the surface as he skated onto the pristine sheet, the Goshawks' crest gleaming beneath him like captured light.

In the booth, Tom leaned into his mic. "I'm Tom Hughes, alongside goalie legend John 'The Hammer' Hamilton. We're moments away from puck drop between the reigning champs, your Portland Goshawks, and the Florida Barracudas."

"You can feel it in your bones tonight," John added. "This isn't just another game; it's a grudge match. Even the fans remember last spring when the Goshawks knocked the Barracudas out of the playoffs. Trembly skating off the ice at the end of the third. That handshake snub still burns."

Ryan skated to center ice, stick tapping with each stride. He could feel Chucky's glare as he approached. Trembly waited on the edge of the Goshawks logo, broad-shouldered, jaw working his mouthguard, a smug curl tugging at the corner of his lip. The Barracudas' new captain wore his C like a dare.

A hush spread through the stands as the lights narrowed, centering on a long blue carpet runner spread across the ice. From the tunnel, Sage walked with Crease at her heel. The Yellow Lab trotted with the puck clamped between his teeth, the '00' on his sweater bouncing with each step.

The Jumbotron highlighted the little guy soaking up the spotlight.

"Well, that's something new," Tom said. "Sage Larson, the team's current media manager, and fiancée of Goshawks goalie Hunter Griffin, with their new mascot."

John's laugh rumbled low. "This should be interesting."

Ryan bent at center ice, stick down as Crease approached. Across from him, Chucky dropped into the same stance, wearing a twisted, greasy grin.

"Cute dog," Chucky said, voice low but carrying. "Guess you needed something loyal in Portland."

Ryan met his glare, mouth curving into a slow smile. "Better than a diving fish with a C stitched on its scales."

Crease gave a brief whine, tail twitching.

"Drop," Sage commanded.

Nikki's shutter clicked as the puck hit the ice between the two captains.

Ryan scooped the puck, gave Crease a quick pat on the head, then offered the disc back like a dog biscuit.

The crowd erupted in applause as Crease trotted off the ice, jersey flapping.

"Clean drop," Tom said.

John's reply came fast. "Might be the last one we see tonight."

Ryan straightened, stick gripped tight, gaze locked on Chucky. Only a ceremonial puck drop, and the war between the two rivals had begun.

First Period

The opening minutes played out like any other ... until they didn't.

Ryan patrolled low in the zone, scanning the Barracudas' setup. Every shift told the same story. Chucky Trembly wasn't chasing goals, he was circling Hunter's crease like a bottom-feeding carp searching for scraps. He slid sideways, bumping Hunter's pad, planting himself in the blue paint like he owned it.

Ryan closed the gap. "You skating or nesting?"

Chucky glanced over his shoulder, a smirk curling slow. "Just marking what's mine."

Ryan didn't bite ... *not yet*. Instead, he skated parallel, shoulder to shoulder, giving Chucky a sharp nudge.

From the booth above, Tom Hughes sounded half amused, half irritated. "Looks like Florida's playing the body, not the puck."

John's voice came through low. "Seen hungrier beer-league teams. They're gunning for Hunter again."

On the next shift, Etan broke up the right side with a clean zone entry. His head dipped for half a second, just long enough for Florida's top goon, Jacobs, to clip him with a high elbow to the jaw.

A whistle shrilled, making this game different from past one-sided encounters with Florida, as the linesman escorted Jacobs to the penalty box.

The Barracudas killed the penalty, returning to full strength.

On the next play, Hunter kicked out a save. The rebound dropped loose in the slot. Chucky drove to the crease, both skates deep, as Florida's big forward, Banks, swept in behind him. Hunter lunged low, stretching across the blue paint. Chucky's knee clipped his shoulder a split second before Banks snapped the puck high glove side.

GOAL! Barracudas–Banks

Coach Harrison threw up his arms, calling for a review.

Ryan didn't wait. He skated straight to the ref. "You're seriously letting that stand?"

The Jumbotron replay rolled in slow motion. Chucky parked square in the blue, clear contact before the puck crossed into the crease. The crowd answered with a wall of boos.

"That's textbook goalie interference if I've ever seen it," John said.

Tom exhaled. "Easy for us to say from up here."

Ryan locked his gaze on the head ref as he skated to center ice.

"After review. The goal stands."

The crowd erupted again. Boos rolled through the arena as curses rained down. A plastic hawk's talon sailed over the glass, skittering across the ice.

Armstrong was tapped to serve the delay of game penalty due to the coach's unsuccessful challenge.

Ryan's grip tightened around his stick. He glanced at the crease. Hunter poured water over his face, expression unreadable, glove hand flexing with slow precision. Moments later Ryan lined up for the kill, heart thudding against his ribs.

Thirty seconds in, Trey cut off a lazy pass near the point. Two strides and he was gone, a blur of motion. He tore down the ice with low balance and perfect control. No deke. No hesitation. Bar down. A breakaway resulting in a clean shorty.

Goal! Goshawks–Moss

The arena erupted. Instead of joining the celebratory glove tap line, Trey raised his stick, sighted down the shaft, and mimed a burst of machine gun fire at the Barracudas' bench.

Tom's voice cut through the roar. "Trey Moss is getting feisty with Florida. I hope he doesn't regret that move."

"You poke the hawk, you get the claws." John responded.

Ryan skated to Trey, tapping his shoulder with a glove. "Nice shot."

Trey gave a quick nod. "They want to play dirty? Let's get gritty."

Ryan's grin came slow. The kid had more edge than he thought. He liked it.

Second Period Intermission

The locker room sat in silence. Too still for a tied game. Even though the Goshawks fought hard and the Barracudas fought dirty, the second period score remained the same.

Tape stretched, snapped, coiled back. The air carried the bite of sweat, ice, and wet gear. Hunter sat in his stall, eyes fixed ahead, breath slow and deliberate.

Ryan removed his helmet, running a hand through his damp hair. They should have been one up. Instead, they were even. Florida never changed their game. They played full contact along with vile chirps.

Third Period

The Goshawks took the ice for the third. Trash talk flew from both benches, voices echoing across the glass. Fans stomped, pounding the glass in a rising roar. On the bench, what Ryan heard behind him locked his spine.

Coach Gray's voice came low, muffled behind a folded bench card. "Harrison, maybe it's time. Wilson's fresh. Kid's quick."

"No." Coach Harrison's reply was flat, like he was batting a fly. "Hunter stays in net."

Ryan clenched a fist near his thigh, small but fierce. *Damn right he is.*

On the next shift, Etan cut through the neutral zone. A freight train in red and gold caught him shoulder-high, driving him into the boards. His helmet popped loose, skidding across the ice.

Ryan skated over as the whistle blew, retrieving Etan's helmet, handing it back.

"Did he get my tooth?" Etan asked, glove off, fingers probing a bloody lip.

Ryan shook his head. "Looks like you bit your lip." He guided him to the bench, eyes fixed on Chucky. The Barracuda captain grinned, followed by a slow wink.

Ryan leaned closer to Etan. "What a dumb hooser. Giving us another opening."

The Goshawks' power play was strong, but Florida's penalty kill proved stronger.

Full strength, they lined up for the faceoff, Florida's trash talk resumed. "I gave your goalie's girlfriend my number." Chucky sneered. "She's meeting me on the Barracudas bus after the game ... with her mangy mutt."

Murphy's lips twitched. "Not happening even in your dreams," he said. "Oh, and is that a new binky you're sucking on?"

Chucky snarled as the ref's whistle blew sharp. "If you two ladies want to stand here gossiping, you can do it outside my circle." He waved them both out.

"Looks like the ref's getting fed up too," Tom said.

John cut in. "The only funny thing on the ice right now is how Trembly's pretending he's the victim."

The period turned savage. Slashes after the play. Elbows high. Goons clogging the crease. Ryan took a crosscheck to the ribs that spun him off balance. He answered with a shoulder hit that sent a Barracuda stumbling backward. Murphy, and the Goshawks' right winger, Sturman, battled to protect the front of the net for Hunter. The ice felt like a war zone. No one raised a white flag. The clock bled down to the final minutes. Game tied.

Then it broke open. A loose puck at the point. A Barracudas' forward whiffed. The puck deflected to Trey at the far wall. He spun, exploding down open ice, locked on Florida's net. His speed blistered. One defender lunged, falling. Another angled wide. He slipped through a third Florida player with Ryan closing fast beside him. Then, Trey snapped the shot. High blocker. Horn blasting. The crowd detonating with it.

Goal! Goshawks–Moss

Tom's voice rose above the noise. "Trey Moss with the silencer! The kid's chasing a record season."

John laughed. "The season's still young. But what a way to start."

The Barracudas scrambled for one last faceoff, but it was done. No seconds left for retaliation. The final buzzer blasted, sealing their loss.

The Goshawks' bench erupted. Players swarmed the ice. Hunter skated from his crease to meet them. First in line, Ryan, bumping helmets before pulling him into a brief, hard hug. The rest followed, faces lit with the same mix that burned in Ryan's chest ... relief, respect, pride. Across the rink, Chucky was the first to enter the tunnel.

Ryan nudged Axel. "Some things never change. He's still running off the ice like a moldy carp chased by an angry hawk."

Axel pressed two fingers to Ryan's C. "Ya, ya. Let them dive. We fly."

Chapter 21
Once Upon a Goshawk

Tuesday, October 31st, Halloween

Margret flew down the grand staircase, one hand gripping the folds of her hooped Cinderella gown, the other clutching a single sparkly high heel slipper. The skirts of her dress fanned behind her like a tidal wave of tulle.

Beyond her reach ... the clatter of claws on marble steps. Crease, dressed in a dragon costume complete with wings and a spiked tail, bounded with Margret's second slipper clenched triumphantly in his mouth.

"Stop him!" she shouted.

Luke stood at the base of the stairs, laughing. Crease ducked under his reach, zigzagging past. Luke lunged, misjudged, landing on his back with a grunt.

"Not so funny now, is it?" Margret said as she reached the bottom step, grabbing her soggy shoe from the Lab.

Crease stood with chest puffed, tail sweeping the marble entryway like a feather duster.

"Where is Sage?"

Luke brushed off his white tights. "She's picking up Hunter and Ryan."

"Why didn't she take her mutt?" Margret shook the slipper. "Gross. It's slimy and warm."

Luke tugged at the front of his waistcoat, adjusting the gold embroidery. "The better question would be ... why am I wearing tights?"

Margret's dark brown hair spilled in loose waves over her shoulders. The soft blue gown shimmered with every breath she took. One hand clung to the banister as she slid the offending slipper on. "You know this is a themed event. I had my dress custom-made months ago. I thought you'd be right at home in shiny leather riding boots and tailored sleeves."

Luke let out a low whistle as he looked her up and down. "Wow. You *are* a fairy princess," he said, stepping into her for a kiss.

“Stop that. You’re going to ruin my makeup.” She pushed him back. “Make yourself useful. Take Crease outside so we don’t have a Petco incident at the hospital.”

Luke gave her a deep bow. From behind him the front door burst open. Etan, Axel, and Trey clomped in. All three wearing Goshawks-blue musketeer tunics with silver trim, the team logo stitched over their hearts. White breeches tucked into polished tall black boots. Stagecraft swords dangled loosely from their belts. Their cavalier hats, adorned with plumes, looked more mangled than majestic.

“I think your hat’s on backward,” Trey said to Axel.

Axel yanked it off, flipping it around. “How can you tell?”

“I wish Ryan was here,” Etan said, turning his hat back and forth. “He’d know which way is front.”

Trey strolled to the foyer mirror, striking a pose. “Doesn’t matter. When you look this good, every side’s your good side.”

The front door swung open again to reveal a towering figure. Finn ducked to clear the doorframe dressed in a Viking outfit. On his head, a silver winged helmet with large, curved horns. His upper body was draped in a furry tunic, a pelted cape slung over one shoulder. His waist was cinched with a wide, studded leather belt. He wore forest-green baggy pants and slouchy boots. In one hand, he held a large plastic battle axe. Long braided extensions clipped into his thick red beard.

Luke blinked. “Who are you supposed to be?”

“I’m Stoick the Vast,” Finn said with a huff, tossing a braid over his shoulder. “From *How to Train Your Dragon*.”

Luke looked baffled. “Is that one of those Pixar things?”

“Even my five-year-old knows who I am,” Finn muttered.

Luke took a step back, lifting his hands. “Hey, I work for a living. I don’t have time to sit around watching Vikings talking to lizards.”

“Dragons,” Etan, Trey, and Axel corrected in unison.

A breeze rushed through the door, as Sage and Hunter walked in. She wore a dark green velvet gown with flowing sleeves, a long golden braid curling across her chest. Beside her, Hunter wore leathers and a dark tunic ... a quiver slung over one shoulder, bracers on his forearms.

Axel danced about. “Robin Hood and Maid Marian.”

Etan nodded. “Nailed it. We just watched that Kevin Costner version last week.”

Margret smiled. “The costume department loaned me the original outfits from the movie.”

Crease leapt up, tail wagging his whole body, as he greeted Hunter with a dragon-suit full-body tackle.

All heads turned when Ryan entered behind them. He didn't say a word. His chestnut hair curled just enough to fall across his brow, his beard neatly trimmed. His tunic, a rich weathered brown, fit like leather armor molded to muscle. He didn't wear the costume, he embodied it.

Margret's eyes narrowed. "Now that the Huntsman has arrived, we can get going." She clapped her hands at Etan and Axel, who were mock-dueling with their swords. "Sheath those before someone loses an eye. Limo's waiting."

Luke offered his arm as she gathered her skirt.

"Where's the rest of the team?" Trey asked.

"There's limited space in the children's wing," Margret said. "So, I picked the ones most likely to behave."

Axel smirked. "You picked us?"

Margret gave him a tight smile. "Yes, and now I'm questioning my life choices."

Crease barked once, then darted out the door, wings bouncing.

The elevator chimed with a soft ding before its doors slid open, revealing a lineup of storybook misfits so outlandish the nurse on duty dropped her clipboard.

Margret stepped out first, the tulle of her Cinderella gown rustling with every step, her slippers clicking on the waxed hospital floor. Behind her trailed the thud of leather boots, the whisper of velvet cloaks, and the swish of a dragon tail ... like a fairytale parade that had lost its route but found its purpose in the children's ward.

Streamers fluttered from IV poles. Paper bats dangled from fluorescent lights. The scent of disinfectant mingled with latex gloves and a trace of chocolate, as though someone had already broken into the good candy.

Crease trotted down the hall, purple wings askew, one slightly bent from the limo ride. His tail wagged in erratic loops, slapping Ryan's shin, Finn's boot, then the wheel of a parked gurney. The sound a rhythmic, thump-thump, thwack-thwack, a percussion of joy in an otherwise too-quiet place.

"Clear the halls," Nikki called from down the corridor, camera raised. "We're under attack." Dressed in full jester regalia, Nikki's bells jingled as he crouched mid-snap. His Italian accent trailed the words like confetti. "Ryan, tilt your head. More brooding. Less D-man."

Ryan, shirt open at the collar, his Huntsman leathers creaking with every shift, leaned in a doorway, arms crossed, one leg bent, foot propped on the frame. Head tilted, he looked into the camera with an intense, unreadable stare. "Broody enough for you?"

A tiny laugh bubbled from behind a curtain. Margret's eyes scanned the faces. Nurses paused their charts. Parents straightened in chairs. A child in a giraffe onesie peeked around a doorway, eyes widening at the spectacle.

Then the trio struck. Etan, Axel, and Trey, formed a triangle in the center of the hallway. Their cassocks bore the Goshawks crest instead of the fleur-de-lis. Their plumed hats bobbed as they unsheathed their swords with flair.

"All for one and one for all!" the three shouted.

A boy in a wheelchair squealed, "It's the real Musketeers!"

Etan saluted with his sword. Axel attempted a spin, almost clocking a nurse with his scabbard. Trey dropped to one knee with signature flair, offering the boy his first hat trick puck from his time with the Nashville Shredders.

Behind them, Sage handed out gift bags stuffed with Goshawks hats, glow-in-the-dark bracelets, and hockey stickers. "Take your pick," she told a girl with a bandaged IV arm. "I'll make sure your favorite player signs it."

"Even the dragon?" the girl asked.

Sage leaned in. "Especially the dragon."

Crease sniffed the air, nose twitching. A toddler in a bumblebee costume waddled to him, shrieking with joy. Without missing a beat, Crease dropped into a play bow. More kids followed, some dragging IV poles, others clutching stuffed animals. They trailed behind him like ducklings following a dragon. For a moment, the ward looked less like a hospital and more like Neverland.

Luke, ever the Prince Charming, extended his arms when a little girl wearing a plastic tiara curtsied to him. "Your Highness," he said, clicking his heels, bowing low.

Margret caught motion to her left. Finn, towering, red beard flowing, knelt as a little girl in a sparkly Belle gown tugged his belt.

"Are you my Beast?" she asked.

He grinned, moving a hand over his heart. "I'll be whoever you wish me to be."

She reached up with trembling fingers, weaving them into his beard.

Near the far window, a boy sat cross-legged in a hospital bed, face pale, hair missing in patches. He watched quietly as Hunter approached, the quiver shifting on his back. The boy didn't move.

Hunter knelt, slipping the bow and quiver from his shoulder, offering them to the boy. "You wanna be Robin Hood today?" he asked, leaning close.

The boy smiled. "I'd rather be a goalie," he whispered.

Hunter turned to Nikki. "Did you bring my backup weapon?"

Nikki was already moving, jogging to the nurse's station. He returned with a goalie stick and a marker pen.

Hunter signed the stick, handing it to the boy as if it were an ancient relic. "Every outlaw needs a backup."

Margret felt a lump rise in her throat. Not from pity, but from something fierce and fragile, as she watched Hunter gift the boy the stick he used during his Cup win.

A nurse sidled up to Margret. "Some of these kids haven't smiled in days," she said, voice hushed, reverent. "Until now."

At Margret's side, Ryan stood silent, back pressed to the wall, his gaze tracking the chaos like he was watching a play unfold in front of Hunter's net. Her breath caught when he swiped a thumb across the corner of his eye.

She stepped back, taking it all in. The rustle of satin. The creak of leather. The bark of a Yellow Lab in dragon wings. A play sword clacking against an IV pole. Above it all ... laughter. Real, unfiltered, from-the-belly laughter.

Nikki's camera clicked again. "Smile, Cinderella," he said, lowering the lens. "Magic is happening."

Margret didn't need prompting. She was already smiling.

The long hallway gave way to smaller rooms, spaces quieter and dimmer, filled with the soft beeping of machines. Threadbare stuffed animals clung to windowsills.

Nikki stayed in the hallway, camera raised, catching moments without intruding. The lens saw everything, but Margret saw more.

In one room, Luke sat at the foot of a hospital bed, his head tilted as a three-year-old in bunny pajamas clutched the gold braids of his royal doublet.

"You're my prince," the girl declared. "You have to marry me."

Luke blinked, his mouth parting in a rare flicker of speechlessness. "Uh..."

The girl's mother stifled a laugh behind her hand.

"Well," Luke said, "I'll have to ask the Queen of Goshawks for permission. But I warn you, she makes all the married ladies do dishes and eat Brussels sprouts."

The little girl wrinkled her nose. "Never mind."

Across the hall, Ryan knelt beside a boy no older than seven, tubes taped to his nose, a blue knit cap stretched over his bald scalp. The boy clutched a stack of crayon drawings, one page held out with care.

Ryan took it, brow furrowing. It was a bright, childlike sketch of Ryan. Number 73 on his sleeve, a C stitched across his chest, standing over a stick figure labeled *Chucky*, sprawled in defeat in front of the crease.

"This is..." Ryan swallowed, then smiled. "This is the best," he said, handing it back. "Will you sign it for me? I want to hang this in my locker for good luck."

"You don't need luck. You have skill," the boy said, a grin breaking across his face like the sun through cloud cover.

Around the corner, a cluster of children gathered in a playroom where Axel and Etan staged an impromptu duel. Their blue musketeer cassocks billowed as they clashed swords with exaggerated groans and stealthy footwork.

"I fight for honor!" Etan shouted, dodging Axel's swing.

"And I fight because you drank the last juice box!" Axel bellowed.

Kids squealed, chanting, "Ax-el! Ax-el!" until Etan faked a fall, clutching his heart like he'd been mortally wounded.

Axel bowed to the cheers.

"Again! Again!" a squeaky voice cried out.

Back in a larger shared room, Finn crouched low in front of a bed where two boys sat. Crease clambered onto the mattress, settling between them, panting. Finn raised a finger. "Now," he said gruffly, channeling his inner Stoick, "to tame a dragon, you must show courage."

Crease flopped onto his side with a moan, baring his belly.

Finn blinked. "Or bacon. You can tame him with bacon."

One of the boys snorted, then coughed, then laughed again.

Margret followed Sage and Hunter as they floated from room to room like couriers of calm, a satchel of Goshawks swag slung over the goalie's shoulder. They offered signed pucks and shirts in exchange for high fives. One girl gasped when Hunter handed her a Goshawks cap.

"Are you really Robin Hood?" she asked, her eyes wide.

Hunter smiled. "I heard you're the sheriff. Please don't arrest me."

"Never," she said, jumping into his arms, giggling.

As Margret ventured down the hallway, she accepted an invitation to sit at a small table with a teapot in the middle. Two girls in tiaras poured invisible tea into cat-shaped cups. Lowering herself took strategy; the hoops of her gown refusing to cooperate. She let out a tiny moan, scrunching the wires into place as she smoothed the tulle. "Delightful," she said, lifting the cup, pinky finger extended.

Across from her, Luke fidgeted in the small chair, knees tucked under his chin. One of the girls studied him with a frown.

"You're crooked." With utmost care, she stood, adjusting his royal crown, then patted his cheek. "There. Now you're all handsome again."

"Thank you, M'lady."

Margret got the giggles, nearly spitting out her fake tea. Yet in her wooden chair, surrounded by imaginary cakes and real children, she felt her heart thump. In that small moment of hope and joy, she knew that no matter how dark the world ... light always finds a way in.

The fluorescent lights flickered with a soft hum as the children gathered for goodbyes. Nurses helped prop the youngest ones on their laps, others sat in wheelchairs, while parents stood off to the side, clutching coffee cups, their eyes red-rimmed ... everyone sporting a smile.

The Goshawks players lined up shoulder to shoulder behind the kids. Swords sheathed, fake mustaches crooked, plumes drooping. Crease sat in front, tongue lolling in a toothy grin, dragon tail curled around a nurse's ankle.

Nikki crouched low, camera poised. "All right, on three! One... two..."

Crease lunged at the nurse beside him, planting a wet kiss on her cheek. She squealed, the kids howled.

Nikki clicked anyway. "Perfect," he said, lowering the camera. "Better than perfect."

Margret stepped to the side, hands folded at her waist, watching it all like a living painting. Sage joined her, cheeks pink, braid loosened, a smudge of glitter on her cheek. Margret leaned in. "Another successful event."

Sage smiled. "Because of you."

Margret's throat tightened. She didn't trust herself to answer.

One by one, the Goshawks said goodbye, each hug a little longer, each step towards the elevator a little heavier.

Ryan lingered, crouched low as two boys clung to his calves like tree frogs. He ruffled their hair, signed the back of one boy's Goshawks jersey, then with great care peeled them off. "I'll come back," he promised. "But you gotta be strong. Like a captain, okay?"

Both boys saluted.

Margret watched as Ryan turned away, eyes fixed on the elevator, jaw clenched like he'd taken a puck to the heart.

Hunter was the last player to leave. He hovered near the exit, gaze searching.

Sage emerged from a side room, arms now empty of goody bags, the hem of her velvet gown trailing behind like a shadow. She looked tired, happy, raw around the edges.

Hunter stepped into her path, pulling her close, pressing a lingering kiss to her forehead. "This..." he said, voice husky, "this was the best kind of win."

Sage's eyes shimmered. "You were amazing."

He shook his head. "No. They were."

As the elevator doors opened with a soft chime, Crease gave a low woof, pausing to look back.

Margret exhaled, the weight in her chest blooming into something warmer, something lighter. In her seasons with the Goshawks, this remained her favorite charity event. Not because it made headlines, but because it made sense. In a world that often felt too sharp, too fast, too cold... today was soft. Today mattered.

Chapter 22
Leather and Lace

Tuesday, October 31st, Halloween

Ryan stifled a yawn behind Sage as she tapped her foot, waiting for Hunter to unlock his door. The children's hospital visit had been rewarding, but it drained him more than any double-overtime playoff game. He admired the kids' grit, their courage ... yet the sight of so many small bodies fighting big battles always left a weight he couldn't shake for days.

"Dear Maid Marian, would you grant me the honor of your company?" Hunter bowed, still dressed in his Robin Hood costume, hand extended to Sage in her flowing medieval gown.

Ryan groaned. "Good grief, you two."

"You're just jealous you don't have a partner to invite into your lair," Hunter teased.

"I tried to rope my own South Dakota cowgirl. We all can't be as lucky as you." Ryan winked at Sage.

She punched Hunter's arm. "Don't be a jerk." Then to Ryan, softer, "The world's full of princesses waiting to be rescued. You'll find yours." She hugged him before following Hunter into the front room.

Ryan walked to his apartment, searching for his key as Jill's door clicked open behind him. He paused, shoulders tensing. The last thing he needed tonight was her barbed comments.

He turned, braced for a fight. The comeback on his tongue vanishing when he saw her.

Jill stood in her doorway, nothing like the sharp-tongued East Coast preppy neighbor he was used to. The sight of her stopped him cold. Her white blouse, laced beneath a blue corset, dipped low. the yellow full skirt swayed mid-thigh. Red lips matched the ribbon tied in her dark hair. Snow White, but not the fairytale kind ... her version was pure temptation in heels.

They both stopped short. A sly smile tugged at Ryan's lips as Jill's gaze swept over his leathers ... boots, pants, vest, every piece cut to fit like a second skin.

Her eyes lingered. She reached out, fingers brushing the hilt of the sword at his hip. "Is that real?"

"Wood," he said, fighting a grin.

"Nice costume." Her voice low, warm, as she drew her hand back.

Ryan slipped into the same brooding pose Nikki had coached him through at the hospital shoot. He leaned against his doorframe, one boot braced on the jamb, arms folded, expression unreadable. "Right back at you, Snow."

"Please don't tell me you're the Huntsman." Her fingers toyed with the pleats of her skirt, as if the movement kept them from reaching for him again. "Or is leather the new standard issue for Goshawks when they're not skating?"

"We just got back from a Halloween event at the children's hospital. Annual visit."

Jill's expression softened. "That's actually sweet," she said, tilting her head.

He gave a small shrug. "Hot date tonight?"

Her laugh came quick and dry. "Supposed to be. My friend's throwing a Halloween bash at her daddy's estate. My date bailed last minute ... client crisis or some Wall Street emergency. Men in power suits with god complexes. You know the type."

"No. Not really." Ryan pushed off the wall, the carpet muting his step. "Sounds like someone I wouldn't want to know anyway."

Jill's gaze stayed fixed on him. "I detest showing up to these parties without a date."

He turned slightly. "Wow. So, you're seeing a guy who'd stand you up for work? I'd rethink that choice."

"I'm not seeing anyone. I just date ... occasionally." Her voice held the faint coolness of someone pretending not to care. "It's different."

Ryan rolled his shoulders, the leather of his vest shifting with the movement. "Still sucks he bailed. I've got early practice. Night, Jill."

"Wait." She stepped closer, her fingers closing around his bicep. The touch stopped him more than her voice. "I figured you might have a thing for rescuing a damsel in distress."

Ryan looked at her hand, then met her eyes. "I don't go out before a game."

"Oh, right. Hockey players and their rituals." The word *rituals* slid off her tongue like a tease. "Besides, your game's not until the day after tomorrow."

His head snapped up, brows drawn. "Jill, I've known you almost as long as Hunter has. I know for a fact you couldn't care less about hockey players or their schedules."

"Hunter's my best friend. I've lived next to your star goalie for six years. I've heard the lectures. I know all about the sacred pregame mindset. I keep track of his games so I can let the housekeeper in when he's gone."

Ryan gave her a slow once-over, gaze unapologetic. "So, you really want me to be your plus-one to a party full of your designer friends ... in this getup?"

She pressed a finger to his chest, a faint smile curving her lips. "You're wearing those leathers like they're wearing you. Trust me, you'll fit right in."

"I don't know, Jill." He rubbed the back of his neck, unsure if he was protesting or stalling.

"You owe me, mister. Remember?" Jill stepped closer, tapping his cheek with her palm. "I'm collecting on that debt."

Ryan caught her finger before she could pull away. "Fine. I'll go ... only if you convince Hunter and Sage to come too."

"Deal." Jill spun, making a beeline for Hunter's door.

Ryan hesitated, bone-deep fatigue tugging at him before he gave in and followed.

"Hey, you guys decent?" Ryan knocked as he cracked the door. Inside, a play-by-play echoed from the TV, the announcer hyping a Goshawks shutout.

"Always," Hunter called, muting the screen. "What's up?"

Jill pushed past Ryan. "I need you guys to come with us, to a Halloween party."

Sage clapped her hands, eyes bright. "That sounds like too much fun."

"No!" Hunter said, reaching for the remote.

"Come on, Hunter. After today, we could use some laughter." Sage snatched the remote before he could react, the TV going dark. "Besides, I know you've never been to a costume party."

Hunter frowned at Ryan. "You think this is a good idea before an early morning practice?"

"As your captain, I don't." Ryan sighed, running fingers through his hair.

Sage rested her hand on Hunter's arm. "Please. Please. Please. Just this once. We're already dressed for it."

Hunter ran a hand over his face. "Fine. Now get out of my blue paint."

"I'll text Luke, let him know I'll be late so he can take care of Crease." Sage unlocked her phone with a quick tap.

Ryan glanced at Jill. "Happy now?"

Jill's smile widened. "You'll thank me by the end of the night."

"Doubt it," Ryan muttered.

"Luke's got Crease covered." Sage's voice lifted with a cheer. "I'll drive."

Ryan unbuckled his sword belt, setting it by Hunter's door. He hoped he wouldn't need it before the night was over.

Sage's SUV rolled to a stop inside the gated estate. Strings of lights curled around every column and arch, glowing like fireflies in the dark. The lawn stretched wide enough to host a golf tournament. Jill stepped out, adjusting the bodice of her dress.

Ryan gave a low whistle, eyes sweeping the mansion's façade. "This isn't a party," he said. "It's a Jane Austen movie set."

Jill smirked. "Try not to embarrass me, Huntsman."

"Who needs a valet for a Halloween party?" Ryan muttered.

At the entrance, a butler opened the door with a polished smile. "Good evening, Miss Markham."

Inside, the air was thick with roses, expensive cologne, and old money. A band hustled through the foyer, hauling instruments. The ballroom shimmered with the trust-fund crowd ... designer gowns, tailored costumes, and laughter that sounded a little too rehearsed.

Ryan adjusted his leather cuffs, suddenly aware of the weight of every head turning their way. Goshawks fans. He could feel it before the whispers started.

"Is that...?"

"No freaking way. It's Ryan Mitchell and Hunter Griffin."

A brunette dressed as Elvira, Mistress of the Dark, pushed through the crowd. Her costume so tight Ryan wondered how she managed to breathe, let alone rush to his side.

"RYAN. MITCHELL. Oh my gosh, Jill, where have you been hiding this snack?"

Before he could react, she pressed in, pink liquid sloshing over the rim of her martini glass. "Hold this," she said, shoving it into his hand while lifting her phone. "Smile," she cooed. "I've got eight thousand jealous followers to feed."

Ryan forced a grin. "Sure. Just one, okay?"

She fired off ten photos and a short video. "Okay, maybe three more. Turn your head a little ... yes, right there. I've always loved your perfect jawline."

Beside him, Jill's fingers crunched her skirt. Ryan caught a flicker of something he'd never seen ... concern, suspicion, maybe jealousy.

Elvira reclaimed her drink, cheeks flushed. "Seriously, Jill, this guy is lethal. If I were you, I'd..." She stopped herself, smiling. "You know what? Never mind. I'm posting this on all my social media pages." She wobbled off, fingernails tapping across her phone screen.

"Close friend?" Ryan asked, brushing pink residue from his sleeve.

"Unfortunately." Jill's voice came tight. "She's always had a severe lack of boundaries, with a passion for too many Cosmos."

Ryan's gaze lingered on her longer than he meant to. Something had shifted. She didn't roll her eyes or toss back a sarcastic quip. She just looked ... thoughtful.

She met his stare. "You handled that with more grace than I thought you were capable of."

"You forget, I'm the team's captain, not just a hunky slab of muscle." He flexed a bicep.

"Well," Jill said, lips curving slow, "that remains to be seen. But I'm intrigued."

Ryan laughed under his breath, stepping closer. "I thought this was supposed to be your crowd."

Jill glanced around the room, the flicker of chandeliers catching in her eyes before she met his again. "It is."

He didn't believe her.

A server approached with a silver tray of champagne flutes, bubbles rising like liquid light.

"Let's find something you'll actually enjoy," Hunter whispered to Sage, steering her to a small bar across the room.

Jill plucked a flute without hesitation, her fingers grazing the slender stem as she lifted it from the tray.

Ryan watched Hunter and Sage disappear into the crowd. A good scotch sounded tempting. When Jill lifted her glass in a small, confident toast, he reached for a flute too.

"To a fun evening," Jill said, lifting her glass.

Ryan clinked hers lightly before taking a sip. The champagne fizzed cold on his lips, sharp on his tongue.

Jill's fingers slipped through his, guiding him away from the noise and glitter of the ballroom. They walked down a wide passage lined with framed oil paintings. Along the walls, entry tables held crystal vases of Black Magic roses, their subtle perfume mingling with the soft glow of candles set inside carved pumpkins.

Ryan slowed near one of the canvases. The art light captured the brushstrokes … fine, deliberate, unmistakably from an Old Master's hand. He could see the age in the varnish, the depth of color only centuries could create. Not a reproduction. "Who lives here?" he asked, lifting his glass for another sip as he studied Jill instead of the art.

"Does it matter?" Her fingers tightened around his, pulling him farther down the hall into the library. She led him to a cushioned bench under a broad picture window overlooking the bay. The night pressed close to the glass, mist giving a surreal feel to the horizon.

"This better not be where you shove me out a tower window," Ryan said, nudging her with his shoulder.

"Tempting," Jill replied, nudging him back. "You've earned a temporary stay of execution." She turned to the window, finger tracing his reflection in the pane.

Ryan nodded to the ballroom. The hum of laughter and music ebbed and flowed soft into the room. "Your friends don't feel like your kind of people."

"Like I said, they are." She hesitated, the words softening as they left her. "Of late, I feel like we're drifting apart."

A comfortable silence stretched between them. Ryan sipped his drink before asking, "So, how come you've never been to a game?"

Jill met his gaze. "I don't find grown men in shorts and long stockings chasing each other on skates particularly riveting."

Ryan laughed. His fingers brushing her arm. "You left out the part where we beat each other senseless for fun."

She smirked. "Thought that was a given."

He nodded, slow and knowing. "That's fair. To outsiders, I'm sure it looks like chaos. Violence wrapped in silly rituals."

Jill said nothing.

He stared into the room when he spoke again, his voice losing its edge. "But for me … it's special." He paused, as if trying to distill something too big into something small enough for her to understand. "It's rhythm. It's grit. It's knowing there's a guy behind you who'd drop gloves for you, whether you deserve it or not. And it's your job to be that guy for him. No questions asked."

Jill remained silent, her focus entirely on him.

"It's the sound of skates cutting into fresh ice at early morning practice. The smell of sweat and victory in the locker room after a big win. The silence after a loss that hits too hard. It's … family. The good, the bad. All of it."

Silence settled between them again.

When Jill finally spoke, her voice was soft, caring. "I didn't realize it meant that much to you."

Ryan turned to face her, the library's low lighting caught the edges of his expression. "No offense, but I don't think you realized it could mean that much to any of us."

He waited for the snark ... none came. She held his gaze, and for the first time he saw someone he'd want to get to know better.

Hours later, they drifted back into the grand ballroom, where velvet chairs lined the walls and a stretch of polished wood gleamed beneath the chandelier. Conversation dimmed as a slow song unfurled through the speakers, a warm, honeyed voice curling around the room like falling leaves.

Across the floor, Ryan spotted Sage tugging Hunter onto the dance area. The goalie resisted for all of two seconds before surrendering with a grin full of defeated affection.

"Look at that," Jill said. "Even Hunter knows when to accept defeat with grace."

"I'm sure I'll hear about it tomorrow," Ryan murmured, glancing at his boots. "Probably lose my captain letter for not stepping in."

She moved in front of him, with a mischievous grin. "Want to?"

Ryan blinked. "Want to what?"

"Dance, silly." Jill tilted her head. "You do know how to dance, right?"

"I can two-step," Ryan said, straight-faced. "It's called covering the crease and clearing rebounds."

Jill laughed. "So, you're saying you'll probably step on my toes?"

"I'm saying ... you've been warned."

"Noted." She took his hand, leading him to the dance floor before he could voice a protest.

They found space near the center just as the music deepened, still slow but richer. Ryan slid an arm around her waist; his other hand still tangled with hers. Her fingers warm against his cool palm. The way her body fit against his made his breath catch.

Jill rested her head on his chest like she belonged there.

His heart stuttered. The scent of her shampoo, something with a hint of spice, hit him like a memory he hadn't lived yet. They swayed together, soft, unhurried. Her breathing matched his as her fingers curled against the leather of his shirt.

For the first time in a long while, Ryan forgot about the next game, the pressures, the expectations. All that existed was the comfort of now, the hush of the music, the pulse of her against him, and an ache in his chest that felt both new and inevitable. He closed his eyes, falling into it.

Three slow songs later, Ryan forgot where he was, what day it was, and why he ever thought leather pants were a bad idea. A tap on his shoulder broke the spell.

"Bro..." Hunter's voice carried a note of urgency. "It's late. We've got practice in six hours."

Ryan blinked, disoriented, Jill still warm in his arms. "What time is it?"

"After one." Hunter checked his phone. "If we're late, we'll both be skating extra laps. Gray needs any excuse to bench me for the next game."

Ryan muttered a curse. "Right. Thanks." He glanced at Jill. "I have to go."

Her body stiffened. "Of course you do."

"I shouldn't have had that last drink." He scrunched his face, trying to clear the fog. "This night's way off my routine." He took a small step back. "You ready to head out?"

"I'll call an Uber," she said, the words spilling out too fast.

"Are you sure?"

"I'll walk you out." She guided him across the dance floor, through the entrance doors. A soft salty breeze whipped multi-colored leaves around their feet. Jill stopped outside the threshold. Porch lights strung along the columns wrapped them in a golden glow.

"Thanks for being my stand-in," she said, voice low, eyes not meeting his.

Ryan leaned his back on a column. "Anytime." To his surprise, he meant it.

Jill looked up, an unreadable expression moved across her face. She pressed her palms to his chest, rising on her toes. Her lips met his, soft ... unsure at first, as if she were giving him a chance to pull away.

He didn't.

Ryan's breath caught, then released as he pulled her closer, deepening the kiss, slow, steady, anchored in something he couldn't name. Her hand slid higher, fingers curling against his collarbone. She tasted like champagne, warm and sweet.

A car horn blared twice. Sage's unmistakable signal.

They pulled apart, breath short. Jill's lips parted, her violet eyes darkened under the porch light.

His fingers lingered against her cheek. "Goodnight, Snow White," he said before walking away. It took all his resolve to keep from returning to her arms.

Chapter 23
Guarding the Goalie

Wednesday, November 1st

A fist pounded Ryan's door. Not once. Not twice. But a relentless, rhythmic BAM, BAM, BAM vibrating through his skull like a bad bass line. He cracked a bloodshot eye, groaned, dragging off the mattress. His feet hit the floor with all the enthusiasm of a post-check hip bruise.

Another knock. "Mitchell! You alive in there?" Hunter's voice carried through the door like an end of game horn. "We gotta go."

Ryan opened the door a sliver, squinting through the crack. "What...?"

Jill's door swung open across the hall. She was in full early-morning glory; hair brushed, lips glossed, wearing joggers with a crisp tee. She looked too put-together for someone who had been out later than him.

"Where's the fire?" she asked, arching a brow.

Hunter didn't miss a beat. "If we don't get to the rink in the next twenty, our butts are going to be scorched."

Ryan blinked at him, then at Jill. "How ... how do you look so ... perfect? Didn't you get home after us?"

Jill smirked. "Practice."

That one word sliced through Ryan's mental fog like a slap shot to the temple.

Hunter shouldered the door wide open, shoving Ryan backward. "No time for small talk with Snow White. Get dressed."

Ryan stumbled to the bedroom. "What time is it?"

"Practice starts in less than twenty."

Ryan's eyes widened. "You serious?"

"Do I sound like I'm joking?" Hunter called after him.

Two minutes. That was all Ryan needed. He yanked on sweatpants over his workout shorts, threw a hoodie over his bare chest. He stumbled into the main room, snatched his car fob off the counter, slinging his gear bag over one shoulder. "Let's go!"

The hallway echoed with their rushed footfalls. From her apartment, Jill's voice rang out, half-laughing, half-scolding. "Where are your shoes?"

Ryan looked down as the elevator dinged open. Feet bare. He glanced back at his apartment door.

"No time," Hunter growled, grabbing Ryan by the hoodie, hauling him inside as the doors slid shut. "I can't be late."

The frigid air bit Ryan's ankles the second he stepped from the car, bare feet slapping against the pavement as he jogged behind Hunter to the Goshawk's practice facility. Wind sliced through the hoodie. The cold cut into his bones like punishment. "Geez, it feels like minus a million." His Canadian accent thickening; voice gravelly with sleep and regret.

Hunter didn't answer. He swiped his access card with the urgency of a man breaking into a burning building to save a life. The door buzzed, then swung open. Inside, the hallway reeked of sweat, strong coffee, and wintergreen liniment. Home sweet home.

The locker room buzzed with rustling fabric and clinking gear. Guys were mid-dress, some half in, some half out of pads. Chirps ricocheted around the room with a tired edge that came with early skates. Ryan's eyes swept the room. Lane's stall was empty. No Coach Gray. He turned to Hunter, who was already stripped to his shorts, pulling on his goalie gear with robotic-like precision.

"You seeing what I'm seeing?" Ryan asked, voice low.

Hunter gave a single nod, mouth tight as he yanked on his goalie pants.

Then came the voice ... gruff, unimpressed, familiar.

"Nice of you two to join us," Coach Harrison said, approaching with a slow shake of his head. His gaze dropped to Ryan's bare feet. "Where the hell are your shoes, Mitchell?"

"Don't ask," Ryan mumbled, rubbing a hand through his spiky morning hair.

Harrison arched a brow, then looked at Hunter. "Gray's on the ice with Lane."

"Figures," Hunter muttered, lacing his skates.

"What was that?" Harrison snapped.

"Nothing, Coach."

"I thought not." Harrison's scowl deepened. "Mitchell. My office after practice."

Ryan gave a stiff nod. His mouth tasted like expensive champagne mixed with bad decisions. He reached into his gear bag for tape. "Axe, you got clear?" Ryan croaked.

Axel tossed a roll to him.

Etan leaned in as Ryan taped his shin pads. "Save some for me."

"Buy your own," Axel said. Then paused, taking in his fellow D-man. "Cap, what happened to you last night after we left the hospital?"

Ryan peeled back the tape, looked up with bloodshot eyes. "Don't ask."

"Oh, we're gonna ask," Etan said, grin splitting wide as he crouched in front of Ryan's stall like a kid waiting for storytime.

"We went back to your old apartment, played CoD with Trey. He's got a full command center in there. You should see it."

Axel pulled his 'Property of Goshawks' practice sweater over his pads. "We miss having you on our floor. Trey's rig though, is sick."

Ryan's eyes flicked to the far end of the locker room. "Where is Trey?"

Finn's voice rumbled like distant thunder. "Little showboat couldn't wait for the rest of us. He's already on the ice."

Ryan turned. Finn sat slouched in his stall, beard still glinting with rogue glitter. He looked like a Viking who'd been mugged by a craft store.

"Enough," Coach Harrison barked. "If you don't want me to bench the whole top line. Shut it."

Silence dropped as fast as the first faceoff puck hitting the ice.

Ryan finished taping, grabbed his helmet, headed for the door. Toes frozen. Jaw tight. He didn't know how this day could get any worse, but it was sure shaping up to.

Before skating onto the ice, Ryan swept a handful of pucks off the dasher. They clattered across the frozen sheet, skittering like startled mice. Their sharp noise drowned beneath the booming bark of Coach Gray.

"From now on," Gray snarled, voice echoing through the near-empty arena, "I want you in front of the net an hour before everyone else. If you've got better things to do than guarding your crease, I'll make sure you have plenty of free time to do them."

Ryan's gaze locked on Hunter.

The goalie stood motionless in the net, chin lowered, pads square. The tension in his frame said everything. Shoulders tight. Stick clicking the posts. Coach Gray skated in front of him, gloved finger stabbing at Hunter's chest with each word. The man wasn't coaching; he was posturing.

Ryan skated over, casual on the surface, boiling underneath. He tapped the blade of his stick lightly on Hunter's leg pad. No words. A signal. *I got you.*

"What do you think you're doing, Mitchell?" Gray snapped, voice cracking like a whip in Ryan's direction. "Leave my netminders alone."

Ryan didn't stop. Didn't slow. "Or what?"

The space between them thickened with heat. Ryan's fists tightened on his stick. Muscle memory burned through him, the urge to protect his goalie rising. His breath hitched, blood hammering in his ears. He didn't drop gloves. Not here. Not now. He tapped Hunter's pad once more, then turned, skating backwards to the opposite blue line.

Seconds later, Gray was back at it. The instant Hunter let in a weak rebound, off a deflection no goalie could have stopped, Gray's voice rose again, loud enough to shake the rafters.

"Square up! That's three this week you've let leak. Want me to draw you a picture of a five-hole?"

Ryan bit the inside of his cheek hard enough to taste metal. He hated standing helpless, watching it unfold. He was their captain, supposed to lead. One wrong move could get him benched with their starter.

Gray pointed to Hunter then to the corner. "Out."

Lane popped onto the ice, smooth, confident. Five seconds into his rotation, he snagged a mid-slot wrister with a flashy glove save; high elbow, cocky snap.

"That's how a net should be guarded!" Gray roared, beaming like Lane had turned water into wine.

Ryan didn't miss the shift in the arena. Players' attention bounced between Lane and the bench, where Hunter stood, ice side, head back, drinking water like it burned going down.

Murphy skated over, breath fogging. "That jerk makes Viktor look like a kindergarten teacher."

Ryan gave a dry laugh. "That's what I was thinking. We all saw what the old Russian put Hunter through."

"Yeah. But Viktor was never so ... antagonistic."

Ryan nodded. Gray wasn't pushing Hunter; he was burying him.

Practice dragged to a close. Gray didn't ease off. Every save Lane made, earned a booming compliment. Every misstep from Hunter brought a barked critique in front of the squad.

Ryan's fists clenched again. He glanced at the bench. Harrison wasn't watching. Maybe pretending not to. The GM was nowhere in sight. Margret, always in the stands during morning practice, was a no show. His skates ripped to a stop at the red line.

Why doesn't anyone else see what's happening? Maybe they do, choosing to ignore it. Something was going on behind the scenes. Ryan was determined to get to the bottom of it, before the bottom fell out.

The stench of sweat and effort clung to the air, thick and sour as Ryan stepped into the locker room. A few players joked near the showers; the slap of wet towels, bursts of laughter echoing off tile. Ryan's eyes went straight to Hunter.

He sat in his stall, legs splayed, mask by his side, knee pads half-off, head down. The fight had drained out of him, leaving nothing behind.

Ryan sank into the stall beside him, elbows on his knees. "You good?"

Hunter didn't look up. He gave a sharp nod, temples throbbing. "He's setting me up."

Ryan wanted to push back, offer something besides the truth. The words weren't there. He knew it too. *Gray was doing his best to destroy his best friend.*

"I'll talk to Harrison," Ryan said, voice low, the words nearly swallowed. "This crap's not gonna keep flying."

Hunter finally moved, jerking off his sweater, throwing it to the floor. It landed with a wet slap, joining the puddle under his gear. "I can fight my own battles."

"Not saying you can't." Ryan sat upright, tapping his fingers on the bench. "I just need to let you know ... you're not alone in this."

Hunter didn't answer.

"Let me know when you're ready to leave." Ryan stood, resting a hand on Hunter's shoulder.

"Don't wait. I'm getting a ride back with Sage," Hunter said unstrapping his chest protector.

Ryan hesitated for a second before returning to his stall. The silence between them said it all. Hunter wasn't only tired; he was bracing for a storm. Ryan knew it was time to ready himself for battle too.

Showered, dressed, running on no caffeine and pure instinct, Ryan jogged up the narrow staircase to the admin offices. His wet hair curled at the collar of his sweatshirt. Cold air cut through the thin fabric. His bare feet slapped the concrete steps.

Inside the head coach's main office, Harrison sat behind his desk, attention fixed on his tablet. Without looking up, he said, "Have a seat, Mitchell."

Ryan dropped into the chair opposite, leaning forward, forearms on his thighs.

"Before you light into me," Ryan began, "I need to ask you ... did you see what Gray pulled out there?"

Coach Harrison pinched the bridge of his nose. "I see everything, Ryan. It's not just about today. Hunter's been off. You know it. I know it."

Ryan leaned back, one brow raised. "You really think that's all on him?"

"He's a goalie. It's always on them. They know that."

Ryan's jaw ticked. "No. This is different. Gray's got an agenda. He's trying to make Lane the Goshawks' starter, whatever it costs."

Harrison raised his head, focusing on Ryan. "Take it up with the GM. This is above me now."

Ryan stared at him. *That was it? No defense. No pushback.* He stood.

"Where are you going?" Harrison's voice sharpened.

Ryan continued walking to the door. "Nice chat, Coach. I'm the one wearing the C. I've got responsibilities to this team that can't wait while you chew me out for cutting it close to practice."

Harrison called after him as he reached the doorway. "Don't do it again."

Ryan didn't look back. He lifted a hand in the air, giving a lazy backhanded wave as he walked out. He had the GM to find. Frustrated, he stormed past George Stonebridge's empty room.

He went straight to the corner office. He knew better. Didn't care. He breezed by Margret's assistant with a wink, followed by a half wave. "I've got it, thanks."

"Mr. Mitchell." Annie called after him, rising from her desk.

Too late. He was already pushing through the door.

Margret looked up, mid-sip of coffee, mouse scrolling through Excel sheets, a stack of papers in a neat pile on the desk. Her eyes narrowed as she looked up.

"You planning on letting Gray break Hunter?" Ryan barked. "Or are you going to stop this?"

Annie dashed in behind him. "I'm so sorry, Ms. VanAlen. He..."

"No problem, Annie." Margret's tone stayed calm, coiled like a spring. "Please close the door as you leave."

Annie shot Ryan a glare. Ryan flashed his best charming smolder back at her, turning to Margret as the door clicked shut.

She removed her glasses, setting them on the desk. "Watch your tone, Mitchell."

Ryan didn't blink. "Then give me a reason not to. Hunter is your most valuable player. Your starter. He won you the Cup. He's not Lane's backup."

Margret let out a slow breath. Clicked the computer off. "You think I don't know that?"

Ryan stepped closer, palms slapped her desk. His voice dropped low, controlled, deadly. "Then do something. Because he can't win this fight alone."

Margret's voice lost its edge. "You have no idea what's going on behind the scenes."

"You're right," Ryan said. "I don't. But, the C on my chest suggests I should."

Before she could respond, the office door creaked open. Luke popped his head in, casual as ever. "Hey, Margret. You want to grab some lunch?" His gaze bounced between her and the captain. "Hey, Ryan. What's up?"

"Nothing," Margret said sharply. "Ryan was leaving."

"We're not done with this," Ryan said, fist landing hard on the desk.

"We are for now." Margret's tone clipped short. "I'll take your concerns under advisement and circle back to you."

Ryan didn't slam the door, though it closed harder than he intended. He walked out, uncertain if he'd helped or made things worse. What he did know ... he wasn't done fighting for his goalie, for his best friend.

In her office, Margret returned to the computer, clicking open a file.

Viktor Volkov. Contractual Archive.

Chapter 24
Brunch and Business

Friday, November 3rd

In Margret's home, the scent of cinnamon scones and rich roasted coffee hung in the quiet air like a well-laid trap. She stood at the doorway to her smaller dining room, surveying the scene like a conductor before a performance. No linen tablecloths. No centerpieces. Only a round walnut table polished to a soft sheen, flanked by high-backed upholstered chairs in slate blue. Two leather-bound folders rested with quiet importance at one place setting, each thick with legal weight.

The men arrived fifteen minutes ago. Now they circled the sideboard, helping themselves to a spread of pastries nestled between two steaming French presses gleaming like fresh-cut glass beneath the recessed lighting.

General Manager, George Stonebridge, rumpled but dependable, poured his second cup of coffee after taking a scone.

Anderson Griffin passed on pastries, holding his cup with lawyer precision, already studying the room like he was preparing to cross-examine each guest.

Sterling Wheatfield, impressive in a dove-gray sports coat, matching slacks, and polished snakeskin boots, lifted the misshaped homemade scone to eye level like it offended him. "Margret," he said, "when are you going to get staff to help you run this place? This isn't a two-bedroom condo."

Luke leaned against the edge of the credenza, cutting in before Margret could answer. "This isn't your ranch either, dad. Margret's managing just fine."

A faint smile curled at the corners of Margret's lips. She was about to add her own remarks when Crease barreled into the room, like he was leading the rush on a short-handed breakaway. Tail high, he sniffed once, twice, then zeroed in on Sterling's boots.

"Good Grief." Sterling danced backward, sloshing coffee on the floor. "What is Sage's mongrel doing in here? And why isn't she watching her dog?"

"Sage's doing media control from last night's loss," Luke said as he reached for Crease's collar. "I'm taking care of him until the dog sitter comes."

"You're doing a lousy job of it." Sterling dropped a cloth napkin on the floor, using the toe of his boot to wipe up the spill.

Anderson took a step back, not quick enough to stop Crease from rubbing against his leg. Yellow hair clung to his navy-blue Armani slacks like static cling.

George, unfazed, crouched, tearing a corner off his scone. "Here ya go, buddy," he said, offering it to the Lab, who took it with a polite chomp, leaving George's fingers smeared with dog slobber.

"Don't you dare," Margret scolded as Crease's nose lifted. His eyes locked on the leather folders.

"No. No. No." She raced to the table.

With a single bound, Crease snatched the top contract folder, bolting like Trey in control of an empty net puck.

"I got him!" Luke said, as he ran down the hallway grabbing the Lab's collar.

"Be careful!" Margret shouted. "Those are original documents."

From the foyer, a new voice cut through the chaos. "Drop it," Margret's assistant, Annie said, calm but firm. She pried the document free, handing it to Luke as she leashed Crease.

"Perfect timing," Margret said. "He was about to sabotage Goshawks negotiations."

"Who's a good boy?" Annie said, patting Crease's head. "I'll keep the team safe from this thief during the upcoming away games." She grinned, giving Margret a quick wave before scooping up the Lab's overnight bag and heading for the door, Crease trotting at her side.

"Now that the menace is gone," Margret said, pressing her palms to the table, addressing her guests. "Please take your places, gentlemen. We have business to resolve before the team plane takes off this afternoon."

She laid the folder flat, smoothing its chomped edge. Margret waited until the final scrape of chairs faded beneath the table. China clinked as coffee cups settled. The French press gurgled when George poured his third cup. She didn't rush. She let them settle, let the moment breathe.

"Shall we begin?" Her voice carried deliberate calm. "Thank you for coming," she said. "We don't have much time, so I'll get to the point."

Margret's gaze moved around the table, assessing each man. Sterling appeared relaxed, but she knew the shrewd businessman behind the charm all too well. George, ever the loyal GM, stayed sharp-eyed, dependable. Luke sat stiff beside her, fingers clutched too tight on his coffee cup. Anderson met her stare with cool detachment, like a man enduring a meeting he considered beneath him. Hunter's father was the only one who intimidated her.

She flipped open the top folder, the one spared from Crease's destruction. A damp corner curled. On the left side, a glossy 8×10 image remained unmarred. It showed a man with sharp Slavic features and an unflinching stare. On the right, a multi-page legal document.

"Viktor Volkov," Margret said. The name hit the room like a puck slapping tempered glass.

Anderson cleared his throat, slipping into lawyer speak. "As we're all aware, When Hunter's contract expired, Viktor's, by default, did as well. Furthermore, there was no mention of Viktor's employment as a condition in Hunter's new contract." He steepled his fingers, eyes fixed on Margret. "Curious, isn't it, how my son's loyalty wavered the moment his bank account grew?"

The insult hit Margret like a spark, quick and hot. She held Anderson's gaze a little too long before responding. "Agents *and lawyers* have a way of sneaking in details or leaving them out." She paused. "We all know Hunter needs Viktor. The team needs Viktor." She leaned back in her chair, letting the silence work in her favor. "That's why I want to honor the intent of Hunter's original contract."

George reached over, tapping the edge of the folder. "I agree. Especially after last night's loss. Hunter needs Viktor if we want this team in the playoffs again."

Margret turned to Anderson. "Do you have Viktor's contact information? Or better yet, are you still in touch with him? Our resource office is having a hard time locating the man."

Anderson didn't flinch. "You want Viktor? Viktor can be found if he wants to be."

Margret's fingers tightened against the folder. She took a slow breath before speaking, "You know Viktor better than anyone, Anderson. You hired him seventeen years ago to coach Hunter. He guided him through every level of his career. He was family."

The room went still. The weight of Margret's words lingered in the air, too heavy for comfort.

"Oh, for goodness' sake, Anderson, stop pussyfooting around," Sterling said, rising to refill his coffee with a muttered exhale.

Without missing a beat, Anderson's gaze tracked him. His voice turned bitter. "Viktor respects results, not sentiment. He's semi-retired. You'll need more than a paycheck to bring him back."

"Oh, I doubt that," Sterling said, returning to the table. "Money has a way of convincing people." He turned to Margret. "So, how much is it going to cost me to get the Russian? More important, what guarantees do we have that he'll benefit Hunter or the team?"

"No one can guarantee that," George said. "But I can assure you, Viktor is the best bet we have to turn our million-dollar investment around."

Margret's stomach tightened at Sterling's arrogant claim of footing the bill. She steadied herself before turning to Anderson. "What will it take?"

"An offer from someone he respects."

Luke leaned forward, brows furrowed. "I'm confused. You're going to get Hunter to call Viktor?"

Anderson's stare cut through the room like a blade. "No. Not Hunter." He stood, adjusting his suit jacket cuff before turning. "I'll make the call." Without another word, he walked down the hall, leaving a trail of unspoken questions in his wake.

Sterling leaned back in the chair, sipping his coffee. "A washed up goalie coach is the reason you brought me to Portland?" He gestured at the folder like it offended him. "Didn't Justin let him go for a reason? Are we paying for nostalgia now?" His words hung in the air like stale smoke.

George didn't hesitate. "Viktor was forced out when Hunter didn't instantly re-sign," he said, glancing at Margret. "They came as a package deal." His tone was clipped, factual. No sugarcoating. No soft edges. Just the truth laid bare, followed by the brittle silence after Sterling's scoff.

Margret glanced at the clock on the wall. "Where's Stan? He was supposed to be at this meeting."

George scratched his head, the motion slow and sheepish. "Yeah ... about that." He gave a crooked grin. "I just got a text from Stan. He can't make it. Practice ran long, but he's available to FaceTime."

Margret squeezed her eyes closed for half a second, temples throbbed with a dull ache. "I understand how important it is for a coach to be with his team. But..." She tapped a fingernail on the other folder in front of her. "The second matter we need to go over involves Stan's input."

"I would think that both decisions on his goaltending coaches need the head coach's input," Sterling tossed out.

"I agree." Margret turned to Luke. "Get Coach Harrison on the line."

Luke blinked. "You want me to...?"

"Now," Margret said, the word sharp as glass. When Luke flushed crimson, she knew she'd crossed a line. She'd undermined him in front of his father. She'd deal with that later.

Luke pulled out his phone, stabbing each number like it had offended him. A moment later, he held it up, speaker on. The screen flickered to life, revealing Coach Harrison standing on the players' bench, his back to the glass. The empty practice rink loomed behind him, hushed. No skates. No pucks. Just silence waiting to be broken.

"Is now a good time?" George called out.

"Yup," Stan said. "Practice just ended. Everyone's in the locker room."

"Good," Sterling said, leaning forward for a better view of the screen.

Stan squinted at the group. "So, George says there are rumors about bringing Viktor back?"

Everyone turned to George, who shrugged, followed by a guilty smile.

"That's right," Margret said, shaking her head. "Are you good with that?"

"Better than good," Stan said.

"Great news." Sterling smiled. "If we let Cal go, it should balance the budget."

"No can do, cowboy." Stan laughed. "If Viktor's willing to return, I'll shift Cal to handle Lane. Let Volkov stabilize Hunter."

Luke lifted a scone halfway to his mouth, hesitated, then spoke. "Does the league allow the Goshawks to have two goaltending coaches?"

Margret inhaled through clenched teeth. "It's not up to the league. It's a team decision. If you'd do your homework like I keep asking, you'd know that."

Luke glared back. Stuffing the scone in his mouth.

"It's not that different from what we did with the Snowman." Stan's voice came through the phone strong, confident.

Sterling sat back, voice edged with curiosity. "Sounds like Cal's getting a demotion. Will he be okay with that?"

George let out a snort. "If he isn't, that'll take care of your money concerns."

Stan glanced down the tunnel at the sound of approaching voices. "Okay, if that's all you need from me, I gotta go." The screen went dark.

Luke tucked his phone away as Anderson re-entered the room. The lawyer wore a frown as he retook his seat at the table.

"Well?" Margret said, eyes locked on him.

Anderson met her gaze, calm as ever. "He'll consider it."

Chapter 25
Shock Waves

Wednesday, November 8th

The locker room buzzed with the usual morning noise. Velcro ripped, rolls of tape tearing, pads clacking. Axel cranked the volume on the Bluetooth speaker just loud enough to drown out any chance of a peace.

Ryan stepped into the swirl of motion and the scent of caffeinated breath, menthol balm, and fabric softener clinging to practice jerseys still warm from the dryer. He ducked a flying roll of stick tape, tossing his gear bag in front of his stall hard.

"Etan, you lose another bet to Axel, or are you just slow because your new skincare routine is clogging your pores?" Liam Armstrong chirped.

Etan smirked without looking up. "Jealous of my glow?"

"One minute faster again. Three days in a row. You owe me big time, Etan." Axel stood, fully dressed in his practice gear.

"Better save your money, Etan," Ryan said, wrapping his stick's blade. "You're getting slower than Murphy when he's hungover."

"At least I don't use half the roll on my knob like you," Etan fired back. "What is that … extra grip or overcompensation?"

"Bold talk for someone who puts his elbow pads on upside down," Ryan muttered, laughing as Etan checked his pads.

Down two stalls, Dylan Gallagher snorted, nose deep in a jar of smelling salts.

Lane sat slouched in the stall next to Hunter, flipping through his phone. "Hey, anyone know if the Rapids have Dubinsky or Keller in the net tomorrow night?"

Finn, lacing his skates with slow, deliberate movements, didn't look up. "Doesn't matter. You'll be riding pine either way."

Ryan didn't miss Lane tensing as the backup goalie gave Finn a side-eye glare.

Trey leaned against his locker, already in socks and shorts, taping his blade. "Ease up, Finn. Nobody knows the lineup yet."

Daniel Murphy looked up, pulling a sock over his shin guard. "That includes you, Rock Star." His thick voice cut the air as he rummaged through his bag. "Axel, got any clear?"

Axel let out a long sigh, reached behind him, lobbing a half-used roll at Murphy. "Next time, get your own damn tape ... that goes for everyone. Your contracts are all bigger than mine."

"Stop complaining," Etan said, grinning at Axel. "Maybe Santa will drop a dozen rolls of clear in your stocking ... right next to that lump of coal where your soul used to be."

Bursts of laughter broke out until Liam clapped once, barking, "Can we go one morning without complaining about tape?"

"I wish," said Dylan, holding up his frayed roll.

Ryan studied Hunter through the noise. Goalie gear on. Gloved hands resting on his knees. Mask high on his head, staring ... not at anyone, not at anything. Fingers twitching. Something was off.

In the far corner, Coach Harrison leaned into a quiet conversation with his assistant coach at the whiteboard, marker moving through diagrams, practice plans taking shape.

"Turn it down," someone shouted when AC/DC blared the first beat of *Back in Black.* In defiance, Axel turned it higher as the metal entrance door swung open. A whoosh of cold air sliced through the locker room buzz.

Every head turned.

A roll of tape slipped from Etan's fingers, hit the floor with a soft *thump,* bounced once, then spun in a lazy arc across the Goshawks logo.

Axel cut the music. The room fell silent.

In the doorway stood a man built like a brick wall. Six foot two inches of carved muscle wrapped in team colors. Warm-up pants swished slightly with each step. The fleece zip-up hugged broad shoulders, the Goshawks logo stitched over his heart. His white buzz-cut was new ... clean, efficient, like his presence. Same stoic expression, giving nothing away. No greetings. No explanations. Pure purpose.

Viktor Volkov walked in like he'd never left.

In his left hand he held a well-used hockey stick, newly taped. Over his right shoulder hung a skate bag, edges frayed.

Ryan held his breath as Viktor scanned the room, his gaze settling on Lane.

He stopped in front of the young goalie's stall, uttering one sharp, deep command. "Move."

Lane scrambled like he'd been called off the ice for a delayed penalty, slipping into the nearest empty stall, no questions asked.

Viktor sat next to Hunter. Stick propped against the locker, he dropped the skate bag to his side. The zipper hissed open with a slow pull. Taking off his sneakers, he placed them beneath the bench with military precision before retrieving his skates. Sharpened blades gleamed beneath worn leather. He laced them tight; each pull steady and exact.

Hunter sat frozen.

Ryan watched the goalie stare, not at Viktor's face but at his mentor's hands ... the same hands that had shaped his game, molded his instincts.

Viktor turned to Hunter. The slightest upturn at the corner of his mouth. Not quite a smile. Not to anyone else. Yet Ryan knew that to Hunter it was the equivalent of a handshake, a shoulder-clap, a homecoming.

Then came the Russian's voice. Low. Commanding. Familiar. "Get on ice. Rest later." He slapped his stick on Hunter's pads before walking to the door.

Hunter shook his head as if waking from a trance. In one fluid motion, he yanked down his mask, grabbed his stick, rushing after his old goalie coach as though chasing a dream that might vanish. The movements reminded Ryan of Hunter sprinting to his first Goshawks practice.

When the door shut behind them, Lane let out a low whistle. "Who was that?" he asked, phone frozen in his hand.

Ryan smirked. "Hunter's salvation."

The room erupted, voices overlapping at once.

"I thought he was gone for good," Axel said, leaning on his stick next to Ryan.

"Why'd he look like he was about to murder someone?" Trey sat, frowning at the door.

"Because he probably was," Daniel grunted, taping his stick faster. "That was Viktor Volkov, Hunter's personal tormentor."

"Old school," added Steve Sturman, shaking his head. "No one trained harder than under that guy."

"You serious?" Trey asked, glancing from face to face. "That man's a legend."

"He told me to move, and I did." Lane sat upright, eyes wide. "I didn't even think. I just ... moved."

"You blinked and teleported." Etan shrugged. "Viktor has a way of making you do the impossible."

"You should've bowed first," Axel added. "Would've been safer."

Ryan felt the shift in the room as the players continued to chirp. An electric current lingered in the wake of Viktor's arrival. Looking around, he knew he wasn't the only one who felt it.

The bathroom door slammed open. Coach Gray stepped into the locker room, adjusting his waistband.

Ryan paused mid-lace, watching.

Cal's gaze swept over the stalls. His brow furrowed when he saw Lane sitting next to Ryan instead of in his usual spot. His eyes narrowed further when he noticed Hunter's stall empty ... no mask, no pads, no goalie.

"What the..." Cal started.

"Gray," Harrison said, motioning him over. "Need a word." Without waiting for a response, the head coach stepped into his locker room office.

Cal hesitated, then followed. The door slammed shut.

The conversation in the locker room ceased as the players exchanged glances.

From behind the closed door came muffled voices ... sharp, tense, angry.

Moments later, the office door flew open. Cal stormed out, face flushed. Walking past Lane, his voice dropped to guttural tones. "Get on the ice."

Lane scrambled to his stall, pulled on his mask, gloves, grabbing his stick in a single clumsy motion. The rookie bolted out without a word.

Cal stalked after him, fists clenched. The locker-room door banged shut.

Coach Harrison stepped into the locker room; clipboard tucked under one arm. "There's been a change to the goaltending roster," he announced.

"We got that, Coach," Finn called from the far end, smirking.

A ripple of low laughter followed.

Harrison shot Finn a look sharp enough to freeze a slapshot midair. The laughter died in an instant when he raised a hand to quiet the room.

"Viktor Volkov is officially back as Hunter's goaltending coach."

"What about Gray?" Ryan asked, adjusting his practice sweater over his chest protector.

"Coach Gray is assigned to Lane."

Trey started to raise his hand. Ryan swatted it down.

"Is that permanent?" Trey asked.

Harrison didn't answer. His gaze swept the room, lingering just long enough on each player to squelch any follow-ups. "Everyone on the ice in five."

Nobody lingered. Gear slammed into place. Pads thudded. Helmet straps snapped. Sticks clattered. The room crackled with nervous energy.

"Move it, divas," Daniel barked at Etan and Axel, tugging on his gloves.

"Someone grab popcorn," Etan muttered.

The banter resumed, lighter now, laced with excitement and curiosity.

Ryan yanked the door open to the tunnel, leading the charge.

On the ice, Coach Gray barked orders at Lane, who shuffled into position at one net.

In the other net, Hunter crouched, laser focused. Viktor skated the blue line, a puck waltzing on the tape of his stick.

Ryan's grin widened as he skated to their net, his gaze locked on the pair deep in a well-rehearsed zone.

Chapter 26
Power Play

Thursday, November 9th
Home Game: Goshawks vs Buffalo Rapids

Margret hesitated a moment before entering through the side door of the Goshawks' locker room. The crisp air from the hallway gave way to the lingering manly stench inside the team's changing area. She glanced at the wall clock. Pregame warmup was about to end. She hoped it would give her enough time to get in and out before the players returned to the ice for tonight's rematch against the Buffalo Rapids.

"Hey, Margret," Assistant Coach Scott said, ushering her to the open door of the coach's office. "Stan's on his way."

"Where's your cowboy?" George Stonebridge leaned halfway out of the head coach's cramped room, one hand on the doorframe, the other spinning a lanyard badge between two fingers.

"Already in the VIP suite." She pushed past, causing him to step back. "Sterling also flew in for tonight's game."

The sound of players coming off the ice ebbed and flowed preceding Stan Harrison's arrival. The head coach nodded to Margret, shutting the door. The windowless room reeked of stale coffee, dry-erase marker, and the familiar tang of pregame anxiety. Overhead fluorescents flickered, casting a pale light across a desk cluttered with rosters and play notes.

He was about to sink into his wooden rolling chair when the office door shot open. Cal Gray pushed into the room. Papers scattered on the floor as he slammed palms on Stan's desk. He bent low, voice pitched a little too high. "We've put in the hours. I've earned that net for Lane. But it's clear now ... I've only been a placeholder until Volkov returned."

Margret stepped to one side as George moved around her. The GM walked with a slow shuffle. Leaning against the filing cabinet near the door as if he had all the time in the world.

Stan settled behind his desk, legs spread wide, posture slouched, a wad of gum rolling in his cheek like a metronome. He glanced at Margret, tilting his chin to the lone chair across from him.

The metal creaked as she sat, hands folded in her lap, one ankle crossed over the other.

Cal kept his back turned to her. He straightened, fists now clenched at his sides. "You're all acting like that Russian didn't stroll in yesterday, shoving me aside. You blindsided me." He slammed a fist on the desk. "If Lane isn't starting tonight, I walk. If there's a loophole in the kid's contract, I'm taking him with me."

For a split second, no one breathed.

George's long, low sigh, like steam easing from a release valve, broke the silence. "You're not coaching a farm team, Cal." His words came out clipped. "Your contract isn't bonded to Lane like Viktor's was to Hunter."

"Be reasonable, Cal. It's a lateral move, not a demotion. Your paycheck's the same." A ping rang through the room as Stan spat his gum into the wastebasket. He unwrapped two more pieces, shoving them into his mouth.

Cal's nostrils flared. The overhead light caught the vein pulsing in his temple.

Margret uncrossed her ankles, slow and deliberate. The fold-out chair's frame shifted as she stood. Clearing her throat, she stepped forward just enough to remind Cal she was the most important presence in the room. "We don't need this kind of off-ice drama." Her voice dropped a notch, quiet, cold. "Especially not before puck drop."

Cal crossed his arms like concrete beams, jaw set. He turned, staring her down, lips pressed in a flat line ... a silent scream of *You don't get to tell me how to run a bench.*

The silence smoldered.

Margret took another step forward, her designer perfume threaded through the stale office air. "I asked for calm," she said. This time her words snapped like a twig. "What I'm getting is ego."

Cal's brows lifted.

She didn't stop. "You want to walk, Cal? Walk. But don't think for one second you're taking Lane with you. Did you forget the words on his warm-up sweater ... *Property of Goshawks.*"

Stan's gum-chewing slowed. George glanced up but remained quiet. The silence thickened ... awkward and charged, like the breath an instant before a slap.

Scott knocked on the door, creaking it open. "Coach. Ref's here for any lineup changes."

Margret's eyes flicked from Stan to Cal. They all knew time was bleeding out.

Stan dragged a hand over his shiny scalp, palm squeaking against the sheen of his skin. Grabbing a notepad, he scribbled a name handing the paper to Scott. "Wilson starts."

The words hit the room like a puck off the crossbar.

Cal's slow, smug smirk said volumes.

Margret stepped even closer. She stood eye-level with Cal. Slender, not slight, her presence cut through the room like a cold front off the bay. She met his stare head-on. Heat simmered behind her glare held just beneath the surface. "If you ever pull this crap again ... especially before a game ... you can pack your skates and not let the door hit you in the ass on your way out."

Cal's mouth tightened. His Adam's apple shifted in a tense swallow. His stance widened as if anchoring for another verbal blow.

Stan's gum paused mid-chomp. George looked at Margret like she'd fired a glass shattering slapshot. The room a pressure keg about to blow.

Margret leaned closer. "Am I clear?"

Cal's nostrils flared. Shoulders tight, jaw locked, temples pulsing, he snarled the words through clenched teeth. "Crystal."

"Good." Margret tugged at the hem of her blue blazer. Her head ached. Pulse buzzed in her ears like a runaway freight train. It took all her willpower to lift her chin, forcing her eyes to soften, her lips to curl upward. She turned to George, tapping a finger on his chest. "Hunter's parents are in the Goshawks' suite tonight. *You* get to explain to them why their son won't be in the net."

Game. On.

Chapter 27
Weight of the Net

Thursday, November 9th
Home Game: Goshawks vs Buffalo Rapids

Sweat and swagger followed the Goshawks players into their locker room after pregame warmup. Ryan stepped in last, lingering in the doorway. He shook his head at Trey as he cut in front of Axel to reach the Bluetooth speaker. A quick tap changed the track to Taylor Swift, the song a little too bright, a little too girlie. Trey lifted his stick like a microphone, belting the chorus ... wrong notes, wrong words, full commitment.

Finn peeled out of his wet sweater, lobbing it at Trey's head. The locker room burst into applause as it hit its target. Without missing a beat, Trey tossed it back, taking a low, exaggerated bow.

Ryan made his way to his stall, smiling at the familiar pregame nerves masked in locker room disruption. It was the right kind of chaos ... everyone loose but on their game. *A good omen*, he thought, until he looked across the room at Lane.

The backup goalie sat hunched, mask by his side. Damp curls clung to his forehead. His fingers worked the leg pad straps. Tighten. Loosen. Tighten again. No reason for it. No purpose. Just a repetitive motion, as if he were trying to keep something inside that yearned to escape.

Ryan frowned. He couldn't recall the last time the young goalie came off pregame ice without a grin, humming a country tune under his breath, tossing chirps like beads from a Mardi Gras float. Tonight? Not a single word. Not a smile. The kid wasn't just fidgeting. He was unraveling.

The bench creaked as Ryan pulled off his chest protector and compression shirt. His gaze drifted back to Lane. He'd looked fine during morning skate, no hint of injury. He'd been quieter than normal, but no outward signs of distress. Now he sat tight, folded in on himself. Goalies had their rituals. Ryan respected that. Over his time as a pro, he'd seen all kinds of quirks. This was different.

Lane's movements came in sharp, uneven bursts. A slight shiver of his shoulders. It wasn't ill-fitting gear causing the restless body shifts ... it was as if his skin didn't fit right.

Ryan reached for his stick, gave the shaft a casual spin between his palms, biding his time. He'd seen this before when kids came up from the farm team. Pressure could unnerve a young player faster than taking a slapshot to the throat. Tonight, Lane appeared to be gasping for air. He leaned back, studying closer. The goalie tugged at the collar of his sweater, as if being strangled. The leg pad strap slipped loose again. Ryan lost count how many times they'd come undone.

He considered alerting a coach, as the starting goalie hadn't been officially announced. His gaze moved to the far corner. Scott stood near the coach's closed office door, speaking with Hunter's goaltending coach in low tones. Viktor's frown was expected. Scott's matched one ... not so much. The usual calm the assistant coach always carried before a game was missing.

Viktor broke away from the conversation, his posture ramrod straight as he crossed the room, stepping with care around the team logo. He paused in front of Hunter's stall, grasping his shoulder. "Keep your head clear tonight, no matter what," he said, both nodded before Viktor walked out of the room without a backward glance.

When the door closed, Ryan turned his attention to Hunter. His friend sat statue-still, eyes locked on the floor like the game had already started in his head. *Yeah, not going to interrupt that.*

Instead, he wandered over to Lane's stall. The young goalie flinched the moment he neared. Subtle, but telling. The kid kept his eyes low, hands fiddling with his leg pad buckle like it needed fine-tuning for the seventh time in five minutes.

Ryan leaned against the locker's edge. "You good?" he asked, soft enough to stay between them.

Lane didn't answer straight away. His gaze darted round the room, then back to his lap as he inhaled, sharp and uneven. "Not that great." The words emerged low, almost a whisper.

Ryan's brows ticked upward. "Yeah?" He leaned closer. "Why're you wound tight? There's a good chance you'll be riding the bench tonight. So, what's up?"

Lane brushed a lock of damp hair out of his eyes. "I dunno," he said, side-eyeing the closed coach's office door. "Feels like I'm getting caught in the middle."

Ryan stayed quiet.

"I've never seen Coach Gray like this before." The words flooded out. "Back when I played with the Eyas, he was strict, yeah, but fair. He always had my back.

Now..." His voice thinned. "It's like he needs me to want the net so bad I'd fight Hunter for it."

A long harrumph escaped Ryan's lips.

Lane glanced up, staring into Ryan's eyes. "I let one goal in during morning skate. Just one. He lost it. Said I was playing soft ... like I wanted to stay backup."

Ryan turned as Coach Harrison's office door opened. Three people emerged, but Gray was the only one who held his attention. Lane's goalie coach leaned against the wall wearing a smirk; arms folded, glaring like a general surveying his troops.

Lane glanced over, dropping his voice lower. "When I told him I was fine backing up Hunter, Gray flipped out. Said I was wasting my shot. That he'd been wrong about me. I didn't have the skill or the mindset to guard the net for a pro team like the Goshawks."

Ryan glared into Lane's eyes, seeing something a player never wants to in their goalie ... *doubt*. "No one believes that." Ryan hoped his words struck home.

Lane paused, fingers tracing the goshawk in flight painted on his mask. "I used to love game nights," he mumbled. "Now I'm afraid of messing up. Like Gray is weighing everything I do. If I fall short, it's over ... I'll be sent down to the farm team."

Ryan wanted to crosscheck Gray so hard he'd have to be carried out of the locker room on a stretcher. Instead, he squeezed Lane's shoulder. "Listen to me. You didn't make this roster by accident. You've earned every minute you've spent in the net."

"I don't feel like I belong up here, Cap."

"You belong," Ryan said, voice steel. "Don't let one man's ego rewrite what you know to be true."

Lane blinked fast. He reached up, fist pumping Ryan. "Thanks Cap. It means a lot that you believe in me."

Ryan glanced over to the next stall. Hunter still sat like a stone, eyes glazed, focused. He was in the zone, constructing the ice wall he built before every game. Ryan pushed off the locker. "You play you," he said, tapping Lane's leg pad with the blade of his stick.

As he returned to his stall, the office door opened again. Harrison stepped out, his expression carved tight with whatever went down behind the closed door. The coach crossed the room; a folded sheet pinched between his fingers. Ryan caught the faint warmth of the paper as Harrison slipped it into his hand. "Tonight's top line." Quiet. Final. Harrison left the room without waiting for a response.

Ryan scanned the list as he walked to the head of the room. "Another grudge rematch tonight, boys."

A hush fell. Etan stopped mid-swig of Gatorade. Finn ripped the cloth tape from the knob of his stick with a snap. Axel muted the music.

Ryan held the paper like it was gospel. A loud group clap followed each name called. "Eklund, Moss, O'Connell, Berger, and myself."

Ryan let the moment hold for a beat before lowering the paper. His gaze darted between the two goalies. "And in net tonight…" He paused, letting the quiet settle. "Making his return against the Buffalo Rapids … Lane Wilson."

Silence.

Lane's body jerked as Hunter clapped hard. The team followed with a surge of stomps and hoots.

Coach Gray joined in. His clap slow. Loud. Stretched. To Ryan, it looked like he'd cashed in a bet. The clap was not a celebration. It was a reminder of who held the net. His gut told him Gray had made this game personal. He hoped he was wrong.

Chapter 28
Sharing the Paint

Thursday, November 9th
Home Game: Goshawks vs Buffalo Rapids

The camera swept over the packed arena, catching fans on their feet, waving towels above their heads, signs rising and dipping through the crowd. The lights lowered as the music muted during the announcement of both teams' starters.

A warm, practiced voice rolled through the broadcast speakers. "Welcome back to Goshawks hockey, folks. I'm Tom Hughes, joined tonight by John 'The Gatekeeper' Hamilton. Big one here in Portland, a rematch between your Goshawks and the Buffalo Rapids."

A hush fell in the arena like a dial clicked off the crowd's energy. Then the murmurs rose with scattered jeers. From one corner, a chant started rolling through the stands like a forest fire.

"Ice Wall! Ice Wall! Ice Wall!"

"Fans are not happy about the starting goalie announcement," John added.

"Not what they were expecting, for sure. Lane Wilson in goal for Portland. The fans like him, but he's not the one they expected to see guarding the net tonight."

John leaned forward in the booth, headset pressed tight against his ear. "This building's not subtle. They love Griffin. We all expected him between the pipes tonight," he said, voice dry. "That's gotta shake the rookie."

Tom's fingers drummed on the edge of his clipboard as he glanced at the overhead monitor. "You have to wonder what's going through Wilson's head. Last time he faced Buffalo, he shut down the Rapids with a three-to-one win. But that was in Buffalo's barn."

John gave a low laugh, short and knowing. "No pressure tonight."

The camera cut to the Goshawks bench. Viktor stood near his goalie, hands clasped behind his back, gaze fixed on the ice.

Tom turned to John. "There's Viktor Volkov, Hunter's long-time goaltending coach, once more back on the bench."

"I watched him earlier working with Hunter during the morning skate," John said, flipping through his notes. "And I tell you, Tom, Hunter's spark was back. He was dialed in, focused."

"The fact that Harrison's not starting him," Tom said, voice low and even, "tells me one thing ... this is a test to see if Lane sinks or swims."

John leaned back in his chair, the leather creaking under his weight. A deep laugh slipped out. "He's going to need a lifejacket if he's going to survive the Rapids' crush."

First Period

"Puck's down," Tom said, voice tight with anticipation. "First period underway here in Portland."

Ryan skated straight into Buffalo's big defenseman, the hit echoing through his gear. His shoulder burned, but he held his ground, pinning the Rapids player against the glass behind the net. The boards shuddered. He wanted that hit to send a message to his team ... protect the crease, protect Lane.

"Puck's loose," Trey cried out as he battled near the crease.

Ryan pivoted, stick sweeping for control as the puck ricocheted off Axel's skate. Buffalo's captain jammed it between Lane's pads.

Goal! Rapids—Jackson

The crowd's reaction fractured between groans and boos; a wave of frustration rolled through the stands.

"That one trickled through the five-hole," John said, voice grim. "I know Wilson wants it back."

"One to nothing, Rapids. Not the start the Goshawks were hoping for," Tom added.

Ryan hunched low near the blue line, stick poised, waiting for Trey to win the draw. The puck dropped. Ryan read the bounce, angling at Etan, streaking up the wing.

"Watch number fifty-eight," John said.

Etan caught Ryan's pass clean on his tape, slipped around a Rapids forward with a smooth toe drag. He snapped a shot that rattled the mesh as the red light flared behind the net.

Goal! Goshawks—Eklund

"What a snip," Tom shouted. "Just like that, the Goshawks respond."

"Tie game," John said, grinning. "That's what you call a counterpunch."

A line change later, the whistle blew. Armstrong sent to the box for interference.

"Penalty kill time," Tom said as the Rapids set up their power play.

Ryan growled as the ref waved Trey out of the faceoff for jumping early. Murphy stepped in, drew the puck backwards. Trey caught it in stride, driving hard up center ice.

"Look at Moss breaking up ice," Tom said. "For a young player, he's got great instincts."

"Chance for a shorty," John added, his voice lifting.

Goal! Goshawks—Moss

"Backhand, upstairs." Tom shouted.

"What a read by Trey Moss," John barked.

"That's the flash he was drafted for," Tom said. "Puts the Goshawks up by one."

Two line changes later, Eddie Bennett battled in front of the Goshawks' crease with Liam Armstrong, both fighting to clear the slot. The puck skittered loose near the post. A Rapids forward lunged, slipping it between Lane's skate and the pipe.

Goal! Rapids—Karlsson

Ryan cursed under his breath when Lane slammed the post so hard he thought the goalie's stick cracked.

"Tie game again. Two-to-two." Tom shook his head. "Pressure's back on."

Hits came harder. Elbows up. Sticks chopped. Bodies slammed into boards, glass rattling with every collision. The Rapids swarmed. Ryan dove after a hard shot, stopping it just short. Lane kicked out a rebound, but the Rapids forward was waiting again, rifling it through the five-hole.

Goal! Rapids—Karlsson

"Third goal for the Rapids," Tom said, voice tight. "That one should've been covered."

John exhaled, tone cutting. "Kid can't seem to keep his knees closed tonight."

Seconds later, the Rapids captain tore down the ice. Lane sprawled, glove reaching, but the puck tipped off the top, bouncing into the net.

Goal! Rapids—Jackson

"Four-to-two. Not a great first period for the Goshawks."

The building rumbled with discontent. Chants rose again, not against the Goshawks but for the goalie sitting silent at the far end of the bench.

"Ice Wall! Ice Wall! Ice Wall!"

On the bench, Ryan stared at Harrison. The coach stood red-faced, barking into Cal Gray's ear. The goaltending coach snapped back, jabbing a finger at the net.

"Bench is boiling," John said. "But not Griffin."

"Ball cap pulled low. Not even blinking," Tom added. "He's locked in, waiting for the call."

The buzzer blared to end the first period. Players filed off the ice into the tunnel, shoulders sagging, jerseys clinging with sweat.

Tom exhaled into his mic. "Harrison's got a big decision to make. Lane Wilson's given up four. Does he let him ride it out, or does the Ice Wall return?"

John leaned forward, elbows on the desk, eyes fixed on the ice. "Portland fans won't accept anything less than Griffin. But as we know that choice isn't theirs."

Second Period

"Welcome back, folks." Tom glanced at John. "As a former goalie, how surprised are you that Lane's still between the pipes?"

"Double-edged. The rookie's getting another chance." John shook his head. "Not sure that's a good thing. I remember being in a similar spot when I started out. Glad I'm in the booth instead of on the ice tonight."

Ryan skated to Lane, tapping his stick against the goalie's pads. "Reset. You've got this."

For the next ten minutes, Lane held the line, turning away clean shot after clean shot. Then the Rapids crashed the crease hard. Bodies piled in the blue paint, sticks clattering, skates slicing. The puck slipped under Lane's right pad, inching across the goal line.

Goal! Rapids—Brett

"From here, that sure looked like goalie interference," John said.

"Close. Real close," Tom replied. "Not sure why Harrison isn't challenging."

The camera cut to the Goshawks bench. Coach Harrison leaned in, slapping Hunter's shoulder.

Without a word, Hunter rose, traded his ball cap for his mask, adjusted his glove and blocker, then gripped his stick. He skated off the bench, pushing off the boards as he glided onto the ice.

The crowd stirred, a ripple of noise rolling through the lower bowl.

Lane skated to the bench; mask high, hair plastered to his forehead. Head down as he passed Hunter. His stick slammed against the boards as he entered the bench and yanked off his mask. The goalie chair creaked as he dropped onto it. His gaze stayed locked on the ice.

The chants in the arena swelled. "Ice Wall! Ice Wall!"

Ryan gave Hunter a wide berth on the ice as the goalie slid into the crease, tapped each post, and stretched.

The crowd had their goalie. The Goshawks had their chance. The Rapids had a problem.

Ryan felt the shift the instant the faceoff puck hit the ice. Hunter's calm spread down the line, steadying the rhythm of every pass, every block. Ryan intercepted a dump-in, reversed the puck behind the net, feeding it up the boards to Etan.

The puck dropped in the final five minutes of the period. The Goshawks continued to be centered under Hunter, who guarded the crease like sacred ground.

"Griffin hasn't missed a beat," Tom said, voice crisp with surprise. "You'd never know he came in cold. Look at that positioning. He's tight to the post, locked in. That's the Ice Wall we're used to."

John let out a low whistle. "This isn't just solid goaltending. He's making a statement."

Etan ripped a one-timer from the top of the circle, clean and ruthless, beating the Rapids goalie high on the blocker side.

Goal! Goshawks—Eklund

The next shift, Eddie Bennett buried a rebound, jamming the loose puck into the net.

Goal! Goshawks—Bennett

On the bench, Ryan glove-tapped Eddie, then turned to Lane with a grin. He nudged the goalie on the shoulder. Lane shifted away until his bulky pads hung half off the chair.

As the clock ticked down, Trey took control of the puck, cutting through open ice before unleashing a laser. The red light flared as the crowd erupted.

Goal! Goshawks—Moss

"Unbelievable. They're clawing their way back!" Tom shouted from the booth. "You can feel the building shake."

"Hunter's the anchor," John said. "Not a single dent in the Goshawks' defense since he skated onto the ice. It's like he slammed the Rapids door shut and tossed the key into the bay."

Tom exhaled. "This push changes everything, but only if they hold it. The third will tell us whether the Goshawks can keep that fire burning."

Third Period

The third opened with tension thick as penalties piled up … high sticking, roughing, interference, even a questionable call on Trey for slashing. Through it all, Hunter stood strong in the net. Pad saves. Glove snags. Stick flat. Nothing slipped past him.

Midway through the period, chaos erupted in front of Buffalo's crease. A wild redirect bounced off a Rapids D-man's skate. Liam was there to cash in on the mistake.

Goal! Goshawks—Armstrong

"That puts them ahead by one," Tom shouted. "And guess who hasn't flinched? Griffin closed his net like a vault door."

With under a minute to play, the Rapids pulled their goalie. The crowd rose, a collective breath hanging above the ice.

The puck dumped deep. Ryan took chase, beating the Rapids' captain, sliding the puck into the empty net.

Goal! Goshawks—Ryan Mitchell

The horn blasted. The fan's cheered. Final score, seven to five.

Ryan was the first to reach Hunter, lifting the goalie off his skates in a bear hug. Skating back to the tunnel, he tapped Lane on the pads as the young goalie joined the back of the appreciation line.

Chapter 29
Collision Course

Thursday, November 16th

Cardboard towers lined the walls like barricades ... half-split, scribbled on, none of them useful. Ryan stood with one shoe on in the middle of his cluttered living room, yanking open a box labeled *Linens* with a grunt.

"Why didn't you find your shoes earlier?" Sage asked, sidestepping a box marked *Bathroom?* ... the question mark scribbled big and bold.

Ryan didn't bother looking up. "Because I didn't need them earlier."

"Pretty sure you did," Hunter called from the kitchen, elbow-deep in packing paper. He wore a tux like he was born in it ... bow tie crisp, cuffs gleaming. "Also, why haven't you unpacked yet? You've been here a month."

"When I'm home," Ryan muttered, pushing another box aside, "I sleep."

Hunter gave a mock-nod of understanding. "Fair."

"Here it is," Hunter called a beat later, tugging a lone black dress shoe from beneath a mound of tangled cords. "Buried next to your toaster. Obviously."

Ryan took it with a sheepish smile. "Thanks." He wobbled, putting on the shoe, like a man trying to perform surgery while standing on a skateboard.

Sage leaned on the kitchen counter. The lights cast a gentle shine over her sleeveless midnight-dark velvet gown. "You know," she said, "most people prepare for charity balls ahead of time."

"Yeah?" Ryan stood, smoothing his tux jacket. "And miss out on all this fun?" He motioned to the clutter of opened boxes.

Hunter grinned. "Better question, how in the world did you get Jill to agree to this?"

Sage tilted her head. "Doesn't she hate anything remotely related to hockey?"

Ryan shrugged, twisting the knot of his bow tie. "It's not really a hockey event. It's a charity thing. Fancy food, live music, boring speeches."

"And you," Hunter added.

Ryan spread his arms wide. "Exactly. How could she resist this?"

A voice drifted from the open doorway. "How indeed."

Ryan turned, forgetting how to breathe.

Jill stood framed in the hall light, a vision in royal blue. Her strapless silk gown shimmered like a lake under moonlight, hugging her in a way that made time stutter. She spun slowly. The back of the dress dipped low, four delicate straps crisscrossing her bare skin. Her bob, swept to one side, glinted with a single diamond barrette. When she turned to face Ryan, her eyes caught the light ... locked on his.

"Do I pass the Goshawks dress code?" she asked.

Ryan let out a low whistle. "No," he said, a slow grin spreading. "You surpass it."

Sage stepped forward, offering a quick hug. "You're stunning."

Jill smiled. "Right back at you. You look incredible."

Hunter checked his phone, giving a nod to the door. "Time to go. Limo's waiting."

Ryan stood staring ... her presence rewired his heartbeat, freezing him in place.

The hotel ballroom pulsed with soft light and curated elegance ... silver drapes mixed with blue uplighting cast fractured halos across the glossy black floor. The Goshawks' logo raised above the crowd, regal but subdued.

Ryan's shoulder twitched as he stepped inside. The last time they'd gathered here, Justin Caldwell had collapsed beside the podium. Now his ghost mingled with tuxedos and laughter.

Hunter drifted a step ahead, Sage on his arm. Her presence commanded the space without effort ... no glitter, no sequins, only clean lines and quiet power. Ryan noted the heads turning. Sage didn't.

Jill moved beside him, poised, eyes sweeping the crowd like she belonged.

From a table by the dance floor, Etan and Axel raised their glasses and waved.

"Looks like the boys beat us here again," Ryan said.

"Should I be worried?" Jill asked, with the hint of a smile tugging at her lips.

"Very." Ryan grinned as he guided her to their table.

Hunter pulled out Sage's chair.

"About time you got here," Etan said, giving Sage a fist bump as she sat down.

Jill arched a brow. "You going to make me guess who those two are?"

Hunter grinned. "Last year's star rookies. Keep an eye on them. They'll either win you over or drive you insane."

"Maybe both," Ryan muttered. He turned to Jill. "You want a drink?"

"Being surrounded by hockey players, I think I might need more than one."

As they walked to the bar, Ryan's hand skimmed across Jill's lower back. Her bare skin, silk soft and warm under his fingers.

Hunter placed his order. "A local pale ale and two scotches, neat."

Ryan gave him a nod of thanks as he looked at Jill.

"I'll take a Cosmo."

Ryan leaned an elbow on the bar's polished wood, glancing back at their table. Sage sat close to Etan, phone in hand, most likely sharing clips from their last two away games ... highlights of Hunter's winning streak. He did a double take when Patty walked in, settling between Etan and Axel. Her curls bounced, hands in motion, animated as always. Next to Patty, Axel looked equal parts amused and bewildered.

He paused when he noticed a figure turned sideways. She wore a sultry strapless burgundy dress, her hair in an elegant upsweep. "Who invited her?" Ryan clenched his jaw so tight he thought he might crack a molar.

"Her, who?" Hunter asked, brows knitted.

"Jessica."

Jill's Cosmo arrived, vibrant pink, served in a chilled martini glass. Her mouth curved, amusement flickering in her eyes. "Tell me this isn't going to be one of those nights," she said before taking a sip.

Ryan didn't answer.

As they walked back to the table, He hesitated, a familiar heaviness pressing against his chest at the drama he knew was waiting. Without thinking, he reached for Jill's hand. Her fingers tightened around his, steady and grounding.

He stopped short as they reached the table; only two seats remained empty. Of course, one had to be next to his former South Dakota cowgirl.

Jessica's gaze drifted over the ballroom like she hadn't clocked their approach. But her posture told a different story ... upright, guarded, chin tipped.

Ryan's body tightened, tension crawling up his spine.

"Didn't see that coming," Hunter whispered to Ryan.

Ryan didn't either. And now there was no option but to take their seats. Jill sat next to Hunter. Ryan took the only remaining chair.

Jessica gave Hunter a polite nod, Jill a once-over. Then her gaze snapped to Ryan, striking like a slap. She smiled, slow and knowing. The same smile that used to undo him. The one he now recognized for what it was ... a snare.

"Small world," she said through pursed lips.

"What are you doing here?" The words slipped out before Ryan could stop them.

Jill smacked his arm. "Rude much?"

Ryan's mouth went dry as he looked for an escape route that didn't exist.

Jill leaned closer. "Are you going to introduce me to your charming tablemates, or am I supposed to guess?"

Instead of answering, Ryan took a slow sip of his scotch.

Sage smiled, using her beer bottle as a microphone. Clearing her throat like a seasoned play-by-play announcer cutting through dead air, she began. "And now ... tonight's starting lineup," she said, deepening her voice. "Leading us off, first-line forward for your Portland, Maine Goshawks and last season's breakout star ... Etan Eklund."

Etan stood, taking a bow before Patty pulled him back into his chair.

Sage didn't miss a beat. "Next to him, visiting all the way from Brookings, South Dakota, my best friend and the reason none of us have cavities ... dental assistant Patty Holt."

Patty offered Jill a warm smile, lifting her beer bottle in greeting.

"The best man protecting my man ... well, besides Ryan, obviously ... is last season's Rookie of the Year ... Axel Berger."

Axel gave a stiff nod, saying something under his breath to Patty, whose response was a gentle nudge.

Sage took a breath, turning to the last woman at the table. "Next to Axel is another of my closest friends, also from Brookings. She's a champion barrel racer who, I know for a fact, feels more comfortable in cowboy boots than heels ... Jessica Blake."

Jessica smiled, cold and wide. "Charmed."

Sage turned her attention to Jill. "And this," she said with deliberate warmth, "is Ryan and Hunter's next-door neighbor, the brilliant computer whisperer, the lovely Jill..." She paused. "Wait, I don't know your last name."

Jill flashed a megawatt smile. "Markham. Jill Markham. Nice to meet you all."

When the table broke into conversational chatter, Hunter leaned into Sage. "Did you know Jessica would be here?"

Ryan scowled at Sage, waiting for her answer.

She took a long sip of her beer, smiled at Jessica, shaking her head once. "Nope," she said with a shrug.

He doubted her denial. When his gaze met Jessica's, a shiver slid through him ... caught once again in her cool, calculating pull he knew too well.

Jill nudged Ryan. "What's going on?"

He forced a smile. "I'll tell you later."

Conversation rose with the music as the ballroom came alive. Tuxedos shimmered under the chandeliers. Dresses moved like whispers across the floor. Waiters glided between tables with trays of miniature crab cakes and bacon-wrapped scallops. Someone on stage tuned a bass guitar.

Ryan took a sip of his scotch, hoping to ease the pressure building behind his eyes. Jill laughed with Sage and Hunter, comfortable and effortless, like charity balls were something she attended all the time. *Who knew? Maybe she did.*

Then the ballroom's double doors opened with a burst of excitement. Margret swept in, her sapphire silk gown swishing with each step. Her hair pinned in a dramatic twist, earrings catching the chandelier's light sent tiny stars shimmering around her.

Luke followed, wearing a tux and confidence. A beat behind them came Stan Harrison with his wife, followed by George Stonebridge and his plus-one. The head coach and GM looked like they'd been pulled from a press conference.

The last pair to enter sent a collective murmur through the room. Sterling Wheatfield strolled in with a woman half his age, blonde, polished, clinging to his arm like an expensive accessory.

Luke stopped at Ryan's table. "Evening," he said, giving Sage's shoulder a squeeze. "Sterling thought it'd be a nice surprise to fly these two here for the event." He nodded at Jessica and Patty, a faint smile tugging his lips. Lowering his voice, he added, "He didn't tell me until this morning."

"Let your father know I appreciate his gesture." Sage patted Luke's hand.

Margret stepped in. "We'll be working the bar tonight."

Luke raised his voice like a bartender on call. "Don't forget to tip your bartenders." Laughter rippled around the table, punctuated by a gigglesnort from Patty.

"Let's go, cowboy. Your fans await." Margret caught his sleeve, tugging him into the flow of the crowd.

"The perks of working for a Goshawks' owner." Jessica smiled, tipping her beer bottle at Ryan.

Ryan's mouth opened, then shut.

Beside him, Jill's gaze slid from Axel to Jessica, then back to Ryan. Her eyes narrowed as if tracking an error code unraveling across a screen.

Ryan swallowed hard.

Before the silence could sprawl into something dangerous, a man in a gray tuxedo stepped onto the stage in front of the band.

"Ladies and gentlemen, welcome!" The master of ceremony's microphone squealed through the speakers before evening out. "Thank you for joining us for the second annual Stick It to Cancer Gala."

The sound of applause filled the room.

"As many of you know, the foundation was created in memory of former Goshawks defenseman Brad Morrow, who lost his battle with pancreatic cancer three years ago. Tonight's proceeds will support research grants and family assistance programs."

Another round of applause.

"We've got a fantastic silent auction set up along the east side of the room. Everything from autographed jerseys to an all-exclusive away game weekend. And a big surprise this year, tickets to dance with your favorite player. And yes, the rumors are true ... there's a custom Goshawks goalie mask in the mix, signed by our very own Hunter Griffin."

Chairs shifted as everyone looked at Hunter, who stood, waved, and blushed as he reclaimed his seat. Sage covered her mouth, muffling a laugh.

"And remember tonight, all bar tips go to the cause. So, when Margret VanAlen and Luke Wheatfield pour your next drink, don't forget, they work for tips now."

Laughter rippled around the room.

Ryan didn't join in the laughter. His shoulders stiffened, caught between Jill's perfume and Jessica's stare. He felt like a player in the penalty box, close enough to watch the play unravel but too far to defend it.

Applause spread through the room as the emcee stepped away from the mic. Behind him, the band tuned up, guitars plugging in, sticks tapping snare rims. Candles flickered across round tables dressed in blue and silver. The buffet line stretched along the far wall.

Ryan tipped back his scotch. "I need another drink." He looked at Jill.

"I'm good, thanks," she said.

"I could use a refill." Jessica took a long swig from her bottle.

Ryan ignored her.

Behind the bar's counter, Luke stood, tux jacket off, sleeves rolled, pouring two pints for an older couple requesting a photo. He caught sight of Ryan. "Hey, big guy," Luke said, slapping a towel over his shoulder. "What'll it be? Scotch again? Or are we ordering for two?"

Ryan blinked. "Two?"

Luke pointed over Ryan's shoulder.

Jessica stood way too close. Her perfume crept in, sticky sweet, impossible to ignore.

"I'm not..." Ryan started, then cut himself off. He glared at Luke before turning around. "Why are you here? Why are you following me?"

Jessica's hands went to her hips. "I was invited. Patty too. I've got just as much right to be here with my friends as you do."

Ryan exhaled, fingers digging into his palms.

Jessica's voice dipped, low and dangerous. "So, who's your date?"

"Here's your drinks." Luke set two glasses on the counter, a Macallan and a Cosmos. "I noticed your date's drink on the table."

"I've missed you," Jessica purred, her lips brushing Ryan's ear.

"Not interested."

"Don't be like that."

"My date's drink is getting warm."

Jessica grabbed the Cosmos, tilted her head, emptying the glass in one swallow. "There," she said, setting the empty glass back on the bar. "Guess you don't have to worry about that anymore." She plucked the garnish, sliding the single cranberry from the skewer between her lips.

Ryan stared at her in disbelief. "Remind me why we were an item, let alone friends?"

She stepped forward, fingernails tracing a line down his lapel. "Want to dance?"

Before he could react, a soft voice cut through the music. "Ryan," Jill said from behind him, her hand slipping into his, "they're playing our song."

Ryan downed his scotch, setting the empty glass on the bar as he allowed Jill to lead him onto the dance floor. The band played a slow song, one demanding closeness rather than perfection.

Jill's head rested against his shoulder. She moved with practiced ease, guiding the first few steps until he matched her rhythm. "I thought you needed saving."

Ryan inhaled her familiar scent. "You can come to my rescue anytime," he whispered in her ear, letting the rest of the world fade.

The band started another slow tune as the overhead lights dimmed. String lights twinkled around the stage as couples drifted onto the dance floor.

Next to him, Etan and Patty swayed in time to the music. The folds of Patty's royal blue ballgown crunched.

"She's got a stack of tickets stuffed in her pocket," Jill whispered, laughing under her breath. "Looks like she spent a paycheck on Etan."

Ryan snorted. "I'll bet she's got an equal stack saved for Axel."

Right on cue, Axel stood, fanning a ridiculous bundle of dance tickets like a winning poker hand.

Etan gave him a narrow-eyed glare. "You're not allowed to buy tickets to dance with Patty."

Unbothered, Axel pulled a ticket from the bunch, handing it to Patty. "Didn't. I'm gifting her tickets to dance with me," he said, his German accent growing thick. He tapped Etan's shoulder, cutting in as he twirled her into the next dance with exaggerated flair.

"Gotta love those guys," Ryan said, pulling Jill close.

Over her shoulder, he noticed Jessica at the bar. She leaned across the counter, saying something to Luke. Whatever it was, he wasn't smiling. His shoulders stiffened. Margret swooped in. Jessica shifted, without another word she took several quick steps away from the bar.

Ryan looked away. He didn't want to witness another of Jessica's scenes. Too late. She tapped him on the shoulder, holding a ticket with his name printed in bold letters.

"Seriously?" he asked.

"One ticket," she cooed. "One dance."

"I'll reimburse you." He reached for his wallet.

Etan called out from their table, "I'll dance with her for free."

Jill smiled, her hand sliding down Ryan's chest. "It's just one dance," she said. "You'll survive."

Ryan frowned, watching Jill walk away as Jessica stepped into his arms. His first thought was to pay the band to switch to a fast dance, something that required no physical contact. No luck. Another slow song started as Jessica linked her fingers behind his neck. He tried to pull them away. Tonight was not shaping up to be a lucky one.

Jessica looked into his eyes. "Why are you being like this?"

He let out a low humorless laugh. "How do you expect me to be, Jessica? You broke up with me in a text. Blocked my number, blocked me on all your social media, even emails. Ghosted me. Then you show up tonight and expect what? That we're back together?"

"I was wrong, okay? I panicked. I shouldn't have done that. When Sterling invited us, I hoped we could pick up where we left off."

Ryan's jaw tightened as he looked past her. Couples swayed around them, music softening the edges of the room, but not enough to loosen the tightness in his chest.

She blinked. "So ... just how serious is this thing between you and Hunter's little nerdy neighbor?"

His stare cut sharp. "That is none of your business."

The music continued, but Jessica stood stone still.

Ryan stepped back, spun on his heel, leaving her alone in the middle of the floor. When he reached the table, he looked at Etan. "She's all yours."

Etan popped up like he'd been waiting all night. "I'm off to save the damsel," he said, adjusting his bowtie.

Without waiting a beat, Ryan reached past Jill, grabbing Hunter's scotch, drowning it in one swallow.

Jill placed her hand over his. "You okay?"

"I am now."

Hunter and Sage returned to the table. "Geez, Ryan, I'm so sorry about that," Sage said, "I had no idea Jessica was coming tonight."

Ryan shrugged. "Not a big deal, Sage. I know you're best friends. You shouldn't have to keep your distance because of me." He leaned back, letting Jill's warmth chase off the remnants of Jessica's icy residue. "Besides..." he added with a sly glance at the dance floor, "...this way Etan and Axel have something to do tonight besides pestering us."

That got a snort out of Sage.

Ryan slipped his arm around Jill, fingers brushing her bare skin. "You smell good," he murmured.

Jill stared into his eyes, sporting a sly smile. Without hesitation, she leaned in, placing a kiss on his lips. Not playful. Not teasing. A soft, deliberate kiss ... light on pressure but deep in intention. Public. Visible. It was the kind of kiss that didn't ask permission.

Ryan was never one for public displays of affection. But with Jill, he'd make an exception every time.

When she pulled away, her lips brushed his ear as she snuggled into his shoulder.

On the dance floor, Jessica stood frozen next to Etan, glaring at their table.

"Just letting her know where things stand," Jill whispered.

The evening rolled into its final hour with clinking glasses, fading music, and the unmistakable buzz of satisfied donors.

Luke returned to the table next to theirs ... beaming, cheeks flushed, his bow tie hanging loose. "I made over five grand in tips," he said, dropping a wad of cash in front of his dad.

Sterling laughed. "Guess working at that sports bar back home paid off after all."

Ryan leaned back in his chair, wearing a teasing grin. "What about you, Margret? How much did you pull in?"

"Better question would be, how much did *you* make tonight, Mitchell?"

Ryan opened his mouth but stopped short when Jill blurted out, "I spent three thousand on his dance tickets."

Both tables went quiet.

"Three thousand?" Etan asked, wide-eyed.

Sterling raised his glass. "Remind me to recruit you next time we do a booster event."

Jill squeezed Ryan's hand. "Money well spent."

"Ladies and gentlemen," the master of ceremonies called out, "thank you for making this night unforgettable. We've tallied the donations. With help from our community, team backers, and the entire Portland, Maine, Goshawks roster, we've raised over two million dollars for the Stick It to Cancer Foundation."

Applause erupted around the ballroom.

"We'd especially like to thank those who gave so generously in advance, including Mr. and Mrs. Anderson Griffin, who donated twenty-five thousand dollars on behalf of their son, Hunter."

Hunter gave a tight nod.

Ryan reached inside his tuxedo jacket, retrieving a slim envelope. "I won this for you," he said, sliding it to her.

Jill opened it with care. As she read the contents, her lips parted in surprise.

"It's a VIP box ticket for our Florida away game on November twenty-second," Ryan explained. "First-class round trip flight from Portland. Five-star hotel suite near the Barracudas' arena. Limo to and from the rink. Non-refundable. So, if you're thinking of skipping ... don't."

Sage gasped in delight. She reached past Hunter, grabbing Jill's hand. "You have to go! You can sit with me. It'll be too much fun."

"I second that," Hunter added. "It's about time you watched a game."

Jill glanced at the ticket, then up at Ryan. "I do have that week off," she said. "So... yes. I'll go. On one condition."

Ryan raised an eyebrow. "What's that?"

"No violence."

"That's one promise he'll never keep," Jessica's words came out slurred. angry, beer in hand, her balance questionable. "Especially not when they're playing Florida." A smattering of laughter rose from nearby tables. Jessica lifted her glass, toasting herself.

Ryan ignored her, keeping his focus on Jill as she studied the ticket, fingers brushing across the embossed Goshawks logo. Her smile bloomed like a sunbeam through a storm. Ryan's nerves settled for the first time since entering the ballroom.

Chapter 30
A Knightly Gesture

Wednesday, November. 22nd

Florida's sun beat down on Ryan's bare chest, baking him in a slow roast that made him grateful for the damp towel draped across his face. He could feel sweat pooling beneath his collarbone, a trickle sliding down his ribs. Lounging poolside sounded like a great idea an hour ago, but it wasn't in his nature to sit still before a big game ... even though each game of the regular season was a big game to him.

The hotel lounge chair creaked as he adjusted his back, angling for the sliver of shade offered by a limp patio umbrella. He lifted the towel to check the time on his sports watch. The waterproof band itched. The numbers didn't flip fast enough.

"Seriously?" Hunter's voice cut through the warm air. "Fifth time you've looked at that thing in three minutes."

"Was not."

"Was too." Hunter looked at Ryan. "Sage just sent me a text. Jill's flight got in half an hour ago. Traffic's a mess. They'll be here when they get here."

"Anyway, I'm not checking for Jill," Ryan muttered.

Hunter laughed. "Sure. Just tracking the weather pattern over the hot tub?"

Ryan grunted, readjusting the towel over his face. Sunlight managed to sneak in around the edges. He did his best to tune out the surrounding voices, the slap of flip-flops, the soft hum of hotel staff wheeling carts and serving drinks.

A shadow suddenly fell over him. "Whoever's blocking my tan better be ready to pay on the ice tonight," he growled.

"I look forward to that challenge."

Ryan whipped the towel off. Jill stood above him, sunglasses perched on the top of her head, raven hair glinting in the sunlight. Her bathing suit clung to her frame just enough to make his mouth go dry. He sat up too fast. "When did you get in?"

"About five minutes ago. Sage did some NASCAR moves in the rental car. We beat the GPS ETA."

Sage flopped onto the lounger beside Hunter, her Goshawks blue bikini turning heads. "She's exaggerating. It was creative driving."

Jill settled on the edge of his lounger, giving him a sideways grin.

A smirk grew into a grin as he devoured her with a long stare. "Where'd you get that tan?"

"Booked some tanning appointments the morning after the charity ball," Jill said, dropping her beach bag on the tile. "I wasn't about to blind half of Florida with my Portland skin." Nodding to the pool, she said, "Come swim with me."

"I don't swim," Ryan said, rubbing the back of his neck.

Jill blinked. "Really?"

He shook his head. "Never learned. Grew up in Canada on skates ... not flippers."

Instead of making a sarcastic quip, Jill surprised him by sliding her sunglasses on, moving to the lounge next to his. "Well, I didn't really want to get my hair wet anyway."

Ryan blinked. "That was ... uncharacteristically kind."

"Shut up." Smiling, she reached into her bag, handing him a bottle of sunscreen. "Here. Do something useful."

Ryan let out a low laugh, unscrewed the cap, massaging the lotion into her shoulders. She smelled like sunshine. The way she tilted her head forward, exposing her neck, made his fingers slow down more than necessary.

"So," she asked, "do you get nervous before games?"

He paused. "Used to. Back when I first turned pro. Now it's more like ... anticipation. Controlled chaos. A shot of adrenaline you learn to love."

She nodded. "Sage said you had practice this morning?"

"Yeah. Morning skates before a game is tradition."

"I don't get it. Why do you have to practice when you play so many games?" Her brows furrowed.

"It's a hockey thing. Gets us mentally locked in. Wakes up our legs, forces routine. Hockey's a muscle memory sport."

Jill was quiet for a beat. He glanced over. She wasn't zoning out. Instead, she was listening. Focused. Even through the sunglasses, he felt her eyes track him. He couldn't help but smile when he noticed her gaze dip down his torso.

"You've got more bruises than tan," she said. "How does your body hold up to that kind of punishment every week?"

"The money helps," Axel called, dripping wet in his board shorts. "Ryan gets paid extra for each bruise."

Trey and Etan shouted "CANNONBALL!" in unison, crashing into the pool seconds later.

Water sprayed everywhere, soaking Jill's face, Ryan's chest, and most of Sage's lounger. Ryan handed a dry towel to Jill. "So much for not getting your hair wet."

She blotted damp strands, then dug into her beach bag again. "I have something for you." She held out a thin royal-blue ribbon. Silk. Frayed at one end.

Ryan reached for it, rubbing the fabric between his fingers. "What's this for?"

Jill cleared her throat. "I know it's silly. But I thought you might like a small token of mine to take into battle tonight."

Ryan glanced up, one brow slightly arched.

She pulled her sunglasses down her nose, just enough for him to see her eyes. "Knights used to ride into battle wearing something from their lady. You know. To keep them safe and victorious."

Ryan's upper lip curled. "So … are you saying you're my lady?" He watched her pull the sunglasses up, but not until he saw the eyeroll.

"Don't let it go to your head, Skater Boy. It's just … when you take the ice tonight, I wanted you to have a reminder that someone's cheering for you. No matter what."

He looked down at the ribbon again, rubbing it between his thumb and forefinger, before asking her to tie it around his wrist. He remained quiet.

Jill leaned back on her lounger, pulled out a paperback, flipping it open like nothing had happened.

Ryan twisted his wrist, examining the ribbon. *Maybe that was all a man needed. Not glory. Not goals. Just someone who believed in him when the game got ugly.*

Chapter 31
Lane Change

Wednesday November 22nd
Away Game: Goshawks vs Florida Barracudas

The screen flickered to life with a booming roar from the crowd at the Florida Arena. The Barracudas' faithful were on their feet, teeth bared, eyes gleaming with the promise of a hard-fought game. The camera panned across the stands where kids pounded on the glass as if summoning demons.

"Welcome to Florida, folks. Where it's eighty degrees outside and it promises to be frozen warfare in Florida's arena," Tom Hughes said in his smooth baritone. "Tonight, your Portland, Maine Goshawks face off against their nemesis, the Florida Barracudas. And let me tell you, John, this one's got some bite."

John Hamilton's voice crackled with dry amusement. "Oh, it's going to be brutal, Tom. But here's the twist ... Lane Wilson's between the pipes for the Goshawks tonight. He hasn't been in the net since being pulled during the Buffalo game. Now the rookie is facing the Barracudas for the first time. Baptism by fire on ice, folks."

"And once again, leading the charge for Florida, their captain, Chucky Trembly. If you've got children watching, maybe put the volume on mute."

John leaned forward in his chair; gaze fixed on the ice below. "Trembly's down there now, chomping on his mouthguard, staring down the Goshawks' goalie like he's already living rent-free in Wilson's head."

"The Barracudas expected to be up against Griffin tonight," Tom added, low and grim. "You know, every sniper in a Florida sweater will be gunning for Wilson. And Trembly? He's not here just to score. He's here to cause mayhem."

John sighed, flipping his game notes. "It's a grudge match for Florida, after their one-to-two loss to the Goshawks last month. They still remember the glove save Griffin made on Trembly's backhand."

"And don't forget Trey Moss with the only goals that game. You know that kid's got a target on his back."

"Payback is on the menu. The question is, who's doing the serving?"

"No pressure on Wilson." Tom let out a low, concerned laugh as the camera cut to Viktor Volkov standing on the bench next to Hunter.

First Period

"We're back for the start of the first, folks. The tension in the stands and on the ice is so thick we can feel it in the booth," Tom said, surveying the rink.

John cleared his throat. "First few shifts are going to set the tone. The Goshawks have to come out strong. If they score first, they'll own the period."

The clack of the first puck drop was swallowed by the roar of the crowd. Their voices pulsed through the ice, through the boards, up Ryan's shin guards, cutting into the back of his skull. The Florida fans were louder than he remembered.

Lane filled the crease, feet wide, blocker twitching. From the red line, Ryan could see it ... the goalie's hands too tight, chest rising too fast. Stick taps against the post came too quick, too sharp. *Not again.*

"Wilson looks tight early, Tom. He's got to find his rhythm fast."

Tom adjusted his headset. "Florida knows it, too. He'd better settle soon, because the Barracudas are going to be crowding his crease."

Ryan didn't need to see the red hair sticking out of the helmet or hear the chirps to know what was happening. Without setting a skate near the crease, Chucky Trembly was already in Lane's head.

As he predicted, the Barracudas' captain skated past Lane with a slow glide, a smug expression, and a tilt to his shoulders. He circled like a shark, nudging the paint, bumping the edge of Lane's pads just enough to irritate, but not enough to draw a call.

Then he did it again. And again.

When the first goal slipped past Lane, far side, glove too slow, Ryan felt heat surge through his chest.

Goal! Barracudas–Trembly

Chucky scored again three line changes later.

Goal! Barracudas–Trembly

The crowd surged to their feet. "ICE! WALL!" the Florida fans sang in a mocking chant.

On the next play, Ryan blocked a shot, dumped the puck, turning in time to see Chucky crash the net, spin out, falling like a soccer player touched by air.

Whistle. Penalty. Mitchell.

Ryan skated to the ref. "That's embellishment. You saw it."

The stripes ignored him, just like they had when Chucky jabbed Lane in the ribs with the butt end of his stick two plays earlier.

Power play, a slapshot from the high slot. Lane never saw it coming.

Goal! Barracudas–Gibson

The air in the arena pulsed with the heat and roar of the Florida fans, their noise barreling down to the ice. Every cheer frayed on Ryan's last nerve.

"Florida's running away with it early, John. This isn't the start Portland expected."

John's tone dropped a notch. "The Barracudas will keep hammering that crease until someone clears Trembly out."

Ryan exited the penalty box, pounding his stick on the boards. As he skated across the ice, he shot a look at Hunter, who only shook his head. The scent of cheap beer sloshing from the stands along with sweat-drenched gear added to Ryan's frustration. On the bench, when the smelling salts came his way, he took a long, deep nose full.

Tom tapped his pen against his notes. "End of the first, and it's been all Barracudas."

John shook his head. "The Goshawks look rattled. If they don't push back next period, this could turn ugly fast."

Ryan glanced at the scoreboard. Barracudas-3, Goshawks-0. *Why were the coaches setting Lane up for failure again?*

First Period Intermission

The door slammed shut as Ryan entered the visitor's locker room. Gear creaked. A few fists hit the lockers. Muttered curses bounced off the concrete walls. He glanced to the far corner where three coaches huddled.

Harrison's jaw flexed as he dragged a marker across the whiteboard. The X in the crease came too hard, too fast. The red streaks looked more like a wound than a play.

Gray grabbed a black marker, ripping the cap off with his teeth. The muscles in his temple twitched, eyes narrowing as he jabbed the board, covering Harrison's red X with a heavy black one. Ryan read his defiance ... *Lane stays.*

Viktor stood to the side, arms behind his back, the calmest of the three ... though the slow rise of his chest betrayed a quiet storm beneath.

Hunter hadn't said a word ... until now. Every player turned to him as he stomped to the center of the room, pointing a finger at each of his teammates. "Chucky lives in the crease. Evict him. Protect. Your. Goalie."

His pupils dilated, chest heaving, fingers now curled into fists. He paused, then began again. "If you can't ... I'll switch out of my goalie gear and do it myself. I'm so tired of this shit. How hard is it to guard the one player who's doing his best to protect your net?"

Ryan hustled to Hunter's side. "You heard the man." He turned to the D-line, words emerging low, hissing. "Block with your body if you have to. I don't want to see a puck, let alone a Barracudas player, near our blue paint."

Axel cracked his knuckles. "Take out Chucky? Hell, yeah!"

Lane lifted his head. The fear in his eyes faded ... replaced by a flicker of something new. Resolve. He nodded. Subtle. Steady.

Good. Ryan thumped his stick against Lane's pads once for reassurance. He fingered the blue ribbon tied to his wrist. He needed a win for Jill. Most important, he needed Lane to know his team had his back. "Let's chum the ice with Barracudas players."

Second Period

"We're underway again, folks. The Goshawks need to shake off the last period and reset fast," Tom announced.

"The first few minutes will tell the story," John said. "If Wilson settles, they've got a chance to climb back."

Ryan adjusted his helmet as he skated onto the ice. His gut told him this period was theirs. They were more than ready. The puck dropped. The tone changed. He felt it in the way the Goshawks moved as one ... tighter, faster, cleaner. Lane's focus mirrored his teammates ... shoulders squared, tracking every bounce of the puck.

One thing stayed the same. Chucky. Still buzzing the crease like a housefly.

Ryan caught his smirk as he coasted past the net. "Miss me, Captain Grit?"

"Like a rash," Ryan muttered.

Axel snagged the puck just above the circle, then wheeled near the boards. Chucky came in hot. Stupid-fast. Too confident. Axel braced for the hit, lowering his shoulder into Trembly's chest. Chucky flew sideways onto the ice hard, limbs pinwheeling. The arena gasped, then roared in collective disapproval when no call was made.

Ryan skated over, glaring at Chucky, now on all fours, coughing. He leaned in, stick over his knees, voice low. "Keep your stinky fish ass out of our crease."

Three line changes later. Bodies collided behind the Barracudas net. Gloves jabbed. Sticks clashed. Ryan squared off against a big Florida player fighting for the puck. In the melee, Axel went after Chucky, twisting the butt of his stick under the pest's chest protector. Not hard enough to injure. Just enough to make him think twice.

When the puck escaped the scrum. Etan caught it, turned and fired.

Goal! Goshawks–Eklund

The crowd flipped from cheers to jeers. In the booth, Tom's voice cut sharp. "And the Goshawks are on the scoreboard. Eklund threads it through traffic. Portland's alive again."

John's reply carried the weight of a man who'd been there. "That's the spark they need. Wilson's settled. His teammates are feeding off it."

Florida fans continued to shout. Garbage rained from the upper deck onto the ice ... beer cups, crumpled napkins, a single flip-flop.

No whistle. No penalty.

Ryan skated to the Barracudas' bench, slow and deliberate. Stick pointing, he taunted, "Who's next?"

Back on the bench, Finn leaned into his captain. "You just kicked the hornet's nest."

"Good. Let's pull out their stingers," Ryan shot back.

The game quickly shifted from shots on goal to how many players could fit in a penalty box. At one point, both boxes held more players than the bench. The Goshawks pressed on. Every pass held a purpose. Every check planned. Lane stopped a clean breakaway with a snap of his blocker. Another with his pads. He was standing on his head, saving shot after shot.

A questionable call on Finn put Florida on the power play.

It only took Trey thirty-seconds into the penalty kill to score a shorty.

Goal! Goshawks–Moss

Seconds before Finn's penalty expired, Trey scored another.

Goal! Goshawks–Moss

Florida's fans fell silent for a beat before chaos erupted in the stands. Tom's call came loud and clear. "Unbelievable. Another short-handed from Moss! You can't script this, folks ... two on the kill evens out the game 3 to 3."

John's words came quick, excitement breaking through his usual calm. "Trey Moss is putting on a clinic and Wilson looks like a brick wall. I've never seen the Barracudas' coach chomp his gum so hard."

As the Goshawks skated off the ice for the second intermission, Ryan glanced at the Barracudas bench. Chucky sat hunched over, sucking air, water dribbling down his chin, looking like an escapee from a nursing home.

Third Period

"Welcome back, folks. If you just tuned in, you've missed an epic turnaround. The Goshawks are back in it, from a three-goal deficit to tie it up." Tom's smile spread wide.

"That last period was all Portland, Tom. A goal from Eklund and two impressive short-handed goals from Moss. But for me, it's the netminder who's got my attention. In the second, he shut out everything Florida's thrown his way."

"We're about to see if Wilson can keep up with what you know is going to be a Florida onslaught," Tom added.

Ryan didn't see Chucky on the ice or the bench for the opening of the third. He imagined him in the locker room, nursing his ego.

Lane crouched in the crease like the net had birthed him. Glove hand steady. Pads square. Eyes calm. The fire Hunter lit inside him between periods had clicked. The kid was locked in, and the Goshawks were feeding off it.

Every line that jumped over the boards brought passion. Etan buzzed like a hornet. Axel laid down textbook hit after hit. Trey dangled through traffic with swagger.

Ryan stayed in the thick of it, commanding the ice like a general. Stick tapping, reading the Barracudas' moves before they made them.

They weren't just playing. They were dismantling their enemy.

Axel fired from the blue line; the puck bounced off a Barracudas' shin pad. Finn muscled into the slot, digging for the rebound. One jab. Two. The third found daylight beneath the goalie's blocker.

Goal! Goshawks–O'Connell

"O'Connell jams it home!" Tom shouted. "The Goshawks lead for the first time tonight!"

John laughed. "Portland's finally got it together. It's not looking good for Florida."

Five minutes later, another rush. Trey to Etan ... backhand shovel pass, clean finish.

Goal! Goshawks–Eklund

Florida's crowd turned ugly, booing louder. Fans pounded the glass, middle fingers raised.

It didn't matter. Every shift, Lane held the line. Kick save. Glove snatch. Rebound control, calm as a ten-year veteran.

With thirty seconds left, Axel fired from the point; the puck redirected to Ryan's blade.

Goal! Goshawks–Mitchell

"Mitchell lights the lamp!" Tom shouted. "That puts Portland up by three, and Florida's out of time."

John's tone carried the calm of a man who'd seen it all. "Now, that's leadership. The captain didn't stop until he made sure this one was put to bed."

When the end of game horn blasted, the Goshawks bench erupted ... gloves raised, helmets tapped, adrenaline spilling over the boards.

The arena emptied fast, the few remaining Florida faithful flinging everything short of their wallets onto the ice. Popcorn rained from the upper bowl. A full water bottle bounced off the dasher, missing Ryan's head by inches as it rolled to a stop near center ice.

Ryan maneuvered through it like a man skating through confetti. Beer foam soaked his jersey. Someone behind the glass yelled his name, followed by curses he'd only heard on HBO.

He smiled. This night, this victory ... it wasn't about revenge. Not really. It was about proving Lane could handle the storm. It was about shutting Chucky down, no matter the cost.

As they skated to the tunnel, Ryan clapped Lane on the back. "Hell of a third."

Lane's grin was filled with exhaustion and pride, his breath catching like he wasn't sure the win was real.

"The Goshawks win another one, 6 to 3. I have to say, that had to be the most intense game of the season." Tom shuffled his notes.

"Couldn't agree with you more," John said, rocking in his chair. "What a comeback, not just for the Goshawks, but more so for Wilson. Good thing he's twenty-one, because I foresee a lot of champagne flowing on the plane ride home tonight."

"Well, that's it for tonight, folks. John and I wish you all a safe and happy Thanksgiving. The Goshawks, and you, the fans, have plenty to be thankful for after tonight's game."

The locker room echoed with laughter and rustling gear. The sting of sweat replaced with eucalyptus soap. The blue ribbon soggy on his wrist. Ryan ran a towel once more over his damp hair. Tugging on his ball cap, he stepped into the darkened corridor.

No lingering fans. Media gone.

Jill stood near the locker room door, arms wrapped tight around herself like she'd been trying to play it cool. Her cheeks flushed when she spotted him.

Before Ryan could say a word, she flung herself into his arms. Her lips brushed the edge of his jaw as she landed hard against his chest ... breathless and laughing.

"You..." she gasped, voice caught somewhere between a whisper and a scream, "...you were amazing. That was the most exciting sports event I've ever seen."

Ryan blinked. "Thought you didn't like hockey."

She pulled back just enough to meet his eyes. Her lips curled, not in mockery this time, but something softer. Something real. "I didn't." Her voice dropped. "Until I saw you play."

Ryan started to apologize for the fights and hard hits, but she intercepted the words with a kiss. It was the most defenseless he'd ever felt ... and he loved every moment. His hands slid around her waist, holding her like he'd won big. Bigger than the final score. Bigger than the satisfaction of silencing Chucky Trembly.

He knew when he recalled the season's games, this was the win he'd remember. In that moment, he realized Jill hadn't come to Florida just to watch a hockey game ... *she'd come for him.*

Chapter 32
Giving Thanks

Thursday, November 23rd, Thanksgiving

Margret stood near the picture window watching a strip of fog rolling in from the bay. When she first joined the Goshawks, Justin insisted she spend Thanksgiving with him. That first year, she expected a holiday feast. She soon learned to lower her expectations when he ordered in from his favorite restaurant. Takeout cartons always littered the kitchen, waiting for the maid to clear in the morning. No holiday music, no cooking clatter, no scents of baking dishes moving in and out of the oven. Only the two of them in the smaller dining room, heads bent over outlines for December's media blitz.

Strange how a place could shift in less than two months. The sharp edges of past holidays with Justin softened, thinned by the warmth rising from the nearby kitchen. Rosemary drifted through the hall, tugged forward by slow-roasting turkey. She followed the scent, steam curling toward the ceiling from pots hissing beneath their lids. A tray clattered in a distant hallway as servers moved through the house, setting out linens and polished silver. Each sound scraped away another piece of Justin's lingering ghost.

Margret turned at the sound of footsteps echoing along the corridor. Crease rounded the corner ahead of Sage and Hunter. His paws slid across the marble floor, skittering until he regained control with a proud little huff. Sage followed with her usual bright smile. Hunter entered next, shoulders loose. Margret caught the steady pace he always carried after a solid morning on the ice. *Funny how a calm goalie always steadied the room.*

Crease ran his nose along the prep counter, inhaling the promise of turkey before the sous chef blocked him with a baking sheet. His tail picked up speed, the picture of a dog convinced patience might score him a victory.

Margret caught the Lab by the collar. "If even one carrot goes missing, mister, I'm banishing you to the wine cellar."

"Get out of the kitchen, you troublemaker." Sage laughed as she guided Crease to her side. "You better listen to Margret. No stealing today."

Hunter eased onto a barstool. "Thank you for inviting the boys, Margret. Tonight's dinner is all they talked about on the plane last night." He plucked an olive from the charcuterie board, popping it in his mouth.

Sage leaned on the counter. "Lane was doing his best to explain Canadian Thanksgiving to Axel and Etan. All three were excited when I told them you'd be serving butter tarts."

"I placed a special order from my favorite local bakery. You'll have to try one. They are so good." Margret opened the pastry box, handing Sage a small tart.

"They taste like heaven." Sage slapped Hunter's hand when he tried to steal a bite.

He wiggled his fingers like he caught a puck without his catcher glove. "You know, Trey won't admit it, but he's more excited than the other three to have somewhere to go today."

"I thought Trey's parents lived in Portland." Margret closed the tart box just in time to keep Crease's tongue from snaking inside.

"They do. But Lane told me Trey's parents made last-minute plans to spend the holidays sailing the Virgin Islands." Hunter pulled Sage closer. "Tough break for the kid."

Margret shook her head, a smile tugging at her lips. It never ceased to amuse her when Hunter lumped Axel, Etan, Lane, and Trey together as kids. "Geez, Hunter, you sound like an old man."

"He may only be twenty-three years old, but we all know goalies are born ancient." Sage leaned in, placing a quick kiss on his cheek.

"Hey, what are you doing? Halftime's almost over." Luke sauntered in ... dress shirt beneath a suit jacket, new jeans, same tousled hair.

"What's the score?" Sage asked, eyes wide.

"Packers are killing them, twenty-two to six, but I have faith the Lions will make a comeback."

"Want to put a wager on that, cowboy?" Hunter pulled a twenty from his wallet.

"Keep your money. Besides, I didn't know you followed any sport besides hockey or golf." Luke pulled the refrigerator door open, stared inside, then grabbed three beers. He handed one to Sage, offered the other to Hunter.

"You'd be surprised at what you don't know about me." Hunter took the bottle, pocketing the bill.

"Do you need help with anything, Margret?" Sage said as a server brushed past with a tray of expensive cheeses and specialty cold cuts. "My goodness, the house smells delicious."

"Does it look like I need help?" Margret swept her arm around the kitchen. The chef seasoned a veggie dish, the sous chefs chopped herbs, servers passed each other in a well-practiced dance. "I even took Sterling's advice and hired a maid ... for the evening."

"Alrighty then. I'll go play referee to Luke and Hunter in the TV room," Sage called over her shoulder. "Please let me know when Mom and Dad arrive."

Crease lingered, licking Margret's hand like she was a sweet treat. "Hey. Don't forget your mangy mutt," she said, nudging the Labrador out of the kitchen before scrubbing her hands.

Margret finished the last sip of her Chablis, considering a second glass before guests arrived. She crossed into the dining room where the staff worked in quiet rhythm, putting the final touches on the formal table. Her laughter fell soft as she looked at the cloth napkins folded to resemble tiny pumpkins. "Justin would be amused."

"What's that, ma'am?" a server asked.

"Oh, nothing. I was just talking to a memory." Margret watched the server return to placing crystal goblets on the table. Although the caterer offered to supply the formal place settings, Margret had spent a full day shopping for the perfect dishes, silverware, and stemware. She hoped her efforts would not be lost on this ragtag group. Her hand paused on the top of a high-back chair as she studied the table. Rows of tall holders with white tapers nestled in fall garland lined the center. Still too early to light with dinner an hour away.

She moved from chair to chair, checking each card in the seating arrangement. Hunter's parents' names rested between her fingers as she paused, weighing where they might fit among hockey players and midwestern farm folk.

A burst of cheers rose from the TV room. Margret glanced at the wall clock, noting that the third quarter of the football game must be kicking into high gear. At the same moment, the front door chime rang. "Puck drop," she said, setting Victoria and Anderson's cards on the table as she rushed to answer the door.

A sudden blast of cold air swirled in from the foyer when the maid opened the front door, followed by the thump of cowboy boots, the tangle of layered voices, ııd the warm rush of familiar laughter. Margret turned from the hallway just as Sage raced past her.

"Mom. Dad."

Margret stepped aside, watching Sage hug her mother. Lilly's smile widened as Sage pulled her close. Jim, a step behind, made a move to tip his hat, though he wasn't wearing one, then folded his daughter into a tight hug.

"Happy Thanksgiving, sweetie," Jim said.

Hunter followed, arms open. "Finally. The out-laws."

Jim grunted, though a grin edged his lips as they clasped hands, bumping shoulders. Lilly pressed a kiss to Hunter's cheek.

Crease barked once, sharp and joyous, then launched himself into the fray. Tiny golden hairs swirled as he pressed against Lilly's skirt, like it'd been years since he last saw her, instead of weeks.

"Welcome, you two," Margret said, handing their coats to the waiting maid.

Patty and Jessica trailed in next, each balancing bakery boxes smelling of cinnamon, butter, and love.

"Straight from the ranch," Patty said. "Lilly's pies survived the flight."

"Where's the kitchen? My arms are about to mutiny," Jessica added, giving Margret a quick nod.

Margret pointed to the kitchen. "Follow your noses, girls," she said, turning back to Lilly and Jim. "How was your flight?"

"I hate flying," Jim grumbled. "Too much turbulence. I swear those small planes were built to rattle a man's bones."

Lilly patted Jim's arm. "Sterling's private jet has ruined me for commercial airlines."

"Did you get settled in the Airbnb?"

Jim shook his head. "Came here from the airport."

"Thank you so much, Margret, for arranging a place for us and the girls to stay over the weekend," Lilly added.

Margret did a quick headcount before asking, "Where's Sterling?"

"He got a call during the flight ... some business crisis." Lilly shrugged. "Your limo driver dropped him off at the hotel on our way."

"The big bossman said not to expect him for dinner. I'm betting after smelling Lilly's pies for four hours, he'll show up for dessert." Jim laughed, the sound rolling through the foyer like gravel in a tin pail.

"I bet you could use something to drink," Margret said, turning to Jim as the front door flung open. A blast of cold air swept in, followed by a tangle of laughter as four bodies stumbled across the threshold.

Axel and Etan swooped in on Lilly and Jim, grabbing them like they'd just scored a game winning goal. The boys clutched the Larsons in a giddy huddle, sneakers squeaking across the marble as their excitement filled the foyer with the same wild energy they brought to the ice.

Lane and Trey lingered near the now closed door. Margret waited until Axel and Etan released the Larsons before stepping in for introductions. "Jim, Lilly, these are the newest members of the Goshawks family. Goalie Lane Wilson, and top line forward Trey Moss. Boys, this is Jim and Lilly Larson, Sage's parents."

Lane stepped forward. "Pleasure to finally meet you." He offered a handshake to each. "My parents run a small cattle ranch in Hamilton, Ontario. Nothing as big as yours. I know the effort that goes into keeping one going. Glad you could get away for Thanksgiving."

Beside him, coat half unzipped, Trey stood with a loose posture and a grin that stretched wide. He stepped in to shake hands as well. "Etan and Axel never stop talking about their adventures on your ranch."

"Nice to meet you, boys," Lilly said. "You're always welcome at our place."

"I'll never turn down free farm labor." Jim let out a hearty laugh.

"Oh! Jim." Axel snapped his fingers. "Margret's limo driver was waiting outside. He wanted to know if he should take your boxes to the Airbnb or bring them here."

"Don't take off your coats, boys." Jim headed for the door without bothering to grab his jacket. "I need help carrying in my homebrew."

Axel and Etan bolted outside ahead of him. Lane and Trey followed in quick stride while Crease barreled past everyone with a sharp bark.

"Some things never change." Sage leaned into Hunter.

Moments later the group returned, each one carrying a box stamped in bold ink with the names of various ales. The cardboard creaked in their arms, a faint hop scent drifting through the room as the cold air settled behind them.

"Goodness, Jim, how many people did you think were coming tonight?" Margret shook her head.

"We'll be here for both games this weekend. I'm counting on celebrating two Goshawks wins." Jim surveyed the foyer. "Where can we stash these?"

"I know just the spot." Luke stepped into the room with a relaxed confidence that always made him look like he owned the place. "Follow me into the TV room. The game's in the fourth, Jim. Lions are making their comeback move."

Everyone turned to Margret. She waved a hand in a scooting manner. "Go. Dinner's a little under an hour away."

"Not going to turn that invitation down." Jim passed his box of beer to Hunter, hustling after Luke with the eager stride of a man chasing a touchdown.

"The TV goes dark when I announce dinner," Margret shouted after Luke.

"What can I do to help?" Lilly offered.

"Nothing for anyone to do, Lilly. Enjoy the game." Margret watched the group funnel to the distant roar of the TV, their laughter blending with the rumble of the broadcast.

Crease sat close to Margret, his nose nudged her hand. "I especially don't need your help." Margret patted the Lab's head. "Go find Etan and Axel. I know they'll sneak you some snacks." She laughed watching Crease bolt into the TV room.

"I need a drink." Margret walked into the kitchen, heading straight to the wine refrigerator.

Jessica nodded at the young, handsome chef lifting a spoon to Patty's lips. "Not sure what's up with Patty this year. Guys can't resist her."

"She's always had a spell on Etan and Axel." Margret pulled a bottle of Chablis from the small refrigerator. "You want some?"

Jessica tipped her bottle of Perrier, shaking her head. "Hey, Margret, I wanted to thank you for inviting me. I wasn't sure you would after the charity event." She took a long swig of the carbonated water.

Margret uncorked a bottle, pouring the wine into a chilled tulip-shaped glass. "To be honest, Jessica, it was Luke who talked me into it." She lifted the glass to her lips, taking a small sip.

"I suspected that. I apologize profusely. The booze mixed with my jealousy got the better of me."

"Apology accepted. Luke promised me you'll keep both under control tonight." Margret's smile faded. "I'm counting on you not to make a liar out of him."

"Miss VanAlen, more guests have arrived." The maid glanced from Margret to Jessica.

"Saved by the bell," Jessica muttered under her breath as Margret set her glass on the counter.

Upon entering the foyer, Margret noticed Anderson Griffin first. His charcoal coat hung in strict lines, the wool so smooth it looked sculpted. Victoria stood beside her husband with the same deliberate elegance, a winter-white wrap gathered at her waist, pearls catching the chandelier's light. Her gaze swept in one slow pass, the kind meant to weigh the worth of a room.

Their driver trailed in with a sealed case of Dom Perignon. He set it on the side table, bowed his head to Margret, then slipped back outside.

Margret turned to the maid. "Please let the others know Mr. and Mrs. Griffin have arrived."

A heartbeat later, Sage rushed in. "You made it," she said, wrapping her arms around Hunter's mother.

Margret watched as Victoria accepted the hug with a measured smile.

Hunter stepped in, hands in pockets, jaw tight, shoulders squared. "Dad. Mom." He offered a brief nod.

Anderson removed his coat, helped his wife out of hers, passing them to the maid. "Margret, you've made a few changes since I last visited."

"Like you always say, Anderson, change is a good thing," Margret said, followed by a shallow smile.

She was relieved when footsteps sounded behind her. Lilly entered first with her easy smile. Jim followed at a slower pace, brows knitted, lips tight. A sure sign he was upset from being called away from the game. The contrast between the two couples struck Margret hard. Dressed for comfort, the Larsons radiated Midwestern charm. Across from them stood polished East Coast professionals.

"You must be Hunter's parents." Lilly reached out with genuine warmth. "So nice to finally meet you."

Victoria offered her fingertips, nothing more.

Sage's dad extended his hand to Anderson. "Jim Larson."

Hunter's father accepted it with a tight, palm-down grip. "A pleasure." He paused a beat too long. "Glad you could get away from the farm for the long weekend. Always impressive when a schedule allows that."

Jim leaned into the shake, wearing a slow grin. "Wouldn't miss Thanksgiving with our girl."

Victoria let out a low huff as she glanced at Hunter drifting closer to Jim.

Margret saw all the tiny signs. Victoria's nostrils flared. Anderson's shoulders stiffen. The envy sat plain as day. Hunter showed the Larsons a warmth his own parents rarely earned. Before the tension could escalate, Margret intervened.

"Let's move you into the front room. Dinner is close. Let me know what you'd like to drink."

"What about the game?" Jim grumbled.

"Not now, Jim." Lilly smiled at Hunter's parents as she snaked her arm through her husband's.

"I need a tall IPA," Jim said, glancing back at the TV room.

Victoria lifted her chin. "Something non-alcoholic for me. I'm on call."

"I'll get it, Margret." Sage offered as Hunter guided his parents into the front room.

Margret returned to the kitchen for her wine. The glass sat on the counter. She despised warm Chablis but drank it anyway. The evening drifted from what she'd pictured. Doubts crept in, thin as hairline cracks. Maybe the guest list was a mistake. Maybe Justin had it right. A quiet DoorDash feast sounded easier. No collisions of families. No clashing egos.

On the other side of the kitchen, the oven door creaked open, releasing a bloom of heat that rolled across the room. The chef lifted the turkey pan, the skin shimmering golden, steam rising in lazy curls. Rosemary drifted through the air. Thyme trailed behind, stirring childhood memories filled with family, friends, love, and laughter. The scent wrapped around her, warm and comforting. Her mouth watered as if she could taste the succulent bird.

Maybe hosting this dinner was what she needed after all.

"This is for you," Ryan said.

Margret jumped, gripping the stem of her wine glass. "Didn't your mother ever tell you not to sneak up on a woman, especially one with a drink in her hand?"

"Nope, I can't recall my mama ever saying any such thing." Ryan's Canadian accent thickened. "This is for you." He handed Margret a bouquet of a dozen red roses nestled in winter greenery.

"Thank you, Ryan. They're beautiful." She looked past him. "Where's Jill?"

"Sage kidnapped her when we walked in. Something about meeting parents?" He shrugged.

Margret stepped close, lowering her voice to a whisper. "You know Jessica is here?"

Ryan sported a cocky grin as he whispered back, "Sage asked me for permission before Luke invited her. So yeah, it's cool."

"Good, good." Margret straightened, taking the bouquet from him. "I'll put these in water."

"Hey, Jessica," Ryan said, leaning in the entryway.

"Hi, Ryan. Sage said you knew I'd be here."

"I knew you were invited. Just surprised you came."

"With Patty, Sage, and the Larsons all here for the holiday weekend, I had nowhere else to go." Jessica's finger touched the corner of her eye.

"Here, Ryan." Margret offered him a scotch, straight up.

Ryan accepted the drink, taking a long swig.

"I apologize for how I acted at the charity ball," Jessica said, picking a paper towel to shreds. "My expectations for a reconciliation were too high. My blood-alcohol content even higher." Her laugh emerged deep, tinged with regret. Her lip quivered as she added, "I expected you to still want me."

"You expected wrong," Ryan said. "I thought you were gone for good."

"I needed time to figure myself out."

"And?" Ryan's grip tightened on his glass as Jill's soft laughter drifted from the nearby front room.

"Apparently, so did you," Jessica sighed.

"Okay, you two," Margret cut in. "When our players have a disagreement, they hug it out." She gestured between them.

Ryan rolled his eyes but gave Jessica a brotherly hug, brief but real. "Friends?"

"Friends," Jessica said.

"Now that we've got that settled, everyone I have not paid to put this dinner together ... get out of my kitchen." She turned to Patty. "Especially you, missy. If you don't leave the chef alone, we'll never eat."

"We're ready to start service as soon as you are, Miss VanAlen," the chef said, wiping his hands on his apron.

"Give me a few minutes to round everyone up."

Margret followed the burst of announcers calling the end of the game. Luke clicked the remote as soon as he saw her, the screen going dark as he crossed the room. He slipped an arm around her waist, pressing a quick kiss on her cheek.

"Not in front of the children." Margret patted his shoulder.

Jessica stood nearby, nursing her Perrier. Patty sat on an overstuffed recliner, looking like a princess holding court. Crease lay at her feet, head tilting with each shift in the conversation, as if he followed every word.

Surrounding Patty ... the Goshawks' first line and the backup goalie. Etan kneeled beside her, a soda cradled in one hand, the other raked nervous paths through his curls. Trey lounged across the opposite armrest with calculated ease. Near Crease, Axel sat cross-legged on the rug, chewing ice from his drink. Lane hovered over the back of Patty's chair like an obedient shadow.

"It's like watching wolves compete to impress a bunny," Margret whispered in Luke's ear.

"So," Trey said, flashing a grin smooth as a breakaway goal. "You ever been to a beach in Maine?"

"Can't say I have." Patty gave each boy a slow, assessing look. "Any of you ever muck out a horse stall?"

Etan's eyes darted to Axel. "Did we do that the last time we were at the Larsons' farm?"

"No idea." Axel recrossed his legs.

"I'm a city boy," Trey said, flashing his best toothy grin. "I have no idea what mucking is."

Lane leaned closer, lips brushing Patty's ear. "I have."

"You're my favorite now." Patty turned her head, noses nearly colliding.

Lane beamed. Trey frowned. Etan growled. Axel grumbled.

Jessica choked on her water. "She's got 'em all on leashes."

Margret smirked behind the rim of her wine glass. "Let's hope she doesn't start adopting them. Not sure Coach Harrison would approve of her hauling the lot back to South Dakota."

Jessica laughed. "Oh, I know she's already giving them pet names."

Etan looked up. "What was that?"

"Nothing," Margret called back.

"We're just discussing your off-ice plays," Jessica added.

A warm drift of roasted herbs rolled in from the dining room. Margret lifted her glass in a subtle gesture of authority. "Game's over. Dinner's ready." The young players scramble to their feet.

The double doors to the ballroom opened to the scent of roasted turkey, herbal stuffing, honey-baked ham, and brown sugar–glazed carrots. The aroma rolled into the hall like a delicious tide. Margret's guests gathered inside the formal dining room as servers wove between them offering flutes of Dom Perignon. Victoria, Jessica, Axel, Etan, and Trey received non-alcoholic bubbly from a separate tray, the same crystal glasses catching candlelight.

Margret lifted her glass, ready to make a quick toast. Before she could speak, Hunter stepped forward with Sage.

He cleared his throat, raising his glass. "We've got an announcement." He drew Sage closer.

"We picked a date," Sage said, bouncing on her toes.

"December twenty-third," Hunter added, turning to Margret, as if daring her to object.

Jim choked on his drink. "That soon?"

"Sweetheart, that's perfect." Lilly's eyes misted.

Margret stood frozen, taking the bait. "You realize the Goshawks are in Minnesota that day?"

"We do," Sage said. "It'll be after the game. We want to spend Christmas together as husband and wife."

Margret opened her mouth, about to voice further objections, when two torpedoes, in the form of Jessica and Patty, slammed into Sage from either side.

"You're actually doing it!" Jessica squealed.

"About time," Patty added, looping her arms around Sage.

Etan smacked Hunter's back so hard he stumbled forward.

Axel raised his glass. "To the lovebirds!"

"Am I invited? I love weddings." Lane grinned.

Jill nudged Ryan. "Did you know about this?"

"Yeah, Hunter told me on the plane ride from Florida."

Laughter rippled through the room. Victoria glided beside Sage, cupping her elbow. "My dear, you must let me host the bridal luncheon at our home."

Sage turned, looking like a deer in headlights. "That would be wonderful ... but we'll have to check the Goshawks' schedule. December's packed."

"Nonsense," Victoria said. "We'll make it work." Her smile drifted past Sage to Lilly, settling like a veil of frost.

"You calling them Mom and Dad yet?" Etan said to Hunter, speaking around a canapé.

Axel high-fived him. "You think when Hunter gets married, they'll adopt us?"

Margret took it all in. Her mind raced through the logistics of a wedding, travel schedules, practice times, media demands, all packed into a single impossible month. She drained her glass. Her gaze landed on Hunter's mother. Victoria's smile looked painted on, brittle at the edges. Her eyes tracked Hunter, noting each laugh and every lingering touch with Sage's family like tally marks in an invisible ledger.

Servers moved through the room with a fresh round of drinks when a sound that didn't belong cut through the room. A buzz. Sharp, persistent.

Victoria reached into the pocket of her skirt. She glanced at the screen, lips pursing. Not in surprise, but in something close to vindication. She exhaled with the weight of someone who wanted the entire room to feel it. "I'm needed," she said, her tone theatrical. "Emergency surgery."

Conversation paused. Lilly blinked, her brow creasing. "On a holiday?"

Anderson set his glass on the table "When you're the top surgeon in Maine," he said, "you're on call twenty-four seven."

"Luke, please get their coats." For once Margret was thankful he hustled without offering an objection, returning within seconds, his arms overflowing with wool and fur.

Anderson slipped on his coat before helping his wife into hers. Margret noted the way he adjusted Victoria's collar ... like a man well-trained in performing husbandly duties.

Margret didn't realize she'd been holding her breath until the door shut, shattering the silence. A pulse drifted back into the room as voices rose, glasses clinked, laughter swelled, and the gentle rise of jazz from the speakers reclaimed its space.

Across the room, Axel said something that made Etan snort liquid through his nose.

"Please take your seats. Dinner is being served," Margret announced. The power couple had left the building. No one was sorry to see them go.

She shook her head, watching her carefully constructed seating chart fall apart.

"Better rethink that," Axel said to Lane, blocking the goalie with an elbow when Lane tried to sit next to Patty. "Remember, I'm the one protecting you and your crease."

Lane raised his hands in mock surrender, settling across the table from them.

Etan shuffled chairs with Trey, earning the seat on the other side of Patty with a triumphant grin.

Jim motioned a server over, handing off his full flute. "Can you swap this for one of my homebrews, please?"

"Whoops, sorry," Trey said as his elbow clipped Etan's arm, drowning Patty's plate in a pool of gravy.

Crease trotted beneath the table with a stolen dinner roll, tail thumping against everyone's legs.

Ryan leaned into Jill, "You okay?" he asked, fingers intertwined with hers on top of the table.

"More than okay," she replied, squeezing his hand. She looked at Margret, "I appreciate you including me tonight. It means a lot."

Margret sported a sly grin. "What do you say Ryan? Do I officially list her as a Goshawks WAGs?"

Jill frowned. "I'd like to know what WAGs is before I commit to being one."

Ryan downed his champagne before answering. "It's slang for Goshawks wives and girlfriends."

"Well, in that case, it would be an honor."

At the other end of the table, Lilly grasped Jessica's hand. "I'm so glad you could be with us this weekend."

"Thank you for making me feel welcomed." Jessica put her head on Lilly's shoulder.

Hunter leaned into Sage, whispering something that painted her cheeks a soft pink.

The warmth radiated through Margret. The plates too full, the voices too loud. Although Justin wasn't one to celebrate holidays, she knew he would have loved this moment of camaraderie.

She stood at the head of the table, tapping a butter knife against her glass. "When the season started, this house was empty. Filled with tears. But tonight..." She glanced from one guest to another. Hunter nodded. Ryan winked. Her voice hitched as she continued, "Tonight, it's everything Justin would have wanted. A team knitted together in the best kind of chaos."

Margret lifted her glass. "To the Goshawks. To our friends for their unconditional love and support. Most important, to finding reasons, big or small, to be grateful."

Her gaze drifted down the table once more, at her players and friends, everyone alive with laughter. For the first time in months, her chest didn't brace for the next disaster. She felt rooted, steady, warm.

This was what a team was supposed to look like. Not just players ... but family.

Chapter 33
Beyond Tonight

Thursday, November 25th Thanksgiving Eve

Margret let out a sigh of relief as the last of the guests left. Clean platters lined the long banquet table. A few chairs remained askew. The caterers had packed up hours ago, even so, the warm scents of roasted turkey and sage stuffing lingered. Candle stubs flickered in their tall holders; some guttered out, others still braved the night.

She walked the length of the formal dining room alone, a half-full glass of Chablis in hand, her heels long abandoned. Sage had taken Crease to the Airbnb with her for an extended visit with Lilly and Jim.

It should have felt hollow. Instead, the quiet wrapped around her like a thick quilt. Comfortable. Earned. She stopped at the glass doors leading to the garden room. Beyond, the moonlight traced silver ribbons across the bay. Portland's skyline blinked in the distance. This house had started the season in despair. Tonight, it held every reason to be grateful.

Margret stepped into the garden room, setting her wine on the low stone ledge. Her gaze drifted to Justin's portrait, still hanging in its original place. She rested her hand on the frame. "I'll do it right," she murmured, "not just for the Goshawks, but for you, Justin, and perhaps, more importantly, for myself."

The faint creak of the side door pulled her from her thoughts. Cowboy boots on hardwood. She knew the sound by heart.

Luke stepped into the room, his silhouette broad against the hallway light. He'd changed out of his holiday garb. Flannel sleeves rolled to his forearms. He looked like he belonged there. Like he always had.

He walked to her without a word, pulling a small velvet box from his pocket. He didn't open it. Just held it between them. "I've been carrying this around all night."

Margret turned, fully facing him. She took a breath. Not of surprise, but of sorrow and affection tangled together.

"I was gonna do this before the turkey. Then after the turkey. Then after the pies. When Etan lit a napkin on fire, I lost my nerve again."

"Luke," she said softly, "I love you."

His thumb brushed the edge of the box.

"I do. I love you," she said. "But I'm not ready. Not for this kind of commitment. It's not because of you." The words rushed out. "It's ... everything. I've just stepped into the biggest role of my life. I'm still finding my footing. Running this team. Fighting for them. It matters more than I expected. It needs all of me right now."

He held her gaze. "I know how I feel about you. I know we haven't been together long, but I've done my best to prove myself to you and to the team while here in Portland."

Margret nodded. "But you've also spent your whole life on a ranch in South Dakota. This world ... we both know ... it's not yours. We started out as friends. We were tossed together as business partners. Somewhere along the way, that turned into more. I need to believe this isn't something we're rushing into because everything's been so intense."

"You don't think I've thought it through?"

"What I think is ... you're only twenty-two." She softened her tone. "I'm twenty-four. We're still young. Look at everything that's changed in just two months."

He shifted the box back into his pocket.

Margret's voice trembled. "Please keep it safe. For now. For us. If one day I'm ready for a lifetime, I hope you'll still offer it to me."

Luke studied her for a long moment. "I'll wait," he said. "Because I want to continue to be a part of your life."

"You always will be."

They moved closer, embracing like a habit. Their kiss was slow, unrushed. Full of a promise neither was ready to break.

A cough echoed in the doorway. Sterling Wheatfield stood, arms folded. "Sorry to interrupt," he said, his tone dry. "Luke, I need a word."

Luke exhaled. "Can it wait?"

"No. I need you back at the ranch. Now. Full-time."

Her stomach turned into butterflies as she looked at them.

"Margret, you can handle things here. You've proven that." Sterling turned to Luke. "You, on the other hand, were born and bred to train horses, not babysit hockey players. I thought I could run the ranch without you, but I was wrong."

Luke's jaw tightened. "That's not your call."

"Yes. Yes, it is." Sterling's gaze shifted to Margret. "I trust her with my investment in Maine. I need you to take care of my investments in South Dakota. I paid for your degree. I need you back home. I didn't raise a benchwarmer."

Luke opened his mouth as Margret placed a hand on his arm. "Go," she said. "He needs you more than I do right now."

He looked at her, searching her eyes. "Do you think this ... us ... can work long distance?"

"Hunter and Sage managed it," she said. "Why not us?"

Luke's smile was faint. "They didn't make it look easy."

"They made it worth it."

"Pack your bags. I'll meet you in the car." Sterling walked from the room.

The front door shutting vibrated through Margret's bones.

Luke reached into his pocket once more. He pulled out the velvet box, pressing it gently into Margret's hand. "Keep it safe," he said. "For us. For the future I still believe in."

Their kiss this time was deeper. Final ... for now.

She watched him walk from the room. The silence rushed in like the blackness of a moonless night.

Margret drifted back into the dining room. One by one, she blew out the candle flames that remained. Small smoke tendrils wisped about as the wax cooled. The house seemed to sigh with her in contentment.

She returned to the garden room, retrieving her wine glass by the picture window. The view stretched wide toward the bay. The same bay Justin loved. The same bay she now stood beside as the home's new steward.

Justin left her a legacy. Sterling gave her freedom. Luke offered her a future. She never imagined any of those things happening. For once, she wasn't afraid of the unknown. Instead, she was thankful for it.

The waves crashed against the rocky shore as she took a sip of her now warm Chablis. She looked at the reflection in the window. She liked the woman looking back at her. She had not said yes to Luke's proposal. Not yet. But her heart had ... and that would have to be enough for now.

Acknowledgements

As with all my novels, *Defense and Deals* grew from my love of hockey and the support of many. My family and friends created space for dreams to take shape, offering the strength to keep those dreams alive. Readers, thank you for stepping on and off the ice with me once again. Your enthusiasm, kindness, and encouragement breathe life into every story.

My gratitude extends to the real-world hockey voices who energize my imagination. The players, coaches, and fans who fuel the spirit of the sport bring a spark to each chapter. A special nod to the NHL goalies who fire my creativity, especially Jeremy Swayman. And always, a quiet thank you to Tyler Bertuzzi, the player who made me fall in love with hockey.

Warm thanks as well to Moritz Seider and Lucas Raymond, whose skill and passion for the game helped mold two of my favorite Goshawks players, Axel and Etan. Deep appreciation also goes to Pete Fry, whose goalie mindset approach assisted in shaping the mental resilience of my netminders.

My heartfelt thanks to my husband, Stephen, whose hockey knowledge sharpened every on-ice moment. Your no-nonsense, hard-hitting critiques brought realism to my game chapters (even when they resulted in a total rewrite of the first seventeen chapters).

To Elise Holt, thank you for your keen edits and unwavering friendship (along with your constant requests of, "When are you sending me the next chapters?"). A special thanks goes to Shirly Holt for her continued support and enthusiasm for my books. Not to be forgotten, a cheerful shoutout to Karat, the big goofy Golden Retriever who lent his doggie enthusiasm and big loving heart to the Goshawks' Yellow Labrador, Crease.

And finally, to Susan Munson, whose love for hockey continues to kindle my drive to write in the hockey romance genre.

About the Author

Dee Marie is an award-winning author, photographer, and artist. Her career in publishing began as a managing editor, eventually advancing to editor-in-chief of an international computer graphics print magazine. She lives in South Dakota with her husband (a former hockey player) and a very loved and very spoiled Labrador.

An avid hockey fan with a special admiration for NHL goaltenders, Dee spends September through June chasing NHL games on her flatscreen. Her passion for the sport shines through in her writing, bringing the excitement and drama of hockey to life for her readers.

Also by Dee Marie

Goshawks Hockey Romance Series

Shots and Shutouts

Defense and Deals

Goalies and Goals

Sons of Avalon Saga

Merlin's Prophecy

www.ingramcontent.com/pod-product-compliance
Lightning Source LLC
LaVergne TN
LVHW010652110826
845149LV00014B/3046